THE LITTLE SEA MONSTER

ALSO BY ELIZABETH K. KING

THE HORRIFIC FAIRY TALES SERIES
Rotting Beauty
Beast By Day
The Little Sea Monster
Seven Hexes
Ghoul Girl (forthcoming)

Don't Go Into the Woods (novella)

THE LITTLE SEA MONSTER

HORRIFIC FAIRY TALES BOOK 3

ELIZABETH K. KING

THE LITTLE SEA MONSTER

Published in the United States by Elizabeth King. For inquiries, please visit the author's website: www.elizabethkking.com

Cover Art by Miblart.

Map by Saumya Singh (@Saumyasvision/Inkarnate).

The text for this book was set in EB Garamond.

The Library of Congress Control Number: 2024910418

ISBN 979-8-9888121-7-3 (hardcover)

ISBN 979-8-9888121-8-0 (paperback)

ISBN 979-8-9888121-6-6 (ebook)

First Edition, July 2024.

*For Kelsey, Audrey, and Lauren. My friends,
and my first readers.*

And for my sisters.

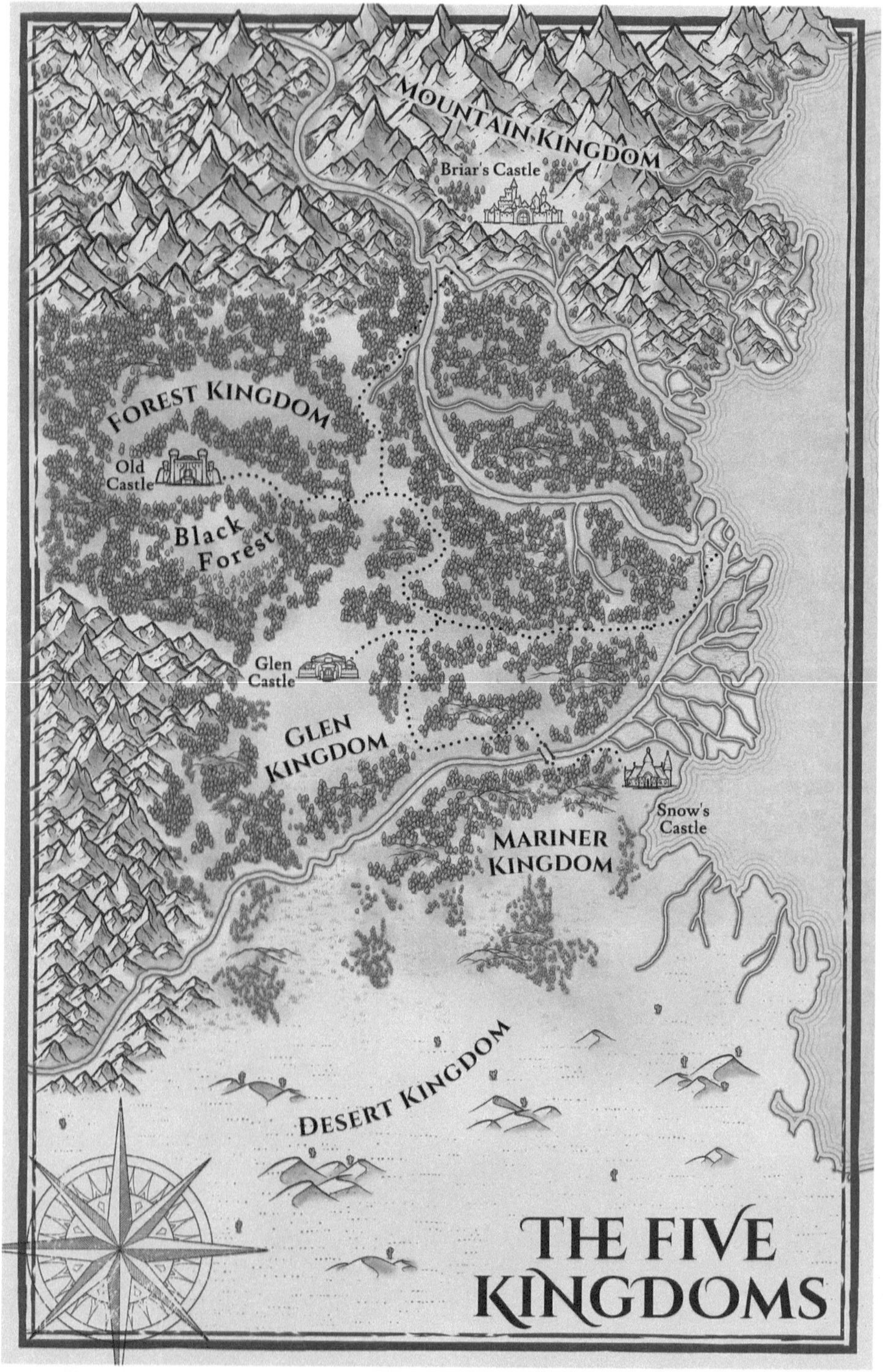

MOUNTAIN KINGDOM
Briar's Castle
FOREST KINGDOM
Old Castle
Black Forest
Glen Castle
GLEN KINGDOM
MARINER KINGDOM
Snow's Castle
DESERT KINGDOM
THE FIVE KINGDOMS

1

STORMY

DEMETRI FLINCHED AGAINST A spray of seawater as a violent wave crashed into the ship. Salt stung his eyes. He wondered, not for the first time, what on earth he was doing out on this floundering vessel, in the middle of the ocean, miles away from the dry, safe shore. And in the dark, no less, for it was nearly midnight. Well, he knew what he was doing, Demetri thought, as the ship swayed over the churning sea. He was trying not to fall flat on his face.

It was his own fault. Demetri had adopted a new rule for his life. He'd tried to live by this rule for the past seven months, ever since he'd left behind the girl he'd loved and let go of the only life he'd ever known. It had seemed like a good idea at the time. But in this moment, as he clutched the ship's rigging, he cursed the stupid rule.

The rule was: *Take every opportunity to try something new.*

Well, hunting sharks was certainly a new experience. When Mason, a saltwater fisherman Demetri had recently met, offered to get him a job with his captain, Demetri jumped at the chance. It would be pleasant, Demetri thought, to be out on the water this summer, the sun blazing overhead, a gentle wind on his face.

Only there was no sun, as it was near midnight. Sharks, apparently, were more active at night. And the breeze was not so much a *breeze* as it was a howling gale. But, Demetri reminded himself, his new rule wasn't the only reason he'd accepted Mason's offer. He'd also accepted it for the money, which he needed these days. After all, he wasn't a prince anymore.

Demetri had been a visitor in the Mountain Kingdom eighty years ago when a curse fell upon the realm, plunging everyone into perpetual sleep—a sleep that had turned its victims into living corpses. Demetri had not fallen prey to this curse, but he'd suffered a fate just as terrible: he'd been locked away to keep him from breaking the curse with true love's kiss. An enchantment had frozen him in time, preserving his life and his youth for those eighty-two years. Most people would have considered that a blessing, Demetri supposed—except he'd been awake all that time, trapped, aware of just how helpless he was, helpless to save himself or anyone else...

And when he'd finally escaped, a lifetime had passed. The world had moved on without him. The Glen Kingdom, which Demetri should have ruled one day, had been conquered, passing into the hands of a new ruling family. That family had welcomed Demetri—well, some of them—but Demetri knew there was no life for him in the Glen Kingdom anymore. He needed to move on.

So gone were the days when everything was provided for him. Demetri had to work. He didn't mind the work itself—not usually. He had to admit mucking out stables had its downsides, and working as a courier hadn't been as interesting as he'd thought it would be. Or, well, it had been *too* interesting. He'd actually had to employ the phrase "Don't shoot the messenger" once or twice.

Those jobs both had another downside—they were solitary, and Demetri preferred to be around people. He'd spent eighty-two years alone—that was all the solitude he needed.

As another wave broke against the ship, sending Demetri reeling, he saw Mason make his way towards him. The fisherman used the rigging to cross the deck, moving hand over hand along the length of rope. Mason was only about an inch taller than Demetri, but he had a broad chest and thick arms that gave him the appearance of a much bigger man. His white cotton shirt was soaked through, plastered to his skin.

As he reached Demetri, Mason grinned and asked, "What did I tell you?"

Demetri managed a weak smile. "Aren't you cold?"

Mason laughed. "Aren't you?"

He had a point. Demetri was not any warmer for wearing his sack coat. He was as drenched as Mason, the cuffs of his sleeves chafing unpleasantly at his wrists. It was nearly summer here on the coast of the Mariner Kingdom, quite warm during the days. But out on the sea at night, with a nearby storm bolstering the wind, Demetri was freezing. His fingers, clenched around the rigging, had gone numb. He couldn't even feel the scratchy rope biting into his hands anymore.

"Cap'n says we don't have to worry about the squall." Mason nodded, indicating the black patch on the horizon. The whole sky was dark, but that patch to the east was like an inky splotch across a swathe of navy blue. Every minute or so, a blinding streak of lightning cracked through the black. "Heading north, it looks like. Shouldn't pass over us."

Demetri eyed the sky anxiously. Even if the storm didn't pass over them, he still worried about it. Given that its proximity was causing these choppy conditions. The storm didn't need to pass right over them to capsize the ship.

Trying to put this thought behind him, Demetri raised his voice and asked, "Any sign of the sharks yet?"

"Remy says no." Remy was the ship's lookout, a short, skinny girl with the bluest eyes Demetri had ever seen. "Anyway..." A dark look passed through Mason's eyes. "That's assuming they *are* sharks."

"What else could be killing people besides sharks?" Demetri asked. That was why they were out here. There had been an uptick in shark attacks lately. People out at sea—sailors, fisherman, and bathers alike—had gone missing. Some bloodied body parts had even washed up on shore.

Mason cast him a glance. "Mermaids."

"Mermaids?" Demetri stared at his friend, wondering if he was serious. Mason did like his jokes, almost as much as he liked doing reckless things—like hunting sharks out on the sea with a hurricane raging nearby. Demetri supposed he'd found a substitute Garrett. He wondered what that said about him, that he always sought out mad thrill seekers for company.

"That's right, mermaids." Mason ran a hand through his dark beard. "You haven't heard the stories?"

"Can't say I have." Demetri wobbled, threading one arm through the rigging for more support. "But I haven't been in the Mariner Kingdom long. I, er—" Demetri strove to keep the incredulity from his voice. "I thought there were no such things as mermaids?"

"So some say," Mason grunted. "My mother always said different though. She said a mermaid killed my father."

"I didn't realize mermaids killed things," Demetri mused. He still wasn't sure how much of this he believed. Fairies and witches and rotting corpse creatures were one thing. But mermaids...? "I mean, I suppose they have to eat, but—"

"Listen," Mason said, his tone serious, "being a landlubber, you've probably heard a lot of pretty stories about mermaids. Well, forget all that. There's nothing pretty about them. People have spotted 'em before—people out on ships or along the coast. And a sighting is always marked by a disappearance or a gruesome death."

Demetri opened his mouth to respond—not that he had anything more eloquent to say than "Huh," because he wasn't sure if he even believed mermaids were real, let alone vicious killers—but before he could say anything, the ship gave another lurch. Demetri gripped the rope so tightly, he thought his frozen fingers would fall off.

The ship teetered, dipping dangerously towards the water. A massive wave tumbled over the bow, breaking against the ship like glass shattering into a thousand pieces. Sailors shouted and scrambled to grab onto something, but when the bow rose up again, water billowing down the sides, there were cries of "Man overboard!"

Mason swore and ran for the bow. Some of the sailors began unraveling a life buoy to throw out. Someone else bellowed, "Stop the ship! Bring her 'round! Tell those boys in the engine room to stop the cursed ship now!"

Demetri followed the rigging as best he could, tottering down the deck towards the bow. Once he ran out of rope, he staggered to the side of the ship and gripped the sea-spattered iron railing. He half-ran, half-fell the rest of the way, wayward waves lapping over the side and drenching him more than ever.

As he joined the sailors at the bow, he addressed the one closest to him. "Where is he?"

The sailor pointed out into the jet-black water. Demetri shielded his eyes from the stinging sea spray and peered out. He couldn't see anything at first, but then he spotted the man, a tiny white speck in the vast ocean. The clashing waves tossed him about like a feather in the wind.

The buoy was thrown out towards the man. Demetri was impressed to see how close it landed to him, considering how far the man was from the ship and how wildly the sea rocked around him. Along the railing, sailors shouted for their flailing fellow, waving and yelling encouragement.

Demetri squinted. It was hard to make out anything in the dark, with seawater pelting him like rain, but then a bolt of lightning flashed nearby, washing the sea in a sickly green luster. In that crack of light, Demetri saw the man paddling for the buoy, saw him fling an arm towards it—

Then he was gone.

Demetri wiped a hand over his face. Brackish seawater burned his nostrils. Had he just lost sight of the man? It would have been easy to do, but somehow, Demetri didn't think so. It was as though something in the water had pulled the man below the surface.

"Do you see him?" Demetri said to the sailor beside him, raising his voice to a near-shout.

The sailor cursed in response. "He's gone under. He was right there, and then—"

Whatever he meant to say next was drowned out by an ominous, earsplitting *cr-a-a-a-a-ck*. Something about the sound raised every hair on Demetri's head. Then the ship pitched sharply, and Demetri mirrored everyone around him as he clutched at the railing. It felt as though the hull had caught on something, jerking the ship to a halt. Alarm rushed through Demetri, flooding every bone in his body.

"By the Gift!" the sailor next to him swore. His face was pinched and white. "That sounded like—"

He was interrupted a second time as the ship began to rattle, *k-thnk-k-thnk-k-thnk-k-thnk*. As though it sat upon a warped axle. Then there was another *crack*, louder this time, the sound as thunderous as the nearby storm. The ship gave another great *lurch*. Demetri fell to his knees.

"Breach!" someone shouted, and the cry cut Demetri to the core. "Breach in the hull!"

Sucking in a breath, Demetri reached for the side of the ship and looked up. Even amidst the thrashing sea, he could tell the ship had stopped moving, no longer cresting over the water. But the ship was not still. Instead, it shuddered around him as though resisting a great pressure. He could imagine the sea swelling into the cracked hull below, filling the ship with water.

It was a terrifying vision.

Screams rent the air as sailors dashed across the deck, rushing to save the ship. Demetri clambered to his feet, the port side of the ship—where Demetri stood—dipping perilously close to the sea. Demetri saw Mason running, shouting at him, but the port side dipped again, and Mason fell towards him. Demetri spun to avoid being flattened by the man, but he lost his footing as the deck heaved beneath him. He pitched backwards.

His head slammed into a sharp edge, and everything went black.

It couldn't have been for more than a minute, but when Demetri came to, he was in the water, his head slipping beneath the surface.

Panic filled him, clogging up his airway. No, not panic. Seawater. He was in the *ocean*. For a moment, there was only darkness as the water closed over his head, as he stupidly struggled to draw breath and only choked on more seawater. It burned down his throat like acid. He couldn't see anything, couldn't feel anything except the smothering weight of the ocean, tugging at him, crushing him as thoroughly as a pile of rocks. He couldn't tell which way was up, which way was down.

He was going to die.

No. Some instinct deep inside him burst to life. *Kick*, it said. *Kick.* So he kicked, he kicked furiously, and he had no idea if he was going the right way, if he was going *anywhere*, or if this was all just futile. But he kept going, kicking and kicking and kicking, and then, suddenly, he broke through the surface of the water.

Demetri spluttered, retching as he struggled to breathe. He nearly went under again as soon as he'd come up, but he kept kicking, flailing his arms, trying to orient himself as he looked for something to save him.

Then he saw it. Bobbing in the water, little more than an arm's length away. The buoy they'd thrown to the overboard sailor. Demetri struggled towards it, pushing his way through the sea. As close as it was, it seemed to take forever to reach it. The water resisted him, leeching all the strength out of his body, turning his muscles to jelly. He felt as though he had a brick tied to each ankle. But he finally reached the buoy, his fingers groping at its slippery edge, and then he had it, and he pulled his whole arm through and held on for dear life.

Relief was there and gone as quick as the tumbling currents, closing in on him and then pulling away. The buoy wouldn't hold him forever, and he was still in the middle of the ocean. The ship. Something had happened to the ship, but if he could get back to it.... He wiped a hand over his eyes and blinked, circling around for some glimpse of the ship.

When he finally found it—a great, hulking shadow in the black night—it looked weird. The shape was all wrong. At first he couldn't pinpoint more than that, and then, as his eyes adjusted, he realized.

The ship had broken apart. Cleaved down the middle, as though some monstrous sea creature, a leviathan from the depths, had sliced through it with gargantuan teeth.

The sight overwhelmed Demetri, his heart seizing in his chest. He couldn't understand. He'd been on that ship, he'd *just been on it*, and for all that it felt like he'd been in the water forever, he knew it had only been a few minutes. He'd been on that ship, and despite the breach in the hull, it had still been whole—dead in the water, sinking, but whole. Now it was nearly in two separate halves, one part almost submerged, the other splintering before his eyes. Distantly, he heard screams, but the ship was too far away and the night too dark to make out anyone on board.

He had to think. He had to *think*. The trouble was, that was becoming more difficult by the second. Demetri's head throbbed; belatedly, he remembered he'd hit it against something. He knew that wasn't good, but he was having trouble focusing on why. He just had to think—he had to get out of the ocean—

Below the water, something bumped against his thigh.

Demetri froze, his flailing limbs going still. Fear gripped him as he thought of sharks, but as he was bumped a second time, he realized whatever it was had to be much smaller than a shark. He threaded his arm through the buoy so he could reach down into the water with his other hand. His fingers closed around something rough and bristling—the rope tied to the buoy. As he felt further, he realized the rope was tangled around something. Demetri grasped the object, foreboding prickling through him. The object had an eerily familiar feel to it, though it was slimy and nubbed on one side. It felt an awful lot like—

A hand.

It was a human hand.

Demetri choked on a scream and dropped the severed hand. Dark blood coated his palm, and now there was blood on the buoy, slick like oil. Suddenly, he felt as though the water around him was streaked with blood, and he didn't know if it was real or just his imagination, running wild with fear. All he knew was he couldn't stay here, hanging onto this buoy, he had to *go*, he had to get out, somehow, he had to *get out*—

And then he saw it. A boat. One of the ferrying rowboats from the ship, miraculously whole, miraculously upright. It sat calmly atop the tempestuous sea, swaying on the surface.

He had to get to it. It was his only chance.

He began to swim. It was hard, harder than it should have been. He tried to tow the buoy behind him, but it slowed him down, and the boat seemed to drift further away every second. Desperate, Demetri released the buoy and plunged through the water. He kicked until his legs ached, he swept his arms back and forth, feeling as though he was heaving the weight of the entire sea behind him. His head still throbbed and all this activity wasn't helping; soon all he could hear was the pounding of his blood in his ears, blocking out the crash of the waves and the distant screams. But he kept his eyes fixed on the boat and pushed forward, forward, even when his eyes began to blur and his chest began to burn.

He was close—so close.

Then something latched onto his ankle and yanked him below the surface.

2

SINKING

PERPETUA WATCHED THE SHIP break apart with little pleasure.

The truth was, she liked ships. She liked the way they moved over the sea, like swans gliding across the water, leaving roiling streams in their wake. She liked the way their sails billowed in the wind, like clouds in a pearly sky. She loved to watch the little sailor up in the crow's nest, looking out over the world. They must really feel like a crow, she thought, perched so high above the sea.

What she really loved about ships, though, was their very existence. It was a wonder that humans could build such things, that they'd discovered a way to traverse the ocean without fins. Even though they couldn't breathe underwater or swim very well. The sea was not a natural habitat for a human; the sea often *killed* humans. But they braved it anyway.

Which made it all the easier to hunt and eat them.

"Imagine seeing you here, Perpetua."

Masking her shock, Perpetua twisted around, seawater spattering the boulder beside her. She'd taken refuge here in this secluded cove to watch the shipwreck. It seemed a safe enough spot, the glossy black pool hidden by encroaching fog and the rocky land bar arching out into the sea. She hadn't realized there was anyone else nearby. Naiads were solitary feeders; they rarely sought out company at mealtimes.

"Candelaria." Perpetua recognized the crimson scales beneath the water. She adopted a cool, even tone. "What are you doing here?"

Dripping golden locks emerged from the water as Candelaria rose above the surface. Seawater drizzled down her scales like rivulets of blood. "I could ask you the same thing." She flicked her tail fin in a nonchalant gesture.

Perpetua refused to be cowed. "I was at the docks earlier. I saw Alamena set the sabotage."

"And you decided to help yourself?"

Perpetua fixed her eyes on Candelaria's too-pretty face. "Am I not welcome here?"

Candelaria's eyebrow hitched, but she didn't press the issue. Perpetua turned away, satisfaction burning hot inside her. Although naiads preferred to eat alone, they did sometimes hunt together out of necessity—taking down a big ship took more than one, and the amount of food that ship would provide was far more than a single naiad needed. Others were welcome to take their fill, even if they hadn't helped with the sabotage.

"I hate to hunt like this," Candelaria said. "It's degrading. Letting them kill themselves, really. And we are the scavengers picking at the wreckage."

"We have to be careful," Perpetua said. "The Ternion dictated we should limit taking prey from the docks. The humans will start to notice if too many of their own disappear."

Candelaria gave a scornful laugh. "The humans. They always talk. That doesn't mean they're clever enough to hunt us."

Perpetua could feel Candelaria's gaze on her, smoldering with anticipation. This, Perpetua thought, was the real reason Candelaria had confronted her here—to rile her up. It was her favorite pastime. And Perpetua wasn't about to let her enjoy it. Striving for a bored tone, she replied, "If you say so."

"You're not going to defend them?" Moonlight arced over the rippling water as Candelaria swam around, placing herself in Perpetua's line of sight. "Your precious humans? Isn't that what you do all day in your cave? Sit around and write poetry about them?"

Perpetua didn't grace this jibe with an answer. Contrary to what her fellow naiads thought, she did not believe humans were "precious." She was just curious about them. Yes, they were prey, yes, they were food. But they were different from other kinds of food. A human was not like a bed of oysters or a school of coal fish. Perpetua marveled at the towns the humans dwelled in, the towns they had built. The elaborate clothing they wore. The things they did, gathering on the beach to eat and talk, working on the docks and sailing in their ships. In truth, Perpetua was not just curious about humans. She was *fascinated* by them.

Unfortunately, all the other naiads knew it. For as long as Perpetua could remember, she had been teased and ostracized for her interest in humans. Perpetua was *strange*, everyone knew that. Most naiads just ignored her, but the worst of them—like Candelaria—loved nothing better than to taunt her.

"You probably have one picked out." Candelaria nodded, indicating the wreck. "Seeing as you were there when Alamena set the sabotage. You've probably had your eye on one since it boarded the ship." She laughed quietly. "I only ask so I know who to stay away from. I don't want to get into a fight with you over food."

"Then stay clear of me," Perpetua growled, "and you won't."

Candelaria snarled back, her eyes bleeding red from eyelid to eyelid. Perpetua stifled a flinch but didn't back down, meeting the naiad's scarlet gaze without allowing her own vision to redden. She wasn't afraid of Candelaria, but she would *not* allow the naiad to provoke her.

Candelaria backed away. With one last sneer, she dove into the water, submerging herself beneath the surface. Perpetua watched her go, her eyes trailing those crimson scales until they disappeared. She only relaxed when Candelaria did not return.

In fact, Perpetua *had* picked out the human she wanted from that ship. She did that sometimes. It was an unusual thing, which was why Candelaria teased her for it. One human was much like another, most naiads would say, but Perpetua didn't feel that way. She could not explain why, not even to herself.

Sometimes, Perpetua wondered why they ate humans. On a physical level, she understood—she had heard stories about what happened to a naiad who went too long without a human meal. The hunger became unbearable, it was said, and Perpetua could imagine it. The hunger for a human was not like normal hunger. It was more of a *need* buried deep inside. Unsated, that need turned on its host, feeding on the naiad instead. It was said that a naiad who did not feed on humans wasted away, no matter what else it ate.

Perpetua knew that. She just wondered why it was.

The white fog invading the cove had deepened, sinking towards the surface of the pool. It was time to go, Perpetua decided. If she waited too much longer, all the humans from the wreck would be dead and drowned. The timing was important. Naiads preferred their prey alive when they ate them, but the entire point of sinking the ship at sea was to draw no attention to themselves. If any of the sailors saw them and escaped on their little boats or a piece of debris, the Ternion would not be pleased.

Perpetua dove a fin's length below the surface and swam towards the ruined ship. She glided along a current, the ocean warm around her. Every now and then, she hit a cold spot, a rush of water that tickled her bare back and rippled over her scales. As she neared the wreckage, the current changed, rolling in every direction. She heard screams from the floundering sailors, filtered through the water; she felt their flailing in the bubbles streaming down from the surface. She glanced around to make sure Candelaria was nowhere near her, then set off in search of the human she'd seen boarding the ship.

Earlier on the docks, she'd watched the sailors board one by one. But one human had drawn her attention because he was *not* a sailor. He wasn't dressed like the sailors in their baggy jackets and rumpled caps. He'd worn a short, dark coat and sturdy boots, and he carried a weapon—something long and thin with a glinting edge. Perpetua thought it was a sword. And he had a quiet, serious face. Even when one of the sailors had said something to him, and he'd laughed, there had been a careworn look in his eyes, as though he could see something the sailor couldn't. Ghosts, hovering at the edge of his vision.

Perpetua couldn't forget that look.

As she reached the midst of the wreckage and swam through it, she searched for him. She wove around sinking netting and iron beams, she ducked beneath bobbing shards of the ship's exterior. But she focused on the humans. The sailors wore loose-fitting trousers and white cotton shirts. Perpetua bypassed them all—drowning, unconscious, or dead. She passed one whose eyes bulged in their sockets as he choked on seawater, sinking fast.

He didn't matter. None of them did. Another naiad would take him, and if they didn't, well, he was still dead and could not spread tales about naiads in the ocean. As Perpetua swam around a large piece of the ship, painted dark blue and bearing golden markings, she spotted a dark shape up above her. An oblong shadow cast through the surface of the water, outlined in glimmering moonlight.

It was one of their little boats, the rowboats they carried on the ship. She couldn't tell if anyone was inside, but she should overturn it. They couldn't let anyone get away.

Then another shape caught her eye, off to her left. A dark, flailing shape—a human. And not a sailor, not in those tall, thick boots. This was him—*her* human. The one she'd picked. She couldn't see his face, for he clutched at something above the water, but below the surface, his torso twisted, his legs kicking frantically. Probably, Perpetua realized, trying to reach that rowboat nearby.

She remembered his serious face from the docks, and her mouth began to water. She could feel every one of her teeth lengthening, sharpening to a point. Her jaw unhinged, stretching wide to accommodate their growth. A filmy, scarlet veil dropped over her eyes, reddening her vision. And a *need* that was more than hunger filled her, expanding from behind her ribcage. It was painful—like a beetle burrowing through her.

She hated this part, right before she fed. When she was on the precipice of losing her mind. Most of the other naiads gave into the bloodlust that welled up inside them, relishing the burgeoning rage and madness. But Perpetua tried not to. It had happened once or twice, and she couldn't understand why the others didn't experience the pure terror that came with it. As though some feral power had reached down into her, yanking her out of her body and leaving her to flounder in the sea, as helpless as any human.

So she struggled to hold the madness at bay as she swam, pivoting up towards her chosen human. A dull ache pulsed in her forehead, just above the bridge of her nose. The price for holding back the mindless killer inside her.

She was three fin lengths from her prey when a glistening shape darted in front of her, snatched her human, and dragged him beneath the water's surface.

Perpetua stopped short. Some of the red faded from her vision as she took in the scene before her, trying to make sense of it. The moonlight cutting through the dark sea cast a luminous shaft over blood-red scales and golden hair.

Candelaria. Candelaria had taken her human.

And it *was* her human. Perpetua recognized him as he struggled, floundering, lashing out with his limbs, scrabbling at Candelaria's grip to pry himself free. His face was screwed up tight as he held his breath. Candelaria wasn't even looking at him as she delved down into the depths of the ocean, her elongated claws wrapped firmly around his ankle.

Perpetua had never fought so hard against the rage inside her. Candelaria. She had probably followed Perpetua; she'd *planned* to take the human Perpetua picked. It was just the kind of thing she would do.

Perpetua lunged forward, throwing herself in Candelaria's path. Her vision reddened even further, so much that she almost couldn't see Candelaria through the scarlet curtain veiling her sight. Candelaria reeled back as Perpetua stretched her jaws wide, baring her teeth and hissing at the golden-haired naiad.

Candelaria looked affronted. What Perpetua was doing—confronting Candelaria, challenging her on this human—was beyond the pale. Even if Perpetua *had* spotted him first, now that another naiad had taken him, the done thing was to let it be. But Perpetua didn't care what Candelaria thought of her hunting etiquette.

She hissed again. Candelaria glared back. For a moment, they faced each other down. Perpetua didn't dare break her gaze, didn't chance a glance at her human to see if he was still struggling or if he'd lost consciousness.

Her persistence paid off. Candelaria, it seemed, didn't want a fight, just as Perpetua knew she wouldn't. Fighting over human prey would be an even worse breach of etiquette. With a derisive flick of her tail, Candelaria released the human and swam off, vanishing into the sea's inky depths. As soon as she was gone, Perpetua shot forward, gripped her flailing human by the arm, and towed him towards the surface. She thought he was still conscious, but he was choking on seawater, flailing worse than ever. She doubted he knew what was happening or even realized she was there.

She broke the surface of the ocean and looked around. Her skin tingled in the blustery air. She'd come up near the little boat she'd seen, and thankfully, it was empty. Mustering all her strength, Perpetua heaved her human out of the water and tossed him into the boat, his body *thudding* against the wooden bottom. She left him coughing and choking as she lowered herself beneath the surface, darting a look around. She could just as easily devour this human above water—in fact, she preferred it—and after all that ruckus with Candelaria, she wanted to make sure no one else disturbed her.

But there was no one in sight, save for a drowning sailor or two, so she resurfaced. Her vision cleared, and her teeth shrank inside her mouth. Her head ached worse than ever as she fought against the bloodlust and hauled herself into the boat. As her fins left the water, they split in two, forming scaled legs and webbed feet.

Outside of the water, naiads walked on two legs, though most of their skin was encased in scales. Perpetua's sea-green scales covered her entire torso and both of her arms, leaving only her back bare. Naiads could take a human form—flesh without scales—but only for a short time to lure their prey. It was more of a glamour than a true form. *This* form, the one she wore now—this was a naiad's true form.

She could hear her human gasping behind her, so he was still conscious. Standing with her back to him, she slicked her dark hair off her face.

"You—you saved me."

Perpetua froze.

The human was *speaking*.

"You saved me," he repeated, his voice raspy.

Perpetua hesitated. Then she turned to face the human.

He sat upright on the floor of the boat. His mousy hair was plastered to his forehead, but he swept it out of his eyes. He coughed again, rubbed a trembling hand across his throat, and said, "Where did you come from?"

Perpetua stared. He was *speaking*. To her? A human had never spoken to her before—not of its own free will. Perpetua always spoke first, and like all naiads, her Voice exerted a control that humans could not resist. When Perpetua spoke, her human prey did whatever she asked, whatever she compelled it to do. Perpetua didn't like talking to her prey. It was unnerving, conversing with someone you were about to eat, so her first command was usually for the human to be silent.

Before Perpetua could do that, the human spoke again.

"Who are you?" The human winced as he struggled to get his feet beneath him. His sopping wet coat trailed water onto the boat's bottom. Groaning, he reached up to touch the back of his head. His fingers came away red with blood. "Where did you come from?"

The ache in Perpetua's forehead sharpened, pulsating against her skull. Her vision began to redden of its own accord, but she blinked rapidly to clear it. Her gums ached too, her teeth protesting as she kept them from elongating. The need to devour human prey was beginning to consume her. It was a swarm of beetles gnawing at her insides, chewing through her veins, scratching at her bones.

But she could not stop staring at this human, this boy, with his serious face and ghost-seeing eyes. She couldn't bring herself to silence him. As though his own, weak human voice exerted some kind of control over her. There *was* something compelling about him, something that pulled at her. It was the same feeling that had drawn her to him when she saw him boarding the ship. As though they were connected. As though she had known him long ago, in another life.

But that was impossible. She had always been a naiad, a hunter and a killer. And he was prey. A human.

He tried to stand, but his body buckled, and he fell to his knees. Before Perpetua could stop herself, she crouched before him, balancing on her webbed feet. Her fingers tensed as she fought the urge to extend them, as she fought the urge to tear into his flesh.

Instead, she just stared at him.

Groaning, he lifted his head. His teeth chattered and he shivered incessantly as the wind gusted past. He seemed groggy—because of his head wound, probably—but he looked straight at her. Even unfocused as he was, she saw that look in his eyes, that careworn look that had first caught her attention.

And for the first time—for the first time *ever*—Perpetua wondered about her prey and what he'd been through. She wondered about his life, about his past. She wondered what had happened to give him that haunted look.

The human took in a shaky breath. "Who are you?"

Perpetua drew her lips together. She watched as a faint moan escaped the human's lips. Then his eyes slipped shut and he sagged forward. He'd blacked out.

Perpetua stared down at him. They were easier to eat when they were unconscious. And the hunger inside her was so painful now, she could barely think.

But instead of giving into it, she held it at bay. She slipped over the side of the boat, allowing her legs to meld into fins. She began to tow the boat away, swimming as fast as she could from the wreckage. She swam for more than an hour, the black storm clouds growing distant on the horizon, the rollicking sea slowly calming around her.

She swam until she reached the shore. She found an abandoned pier near the village and tied the rowboat off there. And then—without sparing another look for the boy inside the boat—she swam off in search of different prey for the night.

3

FORGOTTEN

D EMETRI HAD NO IDEA how he'd survived the shipwreck two nights ago. He couldn't remember anything about it. He remembered boarding the ship. He remembered the stormy sea, the seething waves tossing them about. He remembered the crack in the hull, the ship breaking apart.

Everything after that was a blur.

"Well, that's not unusual," said Doctor Bardot. He was a physician here in Moselle, the little seaside town Demetri was staying in. Demetri perched on the edge of a steel cot in an exam room, sitting patiently as the doctor examined the wound at the back of his head. With summer fast approaching on the coast, the room was warm and stuffy. Even the gear-powered fan in the corner was not enough to dispel the sultry air. "You took quite a bump on your head. Nearly cracked your skull open. I'm not surprised you can't remember what happened after that."

"Everyone else died though." Demetri strove for a neutral tone, but this bothered him more than he could say. Every-

24

one else on board that ship—all the crew, the captain, Mason, Remy—they'd all died, lost at sea. A few bodies had washed ashore, but no one else had turned up alive.

Demetri didn't understand how he'd survived. Some villagers had found him, unconscious and bleeding, in a small rowboat tied to a rickety pier some leagues north of Moselle. The town inspectors thought he must have rowed himself to shore, but Demetri remembered none of that, and anyway, the boat's oars hadn't been seen anywhere. He could hardly believe he'd paddled himself all that way with only his arms.

"Yes, well, that's a matter for the capital guard." Doctor Bardot stepped back. "Don't trouble yourself over it too much."

That was very well for him to say, Demetri thought, as a nurse came in to bandage his head. He wasn't so much troubled over the cause of the shipwreck, though he'd heard rumors that the guard were looking into sabotage. It was just that he felt responsible, even though he doubted he could have done anything to save anyone.

Briar would have said he was being irrational, blaming himself for something that could not possibly be his fault. But he couldn't help it.

His heart clenched at the thought of Briar. The princess of the cursed Mountain Kingdom. Once, she had been his betrothed, and the girl he loved. But he'd left her behind, like everything else in his life.

After responding to the nurse's queries in a monotone voice, he departed from the doctor's house, his thoughts preoccupied and his chest heavy. He squinted up at the yellow sun bearing down on him, unfettered by clouds in a clear, cornflower-blue sky. The cobbled lane before him stretched and curved into the distance, a mosaic of pebbles in grays and tans. As he moseyed down the street, past brick villas with gabled roofs and white-shuttered windows, a hazy image formed in his mind, the memory of a girl's face. It was not Briar's face. This girl had a strong, angular face, sharp cheekbones beneath a pair of hooded brown eyes.

It was the one thing Demetri thought he remembered from the night of the shipwreck, though maybe it was just a dream, something his mind had conjured to make sense of what happened. But he thought—he *thought*—he remembered, just briefly, kneeling on the bottom of the rowboat, sodden and trembling and foggy. And he thought he saw her there—this girl he remembered. She had been in the boat with him. Maybe she had even saved him.

But that was all he remembered, and it made no more sense than paddling himself to shore. There had been no girls besides Remy on the ship, and the face he remembered was not hers. So if there *had* been some other girl out there, where had she come from? And where had she gone?

He sighed as he turned a corner, trying to put it from his mind as Doctor Bardot had advised.

He soon reached the tavern he was staying at—a half-timbered building just off the beach—called LeBeau's. He had no idea who LeBeau was; the innkeeper's name was Pasquier. It was the only tavern in town—well, there were a few others in the dodgier end of town, but they were little more than holes in the wall. LeBeau's was a tavern-and-inn, set at the end of one of the town's main squares, and housing a number of guests. Demetri had taken a room for the summer.

The sprawling taproom inside the tavern was well lit by gear-bulb fixtures latched onto the wood-paneled walls and glass chandeliers hanging from the ceiling. A long, polished bar lined one entire side of the room, rimmed with velvet-cushioned barstools. Box-like, elarium-forged creatures scuttled around the room on spindly legs—auto-waiters, topped with trays for carrying food and with round slots built into their sides for mugs and glasses.

Demetri recognized a few faces in the taproom—mostly sailors and dockworkers, people he'd befriended since he'd arrived. Demetri always tried to find friends when he came to a new place. Right now, though, he was too troubled and tired for company, so he ducked his head and made for the stairs in the back, heading up to his room. It was a small room with sparse furnishings and no window, set on the interior of the building, but he did have a private washroom and a large, lumpy bed.

He sank onto that bed now, the metal frame squeaking quietly. The doctor had instructed him to get plenty of rest and avoid strenuous activities for the next couple of days. As tired as he was right now, he had no trouble with that. He slumped down amidst his pillows, falling asleep quickly.

He dreamed of Briar, as he often did. He dreamed of the days before they'd met, when they'd been betrothed and only known each other through letters. He dreamed of the first time he saw her, when he came to court her in the Mountain Kingdom. He dreamed of those days before the sleeping curse took her, when they'd spent every minute together roaming her castle, stealing kisses in alcoves and laughing quietly as they snuck down to the kitchens.

And he dreamed of what came after. After Briar pricked her finger and slept for eighty-two years, after Demetri escaped from his magical prison. He dreamed of fighting corpse monsters in Briar's castle, he dreamed of the pale, bruised princess Briar had become. Pale and bruised, but no less striking. No less fierce and determined, no less kind and inquisitive.

Briar had been his betrothed, and he had loved her. But she had also been his best friend. And when all was said and done—when Briar had defeated the dark fairy who'd cursed her—Demetri had left. He'd left because Briar did not love him as he loved her. He'd left to find a new life for himself.

Or at least, that was what he'd thought. Now he wondered if he'd just been running away. Trying to escape all the unpleasant memories, all the heartache.

If so, it hadn't worked. His dreams were proof of that. When he woke several hours later, he woke with a twinge of pain. Not in his bandaged head, but deep in his chest. It was a pain he'd become used to over the past seven months. It felt as though—if he breathed too deeply—something would break inside him.

He thought, maybe, it was the pain of regret.

It was a moment before he realized someone was banging on his door. "Just a minute," he called groggily, sitting up.

He found one of his new friends in the corridor outside, a wiry young man named Emile. He was around Demetri's age—well, around the age Demetri looked, which was to say, seventeen or eighteen. "Sorry," Emile said, looking Demetri up and down. "Did I wake you?"

"No," Demetri replied, even though he had. "What's going on?"

Emile flashed a grin, his tanned face half-shadowed in the dim corridor. "Me and some of the others are going to hit up Rue des Saints for some entertainment." Which meant they were going on a pub crawl. Rue des Saints was the street with the most pubs in Moselle. Which Demetri found a bit ironic, given that the street was named for the Saints, the core of the Mariner Kingdom's pious religion. "Thought you might want to join."

"Oh. Well..." Doctor Bardot had instructed him to avoid alcohol. But this advice, he decided, he could ignore. He needed a night out. He needed a distraction. "I'll come. Just let me get my coat."

Emile waved a hand, starting down the corridor. A few minutes later, Demetri hurried after him, and the two clattered down the stairs to join up with a small crowd of people as they headed onto the streets.

It was a muggy night. They made their way down Rue des Saints, a breeze carrying the briny scent of the sea. It was a warm breeze, and by the time they left the second pub for the night, Demetri's cotton shirt was stuck to his back with sweat. Fortunately, he'd had enough to drink by then that he didn't really care, the effect of the sultry night air buried beneath a pleasant haze of alcohol. Thoughts of the shipwreck were forgotten, Briar was forgotten. He laughed and joked and shouted with the others.

A fight broke out in the fourth pub and some of the group departed, staggering drunkenly down the street. Emile stayed at the pub, so Demetri stayed, but when Emile was drawn into a loud, heated argument about the best time for saltwater fishing, Demetri stepped outside, craving fresh air. He wandered down a side alley and emerged out onto the docks. A long, stone quay ran along the coast here, jutting out into the sea. During the day, the pier and the streets were flooded with people: dockworkers, sailors, and traders alike. But right now, no one was around. It must have been near midnight. Demetri glanced up at the sky, but it was smudged over with misty clouds, as though someone had dumped a load of iron-gray paint and smeared it over a deep blue canvas.

A loud splash off the edge of the pier drew Demetri's attention. He ambled towards the water, his stride unsteady. He didn't stop until he reached the end of the pier, the toes of his boots hanging off the edge as he bent to peer into the sea.

There was nothing there. Nothing he could see, but then, the ocean was black and opaque at night, the water lapping gently against the pier.

"You're going to fall in."

Demetri lifted his head and looked around. As he turned, he slipped on a damp spot, and he flung an arm out, grappling for the low stone wall that was *just* out of reach. The briefest presentiment of falling rushed through him—a terrible *swooping* sensation that he felt in the pit of his stomach—and then—

—and then two hands closed around his arms, tugging him forward. He lurched in the opposite direction, away from the water, and straight into the girl who had just saved him.

Without getting a very good look at her, Demetri put a hand on her shoulder to steady himself. "Thank you," he murmured.

"I told you," she said.

"Told me what?"

"That you were going to fall."

Stepping back a pace, Demetri pushed his hair out of his eyes. The girl that stood before him, illuminated by the too-bright glare of a streetlamp behind her, was quite short. That was the first thing Demetri noticed. The top of her head only came up to his chin, and he was not tall. Her arms, bared by the wispy green dress she wore, were a beautiful golden brown, and the long hair that tumbled over her shoulders a few shades darker.

Demetri looked at her face. And as he took in what he saw there—sharp angles, intense, dark eyes—he recognized her.

"It's you!" he spluttered. "You're the girl from the shipwreck!"

Her dark eyebrows drew down, giving her a severe look. But she didn't turn away.

"You *were* there, weren't you?" Demetri pressed. Dimly, it dawned on him that he was being far more forward than was strictly proper, especially with a girl he'd just met, but the combination of alcohol and shock had shoved this concern far and away. "I can't remember anything—what happened there—but I know I saw you. How were you there?"

He stopped abruptly, realizing how close he stood before her, so close that he had to bend his neck to look down at her. She was still frowning, and Demetri noticed she had a small, delicate mouth. She opened that mouth and said,

"Tell me your name." Her voice bore the snap of command, but it wasn't a harsh voice. In fact, Demetri thought distantly, her voice was quite beautiful. There was something hypnotic about it.

"Demetri," he answered.

"Are you a sailor? Tell me."

"No."

"I did not think so. What are you, then? Tell me."

Demetri opened his mouth to answer but faltered. He *wanted* to answer her—he wanted to tell her what he was. But— "I don't really know. That's sort of why I'm here." He clasped his hands behind his head. "To find what I am. What I should be."

The girl looked at him through dark eyelashes. "And why," she asked, her lyrical voice soft and compelling, "do you look so haunted all the time?"

"Haunted?" He dropped his hands. "What do you mean?"

She gestured vaguely. "Like you see ghosts."

"Oh." Something painful jabbed at him, piercing through the lovely fog blanketing his brain. "I do see ghosts." The ghosts of his parents. The ghost of a life lost to him, a kingdom lost to him. The ghost of the girl that was lost to him. He didn't know how to explain, so he said, "I lost...someone. I lost everything. My life. What I was." He shrugged, hoping the answer was good enough. "All of it haunts me."

The girl's eyes pinched at the corners, as though he was a puzzle she wanted to solve. "I don't understand."

"I'm sorry," Demetri said, and he was truly sorry that he hadn't explained well. But then he remembered she hadn't answered his question. "It *was* you, wasn't it? Out at sea. When the ship broke apart. Where did you come from? How were you there? Please," he added, desperate to know. "Please tell me."

The girl's huge eyes widened. "What did you just say?"

Demetri's brain felt fuzzy. "Just now? I said, where did you come from when—"

"No. After that. After you asked me."

"I said...please." This was a very strange conversation. Still, that didn't seem to matter much. "Please tell me. Where you came from. Who you are."

"Why do you want to know?"

"Because you saved me." Demetri swallowed. "I mean, I think you did. I can't remember—but everyone else died. Except me. I don't know how you did it, but I think you saved me. I think I'd be dead if not for you."

"I saved you?" she whispered.

"I thought so." Demetri bent his head a little, his gaze locked on hers. "Didn't you?"

The girl's dark eyes were fathomless. "Yes. I saved you." The words sounded strange on her lips, as though they were foreign to her. As though she was just trying them out.

"Why?" he asked.

"I just did." Again, there was a bit of a *snap* in her voice. But she reached out and laid her hand on the side of his face. Her touch was a whisper against his cheek. "You do not remember me," she said firmly. "You don't remember me from the shipwreck. You don't know that I saved you. You have never met me before this moment."

Demetri's brain felt addled with more than just ale, but all he said was, "All right."

"Good." Her fingers twitched against his face. As though she had been about to pull away, but thought better of it. Her eyes softened. And when she spoke again, her voice was a sweet melody drawn against the strings of a violin. "Kiss me. Demetri."

And though it seemed mad, Demetri kissed her. He was already so close, he barely had to move. A shift of his foot. The merest tilt of his head. And then their lips touched. He brushed a featherlight kiss over her lips, just trying it out. Once, twice. Then he deepened the kiss, drinking in the heady scent of her. She was like the balmy ocean air drifting off the coast, she was like a vine of jasmine blooming in the night. He kissed her, his hands exploring the curve of her waist, the small of her back. He kissed her until there was no thought in his head at all.

He could not have said how long it lasted. But the next thing he knew, she was stepping away from him, and her hands fell away from his face.

Demetri blinked. "I'm sorry," he said. He ran a sheepish hand across his neck. "I must've had more to drink than I thought. Kissing strange girls on the docks."

The girl's eyes narrowed. "How am I strange?"

"I just meant—that I don't know you," Demetri stumbled. "What is your—"

He broke off at the sound of horseshoes clopping against the cobbled street. Demetri stepped past the girl, staring as an elaborate white carriage rolled into view. A few things marked it as elaborate. For one thing, it was pulled by horses. Most carriages were self-propelled these days. The carriage wheels and ironwork were also ornately crafted, the door bordered in green vines. A crest was painted on the door in the same pale green. Demetri felt like he should recognize it, but his brain was still a bit muddled.

The carriage rattled to a halt on the broad street closest to the pier, and a small figure unfolded off the back of the carriage. A footman, he supposed, though when the figure stepped into the lamplight, Demetri realized it was not a man at all. It was a young woman. A girl, really, in snug trousers and a buttoned-up coat. She had dark brown skin and coarse black hair, tightly twisted back and pinned behind her head. "Now what?" she demand-ed, coming around the carriage. She appeared to be addressing someone inside. "Is this it? This can't be it." She looked around. Her gaze swept over the docks, and Demetri. "There's nothing here but a pier."

"I think we're lost," someone called from inside the carriage.

"We are *not* lost," came a second voice.

Demetri frowned. Both voices sounded vaguely familiar, though he wasn't sure why. The footman who was actually a girl rolled her eyes. Then she looked at Demetri. "Excuse me," she called to him, "but do you know of a place called LeBeau's?"

"The tavern?" Demetri eyed the fancy carriage dubiously.

"Unless there's another place called LeBeau's."

"It's just a few streets down," Demetri said. "Keep going straight, and—well, I'm staying there. I could show you."

"Sabine," called one of the familiar voices from the carriage, "who are you talking to?"

The carriage door opened. Someone stepped out. A thin young man with black hair and skin like fresh snow.

Demetri recognized him.

"Kinsley?" Demetri wondered if he was seeing things. "What are you doing here?" Kinsley was a soldier in Prince Garrett's company—Garrett, the crown prince of the Glen Kingdom, and Demetri's friend. But Demetri hadn't seen Garrett or his soldiers since they'd parted ways last autumn.

"Prince Demetri?" Kinsley looked stunned. "I'm—"

But whatever Kinsley was—whatever else he said—was lost. Because someone else stepped out of the carriage then, ducking her white blonde head through the doorway. "So where are we?" she asked, in a voice so achingly familiar, a voice that made Demetri feel like he was stuck in time again, as he had been for eighty-two years.

It was Briar.

4

REUNION

BRIAR HAD NOT HAD the best of days. First, the self-propelled carriage the Mariner counts sent to pick her up from the train depot broke down on the way to the castle. Briar managed to fix it, but she didn't want to be late, so she didn't take the time to change into a proper gown before arriving at the castle. The counts were not at all impressed to meet a princess in a harness vest and trousers stained with axle grease. Not that Briar really cared what a bunch of Mariner nobles thought, but she did need them—or rather, she needed the authority they wielded. So after that disaster of a first meeting, she managed to beg off staying in rooms at the castle and obtained directions to the town nearby—Moselle.

"So where are we?" Briar asked as she stepped out of the carriage. She consulted the compass built into the vambrace on her forearm, then glanced up. They'd come to a halt near a deserted stone pier. "This doesn't look like—"

She broke off. Standing beside Kinsley, looking just as dumb-founded as she felt, was someone she recognized. Someone she knew very well. Someone she hadn't seen in months and had hoped, but hadn't expected, to see again.

"*Demetri?*" Briar's voice came out in an uncharacteristically girlish squeal. She leapt down the carriage steps. When she reached Demetri, she threw her arms around him with enough exuberance that he staggered back a couple of steps. "Demetri! What are you *doing* here?"

His reply was muffled by her blouse, so she released him, stepping back to let him breathe. The last time she'd seen Demetri, he'd been lost and broken, departing for parts unknown to find a new life. He looked *different* now—his hair a little untidier than it used to be, his short coat a little rumpled, his fair face made ruddy by the sun. But he smiled at her, and it was a lighter smile than she remembered, unburdened by the weight of the past.

"It's really you," he said. "I thought I was seeing things. I've been—" His smile faltered. He glanced over his shoulder and then turned, his gaze sweeping the silent, empty pier behind him. A light mist was rolling in, obscuring the long jetty stretching out before them.

"Demetri?" Briar prompted. "You've been what?" When he didn't answer, she asked, "Are you looking for something?"

"Someone," Demetri muttered. "There was someone here..."

"I didn't see anyone here but you." Sabine, one of Briar's new guards, spoke hesitantly. "Er, Your Highness."

Demetri waved the title off with a hand. "She was just here." His smile returned, a little abashed. "I think."

Briar laughed. "Are you drunk?" she teased.

"Possibly." Demetri's smile widened, and Briar noticed his gaze was a little unfocused. "Probably."

"But what are you doing here?" Briar demanded. His clothes were of a more modest quality than the last time she'd seen him. His trousers were baggier, bunching where he'd tucked them into scuffed boots, and his tie was simple, little more than a thin scarf. "Are you living here?"

"For now. For the summer. What are *you* doing here?"

An excited jolt ran through Briar like a sparking current. "I'm here for the next three weeks. I've been working on a design for a steam-powered submarine," she told him. "King Victor—you know, Garrett's father—wrangled a bit with the Mariner counts, and they've given me permission to work on a model here on their coast. I think they're hoping to get some submarines of their own out of the deal," she added, "though the king instructed me to avoid making any indications that might be possible."

"And Garrett?" Demetri glanced towards the carriage. "He didn't come?"

"No. His father wants him home for a bit. He's been away so much in the past six months. I mean, it was one thing when the excursion to come rescue me went from a three-week trip to a six-week trip, but then he was gone for nearly three months hunting this past winter. And his father wasn't happy he was gone so long. I was a *bit* more understanding—but only a bit, since it meant I had to spend all that time *alone* with his father."

Demetri laughed. "Not *alone*, surely."

"Well, I mean, there were other people in the castle, but—not Garrett." It was the longest time she had spent apart from Garrett since she'd met him. "Truthfully, it gave me a chance to get to know the king a little better, which wasn't so bad—but I prefer being with Garrett."

"Me too," Demetri said sincerely.

Briar laughed and tossed her arms around him. "Oh, I've missed you, Demetri. There's so much to tell you! About the Glen Kingdom and what I've been doing and Garrett—" She couldn't believe her luck—that he was here for the summer. "Where are you staying?"

"I think where you're staying—LeBeau's Tavern."

"Oh, it's a *tavern?*" Briar grinned. "Even better. Better than the castle, at least. Come on, then." She linked her arm in his, practically dragging him into the carriage. "You can tell us how to get there. Since I'm fairly sure my guard are all lost."

"We are *not*," said the guard in the driver's seat, a compact young man with dark hair that had grown a bit long over the past several months. That was Alec. Unlike some of her guards, Alec was not new; he had been part of the excursion to rescue her last autumn. The same went for his twin brother, Aden, his quieter counterpart, who sat inside the carriage. Aden's hair was cut close to his head, and it was the only reason Briar could tell the twins apart.

"So you lot are *her* guard now?" Demetri asked as Kinsley settled into the carriage with them.

"We're sort of on loan," Kinsley said, shutting the carriage door.

"Garrett and I are still building up my guard," Briar told him. "I think you met Sabine—" She tipped her head back, indicating Sabine, riding outside. "She's one of mine. And two others are coming on behind us with all my things."

They reached the tavern within a few minutes. Demetri assured her it was a clean and safe establishment, despite the boisterous crowd in the taproom. Briar didn't mind. She'd spent most of her life locked in her own castle, and though she'd been to a few taverns in the Glen Kingdom, she still found the lively environment exciting and new.

While Aden and Alec booked rooms and found a place to park the carriage, Briar and Demetri seated themselves at a round table in the corner. The tabletop's warm veneer gleamed in the light of the shaded gear bulbs. Briar had a cup of tea brought to her by one of the auto-waiters and all the while blathered on, filling Demetri in on everything she'd been doing in the Glen Kingdom—getting to know the court, coming up to date on all the advancements she'd missed, like phonographs and typewriters and bicycles. Not to mention all the steam-powered devices. And she was working on her own inventions, of course.

"A flying machine?" Demetri asked curiously, sipping from his cup. He'd opted for tea as well; apparently, he'd decided he'd had enough wine for the night. "How would that work?"

"I'm still figuring it out," Briar admitted.

"I'll bet Garrett loves that idea."

"He doesn't like to talk about it." Briar laughed. "Oh, but Demetri—Garrett! Wait until you hear what's been going on with *him*."

"You said he went on a hunting trip." Demetri propped his chin in his hand, a few strands of hair falling forward to shade his eyes. "For three months. Which does seem a bit long. I hope he caught some good game."

"Not exactly." Briar pulled one of her feet onto the seat of her cushioned bench, letting the other dangle off the floor. "Though he did run into some were-wolves."

"Were—what now?"

Briar laughed, launching into the whole story of Garrett's trip into the Black Forest and the shapeshifting creatures he'd encountered there. Demetri broke in several times, peppering her with questions, and they had a good laugh about Garrett and the trouble he always found. Then, resting her elbows on the table, Briar asked Demetri, "So what have *you* been up to? You said you're staying here for the summer, but doing what?"

Demetri turned his head away from the warm glow of the light fixture, shadows falling over half his face. His eyes flitted over the large taproom. "Oh, I'm just picking up jobs here and there. Well. I've probably spent too much time pub crawling instead."

"With who? Not by yourself? You were alone when we ran into you."

"No, I've made some friends." Demetri gestured vaguely. "The group had mostly broken up for the night when you came along. I'd just stepped out for some fresh air and..." He trailed off, his forehead creasing.

"And what?"

"There was this girl," he muttered. "I know your guard—Sabine?—said she didn't see anyone, but she *was* there. Weird how she disappeared like that."

"Are you sure you didn't hallucinate her?" Briar asked. "You *had* been drinking."

Demetri threw her a wry glance. "I definitely didn't halluci-nate her." He ran a hand across the back of his neck. "I kissed her, and I definitely didn't hallucinate *that*."

"You *kissed* her?" Briar burst out laughing. "Some girl you just met? Do you even know her name?"

"No." Demetri flashed a reluctant grin. "I didn't mean to. It just happened."

"You *were* drunk." Briar leaned back in her chair. "To think, Demetri Georgas the Sixth, kissing some random girl whose name he doesn't even know..."

"I know." Demetri dropped his gaze, picking at something on the varnished tabletop.

Briar bit her lip. She shouldn't have used his full name. It *was* his name and always would be, but it was also a reminder of the life he'd left behind, the family he'd lost.

She was glad to hear he was moving on. Not just to new places, but meeting new people, making new friends. Kissing new girls. She would have hated to see him still haunted by his past, struggling to break free of everything he had suffered because of her. She would not have begrudged him that, of course. He was entitled to his feelings. But it was nice to sit here with him, chatting and joking as friends. She was glad they could still do that.

"I've missed you, Demetri." She tilted her head, leaning her cheek into her fist. "I'm really glad you're doing so well."

Demetri didn't answer right away, his gaze still fixed on the table. For a moment, Briar wondered whether she'd said something wrong. But then he looked up, smiling. "Yes. Me too." His gaze drifted over the room one more time. "I've missed you too."

———◆○◆———

Demetri retired a little while later. Briar went up to her own room, but she didn't sleep. Still dressed in her trousers and blouse, she lay atop the soft coverlet on her bed. A faint sea breeze crept inside through an open window, cooling her room and scenting the air with salt. It had to be three in the morning, she thought, glancing out the window. She watched the moon peeking through the wispy clouds in the sky, watched as it sank lower and lower, as though it would drop right into the frothy ocean.

Briar flipped onto her stomach, bunching her pillow beneath her head. It was ironic, perhaps, having spent more than eighty years in an enchanted sleep, but these days, Briar did not sleep well at all. She wished Garrett was here. It was easier to pass her sleepless nights when she had someone to talk to. Kinsley didn't mind chatting with her to all hours of the morning, but they'd had a long day. It wouldn't be fair to drag him from his bed now.

She lay awake for another hour. A soothing, gentle roar floated in from outside, and Briar listened to it for a while before she rose from her bed, pushed aside the lace curtain at the window, and peered out.

It was the ocean. Her room looked out the side of the tavern, and her view of the beach was unobstructed. The streetlamp near the back of the inn had wound down to a dim, flickering glow, but Briar could see better in this dark than she could at midday. The ocean lay beyond a sandy beach, black waves breaking upon the shore, driven by a fierce, gusting wind. Briar was captivated by the sight of it. She had never seen the ocean before.

She turned away, but instead of going back to bed, she went for her boots, her vambrace, and her brown leather harness, strapping the latter on over her high-necked blouse.

The back staircase near Briar's room led straight down to an exit facing the beach. Still, it was not so close as it had seemed from her window. She picked her way through scrubby grass. The tavern sat on a slightly heightened crag, so Briar had to scrabble down a short, rocky hillside to reach the shoreline. She found the beach here was quite narrow, little more than a thin strip of sand that vanished into the coal-black water. There must be an easier path, she realized, that likely led to a more attractive beach.

But Briar didn't mind. The last of the clouds were clearing, and the moon was a beacon in the dark. She found a pitted boulder jutting up out of the swirling, foamy water, and she perched atop it, legs dangling in front of her. She tilted her head back as the wind misted sea spray into her face. Her lips soon grew salty, her hair damp and frizzing.

She'd only been sitting for a few minutes when a sharp *snap* sounded out behind her. Briar whipped around, scanning the dark shoreline. Down the way, the beach narrowed even further, coming to a point that vanished beneath a canopy of tall, twisted trees. The trees grew right into the shallows of a small cove, and sheets of pale moss hung from their broad branches, creating a murky entry into a den of shadows.

"Is someone there?" Briar demanded.

There was a moment's silence, a moment in which Briar was sure someone stood within that gloomy cove, just out of sight. Then she spotted movement out of the corner of her eye—not in the cove, but a little ways up the crag. A tall, thin figure stepped out from behind a large rock.

"It's just me," Kinsley said. He wore a resigned look on his face.

Briar's middle caved in as she let out a slow, silent breath. "Why aren't you in bed, Kinsley?" she asked, a little annoyed that he'd scared her.

"Why aren't you, Your Highness?"

"You know why." Briar flicked a small pebble off her rocky perch.

"Let me rephrase." Kinsley approached her, treading carefully around the edge of the shoreline. His black hair was a little tousled, and though he wore his navy blue uniform coat, it was unbuttoned over his cotton shirt. "Why are you out here, on this deserted beach, in the middle of the night, *alone?*"

"Technically, it's morning," Briar pointed out. "And I'm not alone. You're here."

"Only because I followed you."

"I can take care of myself."

Kinsley clasped his hands behind his back. "I know you can. Nevertheless, I would hate to have to tell Prince Garrett that something happened to you, and I wasn't there." He paused. "And even though you *can* take care of yourself...you don't always seem ready to do so."

Briar considered this, brushing wispy hairs from her face. "What do you mean?"

Kinsley looked like he was considering his words carefully. He usually did. "Earlier, when we were on the road to the castle," he said, "and the carriage broke down and got stuck. You managed the repairs well enough, but before that, it took us more than an hour to get the wheels out of the mud."

"And?"

Kinsley lifted an eyebrow. "Well, you could have lifted the carriage easily enough on your own. But you didn't."

Briar shifted. The curse that had fallen upon her had done more than put her to sleep for eighty-some years. Once the sleep had ended, she—and everyone in her kingdom—found they were slowly rotting, becoming living corpses ruled by violence and hungry for flesh. Luckily, most of that had resolved once Briar broke the curse, but some effects lingered. Such as supernatural strength.

But even that was not without drawbacks. "Using my strength would have put me out for the rest of the day," Briar protested. Tapping into her supernatural abilities—the strength, the speed—took a lot out of her.

"Maybe. But we could have caught you a stray snack. There were plenty of those around." By "snack," Kinsley meant a raw animal of some kind—rabbit, mouse, squirrel. Eating raw flesh still fueled her, giving her energy. Another lingering effect of the curse.

"Look." Briar gazed out at the black horizon. "I'll use my strength if I really need to. If I'm in danger. If it's the only defense I have. But I don't think I should get used to relying on it."

"Why not?"

Briar didn't respond. She glanced down at the vambrace clasped around her arm, just above her wrist. She'd installed a compass and a small timepiece in it to make it useful, but the vambrace's real purpose was to cover her ruined forearm—to disguise the gaping hole in her flesh, left there by the dark fairy.

The fairy she'd been forced to kill with her supernatural strength.

She hadn't *really* killed her. That's what she told herself. All she'd done was make the dark fairy mortal. What had killed her was her own curse, rebounding on her for breaking her word.

Briar didn't really kill her. Not directly. And she'd had to do it. It had been the only way to save her people, save herself. Kill the fairy who cast the curse, and the curse was broken. She'd looked for another way until she'd had no more time. She'd done what she had to do.

So why did the dark's fairy death still gnaw at her so?

"I'll use it if I have to," she repeated.

Kinsley took the hint. "Fair enough." He clasped his hands before him. "But I'm still going to follow you around. It's my job."

Briar laughed and slipped off the boulder. "I'm starting to feel I don't do enough to thank you, Kinsley. You should have some time to yourself this summer. Tell you what, I'll find you a beau while we're here."

"I'd rather you not." Kinsley turned to lead the way up the rocky hill. "I don't trust your taste, Your Highness."

"What! What's wrong with Garrett?"

"Well, nothing is *wrong* with him, I suppose. He just isn't my type."

"Well, that's good to know. I'd hate to think I was keeping him from you. That would be a bit awkward."

"Rather, Your Highness."

Briar stepped up to begin the climb back to the tavern, but as a gust of wind blew past her, she paused.

Kinsley glanced down at her. "Something wrong, Highness?"

Briar wrinkled her nose. "Do you smell that?" She pointed, not towards the murky cove she'd spotted earlier, but in the opposite direction, where the beach wended around. A massive rock formation jutted out from the hillside there, cutting off this strip of beach from what lay beyond. "You came around that way. Did you see anything?"

Kinsley went very still, like a watch dog on alert. "Like what?"

Briar didn't answer. She didn't want to voice her suspicions aloud. With a hollow pit in her stomach, she edged around the rocky crag and into the small inlet beyond it, fearing what she would find.

The wind had died down, but the stench Briar had caught still scented the air, stronger in this spot. It was *thick*, rankly cloying, and Briar thought, were it not for the raw flesh she ate on a daily basis, she probably would have gagged. Following close on her heels, Kinsley sucked in an audible breath, covering his mouth and nose with a hand. "Your Highness—"

Briar continued forward, her boots crunching over gritty sand. Her keen eyes traveled over the dark expanse of beach, and then onto the clump of rock protruding from the hillside. The lowest point of the rock was spotted with white growth and dotted with seaweed, as though the water washed over it during high tide.

And then she spotted it. A small opening in the rock, too small to be a proper cave. More seaweed lay strewn within it, half-buried in the wet, clumpy sand.

Then Briar realized. It wasn't seaweed.

It was a mushy pile of bones and clothing, coated in a sheen of blood and viscera.

5

CULLED

PERPETUA RETURNED HOME TO find a death omen in her mirror bowl.

She stared at the stemless flower, floating atop the clear water like some kind of adornment. It was a hellebore, six-petaled and inky black. Black, like her future.

As the full realization of what she was seeing crashed over her, Perpetua sucked in a dry breath. Her arm shot out, ready to crumple the flower, but then she froze. It was a symbol of death—no, a *message* of death—and suddenly, Perpetua feared what might happen if she touched it.

Why was it here? What had she done? She choked on a near-hysterical laugh. What *hadn't* she done in the past three days? She'd spared the life of a human meant for naiad food. She'd sought that human out—spoken to him—*kissed* him—and although she'd had every opportunity to kill him, she'd allowed him to live.

Perpetua let out a long, low breath, recoiling from the stone basin that served as her mirror. Her home here, in this lagoon along the coast, several miles south of Moselle, was a secluded one. Specifically, she lived in one of the caves rimming the lagoon—a great, rounded, yawning cave with dank walls covered in algae that glowed at night. The interior was damp and cold, just the way she liked it, and a shallow pool was sunk into the floor further back in the cave, providing a refreshing place to lounge.

Naiads were solitary creatures. They fed alone, they lived alone. Others rarely ventured into this lagoon, and even if they did, they were not likely to discover Perpetua's cave. It could usually be reached on foot from the coast—a low, rocky bar connected the two—but when the tide was in, the bar was usually covered. Which was to say, Perpetua had always felt safe here in her cave, in her home.

Until now.

Perpetua closed her eyes. Her mind drifted back through her memories of last night on the docks. With *him*. Demetri.

She'd kissed him. Or rather, he'd kissed her, and though she'd told him to do it, she hadn't compelled him. Oh, she had at first—when she'd questioned him, demanding his name, asking what he was. She'd used her Voice to force him to answer honestly.

But when she'd told him to kiss her, she'd dropped her Voice, forgoing any mystical compulsion. She wasn't sure why. Truthfully, she hadn't been sure if she really wanted him to kiss her. It was just...standing there so close to him, listening to him speak about his life and his past...hearing him say she'd *saved* him...such a strange notion, saving the life of another...

In that moment, she had been overcome by the power of his words, the closeness of his body. And she had been curious to see if he would kiss her of his own accord. She had been curious to see what it would feel like.

And he'd kissed her. And it was *glorious*. She reached a hand to her lips, remembering how light and sweet it had been at first. Like a whisper. And then...Perpetua felt weirdly warm at the memory. As though she could still feel his hands on her waist, his tongue sweeping through her mouth. His pulse quickening beneath her palm as she cupped his neck. When it had ended, she'd found herself breathless and quivering, a fluttery sensation in her chest.

Oh, yes. It had been something. Something strange and wonderful.

Now, though, it seemed the stupidest thing in the world. Still, the Ternion would hardly cull her for kissing a human. Or would they? Perpetua doubted anything like that had ever happened before. Naiads didn't kiss. Not each other, and not the human males they mated with. It was a human thing, something most naiads had probably never heard of. Given that most naiads didn't pay as much attention to humans as Perpetua did.

No, it wasn't the kiss that was going to get her killed. She didn't see how the Ternion could know about that anyway.

It was sparing the human's life. That had to be it.

The shallow puddle Perpetua stood in shuddered, water rippling over her webbed feet in a warning. In the next second, a shadow fell across the low opening of her cave, casting itself across the rugged wall, its shape distorted by clumps of algae.

Perpetua's breath stuck in her throat, her gaze darting towards the black hellebore, still floating in her bowl. Then she hurtled towards the cave opening and lunged, her hand closing around the throat of the naiad who stood there.

Only, it wasn't the naiad Perpetua expected. It was someone else.

"Is this some new form of greeting, Perpetua?" The naiad's words were awkwardly formed through her jagged teeth. "Something you picked up from the humans?"

"Tatiana." Perpetua dropped her hand from the naiad's neck and stepped back. She was so rattled, she nearly stumbled. "You should know better than to sneak up on me!"

"I do now." Tatiana stepped away from the wall, rubbing her neck gingerly. Perpetua felt silly. Here at the opening to her cave, the bright morning light clearly outlined Tatiana's long, wavy black hair and mud-brown scales.

"I thought you were—" Perpetua gulped as she turned and walked into her cave. The black hellebore still lay atop her water bowl, and the last thing she wanted was for Tatiana to see it. Allies though they might be, Tatiana was a predator. Just like all naiads. Perpetua didn't want to display anything that could be interpreted as a weakness.

"You thought I was who?" Tatiana prompted, following behind her.

"Candelaria." Perpetua flung a hand up, pointing wildly. "Did you drop that?"

"What?" And when Tatiana looked around, scanning the shallows at the cave entrance, Perpetua hurried back and snatched up the flower, concealing it behind her.

"I see nothing." Tatiana frowned.

"Oh—I thought there was something there." Perpetua crushed the flower's silk petals as she closed her hand around it. "So. What are you doing here?"

"Did you say you thought I was Candelaria?" Tatiana's dark eyes widened. "I thought she didn't know where you lived."

"She doesn't. And she had better never know."

"She won't hear it from me." Tatiana pouted. "You know that. Even if I thought she would let me into her shoal, I wouldn't tell her."

"Her shoal," Perpetua scoffed. "Naiads are not meant to live in *shoals*. That big cave she has with all those others—it will go badly on her, trust me. They will turn on each other, start fighting over food and territory. You watch."

"Speaking of fighting over food." Tatiana ventured further into the cave. "Is that why you thought I was Candelaria, come here to attack you?"

The gills on the right side of Perpetua's neck flared in embarrassment. "What are you talking about?"

"*You* know. I heard all about it. Did you really fight with Candelaria over food? Over a human she had already claimed?"

"*I* claimed him," Perpetua retorted. "I saw him first."

"But she laid hands on him first. Or so I heard. That is all that matters."

Perpetua aimed for a careless look. "All that matters is she gave him up to me."

Tatiana snorted. "*Every*one is talking about you, you know. I hope the food was worth it."

Perpetua's mind skittered over the memory of Demetri's lips on hers. "It was." Or it had been. Before Perpetua came home to a promise of death. "Is that the only reason you're here? To mock me about fighting with Candelaria?"

"I came to ask why you did not tell me that Candelaria and her...shoal...set up a shipwreck." Tatiana's tone was faintly accusing. "*You* went and fed off it without telling me!"

"I found out about it at the last minute," Perpetua protested. "Anyway, I thought you preferred getting your food off the docks."

"I know, but—" Tatiana lowered her voice. "The Ternion dictate."

Perpetua fought to keep her expression clean. The crushed petals in her fist felt hot against her skin. "They did not say we could never take food off the docks. Just to keep the number down. So the humans do not get suspicious."

"Do you think they would? Do you think they would really hunt us?"

"If enough of them went missing," Perpetua said. Humans hunting her seemed like a ridiculous worry, the least of her problems. "They are not stupid. Still, they are also unpredictable, and sailors go off all the time. You can still take one here and there, I'm sure."

"I suppose." Tatiana lowered herself onto a broad, smooth boulder, a shiver rippling through her brown scales. "Still. I don't want to risk crossing the Ternion."

Perpetua's scales felt uncomfortably dry. She retreated further into her cave to sit in her shallow pool, using her free hand to splash water over her scaled legs. "Have you ever known someone who crossed the Ternion? Anyone who received the death omen, I mean?"

Tatiana barked a laugh. "Of course not. The hellebore? I fear the Ternion as much as anyone, but *that* is only a silly story."

Until this morning, Perpetua had thought so too. Come to think of it, maybe it still was. Maybe the hellebore was just a cruel trick. It would be a trick worthy of Candelaria, that was for sure, and much more her style than attacking Perpetua outright. Maybe she *had* discovered where Perpetua lived and left the flower to frighten her. "You've never heard anything true about it? Or about the Ternion, what they do to naiads who cross them?"

"I have not heard of anyone receiving the hellebore. But crossing the Ternion—one of the naiads who lives with Candelaria, we sabotaged a boat together once. Just a small one. And she told me a story about someone who angered the Ternion."

"What happened?"

"I don't know. Only that the naiad disappeared. No one ever saw her again."

Perpetua dug her nails into her palm.

"Why do you ask?" Tatiana cocked her head. "You're not thinking of doing anything foolish, are you?"

"No," Perpetua said. "I am not."

She had already done something foolish.

After withdrawing a promise from Perpetua that she would let her know the next time she heard about a staged wreck or a group hunt, Tatiana left. Perpetua watched her go, still sitting in her pool, and once Tatiana was gone, she opened her hand, letting the crumpled black petals float into the water. She exhaled slowly.

A silly story, a child's tale. Maybe Tatiana was right. Of course, if Candelaria had discovered her cave, that was a problem too.

But nowhere near as problematic as the Ternion descending upon her to make her...*disappear*.

She had been so stupid. Sparing Demetri. Saving him. Perpetua's mouth twisted over the word. It wasn't that she didn't know what it meant—it was just a foreign concept. A thing of humans. One naiad didn't care much for the life of another naiad, and they certainly never cared for the life of one human.

Perpetua flicked at the water with her fingers. She didn't *care* about Demetri's life. She'd fought Candelaria for him on principle. Candelaria had followed her that night just to take whatever human Perpetua wanted. She wasn't about to let that golden-haired shark take anything from her. And as for letting him go...

Perpetua slumped, wilting like seaweed. That was the stupid part, that was the real breach in naiad law. Letting him go. She knew it was stupid, but she could still see him in her mind's eye—the way he'd looked that night on the rowboat, bleeding and drenched and dazed and utterly at her mercy, but in a way she'd never considered before. She could still hear his voice, roughened by seawater, asking who she was.

With a sigh, Perpetua climbed to her feet. She would just have to track Candelaria down and make her confess to leaving the flower in her cave. And if she didn't—

A peal of thunder rumbled outside. Perpetua frowned, turning to look. The thunder sounded close by, but the patch of sky she glimpsed through the opening was the clear periwinkle of dawn.

A thrill of foreboding shuddered through Perpetua. She was suddenly seized by the surest knowing that something was wrong, that the thunder was not natural. Before she could think through what that meant, panic rushed into her, scattering her thoughts, and she turned to run back into her cave—

She didn't make it three steps before a *force* enveloped her, like huge, invisible hands, hoisting her into the air. A scream left Perpetua's lips as she was spun around, tossed back, and slammed into the cave wall. Perpetua's scream died, her breath freezing in her throat. For a moment, her vision went dark. Pain shot through her as the rock jabbed into her skin, slicing her open. But she couldn't move. She hung there, pinned by those invisible hands, webbed feet dangling off the ground.

As Perpetua's breath returned to her, the dark spots in her vision receded. She blinked hard.

Three naiads stood inside the entrance to her cave. Beyond them, Perpetua could see the sky outside was no longer clear. Black clouds had formed, bunching together, and bolts of lightning *cracked*, throwing brilliant, terrifying light over the scene. Over the trio of naiads gathered before her, their hair whipping in the wind gusting through the cave.

Perpetua's stomach clenched so tightly, she thought she would be sick. She recognized each of the naiads, each of the three. She had never seen them before, but she knew instantly who they were.

The Ternion. The mythical, fearsome triumvirate who governed all naiads. Half-gods, half-queens. Few naiads had ever laid eyes on them. No naiad ever *wanted* to lay eyes on them.

There was Nadalia, the youngest of the three; she looked around Perpetua's age, though Perpetua knew she was older. Silky black hair streamed down her back. Her green scales were a shade darker than Perpetua's, green like seaweed. Her gaze was paralyzing in its indifference. On the right side was

Meliora, short and small-boned but no less terrifying, with alabaster-white skin that stood out starkly against her black scales. Unlike impassive Nadalia, her red eyes blazed with fury.

And the last of the Ternion.... Perpetua's heart thumped, beating so hard, she was sure it would break right through her ribcage and burst through her chest.

The last of the Ternion was Sohalia. The sea witch.

She stood in the center. Long and lean, she seemed to tower over the other two, even though Nadalia was nearly as tall as she was. There was a *charge* to her, an occult energy that amplified everything about her, from her blue-black scales to her merciless eyes. As though the magic filling her veins would spill forth, flooding the cave until they all choked on it.

No one knew where the sea witch's power came from. No other naiad possessed magic, not even her Ternion sisters. There were all sorts of dark stories about Sohalia, rumors that naiads only dared to whisper about in the softest voices. That she had made a deal with a demon from the underworld and gained magic in return. That she had discovered an ancient scroll inscribed with words of power. That she had been born with the magic, inexplicably gifted by the sea gods.

But they were all just stories. Until today, the sea witch *herself* had been little more than a story to Perpetua. But here she stood, in Perpetua's cave. And the reality was more terrifying than all the stories combined.

"Where do you think you're running to, Perpetua?" Sohalia asked in a sing-song voice. She stood with one arm stretched forth, gripping that invisible force that pinned Perpetua to the wall. "There is no place you can hide from us."

Perpetua opened her mouth to speak, but another invisible hand wrapped itself around her throat, crushing her windpipe.

"You will speak when we tell you," Meliora said, "and not before."

"We have come," Nadalia intoned, "to sentence you for your crime."

Sohalia arched an eyebrow. "I assume you know what you have done, naiad?"

The pressure against Perpetua's airway loosened. The breath she gulped in hurt, scraping over her throat. Pulse throbbing in her neck, she coughed and tried to speak. "I—I don't—"

"You interfered with another naiad's kill," Meliora snarled.

"You allowed a human to go free from a hunt," Nadalia said, "risking the lives of us all."

"But he didn't remember anything!" Perpetua burst out. "And I made sure he didn't remember me!"

"Not at all?" Sohalia prompted. The amusement in her voice was far worse than Meliora's anger or Nadalia's icy indifference. "Not even the kiss you shared with him?"

Perpetua went cold all over, down to the bone. It was said the Ternion knew everything that happened in the sea—but even if one didn't believe that superstition, it was easy to see how word of what had happened at the shipwreck could have gotten back to them. According to Tatiana, everyone knew about the fight with Candelaria, and even though she'd been careful, anyone could have seen her towing Demetri to safety.

But how could they possibly know what had transpired between her and Demetri on the docks last night?

"My sisters—" Sohalia indicated the two on either side of her "—are of the opinion you should die for your crimes. What do you have to say about that, Perpetua?"

Another burst of wind swelled through the cave. The algae on the walls flared alight, casting a ghostly green glow over the trio of powerful naiads. Terror arced through Perpetua, as swift and hot as the lightning flashing outside.

"Please," she gasped. "Please, I won't—I'll do anything, anything you want. I—"

"Would you kill the human?" Meliora demanded. "The one you allowed to go free?"

"*Yes*," Perpetua answered, though the word tasted like foul refuse in her mouth. "I will, I swear—"

"Unnecessary, if he does not remember the night of the hunt." Nadalia flicked her fingers. "And such a kill would only draw more unwanted attention to our kind."

"Then if there is nothing to be done—" Meliora drew her lips back in a sneer "—I see no course but to kill this naiad for her crime."

Perpetua's heart felt like a stone in her chest. But before she could draw breath for another plea, Sohalia spoke.

"Oh, I think I can come up with an alternative," the sea witch said. "A more *fitting* punishment for this naiad. More suited to her crime."

Nadalia and Meliora looked at her sharply. Sohalia smiled at them both, baring her teeth.

Nadalia shrugged. Meliora's response was almost deferential. "Whatever you think is best."

Sohalia's smile widened, her face a grotesque rictus. Perpetua shriveled beneath the weight of that mad smile. As Sohalia dropped her arm, Perpetua fell, crumpling to the cave floor. She crouched before the trio, too afraid to lift her head to look at them.

"If you love humans so much, Perpetua," the sea witch said, "then you shall join them."

A burst of power, insubstantial but *strong*—like a cloud of bricks—slammed into Perpetua. She tumbled back, sprawling flat. Another blast of wind from the gale outside spiraled through the cave, and the algae flared alight again, so bright that Perpetua was blinded by their luminosity.

Then came the pain. Perpetua bit her tongue against a scream, tasting blood. She felt as though every scale on her body was being ripped from her flesh, one by one. She felt like her skin was on *fire*, raw, scalding, blistering. Her gills burned too, searing as though hot wax had been dribbled down the sides of her neck. Her heart was beating too fast for her body, the pounding so loud, she was sure her eardrums would burst. Everything had gone, her vision cloaked in shadows. She was sure she would black out, she *wanted to black out*, to die, anything to make it stop—

But it didn't. It went on and on. For how long, she could not say. Hours. Days. The whole of her life.

And then—finally—it was over. The pain receded from her body, only the memory of it lingering inside her. The thudding in her head quieted, until all she could hear were her own ragged breaths. Her vision returned, hazy at first, then clearing. The top reaches of her cave came into focus, patches of fuzzy lichen barely visible in the gloom. She had fallen. She lay flat on her back against the cave floor, and it felt strange, cold and damp in a way that was less familiar and almost uncomfortable.

Stifling a groan, she pushed herself upright. Unfiltered daylight stung her eyes, shining through the cave entrance.

She was alone. The Ternion had gone.

Sharp relief pierced her. They were gone. They hadn't killed her, they had let her be. Well, not entirely. The sea witch had caused her such pain as she had never felt before, but it was gone now. Only a tingling remained, like gooseflesh pebbling her skin—

Perpetua froze. Her *skin.*

Suddenly, she realized why the surface of her cave felt so unwelcoming. She dropped her gaze, her eyes traveling over her legs.

They were scaleless. Bare. Entirely human.

Perpetua gaped. She didn't recall assuming human-form. She didn't feel like she *was* in human-form. It took effort to assume and maintain human-form; it took concentration, and Perpetua's mind was as scattered as the wreckage left by a hurricane. Being in human-form was the furthest thing from her mind right now.

Gathering what little focus she could muster, she tried to drop the form. She thought of her scales and webbed feet and gills, but they did not appear. Everything in her body went taut, and she hastened to stand, nearly slipping over the slick rock. Her human toes couldn't grip the pitted surface the way her webbed feet did. Indeed, she caught her big toe against the rock and cried out. Bright red blood welled up through the broken flesh, and she stared at it in disbelief.

She slapped at the sides of her neck, feeling for her gills. They weren't there. She ran her hands over her torso, her hips, her thighs, just in case she was imagining the naked brown skin, just in case the terrible pain had caused her to hallucinate.

The terrible pain. Sohalia's spell. What was it she'd said?

If you love humans so much, Perpetua, then you shall join them.

No. It wasn't possible. It *couldn't* be possible. Perpetua wavered. For a moment, her vision swam, and then she slipped to the floor, her weak, human legs giving out. More blood blossomed at her knee, the rock scraping her flesh, but Perpetua hardly felt the pain.

Human. *Human.*

Sohalia had made her human.

6

CHARGED

DEMETRI WOKE EARLY. As he lay in bed and listened to the *tick-tick-tick* of the clock on his mantel, somehow he knew the sun was not up yet. He sat up slowly, cringing; his head felt like it was encased in iron.

He looked at the clock. It was not yet six.

Demetri groaned. Even after drinking as much as he had last night, sleep had eluded him. He'd tossed and turned for hours, his troubled mind chasing sleep to no avail.

Because Briar was here. Briar was *here*. His ghost become real.

He had thought it a terrible torment, being away from her. It had been Demetri's choice to leave and end things with Briar. But he had regretted it almost every day since. He knew it was for the best—he knew things could not go back to the way they were, and Briar was with Garrett now. But he'd missed her all the same. He'd yearned for her all the same.

Now she was here, and all he wanted to do was run away.

He didn't know how he'd gotten through last night—seeing her on the pier, enduring her hugs, chatting with her at the tavern. As though everything that had happened between them was nothing, as though a mere seven months was enough time to move past it all.

He didn't know how he'd smiled and laughed across a table from her, like he was just fine. He'd felt outside of it all, as though he'd been in some kind of trance.

Demetri sighed, forcing himself to his feet. He felt like death warmed over. He definitely needed a bath and a shave, he thought, retreating into the washroom. Then he changed into clean clothes. He paused before he left the room, wondering why he felt like something was missing. It took him a moment to realize it was his rapier. It was a century old—just like him—and he'd lost it in the shipwreck. It felt odd going without it, but he strapped on a pistol and left the room.

By the time he stepped outside, the sun was creeping up over the ocean. Shades of coral streaked across the horizon, casting a shimmering light over the water. Gulls circled overhead, crying out to each other, and as Demetri watched one dive towards the beach, he noticed a small crowd gathered at the edge of the rocky crag sloping towards the sea. Frowning, Demetri went to join the throng, trying to glean something from the hum of their murmurs. The mood was tense, the faces in the crowd drawn in somber lines, their voices hushed and short. A quick glimpse over the taller heads showed Demetri a mass of figures in sage-green uniforms scuttling over the shoreline below. A patrol of capital guard.

Demetri was just about to ask a stranger what was going on when he spotted a familiar face in the crowd. "Aden?" Demetri ducked around a couple of elderly women and found himself beside Aden, one of Briar's guards. He stood with two young women who must have also been guards, for they were dressed in the navy blue of the Glen Kingdom. Demetri knew one of them—Tory, a short girl with ruddy cheeks who carried an alarming amount of knives on her person. She had been on the expedition to the Mountain Kingdom to rescue Briar last autumn.

The other girl Demetri didn't recognize. She was quite a bit taller than Tory, and a few years older, he guessed, with glossy blonde hair tied back high on top of her head.

"What's going on?" Demetri asked Aden. Aden was the quieter, more serious counterpart to his often-joking twin brother. "Did something happen down on the beach?"

Aden nodded. "Princess Briar and Kinsley found some remains in a small cave. Human remains."

"Briar? She's up this early?"

"I don't think she ever went to bed, Highness."

"You don't have to call me that." Demetri craned his neck to see through the crowd. "Is she still down there? With Kinsley?"

"She's been down there for over two hours." This flat response came from the blonde guard. She had quite an unfriendly stare. Demetri wasn't sure if he had offended her somehow, or if she always looked like that. "One of the Mariner counts was in the area and the capital guard sent word to him. They made her wait until he turned up to question her." She raised a dark eyebrow. "Maybe you could help her out? Being a prince and all."

"Gallia," Aden said in a low voice, looking embarrassed.

"What? He said not to call him 'Your Highness.'"

"Yes, because I'm not really a prince," Demetri said with a small smile. "Not anymore. I don't have any authority to command a Mariner count." His smile disappeared. "Briar does, though. And she doesn't usually take orders from anyone."

Tory said, "I don't think she wants to offend the counts, Prince—I mean—"

"Demetri," Demetri supplied.

"Demetri." Tory looked dubious about addressing him so, but she went on. "Because she's here on their permission, you see."

"To work on her submarine." Demetri nodded.

"I don't think they suspect her or anything," Aden said quickly, "but the count has been down there with her for a while. Maybe—er—maybe you *could*—"

"I'll go check on her," Demetri cut in. All three soldiers looked relieved. Suppressing a sigh, Demetri picked his way through the crowd, murmuring his apologies as he eased past the onlookers and descended the hillside.

A capital guardsman tried to stop him at the base of the crag, but Kinsley turned up and waved him through. Kinsley led him down the narrow shoreline, around a sharp rock formation jutting out into the water. The small, sandy clearing beyond held even more guardsmen, and there as well, Demetri saw, was Briar. She was speaking to an older man who must have been the Mariner count. He wore formal morning dress—a dark, padded frock coat buttoned over his front, and a stiff necktie folded wing-style over the base of his throat. He was a stout man with tightly curled, sable hair and tawny brown skin. As Demetri approached them, he heard the count say, "...questions must be asked. There's been a murder, after all!"

"We don't know it was a murder," Briar responded. She wore the same clothes she'd been in last night. Beneath the glare of the rising sun—especially bright as it climbed over the water—she looked dreadfully pale. She also had a weird smile plastered on her face, but given that she spoke through gritted teeth, the smile gave the impression of a feral fox. "And we *have* answered your guards' questions. Several times. I only—Demetri!" Briar broke off when she caught sight of him, her frozen smile relaxing into a real one.

"Briar." Demetri returned her smile tentatively. As he joined her, a familiar gleam entered her eyes that made his stomach drop. It was the look she got when she had a particularly troublesome idea. "Is everything all right?"

"No, everything is not all right!" the count spluttered. "There has been a murder here, young man!"

Briar drew in a gasp that was decidedly un-Briar-like. "Count Reynard," she said, her hand falling on Demetri's shoulder, "don't you know who this *is?*"

Demetri started, "Uh, Briar—"

Briar's grip on his shoulder tightened. Demetri went silent.

The count pursed his lips. "I can't say that I do, Princess. And I really don't—"

"This is my friend Demetri." Briar pitched her voice over the count's. "My *good* friend Demetri, who—with the aid of Prince Garrett—rescued me from the corpse-ridden Mountain Kingdom. And of course, he is *also* a prince of the Glen Kingdom."

Demetri felt as though someone had run him over with a carriage.

"A prince of the Glen Kingdom?" The count looked confused. "I don't understand how—"

"Much like myself, Demetri is the last of an old royal line," Briar explained. "A direct descendant of the Georgas, actually." This was rather simplifying. By now, Briar's story was well-known; it had been circulated throughout the penny press papers, even here in the Mariner Kingdom. Demetri, on the other hand, was a rather anonymous figure, and he supposed it was a bit much to explain he'd been preserved in an enchantment for eighty-two years.

"*You* know," Briar added, "the Georgas. The family that ruled the Glen Kingdom before King Victor's line."

"An ancient and noble lineage, to be sure." Count Reynard dipped his head, eyeing Demetri with sharp interest. Demetri groaned silently. "My deepest apologies, Your Highness. I didn't realize the princess was accompanied by such an illustrious person as yourself!"

"She isn't," Demetri said. Then he winced as Briar dug her fingers into him again. "What I meant was—" He shot her a quick look "—I didn't accompany her from the Glen Kingdom. I was already here. I've been in Moselle for a few weeks now."

"Have you?" The count furrowed his brow. Briar's fingers clenched around Demetri's shoulder so tightly, he was sure the bone would shatter. But he didn't care. Briar could brag about his lineage all she wanted—for what reason, he was not sure—but he didn't have to play along. Not when he'd made it clear he was done with that life.

"Actually, since you're here—" Demetri glanced around as he addressed the count, his gaze trailing the capital guardsmen as they conferred with each other and encouraged bystanders to keep away. "I wonder if I could ask after any information you've gathered about a shipwreck a few days ago. I was on the ship—"

"You were!" the count cried. Demetri nearly jumped, he was so startled. "You were the sole survivor?"

"Yes. I wonder if you've discovered—"

"Well, that is fortunate indeed, Your Highness," the count said fervently. "Is that why you're here, then? I should have known Victor wouldn't abandon us to such troubles! I'd half-wondered why he hadn't sent that son of his with Princess Briar, everyone knows he's an expert in—well—*strange* occurrences and creatures. But if, as the princess says, you also rescued her from the Mountain Kingdom, then I suppose you will do just as well."

Demetri looked at him dumbly. "I beg your pardon?"

"Mermaids, Prince Demetri, mermaids!" The count shook his head. "Everyone knows that ship was out hunting them—"

"Well, actually, we were hunting—"

"Ever seen a mermaid?" the count barked. "Did you see any that night?"

"N-no," Demetri stuttered. "I mean, I don't think so. I can't remember anything, I hit my head—"

"Everyone knows they sabotage ships," Count Reynard said darkly, "so they can feast. As it is, most of the remains found amidst the wreckage were all in pieces—"

Demetri clenched his jaw. He had not heard that.

"—much like the remains your princess found here!" Reynard threw up his arms. "And people are still trying to tell me it's sharks. Sharks don't bring down whole steam ships, do they, Prince Demetri? Sharks don't leave the bones and the clothes of their victims in caves on the beach, do they, Prince Demetri?"

"Well, I wouldn't think so," Demetri said. "Do they know for certain the ship was sabotaged, then?"

"We're fairly certain, Your Highness." Demetri looked around as one of the guards stepped up to join them. He was older than Demetri, and he had an aristocratic look about him—a square jaw framing his lightly browned face and thick eyebrows set over an aquiline nose.

"This is Captain Gage, Your Highness," Count Reynard said.

"Our divers recovered one of the ship's propellers," Captain Gage explained, "nearly intact. It looked like one of the shafts had been tampered with. I read the statement you made to the guardsmen, of course. Your description of the hull breach when the sailors stopped the engines fits with our findings. The way the shaft was warped, it would have caused such a breach."

Demetri felt numb. So the ship had been tampered with—probably before they'd left the docks. But who would have done such a thing, and why? He wasn't sure what to think of all this talk of mermaids, though certainly, if only bloodied remains had been found amidst the wreckage—but even so, that could have been sharks. But then, the remains on the beach—

"Could I see the remains Princess Briar found?" Demetri asked.

"We've already packed them up for the morgue, Your Highness." Captain Gage looked pleasantly surprised by Demetri's query. "But you're welcome to come by and consult with our coroner. I would welcome your opinion."

"Er...you would?"

The captain nodded. "Of course. If it's true, as Princess Briar said, that you were part of Prince Garrett's foray into the Mountain Kingdom—well, I read about it, of course. The corpse creatures you encountered—I don't know how much of it was true—"

"Probably all of it," Demetri said sourly, remembering the corpse creatures with little fondness.

"—but even if it was only half-true, then of all of us here, you have the most experience with supernatural creatures." Captain Gage's eyes were bright with enthusiasm. "Besides Princess Briar herself, of course," he added, and Briar looked pleased that *some-*one had remembered she'd played a role in the endeavor—beyond that of the damsel in distress. "But I'm sure she'll be too busy with her submarine to help us."

Demetri stared at him. "Pardon, but to help you with…?"

"Investigating these murders. We need to determine if they *are* the work of mermaids, and if so, how to stop them. That is, if you don't mind his involvement, Count Reynard?"

The count, of course, did not mind. Twenty minutes later—once Demetri finally managed to extricate himself, Briar, and Kinsley from the beach—he trudged up the hill towards the dispersing crowd. He supposed he must not have managed to contain his disgruntlement because Briar said, "Well, you were looking for a new job. Weren't you?"

"Don't bother trying to act innocent," Demetri grumbled. "You engineered that whole thing."

"I didn't!" Briar protested. "Really, Demetri, I didn't intend all that. It's just that stupid count kept us there for *two hours,* and he wouldn't listen to anything I said—"

"I can vouch for her on that, Your Highness," Kinsley said.

"Didn't you hear how he went on and on about *you* being a—well, a monster hunter?" Briar asked. "And didn't say a word about me?"

"Well, that was on you," Demetri objected. "You're the one who started gushing about me *rescuing* you, even though you hardly needed rescuing, and the little you *did* need, Garrett took care of. What with the kissing and all."

Briar scowled. "Because Count Reynard is a fool who thinks women can't lift a finger to do anything useful. In fact, from what I've gathered, *all* the counts are like that. I know they're astonished King Victor sent me, a *girl*, to work on this submarine, even though my design for his motor vehicle came in second—"

"Only second?" Demetri said. Briar swatted him on the arm.

"I wasn't getting anywhere with him," she went on. "So I'm sorry, but when you turned up, I *had* to do something. I didn't know they were going to put you in charge of this investigation, I really didn't. Anyway, you could have just said no, you know."

Demetri supposed that was true, though saying "no" had never been easy for him, especially when people said they needed him. Besides, it wasn't being given charge of the investigation that bothered him—he didn't really think he was qualified for it, corpse creatures or no, but he *did* want to discover who sabotaged their ship.

That wasn't the issue. That wasn't why he was upset.

"Briar." Demetri stopped a few paces short of the top of the hill. The sun had fully lifted over the horizon, and the cool damp of dawn was quickly burning off. Wiping his brow, Demetri turned to face Briar. She cast him a quick glance, taking in his sober expression, then nodded at Kinsley. Kinsley continued up the hill, leaving Briar and Demetri alone.

"What is it?" Briar asked.

"I'm not a prince anymore, Briar."

"Oh, curse that." Briar waved a hand. "I know that's what you think, Demetri, but just because you're not in line for the throne—that doesn't make you some peasant. Not that I would care if you were, but…" She sighed. "Demetri, you are what you are. And even I can see, no matter how much time has passed, you're still a prince. And what does that matter, anyway? So what if those counts all bow and scrape to you? *They're* the ones so preoccupied with titles—and *gender*," she added in disgust, "that they can't even see what a person is beyond that. But you and I know better, don't we?"

Demetri wasn't sure that he did. Well, of course he believed a person was more than their class or gender, but that wasn't really the point.

Briar didn't understand. And he didn't think she could.

7

HUMAN

PERPETUA LASTED A DAY and a night in her cave before—with hungry, pained, shivering reluctance—she decided she would have to make her way to town.

Once Perpetua realized what the sea witch had done to her, she
spent most of the day in numb denial, hunched against the wall
of her cave, hugging her knobby knees to her chest. She tried to
convince herself this couldn't be happening, that she was dreaming. That the Ternion would come back and put this right, that
they couldn't really mean to leave her this way. That this couldn't
be *real*, because she could not live this way, she wouldn't survive,
she didn't *want* this. For all the curiosity Perpetua harbored for
humans, for all that she sometimes, perversely, enjoyed walking
around the docks in human-form, she had never wanted to *be*
human.

Rather, she had never wanted to *not* be a naiad.

She felt like something had been stolen from her. She felt like
the *sea* had been stolen from her.

It wasn't until the daylight began to fade that Perpetua climbed stiffly to her feet and ventured outside. There, she crouched on the rocky bar jutting out of the water and tried to catch something to eat. But without claws and fangs, her efforts proved futile. She finally jumped down into the water, and then—after the sun had disappeared, dousing her lagoon in gloomy darkness—she caught a single, small fish.

Her night was cold and uncomfortable. She'd gotten wet fishing for her meal, and with the sun gone, she had no way to dry off. As a naiad, Perpetua was never completely dry; being too dry was unhealthy. But now, as a human, she found her cold, dank cave did not make for good shelter.

As soon as the gulls cried out the dawn's arrival the next morning, she went to sit outside beneath the warm rays of the sun. It might have been pleasant, were it not for the heavy, humid air making her human skin sticky—she would have killed for a breeze—or for the churning in her gut. It seemed her delicate human stomach was not tolerating the raw fish she'd eaten last night.

She sat there, on the black, wet rock, the sea foaming and frothing as it lapped beneath her. She sat and stared at the sun until spots dotted her vision. She sat there for hours, until she was completely dry, her hair tangled and frizzy. And finally—as the sun moved across the sky—she began to accept it. That she was human. That this was real. That the Ternion weren't coming back to fix her.

She was going to need some human resources to survive.

She would need to find food more suited to her human body. And she would need clothes. A naiad's human-form was like a glamour, and as such, clothes were simply part of the form.

It was said a very skilled naiad could manipulate the way the clothing appeared, though Perpetua had never known anyone to do so. But this form she was in now—this very real human body—came with no clothes. She would have to find some.

The trouble was, her cave was a long way out of town, several miles down the coast. And she would have to walk. She could still swim, of course, but she doubted she could swim very far. Not all the way to Moselle.

So, with a hollow ache inside her, she started walking. First, she had to climb a treacherous path up the rocks to the scrubland above her cave. By the time she made it, her hands and feet were scraped raw. Her human skin was easily broken. From there, the land was blanketed in pale grass, but she still winced with every step, leaving a trail of blood behind her. After a little while, her head began to pound too, whether from lack of sleep or proper sustenance or just the stress of...everything.

There was nothing she could do but keep walking.

Soon trees dotted the landscape, just a few at first and then more, as the land sloped gently down, leveling out with the shoreline. The land here was more swamp than beach, small inlets carving through the earth, making wet, fertile ground for the trees. As Perpetua walked beneath their drooping, gray-green boughs, she found herself grateful for the cover they provided. She wasn't sure how she would get into town, naked as she was—she knew enough about humans to know that would draw unwanted attention. Perhaps she could get into the sea a little ways off and swim unnoticed to the outskirts of town, where she might steal some clothing.

But she didn't have to resort to this. Still a few miles from town, she got lucky and came across a small human settlement, close to the shore but well within the cover of the trees. There weren't any humans around, and it wasn't until she heard laughter and shouting, and caught a glimpse of distant figures in the water, that she realized this wasn't a settlement, but just a place where some humans had set up their belongings. While they swam in the bay.

Because the humans were quite far off, it wasn't difficult for Perpetua to take what she needed. Most of the humans had left their clothes hanging on a line tied between two stout trees, and she quickly snatched up a dress and a pair of shoes sitting on a small boulder. She also found a stash of food and took what she could carry—some apples, a jug of water, and something with a strange, musty smell that she thought was called cheese—before hurrying away.

She ate before she dressed, crunching through one of the apples. It was shockingly sweet, in a *sharp* kind of way. She'd never eaten one before, but she'd seen humans eat them often enough. She downed half the water as well—she knew enough to know that humans couldn't drink seawater, so she'd avoided that last night.

Fifteen minutes later, she was dressed and walking down the coast again, carrying the water and nibbling on the cheese. The dress was covered in a weird pattern—something a bit like flowers, though no flowers Perpetua had ever seen beneath or near the sea. The dress was a little tight around her chest and a few inches too long; she had to hold the skirt up to keep from tripping on it. The sleeves were long, covering her arms to the wrist. The shoes pinched her toes, rubbing against her broken skin, but wearing them was certainly better than going barefoot. The marshland ground was plush with moss, but there were things buried in the moss, pebbles and sticks and roots.

When she reached the outskirts of town, she kept close to the coast, wandering until she reached the docks. She'd been to the docks many times, though usually in the early morning or late at night, and usually by way of the sea. Now she was on foot, in broad daylight. It was late in the evening, but the sun hadn't set yet. It hung low in the sky, coloring the sea a deep crimson.

As Perpetua bent to remove her stolen shoes—the stone pier would not be too harsh beneath her feet—she gazed out at the sea, feeling lost, unsure, thrown. She was here now, in town, but she still had no idea what to do and no place to go.

That was when she saw him.

Demetri.

He moseyed down the pier with his hands in his pockets, heading her way, though it was clear he hadn't seen her. His gaze was fixed on the stone beneath him, eyes trailing the ground. As Perpetua watched, he roved to the edge of the pier, just like he had before. But this time, he sat with his legs dangling over the water. He wore a white shirt with his sleeves rolled up to the elbow, and another garment over that—a waistcoat, she thought it was called. He slumped as though he was tired, or—Perpetua wandered closer, peering at his face—as though he was sad.

So she said, "You look sad."

He jumped and looked around. For a moment, Perpetua worried he wouldn't remember her. But then his face broke into a smile, and he scrambled to his feet. "It's you!"

"Yes," Perpetua said, wondering if this was some sort of ritual greeting humans used, given that it was the second time he'd said this to her. "Me."

He laughed, and Perpetua marveled—that he could laugh, when he had looked so sad just a minute ago. "I'm sorry," he said. "It's just, I half-thought I'd imagined you when—well, when we were out here a few nights ago." A red flush crept into his cheeks, and though Perpetua wasn't sure why—it wasn't too hot right now, with the sun going down—she liked the way it looked. "That carriage turned up—with people I knew, no less—and then, well, when I looked again, you were gone."

The gaze he directed towards her was expectant, and she wondered if he wanted her to tell him *where* she'd gone. She didn't have an answer for that, not one she could give him, so she said, "You didn't imagine me. I'm real."

"Good." He rubbed a hand behind his neck and stepped towards her. A little thrill ran down her spine at his proximity. "Look, uh...I'm sorry about that night."

"Sorry?" Perpetua cocked her head. "Why?"

"Well...for kissing you like that, I mean."

Perpetua mulled this over. He was sorry for kissing her? But she had told him to. Why would he be sorry? She felt her face fall as an answer occurred to her. "Was it not...good?"

Demetri's eyes widened. "What? No! No, that's not—I mean..." He scrubbed a hand through his hair, untidying it. "I don't mean that I...didn't like kissing you." His cheeks were bright red now, and he shoved his hands into his pockets. "I just meant—I mean—" He lifted his eyes to her face. "I don't even know your name."

Perpetua wasn't sure what her name had to do with it. Maybe humans didn't kiss people whose names they didn't know. "Perpetua. My name is Perpetua."

"Perpetua," he repeated, and she jerked her head up at the sound of her name on his lips. "Perpetua. That's unusual." His eyes widened again. "Not in a bad way, I mean..." He sighed. "I'm sorry. I'm not very good at this."

"At what?"

"Erm...talking? To people?"

She was somehow relieved to hear him say this, though she didn't really think he was bad at it. She wished *she* could talk more, but she didn't know what things to say, what things humans said. "I'm not good at it either," she confessed. "But I think you're all right."

He smiled. She liked him when he smiled, she thought. He had a face that was nice to look at, and it was even nicer when he smiled. His cheeks dimpled, and his eyes crinkled. Even though it was his sorrow that had first drawn her to him, she liked him much better when he smiled.

"I used to know how to talk to people." He turned back towards the sea, shrugging his shoulder at her. She took that as an invitation to join him and, as he lowered himself back down, she sat beside him. "But I've forgotten, I guess."

What a weird thing. "How did you forget?" Perpetua asked, placing her shoes beside her. The wind breezing off the sea ruffled the hem of her too-long dress, making it tickle her ankles in a pleasing way. "Did you not talk for a long time?"

Something flickered through him—not sadness, exactly, but something worse. Something that made his face crumple, as though he was in pain. But then he cleared his throat, and the look was gone. "Something like that." He gazed across the sea, its surface glittering like diamonds beneath the setting sun. "I used to talk to people all the time. Back in the Glen Kingdom—where I grew up—I had a lot of friends. I made friends easily."

"You have friends here," Perpetua pointed out. "You said you knew those people in the...carriage."

"Yes. Well, I still have friends, I suppose." The corner of his mouth lifted. "But when I'm with them, I don't always feel like talking. I still like to be around people, but when I am..." He swallowed. "Sometimes I feel like I'm not really there. Not a part of them. Like I'm outside it all. Outside of the world."

Perpetua looked at him. Her chest felt tight, and not because of her dress. It felt like someone had grabbed a hold of something inside of her. She couldn't work out if it was a good feeling or a bad one, and that scared her a little.

It was just...what he said. About being outside of the world.

She knew what that was.

"I feel like that too," she said. Her voice sounded weird in her ears. Sort of shaky. "Sometimes." She wished she could explain more—explain it like he had. But she didn't know the words.

Demetri looked at her intently. "I'm sorry."

"Again? Why?"

He laughed. Perpetua liked that she could make him laugh, though she didn't know what she'd said that was funny. "I'm sorry for you," he said, and his voice was soft and nice. "That you feel like that too. It's sort of lonely, isn't it."

That tight feeling traveled up her throat. When she opened her mouth to speak, she wasn't sure anything would come out. But she managed to say, "Yes. It is."

He was quiet for a minute, and she was too. He sat so close, his thigh nearly touching hers, and his arm, bared to the elbow. She looked at him, and she wondered if he would kiss her again. He said he didn't *not* like kissing her, which meant that he did, and she wanted him to do it again.

But he didn't. He just said, "So. Perpetua. Do you live in town? In Moselle?"

Perpetua swung her legs back and forth, watching the blurry shadows her reflection made in the water. She had to think carefully before she answered him. "Not here in town. Outside it. A bit."

"And do you live alone? Or with family?"

"With...some family," she stumbled.

"Oh. Well, that's nice."

She looked up at him, on the verge of asking about his own family. But then she remembered what he'd told her that night he'd kissed her. *I lost everything. My life. What I was.* She still didn't know exactly what he'd meant, but he *did* say he'd lost everything. She wondered if that included his family. Remembering that sad look on his face—and the way she was beginning to dislike it—she decided not to ask.

Suddenly, her stomach gave a sharp *twist*, slicing through her. It was so intense that she clenched her lips shut. She couldn't stop the hand that flew to her middle, clutching at her dress. It was a second before she realized what was happening to her.

She was hungry. Not the normal sort of hunger she'd felt earlier. That hunger had been sated by the food she stole from the beach. This was different.

This was the sort of hunger that drove her to feed on a human.

Alarm coursed through her, her heartbeat thumping. She couldn't be hungry for a human. She *was* human, in every way that mattered. Sohalia had made her that way. How could she still be hungry for humans? She had no claws, no fangs, nothing.

And she had fed less than a week ago, after she'd saved Demetri. Naiads usually only fed on humans every two weeks or so.

Yet she was hungry now. And she knew what would happen if she didn't feed. Madness, agony, death.

Another *pang* rippled through her. Perpetua jumped to her feet. Demetri looked up, and there was that look in his eyes she didn't like—a shuttered look. "I, erm, have to go. Before..." She trailed off, not sure what explanation would make sense.

But Demetri climbed to his feet. "Of course. I'm sure your family will worry if you're not home."

Perpetua looked at him, torn. She had to go, she had to go *now*, but she had the weird feeling that she was doing this all wrong, leaving him like this. He looked...funny. "I *do* want to see you again," she blurted out. "Soon?"

He blinked, his face changing. Lightening. "Really?"

She nodded.

"Well..." His eyes darted from the ground, to her, then back to the ground. "Actually, there's this ball. On Saturday. The Mariner counts are hosting at the castle. I have to go, and I wasn't looking forward to it, but..." He raised his eyes to her face. "Maybe, if you wanted to go with me...it might be fun?"

"A ball?" Perpetua didn't know the word, and Demetri didn't offer an explanation. He seemed to be waiting for her to say something. Whatever it was, she doubted she could go. She very likely might be dead within a few days.

But she recalled that shuttered look in his eyes when she'd gotten up to leave. And she couldn't bear to see it again.

So she said, "Yes. I'll go with you."

8

MEETINGS

B RIAR SURVEYED THE LONG iron vessel before her with satisfaction. "Fifteen meters long," she said, leaning towards Kinsley. "Thirty-two long tons. The biggest submarine built yet."

Kinsley looked amused. "And bigger is better?"

Briar smiled, sharing in the joke. "In this case, yes."

She peered towards the end of the craft, watching as the building crew lowered it into the water. Their worksite here on the bay was about a mile to the north of Moselle, a broad beach topped by a flat cliffside. "Careful on the starboard side!" she called out. "You're coming down too fast for the men over here! Careful!"

Kinsley glanced at her. "Starboard side?"

"Well, it is a boat, after all."

"Not really."

"Course it is." Briar crossed to the edge of the wooden gangplank stretching out into the sea, part of the temporary constructions that had been erected for the project. "Just one that goes underwater."

Kinsley followed her, hands clasped behind his back. "The security around here is a bit lax, wouldn't you say? The armed guard from the counts is useful—" He indicated one of the uniformed soldiers standing on the beach behind them "—but even still, just about anyone could walk up here."

"They'll be erecting a fence. It should be up in another week or so."

"And what exactly do you intend to do with this submarine?"

Briar barely heard his question as the base of the hull touched down into the water. She chewed her lip anxiously, eyes darting back and forth between both ends. It was early in the morning—a bit too early for Briar's liking; she'd only caught two hours of sleep before she had to get up to meet the crew here.

"Do with it?" Briar said belatedly, processing Kinsley's question. "Well, there are all sorts of uses for a submarine. I'm sure I don't have to tell you—they're not exactly new."

"But one with this sort of capability is. How long will it be able to propel beneath the surface?"

Briar flexed her fingers—the four she still had on her right hand—feeling distracted. She took a moment to examine the stitching on her three middle fingers, but as always, it held fast. Kinsley had sewn her fingers back on after they'd fallen off—that had been when she was rotting, of course—and Kinsley was an expert with a needle. "It should go for about four hours."

"You don't sound impressed."

"Well, it's longer than any other submerged vessel has gone," Briar admitted, "but if I could get the submarine to work on an elarium-forged engine instead of a steam-fueled one, then it could go longer. For days, if not months. Of course—" She heaved a sigh "—in order to achieve that, I'd have to solve the Berger problem, and since that's been stumping scientists for years, I have little chance of that."

"The Berger problem?"

"Why elarium can't power mechanical devices over long distances."

"Ah."

"So in the meanwhile, I'm looking into how to power the engine more efficiently with a steam engine."

"I see." Kinsley squinted up at the sun, climbing higher and higher overhead. "I don't suppose you'd mind if I find some shade? I burn faster than a rabbit on a spit."

"Well, you can watch from that staging area over there—see, they've put up a pavilion."

Kinsley departed, but Briar stayed where she was, looking over the vessel. The gangplank beneath her feet bobbed and swayed over the rippling water. Mentally, she began to list and catalog the various tasks she would need to get started on this week.

"It's impressive."

Briar turned around. A woman stood behind her on the gangplank, holding one hand up to shield her eyes as she gazed at the submarine. She wore a white, cotton summer dress with the front of her skirt pinned above her knees, and no stockings, leaving her sun-browned legs entirely bare. She supposed the woman must have come from the beach, though it was a little early for a swim. Then again, for Briar, it was a little early for anything, so she supposed she wasn't the best judge of appropriate morning activities.

"I saw the *Mikkola* down in the Desert Kingdom once," the woman went on, "but it wasn't as large as this one."

Briar's mind pricked with interest. "The *Mikkola?* The first design with an independent engine?"

"Of course, that was nearly twenty years ago," the woman said. "I was just a child then. I suppose this must be the vessel the Glen Kingdom had commissioned? I'd heard there was going to be some work on it in these parts, but I thought maybe that was just a rumor."

"Not a rumor," Briar said, pleased to meet another woman she could talk shop with. "This is it. I'm doing some work on it for King Victor."

"Really?" The woman looked as pleased as Briar was. "I'm sure the Mariner counts must be thrilled the Glen king sent a woman for this job."

"So thrilled," Briar said dryly. "In fact, I was so overwhelmed by their exuberance that I declined their invitation to stay in Mariner Castle. Decided to try my luck at the local tavern instead."

The woman laughed. "I've never met them, of course, but everyone knows what they're like." She held a hand out to Briar. "I'm Sohi."

"Briar." Briar shook the woman's hand.

"Briar. *Princess* Briar, I assume?"

"You assume correctly," Briar said, a little surprised. Then again, the Mariner Kingdom was known for its popular penny press papers, and as Captain Gage had mentioned earlier this week, they were littered with all sorts of stories about her.

She hoped that didn't mean this woman, Sohi, would start bowing and scraping to her—Briar was accustomed to that, but she was enjoying speaking to this woman as an equal. But she needn't have worried. Sohi only said, "Well, it's nice to meet you. I understand you worked on a motor vehicle design for King Victor as well. Turned out quite well, from what I heard."

"You heard about that?" Briar tried not to beam too overtly, fiddling with a buckle on her harness vest. "Dr. Kava's design out-performed mine, of course. Are you familiar with his work?"

"Oh, yes." A warm, salty wind gusted past, rocking the gang-plank, and Sohi gathered her long black hair in her hands, pulling it over one shoulder. It looked a little damp, Briar noted, so she supposed the woman *had* been swimming. "Not only because he's a genius, but he's from the Desert Kingdom. They always boast the latest advancements in technology."

"I've got to make a trip down there sometime," Briar said wistfully.

"Speaking of which," Sohi said, her dark blue eyes sparkling with interest, "I couldn't help but overhear what you were saying a minute ago—about an elarium engine for your submarine. Have you read any of Dr. Ismar's research on the Berger prob-lem?"

"Dr. Ismar?"

"Yes. He's been working in the Desert Kingdom the past cou-ple of years, I think, though he's from some kingdom across the Hyperic Ocean. He's written a couple of interesting papers on elarium and its connection to the locality it's mined from. He thinks the effectiveness of the elarium—particularly with regards to its longevity over distances—may have something to do with its proximity to its original deposits."

"Really?" Briar crossed her arms over her chest, simultane-ously intrigued and befuddled by this prospect. "That *would* explain why elarium-forged machines don't work over very long distances. But it's weird. I've never heard of, say, a train built from steel not working because it's gone too far from the place its parts were mined from."

"True. But then, iron doesn't power anything on its own either."

"I suppose."

"Anyway," Sohi said, her eyes still bright, "I was thinking—if his theories *do* have some merit—then maybe you should try looking for elarium deposits around here. Not on land, I mean, but in the sea caves and rock formations along the coast? Then if you find some, and have your engine built from those specific deposits—"

"Interesting," Briar murmured. "It could work." She'd want to do some more research, but it couldn't hurt to start looking. Of course, she was only meant to be here for three weeks—she wasn't sure she had time to devote to searching and mining for elarium. But it *was* an enticing proposition...

Sohi glanced back at the beach. "Well, I'm afraid I've got to get going. But again, nice to meet you, Princess. Maybe I'll see you around here sometime."

"Sure. And thanks—for the suggestion, I mean."

Sohi smiled and left, heading down the gangplank. Briar watched her go, preoccupied with thoughts of elarium.

She spent the whole of the day down on the beach, working on the submarine. Briar's only break was for lunch—cucumber and dill sandwiches, and a lovely chilled lemon tea—which Sabine and Gallia brought down to the beach for her and all the crew. When she finally finished for the day, and she and Kinsley started their trudge back into town, the sun was rapidly sinking below the horizon.

"I need food," Briar said. Her entire body ached, though it was a delightful, rewarding sort of ache. "And maybe a cold glass of wine."

"I don't disagree, Your Highness," Kinsley conceded.

When they arrived back at LeBeau's, they found a large corner booth down in the tavern's common room, and all of Briar's guard opted to join them—Aden and Alec, Sabine, Gallia, and Tory. They were all so hungry and tired that they scarfed down their food in near-silence—even Alec, who usually wouldn't shut up—but once they were all fed and contented, their moods lifted considerably. As Alec prattled on about the submarine's specs to a clearly disinterested Aden and Gallia, and Tory and Sabine talked about going down to the beach sometime this week, Briar leaned back in her wooden chair, slouching a little.

The atmosphere in the common room was much quieter and more relaxed than it had been the night she'd arrived. This likely owed to the fact that it was much earlier in the evening, and a workday. Rather than the boisterous roar of loud talk and shouts of laughter, the air in the tavern tonight was filled with a low hum of friendly conversation. Townspeople occupied the tables, eating dinner, while the bar was lined with dockworkers and sailors, enjoying a cold drink after a hard day's work. Briar cast her gaze over the room, observing.

"What about him?" she asked Kinsley, pointing to a sailor sitting at the bar. He had broad shoulders and a thick, wiry beard.

"I beg your pardon?" Kinsley said.

"That man there." Briar nodded. "Is he your type?"

"Definitely not."

"Beards aren't really my thing either." Briar reached for her cup and took a sip. "I've never kissed a man with a beard—well, of course, I've only kissed two boys in my entire life, and I think you know neither of them has a beard—but it must feel weird. I don't think I'd like it."

"It's not altogether pleasant."

"So you *have* kissed a man with a beard."

Kinsley shifted in his seat. "I prefer leaner men."

"Like Garrett!" Briar tipped her glass in his direction.

"Prince Garrett not being my type has nothing to do with his physique, Princess." Kinsley smiled at her. "He's just a bit...exuberant. And I do prefer dark hair."

"So you like quiet, broody men," Briar concluded.

"I didn't say broody. And I didn't say quiet."

"By the Gift, you're picky."

"I know what I like, is all. Nothing wrong with that."

"No." Briar smiled into her wine cup. "Nothing at all." She thought of Garrett and wondered what he was doing, right at that moment. It had to be nearly ten—Garrett often went to bed early if he didn't stay up with her. It was possible he was already asleep, unless his father was hosting some kind of dinner or party or other court function.

Alec caught Kinsley's attention then to ask him about changing their guard schedule for tomorrow night so he could meet up with a girl he'd met, and Briar took the moment to wander over to the bar to order another bottle of wine for their table. As she reached the end of the bar, the front door swung open, letting in a burst of muggy air. And as the door swung shut, Briar caught something else.

Something that sounded like a scream.

She spun away from the bar, staring at the door as it bounced shut. No one else around her looked concerned, as though they hadn't heard a thing. But that was not surprising. Briar's hearing was better than most people's.

Without thinking of her guard, Briar left the bar and burst outside.

The cobbled square before the tavern was practically empty, only a few people passing through. But the streetlamps lining the square glowed a bright white, giving a clear view of the surroundings. No one was screaming. No one looked scared or panicked. Briar cocked her head, listening for another sound, another scream. At first, she couldn't hear anything unusual. Then—

A steady *thump-thump-thump* of rapid footsteps, clacking over the paved street. Erratic, hurried. Someone running.

Briar turned right, facing a small alley alongside the tavern. The alley was shrouded in shadow; the streetlamp at the mouth of it had wound down and burned out. But Briar possessed an uncanny ability to see in the dark, and as she crept towards the alley, she saw the shadows there shift.

Someone was coming towards her. Emerging from the alley. Briar stopped and waited, tensed, ready to attack—

Then a girl stepped out of the alley, into the light.

"Oh." Briar stared at the girl stupidly. She was short—a good head shorter than Briar—with long, dark brown hair twisted into a messy bun behind her head. She was dressed in a paisley seaside dress that was much too long for her and a little tight across the chest. She didn't much look like the sort of person others screamed at and ran from.

"Are you all right?" Briar asked, stepping towards her. Perhaps *this* girl was the one who'd screamed, though she didn't look particularly frightened. Maybe a little startled.

The girl's brow furrowed, as though she didn't understand the question. She looked about Briar's age, around sixteen, though her hollowed cheeks gave her a younger look. "Yes," she said belatedly. Her eyes roved over Briar, clearly taking in everything about her. "I'm...all right." Her gaze settled on Briar's face. "Why wouldn't I be?"

Before Briar could answer, she was interrupted by the call of her own name. Glancing over her shoulder, she spotted two familiar figures approaching. Kinsley and Tory.

"There you are." Kinsley's calm demeanor was tainted by his disapproving tone. "What are you doing out here?"

Briar wasn't sure how to answer that. "I thought I heard something," she said lamely, then turned back to the short girl. "I'm sorry," Briar said to her. "If I startled you. I just thought I heard someone scream."

The girl's eyes went a little wide. "No one screamed."

"Well, so long as you're all right."

"I said I was."

"Right."

"You know Demetri," the girl said suddenly. "Don't you?"

"Demetri?" Briar blinked. Of all the things she'd expected the girl to say, Demetri's name wasn't one of them. "Yes. You know him as well?"

The girl nodded, but rather than explaining how she knew Demetri, she said, "I saw you with him—and you—" She pointed at Kinsley "—the night you arrived here. In that carriage. At the docks."

"Oh!" All at once, Briar realized who this girl must be. Demetri had even described her. "You're Perpetua, aren't you?"

The girl looked utterly taken aback. Briar added, "I'm Briar. Demetri told me about you. He said he invited you to the ball on Saturday, didn't he?"

Perpetua nodded. There was something guarded about her—a mistrustful look in her dark eyes, the way she hunched in on herself. Still, given they were having this conversation outside a dark alley, Briar supposed that wasn't so strange.

"Yes," Perpetua said. "The...ball. The party. With dancing."

"That's the one." Briar smiled. "I'm glad you're going with him. He wasn't really looking forward to it—which is stupid, of course, because it'll be fun. I don't even *like* to dance, but it'll be fun all the same. And Demetri *does* like to dance, so I'm sure you'll both have a good time." Stars and stones, she was babbling. Since when did she babble?

It was just a bit weird. Talking to a girl Demetri had kissed. She wasn't jealous; she had no cause to be. But it was still weird. She had kissed Demetri too.

She wondered if Perpetua knew that. She sort of hoped not.

"Were you here looking for him?" Briar asked. "Demetri? He's probably inside."

"No, he isn't," Tory said. "Alec said he went out with friends earlier."

"Oh. Well, then—I'm sorry," she said to Perpetua.

Perpetua gave her an odd look. "I can't stay, anyway." She paused, then added, "My family will worry if I'm not home."

"Of course. I'll see you on Saturday, then."

Perpetua had already turned to go, but at that, she hesitated. "I'm not sure I can go. To the ball."

"Why not?"

Perpetua cast her gaze around, settling it on her skirt, which she fingered. "I...don't know what to wear."

"Oh!" Of course. Briar supposed, judging by her clothes, that Perpetua wasn't from a wealthy family. Demetri said she lived outside of town; she was probably a commoner. Of course she had nothing to wear to a ball. "Don't worry about that. I have plenty of gowns. You can borrow one, if you like." She could have one, for all Briar cared.

Perpetua narrowed her eyes. "Why?"

Briar felt like kicking herself. She didn't mean to sound like she was offering charity, though...she supposed she was. "I just meant—if, you know, you can't find a dress in such a short time, you could—"

"I mean, why would you...offer?"

"Well..." Briar slipped her hands into the pockets of her trousers. "I mean. Demetri would be so disappointed if you didn't come. He's really happy you're coming."

"He said that?"

"I could just tell." Briar waved a hand. "I've known him for a long time. Look, it's no trouble. You could come over a few hours before the ball, maybe? We can figure out what we're going to wear together."

Perpetua opened her mouth to respond, then closed it. After a beat, she said, "Yes. All right. I'll—I'll come."

"Good." Briar beamed at her. "I'm in Room 34. I'll see you then."

9

BARGAIN

PERPETUA SLUMPED DOWN ONTO the pier, her calloused feet dangling over the edge. She huddled in on herself like a crab retreating into its shell, trying to ignore the hunger pains. She'd left the tavern behind, left all the *people* behind, including that girl, Briar, Demetri's friend.

She'd only gone to the tavern to catch a glimpse of Demetri, because he was the only thing that distracted her from her hunger. But she'd come across a girl in that alley beside the tavern, a girl who looked half-starved herself, and before Perpetua had known what she was doing, she'd tried to attack the girl, pinning her against the wall so she could bite her. Not that these pathetically dull human teeth could tear into flesh very well.

But she hadn't gotten that far, because her human arms were stupidly weak. Even that scrawny girl had no trouble squirming out of her grasp. Perpetua might have run after her except Briar had turned up then, which was lucky, really, because her presence had jolted Perpetua back to her senses. Even if she *had* managed to feed on that human girl—killing her *there*, near such a public place, would have been beyond reckless. Especially since Briar had heard the girl scream and come to investigate.

And she said she'd known Demetri for a long time. Briar. A strange feeling rose in Perpetua, an unpleasant, *burning* emotion. It was sort of how she'd felt when Candelaria had tried to take Demetri from the shipwreck.

But Briar had also said she was glad Perpetua was going to the ball with Demetri, and when Perpetua remembered that, the burning abated. Of course, she'd lied to Briar about why she couldn't go to the ball. She couldn't go because her hunger for humans was growing out of control, and she didn't know what to do about it.

She stared into the murky water below, miserable. The water was like black glass, reflecting the lustrous moonlight. It was a clear night, the sky a dark, unblemished dome, bleeding straight through the horizon to meld with the sea. Perhaps she should just jump in and let herself drown, Perpetua thought, before the agonizing pain took over. Starvation was one of the worst ways a naiad could die. Maybe it would be better to return to the sea and die there. She didn't know what else to do. There was no one to help her, no one who *would* help her.

"Don't make a sound," someone said. "Don't move."

Startled, Perpetua jerked around. That voice was like a tremor in the seabed, sending a shockwave through Perpetua. Her eyes fell upon the naiad standing behind her.

It was Sohalia. The sea witch.

Perpetua's mouth went dry with fear. But then she realized the sea witch hadn't spoken to *her*. She was addressing a girl with a freckled face. A girl she held by the scruff of the neck, like an eel she'd caught fishing. Only, an eel would have struggled, flapping about, but thanks to Sohalia's command, this human hung limply in Sohalia's grip. The girl's legs dangled from her body, the toe of one boot scraping the stone pier. Even her head was limp, lolling to one side, as though she was unconscious or asleep.

But she wasn't. Her eyes, wide open, stared mutely at Perpetua.

"This human was following you, Perpetua," Sohalia said.

Perpetua scrambled upright, tripping as her feet tangled in the hem of her dress. Sohalia wore a dress of whispery white lace, though *her* hemline was pinned at the knee, revealing bare feet and smooth human legs.

The sea witch gave the dangling girl a little shake. "Why would this human be following you, Perpetua?"

Still too afraid to speak, Perpetua turned her gaze on the human. Only then did she recognize her. She'd seen this girl not half an hour ago, outside the tavern. With Briar. She recognized her midnight-blue coat with its shiny brass buttons. When she'd seen her before, she'd been unsmiling, her expression almost suspicious.

Now her face was slack. Overcome by Sohalia's Voice.

"She's—I just saw her." Perpetua's voice quavered. The fear making knots inside her intensified. Would Sohalia punish her further for drawing unwanted attention? But then, she reminded herself, there was little even the sea witch could do that would be worse than the fate that awaited her.

Taking a deep breath, Perpetua added, "I just saw her. In town. At the tavern."

"Hmm." The sea witch didn't sound angry. Turning the human to face her, Sohalia said, "Answer me truthfully. What is your name?"

"Tory," the human answered. Perpetua was impressed to see a flicker of a glare in her eyes. Most human minds went utterly blank beneath the control of a naiad's Voice, especially a naiad so powerful as the sea witch. But this Tory was fighting it.

"Were you following Perpetua, Tory?" Sohalia asked.

Tory managed another scowl. "Yes."

"Tell me why."

"There was something off about her. Something weird. I didn't like the way she was looking at Princess Briar."

"*Princess* Briar?" Perpetua blurted out. She hadn't realized Demetri's friend was a princess. She looked so *normal*. She'd been wearing trousers, for gods' sake. Perpetua didn't know too much about princesses, but she was fairly sure they didn't wear trousers. In all the stories, they wore elaborate gowns with lots of gemstones and pearls.

Sohalia looked at Perpetua with special interest. "You were talking to Princess Briar?" she asked. Perpetua didn't like the way her voice sounded—low and smooth, like a hissing snake lulling its prey. "The one who is here to work on the submarine?"

"The what?" Perpetua asked blankly. When Sohalia only looked at her, her gaze expectant, Perpetua shifted, the stone pier scraping uncomfortably against a blister on her heel. "I suppose so. Her name was Briar, anyway."

"Well, then." Sohalia looked at the girl in her grip. "Listen to me, human. Tory. You have never seen me. You did not see Perpetua here on the pier. You came out here after her, but you lost her. You don't know where she went, so you went back to the tavern. Understand?"

There was a struggle in Tory's blue eyes. Perpetua watched it play out, the slightly panicked glare giving way to a vacant stare. "Yes," Tory said. "I understand."

"Good." Sohalia lowered the human carefully, until her booted feet landed upon the pier with a solid *thud*. "Go now. Go back to the tavern."

Tory went obediently, disappearing down the length of the pier. Perpetua watched her go until she passed beneath a blinking streetlamp and into the shadows beyond.

A tense silence hung in the air. Then Sohalia turned to Perpetua. "Well!" She huffed a breath. "I thought she'd never leave."

As though the human had stayed of her own free will. Not that Perpetua minded. In fact, she was rather relieved Sohalia had sent the girl off Perpetua's trail. But there was something so *strange* about Sohalia, something that made Perpetua feel cold inside. The false friendliness in her tone, the demented smile she flashed now and again. Even her mannerisms and the way she walked...it was almost as if she had been a human once, a very long time ago, and half-remembered how to be one.

Perhaps she *had* been human, Perpetua thought. Perhaps that was where her magic came from. After all, Sohalia had turned Perpetua into a human—why not herself into a naiad? Perpetua knew there were witches among the humans. She knew they existed. Whereas no naiad had ever possessed magic like Sohalia's. Was that how she had obtained her power? Was she like all those human witches?

"It's good to see you again, Perpetua," the sea witch said. Perpetua doubted the veracity of these words, considering the last time they'd seen each other, Sohalia had cursed Perpetua. Still, there was no cruelty in Sohalia's voice, nothing to suggest she wasn't sincere. Which only made it more disturbing. "Humanity suits you, I think."

Perpetua bit her cheek. "It doesn't."

That odd little smile played at Sohalia's lips. "And here I thought I was doing you a favor. I gave you what you really want. To be human." Sohalia drifted closer, light on her feet. Her willowy form swayed from side to side. "Everyone knows about you, Perpetua. How curious you are about humans. You remind me of myself, you know."

Of all the things Perpetua had expected the sea witch to say, she had not expected that. "What?"

"You remind me of myself from long ago. When I was just a young thing like you. I, too, was fascinated by the humans. I wanted to walk among them, *really* walk among them. I wondered what it would feel like to be one of them." Sohalia sighed. "So I understand, you see. In a way no one else can."

Perpetua stared at the sea witch. She still wore that mad little smile, and Perpetua wondered if she really *was* mad. Perhaps Sohalia wasn't taunting Perpetua, perhaps she wasn't acting out of malice. It was as though she really thought Perpetua would be grateful to be human.

Sohalia's smile widened. "And now you can pursue that boy you saved."

"No, I can't," Perpetua whispered. "You know I can't."

"What makes you say that?"

"I still need to feed." Perpetua choked on the words, as though her mouth was full of seaweed. "I can still feel—I *need* to feed. On a human. And soon, or I—" She clenched her teeth together.

"Ah." Sohalia did not sound surprised. "Yes. That."

"But why?" Perpetua pushed back the fear crowding in on her. "Why is this happening? You said you made me human. And humans don't feed on each other—"

"Well." Sohalia gave a negligent flick of her fingers. "In point of fact, I didn't *really* make you human. I stuck you in human-form, yes. But you're still naiad on the *inside*."

"But I shouldn't need to feed again so soon."

"You can blame the magic for that." Sohalia lifted a shoulder. "The transformation process likely took a lot out of you. You *will* need to feed soon." She raked her dark blue eyes over Perpetua, her gaze invasive. "I suppose that's why you don't look well. You're just wasting away."

"But I *can't* feed. Not like this. Without my claws or fangs..." Perpetua knew humans killed each other, but she didn't know how. She didn't know how to hunt like a human.

"Well..." Sohalia stepped forward, circling Perpetua. "I suppose there might be something I could do. Something to help you. As I said, you are still naiad on the inside."

"So you can turn me back into a naiad?"

"No." Sohalia whirled on Perpetua. "Naiad you may be, but you broke the law. This transformation was a Ternion dictate. I cannot undo it. Rather, I will not." She paused. "But I *could* restore your ability to grow claws and fangs."

Perpetua's heart thumped in her chest.

"This is assuming, of course," Sohalia added, "that you can prove yourself useful to me."

Perpetua did not hesitate. "What do you want me to do?"

Sohalia's thin lips stretched into another grotesque smile. "Whatever I want."

Perpetua twisted her fingers into her skirt. Then she nodded.

"Good," Sohalia said. "You *will* repay me, Perpetua. You will do what I ask, whatever I ask. Starting with…" She pursed her lips. "This human of yours. The one you kissed. What did you say his name was?"

Perpetua was certain she hadn't mentioned it. "Demetri."

"Demetri," Sohalia repeated.

Perpetua did not like the sound of his name on the sea witch's lips. She did not like that little *twist* in her voice when she said it. It suddenly occurred to her there was something Sohalia could ask of her, something she didn't want to do—and that was anything that might hurt Demetri. She thought of his face, of that pained look in his eyes, and her chest felt heavy.

But Sohalia said, "And this Demetri, he's friends with Princess Briar? Is that why you were talking to her?"

"Yes. I'd gone to see him, but I met her instead."

"What did you talk about?"

"Well…" Perpetua rubbed her fingers together. "We talked about Demetri. And this ball he invited me to—that's a sort of gathering where—"

"I know what a ball is."

"Oh." Perpetua nodded nervously. "Well. We talked about the ball. I told the—the princess—" She still could not believe that girl was a princess "—that I didn't have anything to wear, and she said I could meet her before the ball, and we'd pick something out—"

"Good." Sohalia looked immensely satisfied. "Perfect. Then for now, Perpetua, you can do a simple thing for me. Since you will already be spending time with this princess, you can keep an ear out for any information about the work she's doing on that submarine. And report anything you learn to me."

"The...submarine?"

"It's a kind of a seafaring vessel," Sohalia explained. "The princess is working on it. She should be spending some time searching for a certain mineral. I need to know if she is, because if not..." She clicked her tongue. "I'll have to come up with something else. So. Can you do that?"

Perpetua nodded. Even if they were friends, picking up information about Princess Briar couldn't hurt Demetri, could it? She wondered briefly what interest Sohalia could possibly have in all of this. In Princess Briar and this work she was doing. But then, what did it matter? If it meant the sea witch would restore her claws and fangs so she could feed, then she didn't care.

"And you had better not tell anyone about this," Sohalia added. "Not *anyone*, you understand?"

"Of course." As though Perpetua would tell any other naiad that *any* of this had happened —that she'd been punished by the Ternion and turned into a human.

Sohalia seemed content. "Good. Then, as promised..."

She raised her arm before Perpetua realized what was happening. Something *rushed* at Perpetua. An invisible force, like the one that had pinned her to the wall of her cave. Only this time, the force rushed *into* her, shoving itself down her throat. It felt cold and slick—Perpetua thought again of eels—and she choked. For a moment, she thought she was going to vomit, but then the cold force dissipated through her, like water evaporating into her skin.

When she could breathe again, Perpetua felt a tingling in her fingertips and a slight ache in her jaw. In an instant, that familiar scarlet haze fell over her vision. Her claws emerged as easily as they ever had, and her jaw hinged open wide, making room for her jagged teeth.

"There you are," Sohalia said. "All better now."

Perpetua blinked, the red film clearing from her vision as she dismissed her claws and fangs. "Thank you." The phrase felt awkward; naiads did not go around *thanking* each other. But somehow, she thought Sohalia would approve.

She was right. The sea witch looked pleased. "I've only restored your claws and fangs, you understand," she said. "Not your Voice. You will have to find some other way to lure your prey. Some other way to compel them."

Perpetua nodded. She didn't care. It would be more difficult without her Voice, but not impossible.

"Don't forget what you owe me, Perpetua," Sohalia said in parting. Then she leapt clear off the end of the pier into the ocean, white dress and all.

Perpetua let out a long breath. Her senses rushed back to her, sound and sight and smell. She heard the distant roar of breaking waves as the tide rushed in, and she inhaled the musty scent of the water swirling around the docks. The relief flooding her was so powerful, she felt lightheaded. Blinking hard, she lowered herself to sit at the edge of the pier.

She would be able to feed again. She would not starve, and she would not die. And she would be free, free to go to this ball, free to spend time with Demetri. And all it would cost her was some information about a human girl Perpetua barely knew.

10

DROWNING

DEMETRI WRINKLED HIS FACE before the mirror, fidgeting with his bowtie. The shaded gear-bulb lamps cast a very dim light over his little room at LeBeau's, giving his face a sallow look. He stared at his smudgy reflection, making a desperate attempt at straightening the crooked bowtie.

He hoped this wasn't a mistake. Not the bowtie—though no matter how he messed with it, he didn't like it; it was such a shame cravats had gone out of fashion while he was being held captive for eighty-two years—but this ball. Rather, inviting Perpetua to attend the ball with him.

He liked Perpetua. He liked being around her. There was something so artless about her, something that made her easy to open up to. It was a bit weird for him, because he knew next to nothing about her, and Demetri did not usually go around courting girls he barely knew. Actually, Demetri had never courted *any* girl except Briar, and they had been engaged since infancy. Needless to say, he was used to lengthier courtships.

But thanks to all the wine he'd consumed the night he met Perpetua, he'd kissed her before even learning her name. And somehow that had broken down a barrier between them. Especially as she had seemed so—well—so all right with it.

But there was something else Demetri was beginning to realize, something that made him uneasy. That one of the reasons he liked being with Perpetua was because it was so much easier than being around Briar.

He wasn't still hung up on Briar. He wasn't. It was just...Briar being *here*, and then to top it off, she'd gone and made him a prince again—even if in name only—and thrust him back into this life of court and balls and nobility. It was a life he had enjoyed once, the only life he had known. But Demetri had begun to accept that life lost to him. He'd begun to accept he needed to find a new life.

That was what he was supposed to be doing here in Moselle. And instead, thanks to Briar's machinations, he was playing the prince again.

But he didn't have to be a prince with Perpetua. Come to think of it, Perpetua didn't even know he'd been a prince. When he was with her, he could just be himself—just a boy with no home and no ties, looking for the next job, the next place. That was who he was now, he told himself firmly, no matter what Briar said. At least he could *try* to be that person with Perpetua, who didn't expect him to be anything else.

And so—confident this wasn't a mistake and determined to enjoy the ball—Demetri adjusted his disastrous bowtie one last time, looking himself over. He supposed he passed for what was fashionably formal nowadays, in a dark tailcoat and trousers. His waistcoat was white—a tribute to the style of Demetri's day; dark waistcoats were more in fashion now—but cut in the current style, without the high, stiff collar Demetri was used to. Between that and the small bowtie, his neck felt strangely naked.

He tucked his new timepiece into the pocket of his coat, leaving the bronze chain hanging out—according to Kinsley, that was "all the rage" now—and headed out into the corridor.

Kinsley was already there, dressed smartly in his navy blue guard uniform, along with Sabine and Aden, all of whom were accompanying them to the ball.

"Aren't they ready yet?" Demetri asked.

Kinsley smiled. "Not quite, Your Highness."

"Kinsley," Demetri said reprovingly.

Kinsley shrugged. "You are a prince tonight, aren't you?"

"I suppose." Demetri pulled out his watch to check the time. "I hope they're ready soon. We're going to be late."

"I think that's the plan, Your Highness," Sabine said. When Demetri turned a quizzical eye on her, she explained, "Princess Briar thought if you arrived once the ball was in full swing, people might pay less attention to your arrival. She thought you'd prefer that."

"Oh." Demetri had to admit it made sense. "Well. In that case, they can take their time."

"They," of course, were Briar and Perpetua. Apparently, Briar had met Perpetua a couple of days ago and invited her to come and get ready for the ball with her, which was nice, Demetri thought. Perpetua had probably never been to a ball before, come to think of it. He didn't know where her family hailed from, but he was fairly certain they weren't nobility.

It was another half hour before the girls finally emerged from Briar's room at the end of the corridor. Perpetua came out first, looking taken aback to find four pairs of eyes on her. But then her gaze found Demetri and she smiled, as though reassured by the sight of him.

Demetri returned the smile. Perpetua was beautiful—it was, if he was honest with himself, the first thing he had noticed about her—and here, now, she looked more beautiful than ever. She wore a deep rose-colored gown with ruffled detailing along the bodice. Modern ballgowns displayed a bit more skin than they had in Demetri's day—indeed, the sleeves of Perpetua's gown were tiny, off-the-shoulder things, leaving her sun-kissed arms bare. Perhaps, Demetri reflected, his cheeks growing warm, there *was* something to be said for the fashions of this period after all.

"You look—erm—nice," Demetri said. His flush deepened. Stars and stones, he couldn't even compliment a girl properly. He supposed eighty-two years was enough time to grow rusty when it came to remembering proper graces.

But Perpetua's smile only widened. She had a nice, genuine smile, Demetri thought. Her entire face brightened when she smiled—her dark eyes gleaming, her cheeks dimpling. She didn't just look nice, she looked radiant—and he wished he actually had a spine so he could tell her so.

"Is Princess Briar ready?" Kinsley asked.

Perpetua looked surprised to be addressed by the guard. "Yes," she said after a beat. "She's just finishing her hair." She frowned. "For some reason, it seems very important that her—uh—" She motioned towards her right temple.

Kinsley seemed to understand. "Her bruise?" Thanks to the rotting curse Briar had suffered, she bore a number of strange bruises and injuries that had never gone away—a mottling at her temple where she'd taken a blow to the head, a missing pinky finger from her fight with the dark fairy.

"Yes," Perpetua said. "She wanted to be sure it wasn't covered up."

"She wanted to be sure it *wasn't* covered up?" Demetri repeated, baffled.

Kinsley had an odd expression on his face—sort of tolerantly affectionate. "She likes to, as Prince Garrett told me once, 'weird people out.'"

Demetri groaned. "Well. At least that means people will pay more attention to *her* than me."

Perpetua looked at him. "You don't want anyone to pay attention to you?"

"No one but you," he said unthinkingly. Perpetua smiled again, positively glowing, and Demetri reflected that he *could* be charming when he didn't try too hard at it. That figured.

Briar emerged a few minutes later. "Weird" was definitely the word to describe her. Her gown was entirely black. She showed no more skin than Perpetua—her capped sleeves covered her shoulders entirely—yet her appearance was somehow more shocking. Perhaps it was the contrast between the black satin and the dreadful pallor of her skin, or the silver plating and thick clasps ornamenting her bodice, details that would have been more at home on a factory worker's uniform than a ballgown. Not only was the bruise at her temple extremely visible, but she also wore no choker to disguise the fingerprint-like bruises circling her throat. The bruises there were black, much like the color of her gown, which made them a macabre sort of neckpiece all on their own.

And yet, as Demetri looked at her, he felt a lump rise in his throat. Even without her ill coloring, Briar was not—had never been—as classically beautiful as Perpetua. But Demetri looked into Briar's clear gray eyes, and he felt like he was drowning. Like he had that night of the shipwreck. Only this time, he was drowning in a hundred different emotions he couldn't begin to pick apart.

None of this must have shown on his face because Briar only smiled. "Ready?"

"Yes." Demetri was amazed how normal his voice sounded. He quickly turned to Perpetua. "Let's go."

The Mariner counts had sent a self-propelled carriage for them, identical to the white carriage that had first brought Briar to Moselle. Demetri and Kinsley helped the ladies inside, giving them time to settle their draped-up skirts on the velvet benches. Then Demetri took his seat beside Perpetua and Kinsley beside Briar. Aden rode up front with the driver and Sabine on the rear, taking the place of the footman again.

It was nearly an hour's ride to Mariner Castle along a broad road curving up the coast, through the marshy woodland separating the castle from the beaches. Even through the trees, the rumbling of the sea could be heard as it crashed against the cliffs, a soothing backdrop to the long carriage ride.

Briar, thankfully, spent most of the ride chatting with Kinsley—leaving Perpetua and Demetri to talk alone. Only for some reason, Demetri struggled to think of anything to say. It had been so easy to talk to Perpetua before. He had told her things he'd never told anyone. But now he couldn't find that ease. He didn't know if it was because they had an audience—though Briar and Kinsley weren't paying them any attention—or if he was just nervous. But the more he fretted about it, the harder it became to think of anything.

Luckily, after a short silence, Perpetua said, "Have you been to many balls?"

"Oh, yes." Demetri answered with more relief than the question called for. He hoped he didn't sound like an idiot. "Many. Ever since I was old enough to attend them."

"And did you dread them all as much as this one?" she asked baldly.

"I'm not *dreading* this one," he protested. "Did Briar say I was dreading this one?"

"*You* said you weren't looking forward to it."

"Oh." So he had. "I don't mind balls. Actually, I used to enjoy them. It's just…" In the confines of the carriage, with Briar and Kinsley so near, he couldn't imagine explaining how he felt about being dragged back into this life of a prince. "The Mariner counts are hosting the ball," he said instead, "and they're not very pleasant. Well, I've only met one of them, but that's what I've heard."

"But there will be a lot of people there, right?"

"Oh, yes. So it shouldn't be hard to avoid them. And besides, I hope we'll be too busy dancing to talk to anyone."

Perpetua twisted around to face him head-on, her dark eyes serious. "I have to tell you something," she said in a low voice.

Demetri, slightly alarmed, tilted his head towards her. "All right."

"I…" Perpetua fidgeted with the lace cuff on one of her gloves. "I don't know how to dance."

"Oh." Judging by her somber tone, Demetri had been expecting something much worse. "Well, that's all right. I can show you. It isn't difficult, and all that matters is that you enjoy yourself."

Perpetua looked at him through dark lashes. "So long as I'm dancing with you, I will."

Warmth flooded Demetri again, but it wasn't an entirely bad feeling. And he tried, as he glanced across at Briar, to hold onto that feeling.

As they finally approached the castle, the carriage trundling up the long, winding driveway, Demetri glanced out the window. The castle sat upon a wide promontory, the dark sea spread beneath it, glistening like a jewel in the winking starlight. The castle itself was picturesque. Briar's castle in the Mountain Kingdom was a sprawling, lavish construction, while Glen Castle's tall stone walls gave it an imposing look. Mariner Castle, on the other hand, was like something out of a pretty tale, built from pale stone and boasting perfectly round towers topped with blue spires. Two of those towers flanked the entrance of the castle, and as they stepped out of their carriage, Demetri noticed ornate trimming carved into the stone, a detailed pattern that resembled the whorls of a seashell.

Briar gazed up at the castle. The warm light glinting out of every window fell over her pensive face. "This was where she lived, you know."

"Who?"

"Princess Snow."

"Oh. You're right." Demetri hadn't really thought about that. Snow—the princess Garrett had been betrothed to—had been the daughter of the last king of the Mariner Kingdom. His death, and the deaths of his two daughters, had plunged the kingdom into a succession squabble that had been settled by the Mariner counts when they'd stepped forward to govern the country. Still, it was a tenuous hold they had on the kingdom, and there was no telling how long it would last. Hopefully long enough for the debates over who should hold the throne to settle.

"Garrett lived here with her for a little while." Briar peered up at the tallest reaches of the towers. "Before she had to flee."

Demetri knew the story, though he wondered what more Briar knew. How much Garrett had confided in her.

"Who's Garrett?"

Briar and Demetri both turned. Demetri hadn't realized Perpetua was listening. Briar opened her mouth to respond, then cut her eyes in Demetri's direction. "A friend," she said. "He's the prince of the Glen Kingdom."

The castle's inner courtyard was modest and modern but bedecked with hundreds of glittering lanterns, giving it a sumptuous air. The winding staircase up to the ballroom was white marble, and rich sage-green tapestries hung over the walls.

The ballroom was a striking sight. The arched ceilings were also marble, but rather than tapestries, the towering walls were hung with modern art pieces, portraits of kings and queens pasts. Some of the portraits were quite enormous, ornately framed in gilded metal and carved mahogany. Still, Demetri thought them sparse decoration compared to the halls of Briar's castle, where the walls were covered in colorful, elaborate murals from an old medieval period.

But there were enough similarities to make Demetri's heart ache and not in a good way. The low, cozy lighting. The long tables piled with banquet food on glittering platters and sparkling crystals of wine. The people in their colorful frippery, dotting the room like children's baubles left lying about. The string quartet crafting graceful melodies with their bowstrings. It was all so familiar, like every ball he had ever been to—and he had not been to one since before Briar fell to her curse. Before he'd been imprisoned for eighty-two years. Before it all went wrong.

"Well," Briar said as they entered the room. "If you'll excuse me, I'll just be off somewhere avoiding all the Mariner counts."

Demetri lifted an eyebrow. "I thought you wanted to antagonize them? Isn't that why you're dressed the way you are?"

"I'm *dressed* the way I am, Demetri, because I wanted to dress this way. And anyway, I'm hoping to antagonize them from afar." With that, she began weaving through the mass of people, trailed by Kinsley and Sabine.

Demetri felt as though a weight had been lifted from him as soon as she was gone. Though now he realized he was alone with Perpetua. His palms felt sweaty. Reminding himself that he had invited Perpetua here—because he liked her, because she was guaranteed to make this night more enjoyable—Demetri turned to her, mustering a smile.

She returned the smile, and the radiant effect made Demetri's knees tremble. "Should we dance?" she asked.

Demetri managed to hold onto his smile, but for some reason, the word *dance* sent a panicky shiver down his back. "Sure. But maybe some drinks first? It's a bit hot in here." He had no idea if it was actually hot, or if that was just him. He felt flushed from the inside out.

Perpetua said, "All right. I can get us drinks."

"Oh, wait, you don't have—to…" Demetri trailed off as she vanished into the crowd. Some gentleman he was, letting her fetch their drinks.

Left alone, Demetri ran his fingers through his hair, then immediately regretted this action. As he hastily smoothed his hands over his head, he wondered what was *wrong* with him. Of course, he had not been looking forward to this ball, not in the slightest. He had expected to be miserable and annoyed by the whole affair.

He hadn't expected to feel so *shattered*.

He closed his eyes, inhaling deeply. But all he breathed in was the aroma of roast duck blended with dozens of perfumes, sickly sweet, thick and musky.

The smells made him want to vomit.

He repeated to himself what he'd told Perpetua, that all that mattered about dancing was that you enjoyed yourself. But when he opened his eyes and caught a glimpse of the waltzing couples gliding across the floor, these were not the words that flashed through his head.

"Dance with me again, Demetri."

"Princess Briar, are you asking me to dance with you? Princess Briar, who never, ever dances?"

"No, I'm not asking you. I'm telling you."

Demetri felt his mouth go dry. He watched the dance floor like a bystander transfixed by the site of a carriage crash. Everything inside him sped up, his mind racing, his heart pounding faster and faster. But around him, everything seemed to slow. The dancing couples moved as though in a dream, blurring until they were no more than scraps of color flitting across the floor. The lively music played by the quartet muted, as though he was hearing it through a pane of glass.

The corners of his vision darkened. Sweat beaded his hairline. Yet he felt cold. Cold and shaky.

The last time he had danced, he had danced with Briar. Minutes before he'd ended their relationship.

"Demetri."

The sound of his name pierced through it all. The sound of her voice.

"Are you all right?" Briar asked. "You don't look well. Where's Perpetua?"

Demetri gestured vaguely. "She went to get drinks."

Briar looked amused. "You sent her to get drinks?"

"No."

"Are you sure you're all right? You really look like you might be sick."

It took a few seconds for Demetri to process her words. Distracted by a warm weight on his arm, he looked down. Only then did he realize Briar was touching him, her white fingers wrapped around his elbow.

"No," he said, his voice faraway, "I'm not all right."

Thankfully, Briar let go of him. She stepped back, her concerned eyes sweeping over him.

Demetri took in a shallow breath. "I can't *be* here, Briar."

"Look, I know you didn't want to come. I didn't want to either. But it's just a ball, Demetri. We don't have to be here long—though I don't know how Perpetua will feel about that—"

"I haven't been to a ball," he said, his words rough, "in over eighty years, Briar."

Briar fell silent. Her gaze was too knowing. Demetri doubted she could commiserate with him over *this*; she had likely been to dozens of balls in the Glen Kingdom since they'd parted ways.

Finally, Briar said, "I'm sorry, Demetri."

"Why? For what?" Demetri couldn't contain the rancorous note in his voice. "I'm the one who walked away from this life, Briar. I'm the one who decided not to return to the Glen Kingdom, I'm the one who decided to go off alone, I'm the one—" He broke off. His eyes cut to Briar, and again, her eyes said it all. She knew exactly what he was going to say.

I'm the one who ended our relationship.

Demetri wiped his hands over his face. "I don't know how to let it all go, Briar. I want to, but I *can't.*"

She said softly, "Not even me?"

Demetri dropped his hands and looked at her. His insides felt like a tangle of spiders. "You least of all."

"I thought..." Briar bit her lip. "I thought you *had*—you seemed like—"

A laugh croaked out of this throat. "Like I wasn't still in love with you? Because I am."

The words were out before he could stop them, but even as they sat there between them—huge, unwieldy, difficult—he didn't regret saying them. It was such a relief to have it said, such a miserable relief.

"I tried to pretend I wasn't." Demetri clenched his hands into fists, trying to stop their shaking. "But it's not that easy, Briar."

"But you seemed—I mean, Perpetua—"

"I *like* Perpetua. I do." The words sounded weak to his ears. "But I shouldn't have brought her here. It was a mistake."

"Demetri," Briar said, her voice pained, "you know I'm—"

"I don't *want* anything from you." He didn't mean to sound unkind, but his words were tainted with resentment. "I know you're with Garrett, I'm *glad* you're with Garrett. But I shouldn't have brought Perpetua here. To this—" He gestured around the looming ballroom "—and with you—" He indicated her. "It's not fair to her."

"Look, Demetri, I'm *sorry*." The fierce look in Briar's eyes undercut the hurt in her voice. "But I didn't know you were here, you know. I had no idea, when I accepted this commission, that you'd be here."

"Would you have turned it down if you did?"

Briar pursed her lips. "Probably not. Because it's been nice to see you again. Even if you don't want me here."

"You don't get it, do you? Don't you remember, back in your castle, after you woke from your curse? Do you remember when I said that all I'd done for eighty-two years was think of you?"

"Ye-es."

"Well, I *meant* that, Briar. I spent all that time thinking about you, and it was *wretched*. Because you were the only thing I *could* think about without going mad, without losing myself to fear and thoughts of revenge." He took a step back, putting distance between them. "And it wasn't healthy, and it wasn't all right, and it's *still* not all right. It's not something I can just get over in a few months."

He turned away before she could respond. He turned away before he could process the look on her face. He didn't want to see it. He didn't want to know it. He just wanted to find Perpetua and get out of this castle, and maybe, just maybe, find some peace somewhere out in the warm, black night.

11

DISILLUSION

PERPETUA'S SENSES WERE FLOODED with more than she could take in. More than she had ever experienced. The intoxicating aroma of sweet cakes. The warbling of the string instruments. The vibrant flash of swirling skirts across the dance floor. The softness of the gloves encasing her hands. The low hum of hundreds of voices, punctured by trills of laughter. The pinch of her shoes.

That last sensation she could've done without. But she was so overwhelmed, so distracted by a million other things, she hardly noticed the discomfort in her feet.

It was all so gorgeous. So heady. So brilliant.

She nearly forgot that she was meant to be retrieving drinks for herself and Demetri. Even the thought of Demetri couldn't punch through her awe at everything around her. She recalled her hope that Sohalia might make her a naiad again, but here, in this moment, Perpetua couldn't have cared less about being a naiad.

She managed to tear herself out of her transfixed reverie long enough to locate a table with delicately wrought glassware, each cup filled with a plum-colored substance. As she turned to look for Demetri in the crowd, she raised one of the glasses to her lips and took a sip. The liquid traveled down her throat, warm, bitter, and wonderful.

"Oh, come now, Theta. There's no such thing as mermaids!"

Perpetua spluttered, looking around for the source of this exclamation.

"I mean, really." The person speaking stood nearby. She was a tall woman, and old, judging by her coiffed gray hair. "Where you find such stories, I've no idea."

"But it's not just a story! It's true!" A second woman, bedecked in a foamy sea-green gown, protested her companion quite loudly. "My boy Eric told me so himself, and he heard it straight from the capital guard. They *are* hunting for mermaids."

Cautiously, Perpetua meandered closer. She'd heard humans talk of "mermaids" before, and she knew exactly what they meant—her and her kind. Naiads. Where they'd come up with *mermaid*, she had no idea.

"Well, Eric is making up stories then," said the older woman, but she did not sound so sure of herself now. "Though he is usually quite sensible. Perhaps he misunderstood."

"He did not. There was a ship sabotaged, you know, last week. Everyone died. Well, I think there was one survivor."

Perpetua's mouth felt dry. She took another sip from her cup.

"And *then* they found those horrible remains on the beach just a few days ago! I *know* you heard about that."

"Well, of course I did, but one does not usually speak of such grisly affairs. And I still don't see how either of those things points to *mermaids*, of all things. There could just as easily be people responsible."

"Not from what I heard." The green-gowned woman shuddered. "It's true, I tell you. That's why the counts employed that foreign prince. Apparently, he has some kind of experience with...well...*unnatural* affairs such as these."

Perpetua frowned. A prince? Hunting naiads? She hadn't heard anything about this, and she wondered if the Ternion knew. They probably did—somehow, they managed to keep abreast of human affairs, at least where they concerned the naiads. But if they didn't know, then Perpetua was sure they would want to—and Sohalia would surely be grateful if Perpetua told her about it.

"Excuse me," Perpetua said to the two woman, pitching her voice loudly enough to be heard through the crowd. She'd learned the phrase earlier that evening from one of Briar's guards.

The two women turned to her with strange looks on their faces, eyes wide and lips pursed. They looked a bit like blowfish.

"Who is this prince you're talking about?" Perpetua asked.

The green-gowned woman's eyes went even rounder. The older woman frowned, her dark eyes sweeping over Perpetua from head to toe. "Excuse *me*," she said. "Have we been introduced?"

"No," Perpetua said. Obviously, she didn't know the woman, and the woman didn't know her. What did that matter? "I just wondered who this prince was. That you were talking about." She looked to the green-gowned woman since she was the one who'd mentioned the prince.

"Well." The woman glanced at her companion, who sniffed, clearly bothered, though Perpetua still had no idea why. But her friend, who had an open face, didn't seem to mind. "He's here tonight, you know. What *was* his name—he's from the Glen Kingdom, as I understand it."

This struck a familiar chord. Perpetua thought for a moment, then remembered where she'd heard mention of the Glen Kingdom. "Prince Garrett?"

"Oh, no, not the crown prince." The woman shook her head. "Poor boy, I don't think he's been back *here* since Princess Snow died. Though from what I understand, he would be quite a help with this sort of thing. No, this prince is from some older royal line. What *was* his name...?"

"Oh, for the Gift's sake, Theta," the old woman snapped. "He's descended from the Georgas line, and his name is Demetri."

"Demetri?" Perpetua said dumbly.

"Yes, Prince Demetri." The younger woman beamed.

"He's right over there." The old woman tipped her head in a stiff nod. "Talking to that girl in that scandalous gown."

"That's Princess Briar, Christiane!" her friend exclaimed. "Not some girl!"

"Well, whoever she is, she looks atrocious."

As the two women began to bicker, Perpetua turned, slowly, in half a circle. There, about five fin lengths away, was Princess Briar—talking to Demetri.

To Demetri.

To *Prince* Demetri.

The mermaid hunter

The *naiad* hunter.

The feeling that swept through Perpetua was unfamiliar and unwelcome. Her stomach plummeted. Her heart shriveled in her chest. She was dimly aware of setting both drinks aside on the tray of a passing human. She thought about what Demetri had said when she'd seen him on the docks the other day. He'd said he *had* to go to the ball. The ball that the Mariner counts were hosting. She hadn't really thought about that, but now she felt stupid for not realizing, even if she didn't know much about humans and why they did things. Why would he have to go to a ball? They were obviously for rich humans, for important humans, for *royal* humans.

It wasn't so much that he was a prince that bothered her, though. She felt stupid for not knowing, but it wasn't important. Not really. No, what was important was that he was *hunting* her kind. It was his *job*. And he'd never said.

But then, he didn't know what she was. What she'd been. And that was probably a good thing.

She didn't know what to do. She felt weird. Shaky, as though her legs were too tired to hold her up anymore. Before she could think better of it, she began threading through the crowd, towards Demetri. She wanted to talk to him—no, she wanted to confront him. She didn't know how to ask about him being a naiad hunter—that would sound too strange—but she was fairly sure he should have told her he was a prince, and he hadn't, and besides, maybe none of it was true, maybe those two stupid women had no idea what they were talking about...

She ducked around a group of young men, coming within a fin's length of Demetri, who stood with his back to her. He was still talking to Briar, who had such an odd, pinched look on her face that Perpetua drew to a halt, hanging back. As she watched,

Demetri ran his hands over his face. He was saying something, but his words were a distant hum. Perpetua couldn't make them out over the buzz of the crowd.

Briar's next words, though, she caught. "I thought you *had*—I mean, you seemed like—"

Demetri dropped his hands from his face, a weird sound escaping his lips. "Like I wasn't still in love with you? Because I am."

Perpetua froze.

It was like a wave crashing into her, sweeping her legs out from under her. A riptide sucking her in. A sickening, staggering blow.

"...like it wasn't true." Demetri was still talking. "But it's not that easy, Briar."

"But you seemed—I mean, Perpetua—"

"I *like* Perpetua," Demetri said, and the spark of hope that flared inside Perpetua was cruel, loathsome, vile. She wanted to stamp on it until it smoldered and died, because somehow she knew she wasn't going to like what he said next. "But I shouldn't have brought her here, Briar. It was a mistake."

Perpetua bit down on her lip, hard. A gaggle of women swept in front of her, and she was glad, because she was half-afraid Briar or Demetri would catch sight of her. And she didn't want them to see her. She only wanted to get out of here, to leave, to use these glorious legs Sohalia had cursed her with and run as fast as she could.

She couldn't run, though. Because her shoes were pinching her toes, and her dress was constricting and cumbersome, and there were so, so many people. Too many people. She wove through them as quickly as she could, shoving past one or two, ignoring the indignant exclamations they hurled after her. She kept going, her shoes slipping over the polished floor, until she reached the doors at the front of the room.

In the corridor outside, she stopped. Her breaths came rapidly, short and shallow, and not, she thought, because of how tight her corset was. She took a moment to lean against the wall.

"Are you all right, Miss?" a human passing by asked. He wore a uniform like others in the ballroom—he was one of those serving people or whatever they were called. "Do you need help?"

"Yes." Perpetua fixed him with a hard stare before she remembered she didn't have use of her Voice. "Tell me how to get out of here."

He gave her hasty directions that she knew she'd never remember. He offered to accompany her, but Perpetua waved him off and started down the twisting corridors. The lights in the castle had dimmed, but the walls were such a brilliant, blinding white, they shone brighter than the lights.

After taking what seemed like her thousandth turn, Perpetua staggered out into the castle's courtyard. She felt like she'd been walking in that castle for hours. Still, the air out here was cool, whispering over her flushed cheeks. The castle stood on the coast, overlooking the sea, and Perpetua inhaled its salty scent, trying to take comfort in it.

The courtyard before her was dotted with people, mostly couples standing close together, half-hidden behind thick shrubs or backed into shadowy corners. Perpetua watched them all resentfully, hanging back beneath a stone overhang. After a moment, she bent to remove her shoes. The first one came off quickly, but the second was so tight, it felt welded onto her foot. With a huff of frustration, Perpetua *tugged* the second shoe off and chucked it into the shrubbery beside her.

She was still trembling and short of breath, and not, she thought, from her exerting trek through the castle. Balling her hands into fists, she tried to calm herself.

She couldn't understand what was wrong with her. Why she felt so rattled. She couldn't stop hearing Demetri's voice in her head, professing his love for Princess Briar. This feeling inside her was so big, so primal, but so entirely foreign. Her chest felt full. Her eyes stung, and when she reached a hand to her face, she realized her cheeks were wet.

The tears unsettled her even more. Perpetua had cried before, but only when she was in physical pain. This...she couldn't explain this.

She dashed a hand across her face, but it didn't help. It didn't stop the tears. Standing in the shadows, out of sight, Perpetua held her hands in front of her chest and summoned her claws. As her fingers elongated and sharpened, her vision turned scarlet, and the tears vanished in an instant.

"Well, you look like *you've* had quite the party."

Perpetua jerked her head up, staring into the courtyard. But there was no one in her immediate vicinity. Only the myriad of couples, arrayed in the distance.

That voice had come from *behind* her.

In an instant, Perpetua retracted her claws, and the red curtain veiling her vision lifted. Fully human again, she turned to face the man who'd addressed her.

He was a young man, and definitely a man—that was to say, definitely human—but there was something very...eel-like about him. He had a slippery, sinuous look, just like an eel, and his penetrating gaze was dark and cunning. His skin was a golden brown, perhaps a shade lighter than her own, and he was tall and lithe—long, like an eel.

"What makes you say that?" Perpetua asked, registering what he'd just said. *You look like you've had quite the party.* She brushed a careless hand over her cheek to make sure the tears were gone. Tears were a weakness, and she had the distinct impression, as a predator, that she didn't want to show any weakness to this man.

The man gestured. "You've lost your shoes. And your gown is ripped."

Perpetua glanced down. She hadn't even noticed the long rent up her skirt. It had been draped back so tightly, she'd felt like her legs had been encased in her fins. She was surprised she'd been able to walk at all.

She straightened, meeting the man's gaze. "That's nothing. And the party was boring."

"I quite agree." The man stepped forward, one hand in his pocket, the other dangling by his side. He had an indolent air about him, but Perpetua did not think he was as careless as he seemed. "And there's nothing I hate worse than a boring party. I don't suppose you'd like to find a better one?"

"A better one?" Perpetua asked warily.

"A better party." He stepped past her, beneath the overhang, and peered up at the starry night sky. "One that isn't so buttoned up as this one." As though to punctuate these words, he tugged his bowtie loose until it hung around his neck, then removed his coat and slung it over his shoulder. "The kind of party where you can really *live* a little."

Perpetua turned, following him with her eyes. She didn't know what he meant by *live a little*, but it struck her. She felt at once that this was what she wanted to do—to *live*, stuck in this human body as she was. And if she couldn't do that with Demetri—and that seemed so impossible now—then why not take this man up on his offer?

There was one good reason not to, of course. Perpetua wasn't an idiot. "And what is it that you want?"

The man turned to her, and his innocent face was anything but. "What do I want?"

"If I come with you to this better party," she said. "What do you want from me?"

The man laughed, and Perpetua, feeling that he was laughing at her, flushed. "Trust me, my dear, I don't want *you*. At least, not in the way you're thinking. I have no interest taking up with anyone of the female variety."

Perpetua, who had just begun to wonder what was so wrong with her human body that nobody wanted her, suddenly understood. "You're only interested in males."

"Right in one, princess."

"I'm not a princess." Perpetua's chest went tight at the thought of Princess Briar.

"I never said you were."

"You didn't answer my question. What do you want with me?"

The man gave a shrug. "I just want some company. Someone who can appreciate a little fun. Someone who's not afraid to live on the wild side. And something tells me *you* are just the person I'm looking for. So." He fixed her with a direct stare. "Am I right?"

Perpetua didn't know what constituted as *fun* among humans. She didn't know what this man perceived of as *wild*. But just as before, she wanted to know. Because she could still feel that horrible thing inside her—pulling at her breath, weakening her knees, pricking at her eyes. And all she wanted was something to chase it away, far into the darkness, where it could never find her again.

Perpetua tugged at her overly full skirt. "I want out of these clothes."

"I believe I just told you, love. I'm not the man you want for that."

"I *meant* I want some different clothes. I can barely walk in this." And they were Briar's clothes, Briar's gown, and Perpetua didn't want anything that belonged to Briar.

"Oh, I don't think that should be a problem," the man said airily. "I'm sure we can find you something somewhere. So. Does that mean you're coming with me, then?"

Perpetua pinned him with her own stare. Predator to predator. "I believe it does."

"Lovely." The man drew the word out, long and low. "Have you got a name?"

"Perpetua."

"Perpetua," he repeated, and Perpetua felt a little thrill. Not the same kind of thrill she felt around Demetri, but a thrill all the same. This man said her name like he *knew* her, like he knew all her secrets and what she was capable of, and even though that would have been a disaster were it true, Perpetua liked it.

"I'm Castel," the man said. "Very pleased to make your acquaintance, Perpetua. So. Now that we've got the niceties out of the way, shall we leave this sorry party behind?"

12

COMPULSIVE

B RIAR PEELED AN ORANGE as she eyed Kinsley, propping her feet up on the empty chair beside her. "So. We're still on for that boat party tonight, aren't we?"

Kinsley's sigh held a mournful note. "I suppose."

"Kinsley. You're not backing out on me, are you?"

"I don't really have that choice, do I, Your Highness?"

"I suppose you don't."

"It's just," Kinsley said, and Briar knew exactly what he was going to say, because he'd already said it about ten times, "these *boat* parties have an unsavory reputation, Your Highness."

"Oh, Kinsley," Briar scoffed. "Sometimes you are such an old maid. What exactly do you think is going to happen? Some drunken sailor might take advantage of me? They won't get far. Only, weren't you the one lecturing me the other day about using my corpse strength when I need to?"

"It's not your virtue I'm worried about, Princess. Only your reputation. But then, given what little there is left of that after last week, I don't know why I bother."

Briar waved a dismissive hand to show just what she thought of *last week*. All that happened at the ball last week was she had shocked a few old biddies and some of those chauvinist counts with her weird appearance. It was hardly scandalous.

Well. That wasn't *all* that had happened, Briar reflected gloomily. But all that affected her reputation.

She hadn't seen Demetri since that night, aside from glimpses of him as he passed through the tavern's common room. He was avoiding her, and it was miserable. She couldn't blame him, she supposed—and he *was* busy with his new job. These days, he spent half his time in the library at Mariner Castle, searching for any mermaid lore he could find, and the other half he spent interviewing locals who claimed to have heard something about mermaids. On top of all that, Briar knew he was worried about Perpetua too, as she had vanished from the ball that night without a word.

But still. It would have been nice to talk to him again, and Briar was beginning to think that was never going to happen.

When they arrived for their boat party that night, Briar could tell it was going to be just as unsavory as Kinsley had promised. She'd heard about it from one of Demetri's friends and was instantly intrigued. It wasn't really her sort of crowd, or her sort of party, but then, less than a year awake from her curse, Briar was still figuring out what "her sort" was. And she didn't ever pass up an opportunity to test new waters.

These parties were held by some dandy lordling with a poor reputation and a penchant for "slumming with the lower class," as Demetri's friend had said. But poor as the young lord's reputation might be, the steamboat where he hosted his parties was anything but. The boat was docked at a private mooring for the evening, allowing guests to come and go as they pleased. Briar alighted the ship around nine o'clock with Gallia, Tory, and a resigned Kinsley in tow.

"Oh, do cheer up, Kinsley," Briar said as they stepped onto the deck. "Just look at this boat!"

"It's a bit hard not to, Your Highness," Kinsley observed.

That was true enough. The boat was bedecked with colored gear-bulbs, strung up on every deck and along the railings. Briar was pleased to see the party was comprised of all sorts of people, upper and lower class, mingling freely. As such, the dress code was practically nonexistent—some people dressed in their finest, others in much plainer garb. Briar herself had chosen tailored black trousers paired with suede boots and a high-necked blouse bound in a corset. The corset displayed dark violet boning on the outside, set against a pattern of black roses.

"Looks like the bulk of the party is up on the hurricane deck." Briar squinted against the lights as she glanced at the top deck. "Though there are a few people milling about on the boiler deck."

"I'm sure most of the people on the boiler deck are in the passenger rooms, Your Highness," Kinsley said blandly.

"No!" Briar pretended to be appalled by this. "Do you think he's right, Tory?"

"I suppose so, Your Highness."

Up on the hurricane deck, a phonograph played recorded music featuring an instrument Briar had never heard before—Kinsley said it was a saxophone. Nearby, a large crowd of men and women competed in a drinking game. Evidently, some part of the rules involved losing one's clothing, because three of the men were bare-chested and one woman, whose skirt was hitched up around her thighs, wasn't wearing any stockings.

"You're staring, Kinsley," Briar noted as they passed the bare-chested men.

Kinsley coughed and averted his eyes.

Briar passed the next hour flitting from crowd to crowd, chatting up common and noble women alike, investigating every part of the boat that she could, and even partaking in some dicing. Kinsley, Gallia, and Tory followed her everywhere, and though Gallia and Tory deigned to take part in the dicing at Briar's insistence, Kinsley remained vigilant, keeping a wary eye on anyone that came close.

"Kinsley," Briar said at one point, as she lounged against the iron railing on the hurricane deck, "will you do me a favor and see if you can find out the rules of that drinking game?" She pointed towards the raucous group nearby.

Kinsley eyed her. "You're not thinking of joining, are you?"

"No," Briar said flippantly. "I'm just curious. Oh, and before you come back, can you see what those people over there are doing?" She pointed out a smaller crowd on the far side of the deck.

"All right." Kinsley cast her a suspicious glance, but he left, vanishing into the crowd.

Briar hummed to herself, turning to lean out over the railing. It was a sultry night. The cooler air they'd enjoyed for a few days had been driven off by the humidity that was said to be common here during the summer. But at this moment, Briar didn't care. She was enjoying herself too much, reveling in the lively atmosphere—the bursts of laughter, the stale smell of alcohol, and the sight of the dark, endless ocean, stretching before her like an abyss. A light mist had begun to form out in the bay, gray and wispy, hovering over the water.

Gallia leaned towards her. "Confess, Princess."

"What?"

Gallia jerked her chin in the direction Kinsley had gone. Her vibrant yellow hair, secured in a long braid behind her head, nearly whipped Briar in the face. "You have no problem finding out what people are doing on your own, so why send him? You're trying to get rid of him."

"I'm not trying to get *rid* of him, Gallia." Briar inched away to put a little space between them. "Honestly, I'm quite used to his hovering. It doesn't bother me. But he deserves a little time to himself, don't you think? And he was never going to leave my side to mingle if I didn't send him off."

"That's because it's our job to stay at your side, Your Highness," Tory pointed out. "And anyway, I don't think these people are really Kinsley's sort."

"You never know." Briar glanced aside as a strong whiff of sweet perfume trailed by, a scent like candied fruit. A small cluster of young women approached, gathering against the railing a few paces away. They each had tiny shot glasses in their hands containing dark liquid, and as Briar watched, they tossed their drinks back, downing them at once. One of the girls, standing closest to Briar, looked very much like—

"Perpetua?" Briar blurted out.

Sure enough, the girl turned to face Briar—and it *was* Perpetua. She wore a gauzy white skirt covered in black tulle and a longline corset, giving her compact figure the illusion of a longer, leaner look. Her long, dark hair tumbled loose around her face in waves. Her expression did not alter when she saw Briar, save for a slight narrowing around her eyes. For a moment, Briar thought Perpetua hadn't recognized her. But then she said,

"Princess Briar." Handing her shot glass off to one of her companions, she stepped forward. Her inscrutable gaze ran over Briar openly. "Did I ever mention you don't look like a princess?"

"Erm—no. But Perpetua! I can't believe you're here. My guard Sabine said she saw you leave the ballroom—you know, last week, at the ball—but we had no idea where you'd gone! We were worried about you."

Perpetua regarded Briar in that curiously frank way of hers. "You were?"

"Yes. Well, Demetri especially." Briar could not get over that Perpetua was *here*, and apparently lost to the fact that her abrupt departure from the ball had caused them all some distress and confusion. "But, so, where did you go? I mean, why did you leave like that? Without telling Demetri?"

Perpetua's eyes—which were a tad unfocused, probably due to the alcohol she'd just consumed—suddenly fixed on Briar with alarming directness. "I didn't think Demetri wanted me there," she said, "since he's so in love with *you*."

"What—? Oh. *Oh.*" Realization crashed into Briar like a train run off its tracks. She cast a sidelong glance at her guards, wishing they were elsewhere, but Gallia was looking on with interest and Tory with a hard gaze. "Erm—you heard that, did you?"

"I did." Perpetua tapped the side of her head. "I have ears."

"Yes, but—well." Briar rubbed a hand over her bruised temple. "I'm so sorry, Perpetua."

Perpetua's gaze flared with exasperation. "Are *you* in love with *him?*"

"No." Briar waved both hands to emphasize this. "No, I'm not. He's my friend—I've known him for a long time. But no, I'm not in love with—"

"Then why are you sorry?" Perpetua rolled her eyes. "Why are all you people so *sorry* all the time?"

"I just mean—I'm sorry you heard that. Or rather, that he said it at all." Briar ran a hand over her head, clutching at the knot of hair pinned behind her ears. "Look, you have to understand—Demetri, he said it was a mistake inviting you—"

"I heard that too."

"No, but, not because he doesn't like you," Briar hastened. "Because he didn't want to hurt you. Because he *does* like you, and he realized he shouldn't have invited you when—well—"

"When he's in love with you?"

Briar chewed her lip. How to explain this? It was not so easy a situation to explain. "Look. Demetri and I *were* involved once. We were betrothed. But that was a long, *long* time ago, and there's nothing like that between us anymore. Actually, it was Demetri who ended it."

Perpetua eyed her, though with less hostility now. The look on her face was a more vulnerable one—like she was truly listening, trying to understand. "Why? If he still loves you?"

Briar shrugged. "You can love someone, but that doesn't mean you should be with them. I think he felt like there was too much bad between us. Too much bad that had *happened* to us. And honestly, I...didn't love him the same way he loved me. And I'm with someone else now, and—" Rambling. She was rambling. "He doesn't *want* to be in love with me. He's trying to move on."

Perpetua looked at her. There was something still unsettling about her gaze. She was like a hawk, trying to decide whether or not to devour its prey. Then she asked, "Who are you with?"

"What?"

"You said you're with someone else now. Who?"

"Oh. Prince Garrett. I think I mentioned him before?"

Perpetua nodded, then frowned, her eyes flitting towards something behind Briar. Standing on tip-toes, she pointed into the crowd. "Isn't that your guard?"

Briar looked. It took her a moment to spot Kinsley in the crowd, and when she did, she found him talking to a rather handsome, dark-haired young man. They were matched almost exactly for height, and, Briar noticed, standing quite close. "Yes, that's Kinsley."

"You should tell him to be careful with that man."

"Why?" Briar spun around. "Is he dangerous?"

"He's a...what's the word?" Perpetua tapped an impatient foot against the deck. "A rake."

"Ah." Briar relaxed. "You know him?"

"You could say that."

"Well, thanks for the warning. I'll let Kinsley know."

"You should."

"Look, about Demetri." Briar forced her hands down by her sides. "It's up to you, of course—and I can't, really, in good conscience, advise you to pursue someone who's in love with someone else—"

"Meaning you," Perpetua said.

"Meaning me." Briar nodded. "But like I said, he is *trying* to move on. And he *does* like you, and he didn't mean to hurt you. And you should absolutely do what *you* need to do for yourself, but maybe—if you could manage it—maybe you can just try to be his friend?"

Perpetua leveled that hawk-eyed gaze at her. For a moment, Briar thought she was going to snap at her, maybe tell her to mind her own business or leave her alone. But all she said was, "I'll think about it."

She left before Briar could say anything else, rejoining her companions and disappearing into the crowd. Briar turned and found Tory staring after Perpetua with that hard look in her eyes.

"Tory?" Briar waved a hand in front of her face. "Are you all right?"

Tory blinked and looked at Briar. "There's something off about that girl, Your Highness."

Briar shrugged. "She's a little weird, I'll give you that. I like her though."

Tory frowned. "There's just something—I don't know. I feel like I know her from somewhere, but I can't remember..."

Gallia suddenly asked, "Do you see Kinsley anywhere?"

Briar flicked a glance in the direction she'd seen him before, but he was gone. She scanned the crowd—Kinsley was tall enough that he was easy to pick out—but she didn't see him anywhere. She shot Gallia a sly glance. "Maybe he went somewhere private with that man he was talking to."

Gallia arched a dark eyebrow. "Maybe he went down to the passenger rooms on the boiler deck."

"Please." Briar snorted as she started across the deck, motioning Gallia and Tory to follow her. "Kinsley would never. I don't care how handsome that man was."

"Was he?" Gallia asked, her tone disinterested. "Handsome?"

"I thought so."

Fifteen minutes later, after searching the top deck, Kinsley was still nowhere to be found. A small, worried knot formed in the pit of Briar's stomach. She was not really afraid something had happened to him, but there were only so many places he could be, and he would not have left the boat without alerting them first...

"Maybe he really *has* gone down to a passenger room," Gallia suggested, though she looked baffled at this notion.

"I doubt it, but he may have gone all the way down to the main deck. Let's go take a look."

Tory remained up top in case Kinsley turned up there, while Gallia and Briar descended to the lower decks, passing through the boiler deck first. The lights on the boiler deck were especially dim—Briar took a second glance and realized they were oil lamps instead of gear bulbs—strung out scarcely along the corridor. They pulsated with a sensuous bronze glow, casting flickering shadows over the floor. It was quiet here, the shouts of laughter and clamoring voices a distant hum. The fog in the bay had risen, coalescing into a thick haze floating below the deck, obscuring the water below.

As Gallia reached the stairs and started down, one of the doors behind Briar slammed shut. Briar turned. A girl crouched on the floor there, in the middle of the corridor. She was dressed in a low-cut, thin brown dress, and she was crying softly.

"Are you all right?" Briar asked, starting towards the girl.

"Princess?" Gallia called up. She was halfway down the stairs. "Where are you going?"

Briar knelt beside the girl. "Are you all right?"

The girl looked up, her face tear-streaked. Her black hair was loose and tangled around her face, her eyes red-rimmed. "Can you help me?" she whispered.

"Of course." Briar glanced at the room she had just come from, but the door was shut tight. "Did someone hurt you? Are—"

The girl closed her hand around Briar's shoulder, her grip like iron. Startled, Briar looked at her.

The girl said, "Don't talk. Don't make a sound."

This was a weird thing to say, but that fleeting thought was lost beneath the sound of the girl's lilting voice, which Briar found oddly...intoxicating. A pleasant haze settled over her mind.

"Come with me," the girl said. She took Briar's hands in hers and pulled Briar to her feet. Briar didn't fight, enthralled by the girl's lyrical voice. It was the sweetest music, notes plucked on a violin string, touching someplace deep inside her. Distantly, Briar noticed the girl wasn't crying anymore, but it didn't seem important. All she wanted was to follow this girl wherever she went.

The girl stepped backwards and pushed open the door to the passenger room behind her. Briar glimpsed a narrow, cot-like bed and a small table, but otherwise, the room was empty. There was no one inside. For some reason, this tugged at Briar's brain, piercing through the lovely haze in a way that was almost painful. But then the girl squeezed Briar's hands in hers, and Briar shoved the niggling thought away. She took another step, following the girl as she backed into the passenger room.

Then someone called, "Princess? What are you doing?"

Two paces from the doorway, Briar glanced aside. Gallia came down the corridor towards her, her clanking footsteps a hasty beat against the iron floor.

The girl in the brown dress tugged at her again. "I *said*, come with me."

Briar looked back at her. The girl's eyes had turned red from brim to brim, as though they had been filled with blood. Her words were almost unintelligible, coming through a row of serrated teeth edging out from behind her lips.

Briar took another step, but then Gallia was there. She grabbed Briar by the arm. "Princess, what—"

Gallia broke off. Her eyes widened as they fell upon the red-eyed girl.

The girl hissed at Gallia. She opened her mouth to speak, but before she could, Gallia yanked Briar away, tossing her into the iron railing. Briar hit hard, her face smacking against the metal. Pain rattled through her cheekbone and down her jaw, and somehow, it righted her jumbled brain, knocking out that hypnotic haze. *Go with her...no...red eyes,* red *eyes...Gallia—*

Briar shook herself. She felt strangely cold, a cold that sank right into her insides. As though she'd plummeted into a frozen lake. Steadying herself on the railing, she looked up.

Gallia was on the floor, spread-eagled. Her yellow hair was matted with blood. Unconscious, or—*no,* Briar thought frantically, *not dead, she can't be*—and the girl was still there, the girl with *red eyes* and teeth like a shark. She had Gallia by the ankle and, as Briar watched, began to drag her into the empty passenger room.

"Gallia!" Briar's voice was a croak. She grappled at the railing, struggling to get to her feet, but it was like moving through molasses. "Gallia!"

The red-eyed girl looked at her. No—not *at* her. Behind her.

"You take that one," she rasped.

Briar's heart lurched. She looked up and around.

There was a second one. A second fanged, red-eyed girl. A second monster. This girl had golden hair and a flimsy red dress, and she perched atop the railing like some enormous vulture. Fixing her crimson gaze on Briar, she let out a snarl from her enormously wide jaw, pointed teeth glinting. One of her hands shot towards Briar. But though Briar still leaned heavily into the side of the ship, she was ready.

She had a little monster in her too.

Briar caught the girl's wrist, infusing so much strength into her grip, she felt bone *crunch* beneath the skin. The red-eyed girl let out a guttural scream, and she didn't stop screaming as Briar yanked her off the railing. More bone snapped as Briar twisted the girl's arm and pinned her to the floor. As she loomed over her, Briar swore she saw a glimmer of fear in that red-eyed gaze.

A heady, potent feeling swept through Briar, chasing away the cold inside her. It was a feeling of *strength*. It was a feeling of power. She could kill this little red-eyed monster easily, she could slam her fist through her throat and crush her windpipe, smash right through her ribcage and tear out her beating heart—

The gruesome thought brought a terrible image to mind. A memory. Another monster, in another place, with pale skin and black eyes, broken and wretched on the floor. And Briar standing over her, two enormous black wings in either hand, dripping blood...

In an instant, the heady sense of power was gone. Briar felt cold again, cold and hollow. She didn't realize she'd loosened her grip on the red-eyed girl until the monster shot up straight, slapping Briar's hand away. Startled, shaking, Briar stumbled back. Grimacing with pain and hatred, the red-eyed girl lurched for her—

Blam.

The shot scorched past Briar's head, so loud that it snuffed out all other sound. Briar gaped, dumbfounded, as the bullet took the golden-haired girl in the shoulder. The scream the girl let out was muted, as though Briar heard it through water. Then the golden-haired monster flipped herself over the boat's railing and dove off the edge, vanishing into the thick fog.

If there was a *splash* as she hit the water below, Briar didn't hear it. A persistent, tinny ring echoed in her ears, blocking everything out.

Suddenly, she remembered Gallia. But when she spun around, she found Gallia alone, still prone on the floor. The other monster. There had been another monster, the girl in the brown dress. Where—

There she was. Further down the corridor, near the stairs. She stood cornered, baring her teeth at someone—someone small and dark-haired who faced the monster with a pistol. A tendril of smoke curled up from the barrel of the pistol, and Briar realized this person must be the one who'd shot the other monster. But before they could let off another shot, the girl in the brown dress turned and leapt over the railing, just as the other monster had.

The small, dark-haired person with the pistol turned around.

It was *Perpetua.*

"Perpetua?" Briar's voice was ragged in her throat. "Where did—how—"

"I'm sorry," Perpetua said. The phrase sounded awkward in her mouth, but then, Briar could barely hear her. That tinny buzz still rang in her ears, though it was faint, dying away. Perpetua held up the pistol, pinching it between two fingers. "I tried to shoot again, but I think it jammed. I'm not very good with this thing. It's a miracle I hit the other one. Here." She proffered the gun. "I took it from your guard." She indicated Gallia.

Gallia. Rather than take the pistol, Briar dropped to her knees. She swept Gallia's bloodstained hair back, feeling for a pulse. "She's alive," Briar whispered. "Thank the stars." She sagged, thumping back onto the floor. She felt dizzy, and despite the warm, muggy air, that cold inside her persisted. She looked at Perpetua. "Where did you come from?"

"Up there, of course." Perpetua pointed towards the hurricane deck. "I was coming down."

Right. Of course. What else would she be doing? "Well, thank the stars you did," Briar said shakily. "Stones, Perpetua—if you hadn't been here—"

"I saw you break that girl's arm," Perpetua said. "Easily. I thought you were going to kill her."

"I thought I was too." Briar ran a hand over her head, then down her face. She flinched as her fingers slid past her tender, bruised cheekbone.

"But you didn't." Perpetua sounded puzzled. "Why?"

Briar squeezed her eyes shut. "I don't know," she said. "I don't know."

13

FAIRWEATHER

PERPETUA WOKE WITH A blinding headache. Literally. The throbbing behind her eyes was so intense, it blinded her. Or, no, that wasn't the headache. It was the strip of light glaring through the gap between her plum-colored curtains. Perpetua groaned, shying away from the light.

"Perpetua? Are you awake in there?"

Perpetua bit back another groan as she buried her face in her pillow. The pillowcase was smooth and cool against her clammy forehead. It was silk, of course, the finest silk money could buy—just like everything else here at Castel's house.

"Perpetua?"

And there he is now, Perpetua thought grumpily. Lifting her head as best she could, she called back, "What time is it?"

"Nearly six o'clock," he said through the door.

He meant in the evening. As a naiad, Perpetua had been mostly nocturnal. She knew humans were largely *not* nocturnal, but Castel seemed to be. She also needed a lot more sleep as a human than she had as a naiad. And since she and Castel hadn't returned home from last night's revelries—a private party at an upscale bar—until dawn, Perpetua was not surprised she had slept the day away. It was a common occurrence since she'd taken up with Castel.

Dropping her head back, Perpetua turned her cheek into the cool silk and asked, "What do you want?"

"I'm going out, love," Castel called back. "Won't be back until late—maybe not until tomorrow. I'll see you then."

Perpetua took a moment to digest this information. Perhaps more than a moment. It was hard to think with her head pounding. Then—with another little moan— she heaved herself out of bed, staggered across the room, and threw the door open. "Where are you going?" she asked.

Castel was already halfway down the corridor. There were no lights in the corridor, thankfully, though the walls were a bright, pearly champagne color. Gilded pillars lined the corridor, adding a luxurious touch. Just like the rest of the house. And like Castel himself. As always, he dressed smartly, in a black waistcoat with subtle embroidery and a peacock-green ascot tie. He turned to Perpetua, smiling secretively. "I have some work to do, darling. Then I'm going out later."

Perpetua had no idea what kind of work Castel did, but she didn't particularly care. The fact that he was going out tonight, though, was quite interesting—particularly because he hadn't invited her. "Another party?"

"Not exactly."

She waited until he'd turned his back and started down the corridor again before she asked casually, "Are you seeing that man again? What's his name..." She knew very well what his name was. "Kinsley?"

Castel came to a halt. He turned to face her, but this time, his face was a controlled mask. "As it happens, yes."

"So this makes the fourth time you've seen him?" Perpetua leaned against the doorframe. "If you count the boat party last week."

Castel examined the cuff of his sleeve. "Are we keeping count?"

"It's just, in all the time I've known you—"

"Which is a grand total of two weeks."

"—I've never seen you spend more than one night with a single man."

Castel flashed a coy smile. "I haven't spent even one *night* with Kinsley yet."

"For you, that *is* weird."

"What it is, my dear, is a challenge." Castel waggled his fingers at her in a wave. "I'll see you later."

He closed the front door with a tad more firmness than Perpetua's aching head could take. She winced, then crept back into her room. She was still wearing the striped skirt and ruffled blouse she'd worn last night, though the skirt was rather more wrinkled than it had been before. Well, she wasn't going to change clothes now. She'd have a bath in a bit—right now, she just wanted more sleep.

She collapsed onto her bed. Covered in the finest silk it might have been, but it was also a bit lumpy. Perpetua loved it anyway because it was *hers*. Certainly preferable to sleeping in her damp cave, which she'd all but abandoned once Castel took her in. Not that it was a hardship on him—it was a massive house with endless winding corridors and a dozen bedrooms. But then, Perpetua had quickly learned Castel didn't do anything by small measures.

Still, his kindness—or maybe *generosity* was a better word, because "kind" was a strange concept to apply to Castel—made her a little suspicious. But Perpetua didn't have the luxury of questioning it much. Besides, judging by the house and the clothes and how easily he got into any party anywhere, Castel obviously had quite a bit of money. And one thing she had learned these last couple of weeks, as she'd navigated the ins and outs of human social circles, was that rich people could be quite careless with their riches.

Perpetua scrunched down into her bed, reaching to pull the frilled sheets over her head. She still felt clammy, her skin coated in a sheen of damp sweat. A common effect, she'd learned, from drinking too much. She'd been to many a party and pub over the last couple of weeks, almost every night. She drank and danced and chatted and gambled and hadn't stopped except to sleep. For the most part, she'd accomplished what she'd set out to do—forget her miserable existence, stuck in this human body, and forget Demetri. The one exception being the night she'd run into Princess Briar on that boat.

Briar had nearly become Candelaria's meal that night. Until Perpetua had stepped in. She still wasn't sure why she had, aside from the fact that it had been extremely satisfying to shoot Candelaria. She'd told herself Sohalia wouldn't be happy if Briar were killed, given the interest she'd taken in her, but the fact was, Perpetua didn't want Briar dead either. She wanted to hate the princess after what happened at the ball. But after talking to her on the boat, it seemed so pointless. It was clear Demetri was Briar's friend, but Briar wasn't in love with him. And the sad picture she'd painted of Demetri—the boy who'd lost everything—made it difficult to hate him too. She'd thought, more than once, about taking Briar's suggestion and seeking him out. Trying to be his friend.

Another knock sounded out, interrupting her thoughts. Perpetua frowned, tilting her head back. Her bedroom door was open, and anyway, there shouldn't be anyone else in the house. That was when she realized the knock had been more distant—not on her bedroom door, but on the front door, down the corridor.

The knock came again, more insistent this time.

Disgruntled, Perpetua rolled off her bed. She padded down the corridor to the vestibule, the tiled floor like ice beneath her bare feet. "Castel," she said, yanking the door open, "did you forget your—"

But it wasn't Castel standing on the stoop outside.

It was a naiad.

Nadalia. One of the Ternion.

"—key," Perpetua finished faintly.

Nadalia eyed her in a predatory fashion. She looked different from the last time Perpetua had seen her—back in her cave, when the Ternion had passed their judgment on her. She looked different because she was in human-form. Her sable hair was twisted back at the nape of her neck and draped elegantly over one shoulder, and the simple silk dress she wore was bottle green, just like her scales. That was usually the easiest kind of garment to glamour, though Perpetua would've thought the Ternion, powerful as they were, could manage something more elaborate.

That's what she *would* have thought, if her thoughts had been anywhere near the vicinity of what Nadalia was wearing. Instead, they scrambled around like a fish flapping on the docks, trapped and panicked, as she wondered what one of the *Ternion* was doing here.

"Hello, Perpetua." Nadalia's voice was like the sea on its calmest day, smooth and inexpressive—but concealing treachery within. Without asking for permission, she stepped neatly past Perpetua and stalked into the house. Her bare feet left damp imprints on the glossy white floor, as though she'd just left the sea and come straight here.

Nadalia flicked a careless glance around the vestibule and the parlor beyond it, taking in the gleaming marble and sumptuous furnishings in a single second. Then she turned to face Perpetua. "Close the door, Perpetua."

Perpetua did so, letting it swing shut with a too-loud *crack*. "What—what are you doing here?"

Nadalia raised an eyebrow.

"I mean—" Perpetua stammered. Just because the Ternion had declined to kill her before didn't mean they still wouldn't, and she was much more helpless now. "I haven't done anything. I mean, since you turned me human, I haven't done anything—"

"Since *Sohalia* turned you human." A hint of ire touched Nadalia's unfeeling tone. Perpetua thought she caught a flash of claws at the naiad's fingers, but if so, they were gone in an instant. "And I imagine you've done quite a bit since then—for Sohalia, that is."

Perpetua schooled her face into a blank expression. She'd always thought of the Ternion as a single entity, even if it was comprised of three individuals. So she had assumed what she did for Sohalia, she did for the Ternion. But the way Nadalia spoke—well, it didn't sound that way at all. "For Sohalia?"

Nadalia didn't move an inch, but her eyes flashed, bleeding red. That scarlet gaze pinned Perpetua just as well as her claws might have. "Don't play games with me, naiad. I know Sohalia granted you the ability to kill, the ability to feed. She wouldn't have done that without extracting something from you first. Something she wanted you to do for her."

Perpetua's frantic thoughts ran over what Sohalia had told her. She thought of the promise the sea witch had required from her—that she not tell anyone what transpired between them. Perpetua hadn't thought that extended to the other two members of the Ternion, but now.... She was sure if she told Nadalia anything, she'd risk Sohalia's wrath—and her future as a naiad.

"She didn't ask me to do anything," Perpetua blurted out.

This time, Perpetua didn't imagine the claws that emerged from Nadalia's fingers. "Do not lie to me—"

"I'm not," Perpetua hastened, backing up into the door.

"So she just gave you back your claws and fangs and sent you off?" Nadalia shook her head. "That is clearly not the case, seeing as you're staying here with her human *pet*."

"Wh-what?" Perpetua stumbled. What pet? "Who?"

"Castel. Sohalia's witch. That you're living here with him is proof enough you're tangled in her schemes."

Perpetua stared at her, uncomprehending. The words washed over her several times before they began to sink in. "I...Castel? He's not a witch—and he doesn't know Sohalia—"

"Of course he does." Contempt twisted Nadalia's features. "He *works* for her. She's always had a human servant to aid her with witchcraft. It is necessary. There are certain ingredients she needs, things than only can be obtained on land, far from here. Castel retrieves those things for her, and does much more besides that."

Perpetua felt like the floor beneath her was crumbling. The human life she'd put together here, this house, the parties, all of it—it all came down to Castel. And if what Nadalia said was true—if he really worked for Sohalia—then there was no way he'd run into her by chance at that ball.

"You really didn't know." The suspicion in Nadalia's voice turned to scorn. "I suppose you thought he had befriended you out of the kindness of his heart—"

"I told him my family exiled me," Perpetua whispered. "He said I could stay—"

"Of course he did. Just as Sohalia instructed, I'm sure. Now why would that be? Is she trying to keep an eye on you, naiad? Trying to make sure you follow through on whatever she asked you to do for her?"

Probably, yes, Perpetua realized. Even though half of her still didn't believe it, even though she clung to the notion that Castel was just her friend. "She didn't ask me to do anything for her," she repeated numbly.

Nadalia closed the distance between them in a flash, her claws inches from Perpetua's face. "If you persist in lying to me—"

"I'm not—she said I would owe her a favor."

"Naiads don't ask for *favors*."

"I only meant...she said she would require something of me in the future. But she didn't tell me what." Perpetua was so tense, her jaw began to ache. Or perhaps that was just her headache, migrating down her face. "And I swear, I swear, I haven't done anything for her yet." That much was true.

Nadalia eyed her a moment more, eyes scarlet, claws extended. Then she stepped back, assuming her dismissive demeanor once again. "Very well. That does sound like Sohalia. But you will tell me, Perpetua, what Sohalia wants of you the moment she asks. Understand, naiad?"

"N-no." When Nadalia raised her clawed hand again, Perpetua hastily added, "I mean, yes, I'll tell you, but...I don't *understand*. You're the Ternion, you're both Ternion, so why—"

She trailed off, fearing she'd gone too far. But as the red faded from Nadalia's eyes, Perpetua saw there was no anger in her face. She seemed to consider Perpetua, her dispassionate gaze sweeping over her. Then she said, "You know why they call Sohalia the sea witch, do you not?"

"Because she's a witch?"

"Yes, of course. But more than that, she is the only naiad to ever possess such magic. *Human* magic." Nadalia's tone turned distasteful. "Oh, I know all the stories about her. But her magic is as common as any human's. She gained it the same way human witches do, by making a deal with dark forces. It was never meant to be. A *naiad*, dabbling in such human affairs, taking power from the land. It has twisted her. It has driven her insane."

Perpetua thought back to the night she'd met Sohalia on the pier. The night the sea witch had restored her claws and fangs. She thought of that demented smile on Sohalia's face, how wildly she'd swung from sympathizing with Perpetua to threatening her. She remembered thinking the sea witch was mad.

It seemed she'd been right.

"She is insane," Nadalia said, her voice soft and lethal, "and yet she wields such power. I *must* be kept apprised of her doings. Do you understand now?"

A puff of air escaped Perpetua's lips. "I understand."

"Good. To contact me, emerge yourself within the sea," Nadalia said, "and call for me by name. Difficult to do, human as you are, but I will receive the message. And I will meet you in your cave."

Perpetua nodded mutely.

"Then we're done here." Nadalia swept past Perpetua, who scuttled out of the way. With one hand on the door, Nadalia turned that frighteningly impassive gaze on her one more time. "Don't toy with me, Perpetua. Sohalia is dangerous beyond your imagining, and whatever it is she wants of you—whatever it is she's *planning*—will be dangerous too. For all of us."

She was gone so quickly, the door *clicking* shut behind her, that Perpetua could almost pretend she had imagined the entire encounter.

But she hadn't. Her knotted stomach was proof of that. Stunned, Perpetua shuddered into the wall and sank to the floor. The icy cold of the tile bled straight through her satin skirt, but Perpetua barely felt it. She was flushed with fear, her heart racing. Closing her eyes, she tried to calm the storm in her chest.

That she had become caught between Sohalia and Nadalia, two of the Ternion, was a distant thought right now, a niggling concern in the back of her mind. At the forefront was Castel—*Castel*, who was not only spying on her for Sohalia, but who, probably, had known all along what she really was.

No. It didn't track. It just didn't. She couldn't accept it. Perpetua clambered to her feet, slipping amidst the folds of her skirt. Her footsteps sounded a silent, rapid pace as she started up the winding staircase to the second floor, and by the time she reached Castel's bedroom, she was running. She burst into the room, flinging the door open, and looked around desperately. The room was plunged in darkness, heavy curtains pulled shut over the windows. Perpetua stepped inside and wound the lever on a large gear-bulb lamp just beyond the door. It flickered on, a low light slanting across the room.

A witch. Castel couldn't be a witch. Witches were terrifying. And Castel wasn't that—though something told Perpetua he could be if he wanted to. She remembered sensing the threat of him the night they'd met—like she was facing down a fellow predator.

She tore through his room, heedless of the mess she made, leaving his silk sheets rumpled and his mattress askew, his drawers half-open and his books scattered on the floor, after she'd rifled through them. She took special care with the books, but that was all for naught; she couldn't read, and given the lurid illustrations in some of them, they were probably all romances, or maybe mating instruction manuals, if humans had such a thing. Her heart pounding faster by the second, Perpetua wrenched open the door to his blackwood wardrobe and began shoving his shirts aside. She was just about to give up when her hand bumped against a small knob in the side of the wardrobe, mostly hidden by a long coat.

She twisted the knob. Nothing. She pushed at it. Nothing.

She gave it a tug.

A drawer popped out from the back of the wardrobe.

Perpetua peered into the drawer. She didn't know much about being a witch, but she knew they used potions and herbs, and this drawer was full of them. She also knew Castel sometimes used such things for fun at his parties, but she had seen those herbs and powders, and these looked nothing like them. And there were other things too—a small bag of human bones, a pouch of odd-looking coins, a pitted stone bowl with strange markings. Perpetua lifted a dark jar filled with gelatinous liquid; when she brought it close to her face, she found herself staring into a single eyeball.

Shuddering, she put the jar back. That was when she noticed the last thing. Beneath all of this, at the bottom of the drawer, was a small, thick book. Perpetua extracted it with trembling hands, knocking a jar out of the drawer. It smashed onto the floor, scattering a fine blue powder everywhere.

Perpetua hardly noticed. She clutched the book in her hands. It seemed old, the edges of the pages frayed and scorched, and it wasn't bound so neatly as the other books she'd seen—no, this one was loosely bound with thick thread, holding the pages together tenuously.

She couldn't read it. But she didn't need to. There were no letters on the leather cover, only another strange mark. But this mark, Perpetua knew. All naiads knew it.

The mark of Sohalia, the sea witch.

Dimly, Perpetua realized it must not be Sohalia's mark alone, but a mark of all witches. Which meant Nadalia was right. Castel was a witch.

Perpetua dropped the book and stumbled back from the wardrobe. She darted a glance around the room, suddenly terrified Castel might appear, even though he'd said he wouldn't be back until tomorrow. But he was a witch, and witches *knew* things, and with this in mind, Perpetua fled his room, tore down the stairs, and ran out of the house, slamming the door behind her.

She didn't stop running until she was a block away, where she skidded to a halt and caught hold of a black lamppost, leaning into it. Castel. *Castel.* He knew what she was, he worked for Sohalia, he was a witch, he'd been *spying* on her—

She'd thought he was her friend. What a fool she was. What a naive, human *fool.* This whole time, Castel had only befriended her so he could report back to Sohalia.

Perpetua rubbed at her eyes with one hand and started aimlessly down the street, completely unaware of where she was going or why. If people gawked at her as she ambled, barefoot and lost-looking—and they probably did, in this upscale neighborhood—she didn't notice.

Maybe she could go to Briar. Tell her everything about Sohalia, about Castel. But the brief hope this sparked inside her died at once; of course she couldn't go to Briar. Telling her about Castel and Sohalia would mean telling the princess about *herself*—that she, Perpetua, was a naiad. And given that Demetri was hunting naiads, that didn't seem like a good idea.

Sometime later—how much later, she wasn't sure—Perpetua found herself at the docks, blinking beneath the dying orange sun. She'd been walking for longer than she thought; it was more than a mile from Castel's house to the docks.

Trudging to the edge of the pier, she lowered herself down to sit. Her thoughts swirled round and round in her head like a whirlpool. She had to do something—she had to figure out where to go—but for now, right now, she didn't want to do anything but sit here and watch the sun sink away.

14

REFUGE

PERPETUA SAT ON THE docks for hours, trying not to think or feel. Thinking made her panic. Feeling made her hurt. But she couldn't stop either, and so she sat there and went over her options again and again, each thought of Castel and his betrayal bringing a fresh surge of blistering pain.

She would just have to return to her cave. The thought of spending the night on that dark, wet rock in that isolated cove was depressing, but it had been her home once, and she had nowhere else to go. Still, it wasn't exactly safe there. Both Nadalia and Sohalia could find her there, and Sohalia might grow suspicious, wondering why she'd left Castel's place.

Maybe she should just do what Sohalia told her to. If she told Sohalia about Nadalia asking after her, then the sea witch could probably handle her Ternion sister on her own. After all, did the truth about Castel really change anything? It scared her, the thought of what he was—but if she ever wanted to become a naiad again, Sohalia was the only one with the power to do that.

And she did want that. She *missed* it. She missed the sea and her scales and just...the simplicity of that life.

Being a human was so complicated.

A shiver arced down her spine, and she wrapped her arms around her chest. The night was breezy, the air drier than usual. The result was a faint chill that Perpetua did not welcome, for the sleeves of her lacy white blouse barely covered her shoulders.

Somewhere behind her, a door banged open and a shout of laughter punctuated the night, followed by a stream of boisterous chatter. A group of humans, exiting the pub nearby. Perpetua ignored them as the voices faded into the distance, her eyes fixed on the horizon.

"Hello, stranger."

Perpetua looked up vaguely, her thoughts as far away as that horizon. Then she saw who stood over her, and her gaze sharpened. "Demetri!"

Demetri smiled a crooked smile. Perpetua's heart felt like a rock in her chest, heavy and craggy. Her eyes swept over him, taking in his floppy brown hair, his smart black coat, nicer than the one he'd worn before. She realized he must have been with the group that had come out of the pub.

"This feels like *déjà vu*," he said.

"What?"

"*Déjà vu*. You know, that feeling that you're experiencing a past moment over again." He gestured at their surroundings. "You know. Because this is where we met." His cheeks had gone faintly pink. Perpetua had since learned to identify this phenomenon as *blushing*, a sign that a human was embarrassed or drunk or uncomfortable or happy or exerted, or possibly, any combination of those things. Demetri blushed quite a lot.

"Oh," she said. "Yes." This was not, in fact, where they'd first met. But since she'd compelled Demetri to forget her from the shipwreck, this *was* where they'd first met—to him.

Demetri shoved his hands into his pockets and gazed down at her, apparently at a loss for words.

Perpetua frowned. "Why did you call me a stranger?"

"Pardon?"

"Just now. You said, 'Hello, stranger.'"

"Oh. It's just an expression."

"Oh." Of course. Over the past couple of weeks, she had learned that humans had many weird expressions, most of which she didn't know or understand. Her cheeks grew a little warm, and she wondered if she, too, was blushing.

"Erm. So." Demetri rocked back on his heels, glancing out at the water. Then he drew in a breath and lowered himself to sit by her side. He was not too close—not as close as that first time they'd sat together here—and Perpetua wasn't sure how to feel about that. "I apologize if it's none of my business, but...where did you go that night at the ball? I was worried about you."

Perpetua blinked. That night at the ball. It felt like a lifetime ago. "Didn't Briar tell you?"

"Oh, yes, she told me she ran into you last week. And she told me you had a family emergency. I just wondered if everything was all right. If you were all right." He mumbled this last bit, his gaze fixed on his knee.

Perpetua realized she was staring at him. Castel had pointed out this habit she had of staring openly at people, which apparently was quite strange and sometimes considered rude. Since then, she'd tried not to be so obvious about it, but right now, she didn't much care. "A family emergency," she repeated. That wasn't what she'd told Briar. Why had the princess lied?

"Yes. Why? Was that not true?"

The oddest thing happened. A laugh bubbled out of Perpetua's throat, though it came out hoarse and shaky. "I don't have a family."

She wasn't sure why she said it. All she knew was that she didn't regret it. It had never been truer.

"What?" Demetri sounded startled. "What do you mean? I thought you lived with them—outside town, I mean—"

Perpetua gripped the edge of the pier on either side of her, the slick, damp stone reminding her of her cave in the lagoon. She wanted so badly, in that moment, to tell him everything. When he'd appeared a few minutes ago, she'd waited for those same feelings to crash over her, the feelings she'd experienced at the party—the hurt, the resentment at hearing he loved Briar. But those feelings didn't return. Demetri's love for Briar seemed so unimportant compared to everything else she faced now, and she just wanted someone she could be honest with, someone she could explain everything to.

But she couldn't do that. It would do more harm than good.

"I...used to have family. I used to live with them, I mean." She kicked one leg aimlessly, her eyes glued to the dark, purling water before her. "But they exiled me. They turned me out," she amended, using the phrase Castel had when she'd told him the same story. "I made one mistake and they—" She broke off as her voice grew tremulous. A sign of weakness. She didn't want to show Demetri any weakness.

"They turned you *out*? Onto the streets?" Demetri's voice was incredulous. "Wait, when did this happen?"

Perpetua replied unthinkingly. "Around the same time I met you." *Because I met you.*

"Before the ball, you mean? Perpetua, why didn't you say anything? Why didn't you—"

"—tell you?" Perpetua tore her gaze from the sea and looked at him. Her voice turned hard in an attempt to shut out the shaking. But Demetri didn't flinch; he met her gaze. "I didn't really know you that well. And what could you have done?"

"I don't know," Demetri admitted. "Given you a place to stay maybe—where *have* you been living? I mean, surely—"

"I was staying with a friend. But I just left there. It turns out he wasn't such a good friend. Not my friend at all, actually."

"I'm sorry, Perpetua."

Perpetua's rock of a heart dug at her. His words were so sincere, so heartfelt, just like he always was. She had never blamed him, she thought, and this was a weird thing. Saving his life had caused all this, but even at the ball that night, she'd never regretted it. Perpetua had met so many different humans since that ball, and it was gut-wrenching to confirm what she'd already suspected—Demetri was an unaccountably, unbearably *decent* human.

"The worst part," she found herself saying, a wistful note in her voice, "is that I'm not even sure I agree with them. My family. That what I did was a mistake." Her voice dropped to a near-whisper. "I don't know anymore. All I know is that everything has been so *complicated* since then, and I..."

She wasn't sure what she meant to say next, but whatever it was went out of her head as Demetri lay his hand over hers, enclosing it in a gentle grip. Exerting just enough pressure to remind her he was there. Perpetua swallowed, trying to dislodge the inexplicable lump in her throat.

"Where are you going to go now?" he asked quietly.

Perpetua shrugged. "I have a place. It's not close by, some ways out of town, but—"

"How far out of town?" Demetri tugged at her hand, and Perpetua turned to look at him. His brown eyes were soft and troubled. "It's so late already. And you're not even wearing shoes." He tipped his head to indicate her feet, and a small smile came over his face. "Even if that's not particularly strange for you."

"I don't have anywhere else to go."

"You could stay with me." When Perpetua looked at him, Demetri hastily added, "Stay at the tavern, I mean. It wouldn't be proper if you stayed with *me*, of course, but Briar's there as well—which you know, of course, you've been there—and you could stay with her, I'm sure—" His cheeks had gone pink again.

Perpetua knew enough of humans by now to know they were often concerned with what was "proper," but she didn't understand why it wouldn't be proper for her to stay with him for the night. Still, that hardly mattered. Staying in a room *anywhere* was preferable to going back to her cave. "Do you really think Briar won't mind?"

"Of course not. Honestly, she probably won't mind if you stay forever."

Perpetua considered. Thinking beyond tonight still made her dizzy—her problems went so far beyond where to sleep, what with Castel working for Sohalia, Sohalia demanding reports about Briar, Nadalia threatening her about Sohalia. She still didn't know how to fix any of it. But she was tired of thinking about it, tired and hungry and cold, and it couldn't hurt if she stayed with Briar for just one night.

So it was decided, and Perpetua felt, at once, oddly light and warm. She suddenly realized her headache was gone. Perhaps the panic at discovering the truth about Castel had driven it out. Either way, she felt a million times better as Demetri gave her his coat and they walked down the pier.

He did not let go of her hand, not until he realized she hadn't eaten anything all day, at which point, they stopped so he could buy them some meat pasties from a cart that was open late. While he trotted across the street to fetch the pasties, Perpetua sat on an iron bench beside the water to wait, gripping the edges of his fine coat. It was full dark out, the moon a sliver in an overcast sky, but the streetlamps shone brightly, their white lights like crystals. The night, which had been so cold and bleak before, now seemed cozy and safe—

—until a cold hand gripped her from behind, closing around her arm.

Perpetua whirled and found herself staring into a pair of dark eyes.

"Don't scream," the owner of the eyes commanded.

"Tatiana!" Perpetua jerked free of the naiad's grip and jumped to her feet. "What are you—your Voice doesn't work on me, you twit!"

"So I noticed. On that boat last week." Tatiana's eyes reddened, hooded with venom. "Even though you are living as a human." She cocked her head to one side. "What is a twit?"

Perpetua bit back a juvenile response. Dashing a glance over her shoulder to make sure Demetri was still across the street, she faced Tatiana with her own red-eyed glare. Her claws emerged as well, and she flashed them discreetly at Tatiana before tucking them into the sleeves of Demetri's coat. "I am still a naiad," she growled.

"I don't think you are." Tatiana's eyes cleared, returning to their usual black. She was in full human-form, a glamoured dress over her boyish frame, the hem flapping gently in the wind. But she was menacing even so, which was odd for hapless Tatiana. "Not entirely. Because I don't know why a naiad would save two human lives and prevent *other* naiads from feeding." She added, almost as an afterthought, "Though I suppose I understand why you injured Candelaria. Given how you feel about her."

"How *I* feel about her used to be how you feel about her too," Perpetua accused. "I don't suppose she's dead now." Unlikely. Perpetua's bullet had taken her in the shoulder.

Tatiana scowled. "No."

"Well, since when do you run around with *her?*" Perpetua dropped her scarlet gaze too, her claws retracting. "Don't tell me you live in that cave of hers now, that you're part of her *shoal*—"

"So what if I am?" Tatiana edged closer, and Perpetua fought the urge to take a step back. No weakness, not like this. Facing a predator. "It hasn't been very easy these past few weeks, Perpetua, especially since *you* disappeared. You used to help me find human food when you could. And now the humans have this hunter of theirs, hunting *our* kind—"

"You heard about that?" Perpetua forced herself not to look around for Demetri. If Tatiana only knew that hunter was right here, footsteps away...

"Of course I did. The Ternion made sure everyone knows." Tatiana narrowed her eyes. "You obviously know. Even though your cave has been completely deserted. Even though you've been capering around *with* humans night and day."

"I'm not *capering* with—"

"I've been watching you, Perpetua." Tatiana tossed a nod over Perpetua's shoulder. "You're with one of them right now. Maybe he's just your meal for the night. But I've seen you with others. Those girls you saved on the boat that night—one of them called you by *name*. And that male you're living with in that big house—"

Perpetua's throat felt dry. How could she know *that*? Stones, how much time had she spent watching her? Castel's house was several blocks into town; naiads didn't usually venture that far from the sea. "I don't live there anymore."

"What I don't understand is how you're managing it. How can you stay with one human for so long without him seeing your true form?" Tatiana's gaze swept over Perpetua from head to toe. "Unless I'm right. Unless you're really not as naiad as you seem. What did you do—get the sea witch to give you a potion to make you human?"

This was so scarily, ridiculously close to the truth that Perpetua let out a trill of laughter. Which she hastened to get under control when Tatiana took her arm in a bone-cracking grip.

"I don't hear you denying it." Tatiana's eyes widened. "It can't be true. You wouldn't, not even you—"

"Tatiana—"

"Sorry that took so long."

Perpetua whirled around, wrenching out of Tatiana's grasp.

Demetri had come up right behind them.

"I couldn't decide between the—oh, hello." Demetri broke off when he saw Tatiana. The smile that came over his face faltered as he looked at the naiad, his gaze slipping from her to Perpetua. "Erm—everything all right?"

"Yes," Perpetua said.

Demetri nodded, reassured, but now he looked between the two of them with an expectant air, and Perpetua realized he was waiting for an introduction. Humans placed a lot of importance on their introductions. "Demetri, this is...my friend. Tatiana."

Demetri proffered a smile—not his real smile, she noticed, but just a polite one—and said, "How do you do?"

Tatiana's eyebrows drew down over her face. "How do I do what?"

Perpetua forced a laugh. "She's always making jokes," she said to a puzzled Demetri. "Anyway, she really has to be getting home, don't you, Tatiana?" She turned her back on Demetri to face Tatiana fully. Curling her fingers into the coat sleeves, she allowed that scarlet haze to flash over her eyes as she shot the naiad the most murderous glare she could manage.

Tatiana looked from Perpetua to Demetri. It was impossible to tell what she was thinking, and Perpetua did not like that. She didn't drop her scarlet gaze until Tatiana stepped back. "Yes. I have to go." She cut one last glance in Demetri's direction, then stalked away, down the pier.

Perpetua dropped her red-eyed gaze, letting out a low breath.

"Are you sure she's your friend?" Demetri asked dubiously. Apparently, the tension between them had not been lost on him.

"She was," Perpetua said shortly. "She's always been...close to my family."

"Ah." The frown creasing his forehead lingered another moment. Then he shook his head, handing her a warm, flaky pasty. "Well. I hope you like ham and cheese."

Perpetua managed a smile. "My favorite." She would've eaten one full of mud, she was so hungry.

Demetri chatted the rest of the way to the tavern, but Perpetua barely listened, her thoughts on Tatiana. She wished Tatiana hadn't seen her with Demetri. Now the naiad had seen him up close, now she knew his name. She may not have realized he was the one hunting naiads, but that Tatiana knew him at all worried her. Once, it might not have—but Tatiana had been so *hostile*, so unlike herself. She used to be Perpetua's friend.

As soon as that thought crossed her mind, Perpetua realized how silly it was. Naiads didn't have friends. She was even starting to *think* like a human.

When they finally reached the tavern, they encountered a small problem. Princess Briar was not there, and neither were her guards. They were all out, so of course, they had no way to access their rooms.

"I vaguely remember Alec mentioning some kind of party this morning," Demetri said ruefully. They stood at the end of the corridor, outside Briar's room. He rubbed his hand across his forehead. "She could be out all night. I think Kinsley's off duty—"

"He could be out all night too," Perpetua said, remembering, suddenly, Castel and his plans.

"He could be." Demetri sounded glum. "Well—" He edged a glance at her from the corner of his eye. "We could wait in the common room and see if any of them come back."

Perpetua nodded. Not with much enthusiasm.

Demetri's gaze turned knowing. "You're exhausted, aren't you?"

He wasn't wrong. Though her headache had gone, Perpetua could still feel the hangover lingering. She may have only been up for about four hours, but a lot had happened in that time. And now that she was comfortably fed and full, Perpetua yearned for a soft pillow beneath her head.

"Come on." Demetri started down the corridor. "You can stay in my room—I mean, if you don't mind." He turned to look at her. "I don't want you to feel uncomfortable—but then, you said you were staying with a man before, so—" His eyes widened, another flush suffusing his cheeks. "Not that—! I didn't mean to imply, erm, well—"

Perpetua goggled at him, trying to process all these twists and turns in his thinking. Why should she feel uncomfortable in his room? Was it not a nice room? And what did Castel have to do with...

Then it clicked. "Oh. You thought, because I was staying with a man, I might have been bedding him."

"What?" Demetri's eyes went so wide, Perpetua thought they were going to pop out of his head. "No! No, I didn't think—I just meant—"

"I wasn't bedding him," Perpetua said. "He doesn't like women. He only lies with other men."

"I can't believe I'm having this conversation," Demetri muttered.

"Is that why you said it wouldn't be proper if I stayed in your room?" Perpetua understood now why he was acting the way he was, and the clueless note she injected into her voice was a bit of an act. She had come to understand that mating was an entirely taboo subject among humans, which Perpetua thought the weirdest and most hilarious thing. So it was to fuel her own amusement when she went on, "Because people might think we're having sex?"

Demetri's face was as red as a tomato. Perpetua rather enjoyed that too.

"I don't care what anyone thinks about me," she told him. "So unless *you* care what people think, then I don't mind staying in your room."

Demetri ran a hand over his face. "Erm. No. I don't care. Not a bit. Not at all." He coughed. "Well...I suppose that's settled, then."

He led her down the corridor to his room, which was *not* as nice as Briar's, or as large. Briar's room sat on the corner of the inn, boasting a separate sitting room and a dressing room, not to mention several large windows. Demetri's room was a small, single room—though there was a private washroom—and had no windows. But Perpetua didn't mind. All that mattered was that it was warm and dry, and there was a bed tucked into a small, dark alcove in the far wall, perfectly large enough for two people.

Demetri provided her with one of his shirts and an extra pair of pajama bottoms, and Perpetua disappeared into the small washroom to change. When she emerged, she found Demetri sitting in the chair in the corner. "You can take the bed, of course." He pulled off one of his boots. "I'll sleep here."

"In the chair?" Of course. If he didn't think it was proper to sleep in the same room with her, then he wouldn't even consider sleeping in the same bed. Still, she eyed the chair uncertainly. It was not like any of the large, plush armchairs in Castel's house; this was a simple, straight-backed chair, like those at Castel's dining table. But not even as nice as those. "Is it even possible to sleep in that?" she asked. She couldn't imagine getting comfortable enough in that chair to fall asleep, no matter how tired she was.

Demetri smiled. "I'll be fine."

"I really don't think you will be."

"Well—I could sleep on the floor, I suppose."

Perpetua experienced a strange sensation then. A plummeting feeling, as though her heart had dropped into her stomach. It was a moment before she recognized the feeling as guilt. She felt bad for him. She was depriving him of his bed just by being here, even if that *was* because his human proprieties wouldn't allow him to sleep beside her.

Something of this guilt must have shown on her face because Demetri smiled again. "Perpetua. I'll be fine. I've spent many a night sleeping on the ground. I can handle the floor."

"Here." She immediately crossed to the bed and pulled off the thick quilt folded at its foot, and one of the two lumpy pillows. "You take these. You can have the other pillow too."

"That's all right. You keep it."

He disappeared into the washroom to finish changing, and Perpetua crawled atop the bed, burrowing beneath the sheets. They felt soft and fresh and smelled faintly of Demetri—a scent she didn't even realize she could recognize until now. She thought she would fall asleep as soon as her head hit the pillow, but instead she lay there, her gaze lingering on the light creeping out from beneath the washroom door.

When Demetri emerged, clad in his pajamas, she said in sleepy voice, "I'm sorry."

Demetri closed the door behind him. "About what? I really don't mind sleeping on the floor—"

"No." Without lifting her head from the pillow, she waved a vague hand above her face. "That I don't always know—about what's proper and such."

She heard Demetri let out a slow breath. Then he chuckled.

Perpetua rolled onto her side to look at him.

"Honestly—" He shook out the quilt to lay it over the floor "—all of that—what people consider proper, what isn't—it's all a bit silly, Perpetua." He spared her a sidelong glance, and the look in his eyes was one she hadn't seen in a while—that haunted look that meant he was seeing ghosts.

She hadn't missed that look, even though it had drawn her to him in the first place. It was too sad.

"It's just the lies we tell ourselves," he said softly, "to pretend we have some kind of control over the world. But we don't have much control at all."

Sleep was encroaching on her, shutting down her thoughts, but the pained understanding she felt at these words was sharp and clear, like the jab of a knife.

"Goodnight, Demetri," she murmured.

"Goodnight, Perpetua."

The last thing she saw, before her eyes fell shut, was Demetri as he lay down on the floor, so close that she could have stretched her arm out and touched the top of his head.

15

AMENDS

BRIAR HAD DECIDED SHE'D had about enough of this weird silence from Demetri. Two weeks had passed since their confrontation at the ball, and that was enough time to make Briar forget whether the silence had begun because things were awkward between them, or because they were angry at each other. At any rate, she wanted to talk to him about his investigation and ask whether he'd made any progress since those two monsters had attacked her at the boat party.

They still weren't sure if the monsters were actually mermaids—they'd looked like human girls, save for the claws and fangs and red eyes—but they were definitely *something*. And whatever they were, they had the most unnerving power of mind control.

Briar shuddered, remembering how that had felt. It had been far too similar to what she'd experienced when she was rotting. That fog stealing over her mind, her thoughts turning muddled, incoherent, senseless.... Yes, it had been a frightening reminder of what it had felt like to slowly lose herself, to lose her mind.

But thanks to Perpetua, she had escaped unscathed, and now they knew those monsters were out there. And Briar wanted to know if Demetri had come up with any information about them.

So as soon as she was up that morning, she threw on a pair of trousers and a clean shirt, smoothed a hand through her mussed hair, and stalked down the corridor to his room. Rapping on his door, she called out, "Demetri! Are you in there?" She paused, but it was a short, impatient one. "Demetri! If you don't answer this door, I will—"

The door flew open. Briar nearly lost her footing as it gave way. And a voice—a very *feminine* voice—said, "Oh, it's you."

Briar stared at the girl in the doorway.

It was Perpetua. And she wasn't wearing anything except what looked very much like one of Demetri's shirts.

"You can come in, if you want," Perpetua said. "But Demetri isn't here."

Briar blinked. She felt like she'd knocked her head into something. "Where...uh, is he?" She didn't know what else to say. Well, no, she *did*, but she couldn't imagine saying it.

"He and Sabine left about an hour ago. Something about a murder. He had to go investigate." Perpetua stepped back, allowing Briar to come in.

Briar didn't, still standing in the doorway. The name *Sabine* reverberated in her brain for about ten seconds before she realized Perpetua was talking about her guard Sabine. Who had been off duty last night. Who had left *here*, with Demetri...?

"Erm." Briar cleared her throat. "Sabine was here too? In Demetri's room, I mean?"

"Yes."

"She...spent the night here? *You* spent the night here?"

"I did." A wrinkle appeared between Perpetua's eyebrows. "Sabine didn't."

"Oh." A weird, dizzying relief washed over Briar, leaving her lightheaded. Not that she thought Demetri would ever...with *two* women...but— "What was Sabine doing here, then?"

"Well, we left a message for you with the man who runs the tavern—Pasquier?—because—well, it's a long story. Basically, Sabine was down in the common room this morning when one of those guards came to get Demetri. Because they found a dead body. So Sabine went with him. Anyway, are you coming in or not?"

"Well. Yes." Still not quite comprehending everything, Briar rubbed a hand over her eyes and stepped inside. "I guess I'd better."

There was a tray of food sitting on the rustic round table in the corner, filled with croissants and fruit and a tureen of porridge. "Breakfast?" Perpetua asked, snatching a croissant from the table and flitting over to the bed—the unmade, rumpled bed—where she sat, her bare legs dangling off the edge of the thin mattress.

"Sure." Absently, Briar plucked an apple from the tray and bit into it. Briar usually ate a raw critter for breakfast—that typically jolted her out of her morning sluggishness—but the crisp crunch of the apple and its sweet juice had a clarifying effect too. "So they found more remains somewhere? And Demetri went to investigate. But why did Sabine go with him?"

Perpetua tore off a flaky piece of croissant. "She seemed interested. In the murder, I mean."

"Huh." Briar sank into the chair beside the table. "And why had you left a message with Pasquier? For me?"

Perpetua proceeded to explain what had passed between her and Demetri last night—that Demetri ran into Perpetua, who was now homeless. That he'd suggested she stay with Briar, but when they'd returned to the inn, Briar and her guard weren't there. "So we left a message with the innkeeper, but it was late and I was sleepy, so Demetri let me stay in here, and he slept on the floor."

"Ohhhh." This made *so* much more sense. "He slept on the floor."

"Yes." Perpetua cocked her head to one side, then let out a trill of laughter. Briar was rather taken aback. She had never heard Perpetua laugh before. "You thought we slept in the bed together, didn't you? Not that it matters. You people are so funny sometimes."

Briar leaned back in her chair, taking another bite of her apple. "What do you mean by *you people?*"

"You, uh—" It was hard to tell in the dim light—stars, Demetri didn't even have a *window* in this room—but Briar thought she saw Perpetua blush. "You know. You royal people."

Briar reflected sourly, "I suppose we do have an overabundance of societal rules programmed into us from birth." She shrugged. "Honestly, it's nothing to me if you *had* shared the bed. I was just surprised because—well, Demetri's sense of propriety is *far* beyond mine."

"I know."

"But, Perpetua, of course you can stay with me," Briar assured her. "You can stay as long as you want. I had no idea about your family. I wish you'd—I mean, you could've told us, you know."

Perpetua looked at her. There was a hard look in her dark eyes—not an unfriendly look, but the hardness of a person faced with stark reality. "I really had no reason to trust either of you."

"I suppose not." Briar understood. She didn't know what kind of life Perpetua had led before now, but it didn't seem so odd that she might have mistrusted the generosity of two nobles she'd just met. "But you trust us now?"

Perpetua scooted back onto the bed, leaning against the metal frame. "I suppose I do."

"Well, I certainly trust you." Briar plucked a grape off its stem and plopped it into her mouth. "You saved my life, after all. So you can stay with me for however long you want. This is perfect timing, actually—I was meant to finish up my work and head back home in a few days, but it looks like I'll be staying for another couple of weeks." She had just gotten the extension approved by the Mariner counts yesterday, so she could have extra time to search for elarium from the coast. "And even once I *do* leave—well, I'm sure you can work something out by then. Or you can come with me to the Glen Kingdom."

"I can?"

"Sure. Garrett is always bringing people home when *he* goes out gallivanting around the Five Kingdoms. The last one was a surly hunter. You'd be quite the improvement over *him*, I promise you."

Perpetua leaned forward a little. "Do you love this Garrett?"

Briar was taken aback again, though she was becoming accustomed to Perpetua's abrupt queries. "Well...yes. I do." She plucked another grape.

"How do you know? That you love him?"

Briar shrugged. "I just do."

A flicker of frustration passed through Perpetua's eyes.

Briar laughed, then wished she hadn't. She didn't want Perpetua to think she was laughing *at* her. "I'm sorry. I don't think I can explain it better. You'd be better off asking Garrett himself. He thinks about that kind of thing more than I do." Briar leaned back, balancing her chair on its rear legs. "He was rather put out when he finally told me he loved me and I behaved as though it was no big deal. It *was*, of course, but I fell in love with him very quickly, and once I did, I knew it. It was simple for me. Him, not so much."

Perpetua's cheeks pinched in a frown.

"Is this about Demetri?" Briar's eyes widened as she allowed her chair to fall back onto four legs. "Did you talk to him about me? About what he said at the ball, I mean."

"I didn't mention it. I sort of thought you had."

"I was going to," Briar admitted. "But it seemed like it wasn't my business to mention it. I thought if *you* wanted to let him know what you heard, you could. I didn't want to interfere."

Perpetua's mouth twisted ruefully. "It doesn't seem so important now. I have bigger problems."

"Not anymore, you don't." Briar bounced to her feet. "Now. I'm not at all averse to sharing my bed with you, but I'll wager I can get us a second bed if I talk to Pasquier. Want to come?"

⸻ ◆ ⸻

After her morning with Perpetua, Briar nearly forgot about speaking to Demetri. Until he walked into the tavern later that day while she sat in the near-empty common room, eating a late lunch with a bleary-eyed Kinsley.

"What were *you* up to last night?" she'd asked Kinsley, when he'd joined her a few minutes ago. According to Aden, Kinsley had gone out last night—for the third time this week. Each time, he'd come home very late.

"Nothing good," Kinsley muttered, rubbing at his eyes.

"Somehow, I don't quite believe that."

"Somehow, I think it's none of your business, Your Highness."

Briar raised her teacup to her lips. "Really, I don't know what's gotten into you, Kinsley. Staying out all night, coming over all hungover—"

"I'm not hungover. This time. And I might remind you that *you* were the one who started all this, Princess."

"I really don't know what you're talking about. *I* didn't introduce you to Castel. Speaking of introductions, when do I get to meet him? Properly, I mean."

"What makes you think you get to meet him at all? I've only known him for a week."

"And been out with him three times. Wait, does the time I caught you kissing him at the boat party count? You know—when I was being viciously attacked by a mind-controlling monster, and you were off snogging some man you'd just met?" After all his nagging about protecting her at the boat party, she was *not* about to let him live that incident down.

Kinsley muttered something unintelligible into his cup of tea.

That was when Demetri walked into the tavern. His wardrobe had improved slightly since he'd taken on his new job with the counts. He wore a navy blue waistcoat and a tailored sack coat, paired with a black tie and black trousers. The new clothes, however, could not disguise how weary he looked. There were deep bags beneath his eyes. As soon as he walked in, he spotted Briar and, after saying something to Sabine, made a beeline for her table.

"Kinsley," Briar said in a low voice, "could you give me a minute?"

"A minute of what?" Kinsley asked blankly.

"Just shove off, Kinsley," Briar muttered as Demetri reached their table.

"Princess, I—oh. Demetri." Kinsley stood. It was the first time Briar hadn't heard him stumble over the lack of "Prince" before Demetri's name. "I'm going to check in with the others. Alec wanted to change shifts again, and I need to make sure they sorted it out." With that terse explanation, he left the room with Sabine, making the kind of smooth exit only Kinsley could manage.

"Demetri," Briar said as he plopped down opposite her. It was difficult to summon a smile beneath the roiling churn of emotions he created in her, but she managed it all the same. Or she thought she did.

"Briar." Demetri eyed her with a slight frown. "Your smile is ghoulish. Please stop."

Briar dropped her smile, assuming a more neutral expression. "You've been, erm...quite busy lately."

"No, I haven't." Demetri dropped his head into a hand. "I've just been avoiding you."

"Oh. Right." Briar didn't know whether to be pleased or offended by this honest admission. "And you decided to stop because...?"

Demetri lifted his head and met her gaze. "I owe you an apology, Briar."

Briar privately agreed, though now he'd said this, a part of her wished he wouldn't. It wasn't her fault, running into him here in Moselle—but he'd been through so much, and she knew he was trying to get past it all. It wasn't his fault he hadn't yet.

"It was just—that ball, that place, the way it all was...but that's no excuse." Demetri rested an arm over the tabletop, and there was such an earnest light in his eyes that Briar's heart went out to him. It made her want to sag with relief. He was still Demetri, the same Demetri—just with a lot more baggage. "I shouldn't have laid all that at your feet. And it's not true I don't want you here."

Briar nodded. She hadn't realized how much it hurt to think that until just now.

"But I'm *not* sorry for telling you the truth. All of it," he said. "Because it was too hard, pretending to be fine when—when—"

"When you're not?"

Demetri shrugged, and it was such a helpless gesture. "I'm trying."

"I know." Briar resisted the urge to take his hand. "I know you are."

"You said..." Demetri gazed at the bar over her shoulder. Glasses clinked as the bartender tidied up, but Briar kept her gaze on Demetri. "Last fall, when we parted ways at the train station. You said if nothing else, I was your friend. I'm—can I still be?"

"Of course." Briar couldn't imagine the circumstances that could keep her from wanting his friendship. "And am I yours?"

Demetri flashed her a smile. "Always."

Briar felt lighter than she had all week.

Unfortunately, Demetri didn't have any further information on the monsters that had attacked her on the boat, or on mermaids in general. The grisly remains that had turned up this morning were similar to the ones Briar found on the beach, but aside from that, there wasn't much to go on. So Briar let Demetri know she had spoken to Perpetua and sorted everything out, and then she took Alec with her to spend the rest of the day working on the submarine.

It was a curiously balmy day. Another blast of dry air had pushed out the humidity last night, and Briar enjoyed the reprieve. Still, it was plenty warm, the sun beating down on them all day. Even working inside the submarine wasn't particularly cool; it was stuffy and airless inside.

Briar had taken the advice of that woman she'd run into—Sohi—and instructed her people to look for elarium deposits in the sea caves along the coast. The trouble was, there was a *vast* network of caves up and down the coast, and even with their equipment, it would likely take time to find any—which was why Briar had decided to extend her stay here.

It was dark by the time they finished for the day, the ocean a deep blue and oddly calm. Briar was sticky with sweat, but Alec, who had been working on the engines, had come all over covered in grease and grime. So while he went to clean up, Briar waited outside the barbed wire enclosure, where the beach cut off at the sheer cliff rising above the sand. She leaned back to perch on a large boulder and closed her eyes, listening to the waves lap upon the shore.

She thought of Perpetua and the conversation they'd had about love, and her thoughts turned to Garrett. She'd been in the Mariner Kingdom for three weeks now, and she missed him. She'd been surprised, when he left for his hunting trip last winter, to find she missed him quite a lot. She'd known even then that she loved him, but she hadn't realized how it would feel to be away from him for so long. It was like being away from a part of herself.

She'd been left on her own for most of her life, and it had been lonely, but she hadn't really known what it was like to miss a specific person. To miss all the things about *Garrett*, to miss his smile and his kindness and the warmth of his arms around her and all their late night talks, when she was too wired or too wary for sleep.

They'd spent entirely too much time away from each other in the past six months. He'd been home from the Black Forest only a month before she'd left for the Mariner Kingdom. She'd have to make sure they saw more of each other when her business here was over. She knew he wanted that too.

"Princess Briar."

Briar peeked one eye open. She'd been too caught up in her thoughts to realize the voice did not belong to Alec, so when she saw the stranger standing before her, she opened both eyes and straightened. The man was vaguely familiar to Briar, but she couldn't quite place him. "Yes?" she asked blankly. "Have we met?"

The man smiled, and it was a certain kind of smile. Calculated. A little self-satisfied. "We have a mutual friend." He was incredibly handsome, with dark hair and dark eyes, and he was long and lean, a good head taller than Briar. Nearly as tall as Garrett. As tall as Kinsley.

Kinsley. That was when she realized who he was.

"You're Castel," she said, probably sounding a little too pleased with herself. "I'm sorry. I should have recognized you from the boat party. But then, I didn't get a very good look at you while you and Kinsley were...how should I put it..."

Castel's smile widened, revealing a set of very white teeth. "Getting acquainted?"

"I was going to say engaged in a passionate embrace, but perhaps that's too crude."

"Passion is never crude, princess." There was something about him—a sort of *charge* in the air that made it difficult to draw her gaze from him. Almost without realizing it, Briar smiled at him.

Castel smiled back. He had never stopped. "So? Do I meet your approval?"

Briar made a point of looking him over, noting his expensive leather shoes, his tailored trousers, the fine cut of his dark coat and his lemon-colored ascot tie. "Well, I've only just met you."

"Yes. But you strike me as someone who can make up your mind very quickly about a person."

Something about these words prickled at Briar in a disconcerting way. They were a bit similar to what she'd said to Perpetua about how quickly she'd fallen in love with Garrett. Which had to be a coincidence, of course. "I would say that's true." Briar twisted her head to one side, surveying him. "Still, you're not quite what I expected. Not the sort of man I thought Kinsley would like."

"He doesn't like dashing, handsome, clever men?"

Briar laughed. "Well, I don't really know, I suppose."

"*You*, on the other hand, are quite what I expected."

Briar's laughter died in an instant. She was not imagining it this time, the sense of disquiet within her. "Am I?" She tried to smooth out her voice to disguise how unsettled she was. "I didn't realize Kinsley had said much about me. In the little time you've spent together."

Castel shrugged. It was a distinctly blasé gesture, as though he'd realized he'd made her uneasy and was trying to backtrack. "Not so much from Kinsley. But everyone knows your story. It's all over the penny presses, and they're *most* popular. The long-lost princess from the Mountain Kingdom, asleep these hundred years—"

"Eighty-two years."

"—the damsel in distress, rescued by the courageous princes who braved fairies and corpse monsters to save her."

Briar frowned. "And that's what I seem like to you?"

"Not at all," Castel's grin was roguish. "But that's because I realize any princess stuck in a monster-ridden kingdom must have done *some* of the saving herself."

Briar was slightly mollified by this, but only slightly. Something had cut through his charming demeanor, something that still gnawed at her.

"But I'm not here about you, princess." Castel slipped his hands into his pockets. "Or about Kinsley, I'm afraid. I wanted to talk about Perpetua."

"Perpetua?" Briar echoed. Then she remembered. "That's right. She said she knew you, that night on the boat." She raised her eyebrows. "She said you were a rake."

"Hardly that," he said carelessly. "What I am is Perpetua's...brother."

"Her brother?" Briar's unease sharpened. "She told me her family turned her out."

"I didn't." Castel spread his arms wide. "I took her in when that happened. She was staying with me until last night. I was out, of course—with Kinsley—so I didn't realize she'd gone until I got home earlier today. I'm not sure why she left, but. I think she must have been upset about something."

"And what makes you say that?"

Castel grimaced. "She left quite a mess." He fixed his gaze on Briar. "I was hoping you might have seen her. A friend of mine saw her round LeBeau's earlier today."

Briar crossed her arms over her chest. "She's staying with me. *She* said she had been staying with a friend, not a brother. And she said she left because she'd realized that friend *wasn't* her friend after all."

"I was afraid of that." Castel tugged a hand through his hair, looking vexed.

"So may I ask," Briar said, "what exactly happened to make her feel that way?"

Castel's gaze darkened. "You may ask. But I don't think it's any of your business. If Perpetua didn't tell you."

Briar bit back a retort. Much as she hated it, he was right; whatever had happened, Perpetua had chosen not to share. "Fair enough."

Castel dipped his head. "I'll be on my way, then."

He turned to go, but Briar shot an arm out and grasped his wrist, twisting him back to face her. She caught a flash of shock across his face—she'd exerted *just* enough supernatural strength to keep him from pulling free. Still, she did not think this man was easily surprised, and it was satisfying to see.

"If I find out you did anything to hurt Perpetua," she said, "*or* if you do anything to hurt Kinsley, I *will* hunt you down. Understand?"

A most curious expression came over Castel's face. "You care about Perpetua?"

This caught her so off-guard, she almost lost her grip. What an odd question from a man who was supposed to be Perpetua's family. "Well, yes. I do."

He laughed quietly. "Isn't that just a thing." He said *thing* in a most significant way. "I understand, princess. Perfectly." He gave the smallest tug at his arm.

Briar let him go. He did not rub his arm, as some people might have. He only flashed her another smile and turned away, melding into the shadows beyond the beach.

16

FEARLESS

DEMETRI GAZED DOWN THE shoreline, studying the marshy landscape. The bay curved in on itself here, creating a little cove lined with windblown poplar trees. The trees were spindly, looking as though one good gust would knock them all down. But they grew thick here, clustered close together, giving the spot an air of seclusion. They were also a couple of miles from the outskirts of Moselle, which made this the perfect spot for a murder.

Or at least a dismembering, as it were.

Demetri glanced down at the...remains...before him. He bit down hard on his tongue, trying to keep from gagging. A small crowd had gathered—somehow they always did, even when they *were* a good ways out of town—and not for the first time, Demetri wished he could have gone to stand with them, corralled by the capital guard a good distance from the pebbly beach here.

"So…" Sabine squinted up at him. She was out of guard uniform today, since she was off duty. She wore simple brown trousers paired with a fitted blouse and a short coat. Her black hair was slicked back and pinned in a knot at the nape of her neck. "Is this what I think it is?"

"Were you thinking mermaid?" Breathing in through his mouth, Demetri crouched beside her. "Because I was thinking mermaid."

Sabine grimaced. "I was thinking *part* of a mermaid."

Sabine had the right of it. Because the remains before them, the remains that had been discovered around dawn this morning, could hardly be called remains. It was, in point of fact, a severed arm.

A severed arm covered in bottle-green scales, ending in a hand with claws.

"You know," Sabine said, "you're being a bit blasé about this. I mean, I realize you've dealt with monsters before, but until recently, you also weren't convinced mermaids are real."

"Well, *something* supernatural attacked Briar on that boat."

"Yes, but not something with scales. Rather, something with red eyes and ginormous teeth."

"And mind control," Demetri reminded her. "Don't forget the mind control."

"How could I?"

One uniformed guard broke away from the crowd and trotted across the beach towards them. He carried a small notepad and slowed to a walk once he reached them. "Your Highness." Captain Gage's tone was a weird mixture of grim excitement. "I've just finished interviewing the couple who discovered the arm. Not much to report—they didn't see anything strange, nothing to indicate what might have done this." He rubbed his chin. "When were the last remains found?"

"Four days ago," Sabine answered. She had been present for that investigation as well, the morning after Perpetua spent the night in Demetri's room.

"We haven't found any remains so close together," Captain Gage noted. "Though I suppose *these* remains are—er—quite different than the others." He looked at Demetri. "What are we thinking? A vigilante killing?"

Demetri peered up at him, using a hand to shield his gaze against the sun. "I was thinking we should rule out some kind of hoax first."

"Hoax?" Sabine repeated. "You think someone faked this?"

Demetri glanced down at the scaled arm. It was entirely possible, so far as he was concerned. By now, the town and surrounding area was abuzz with talk of vicious mermaids attacking and killing people. Someone might have done this for attention. Or as some sick joke.

Or, maybe, to rile everyone up. Not that anyone needed much help in that department. The story about these creatures possibly having mind control had already spread. Demetri had heard some of the soldiers talking about what they would do if they caught a mermaid. Cutting out their tongues was their first idea.

"We'll have the body authenticated, of course, by the coroner." Captain Gage sounded disappointed, but he didn't allow it to overcome his professional demeanor. "The couple that discovered her, at least, seem sound enough. Their story doesn't have any glaring holes in it. Nor do they seem like sensationalists or fame-seekers. If it *isn't* a hoax—"

"Then we may have a mermaid," Demetri admitted. "Or at least, the arm of a mermaid." He rose to his feet and raked a hand through his hair. The humidity was unforgiving at this time of day; beads of sweat dotted his forehead. "At any rate, you can take the remains. I'll come by the coroner's tomorrow."

Captain Gage saluted—Demetri rather wished he wouldn't, though at least the man didn't bow—and went to retrieve some of his men from up the beach.

Sabine eyed him with scrutiny. "Always the skeptic."

Demetri rolled his shoulder. "It's the only way to investigate properly." He started down the beach towards town, keeping close to the water's edge to avoid the crowd.

"What exactly is your interest in this, Sabine?" he asked. This was the third time she had volunteered to accompany him on an investigation. "Not that I mind your company—but observing dead bodies and interviewing locals seems an odd way to spend your time off."

"I don't know." Sabine looked at him, a strange gleam in her eyes. "It's rather exciting, don't you think?"

"Oh, stones." He barely held back a groan. "Don't tell me you're one of those mad thrill-seekers like Garrett."

Sabine permitted herself a small smile. She was not a particularly effusive person, so in that way, she was nothing like Garrett. "Not really. I just have an interest in...the weird and supernatural. It *is* part of what drew me into service to Prince Garrett and Princess Briar, but not for the adventure. It's more of an academic interest."

It was a long walk back into town with very little shade. Demetri and Sabine managed to avoid any onlookers and reporters as they entered Moselle, but even so, Demetri was exhausted and starving by the time they reached LeBeau's.

The investigation was wearing on Demetri. He'd been looking into these incidents for nearly a month now. In that time, two small fishing vessels had been overturned and their passengers gone missing, though only one showed obvious signs of sabotage. And the arm discovered this morning was the third set of remains found. He'd done what research he could on mermaids—both with the resources provided at the castle library and by collecting tales from locals. But everything turned up little more than fairy stories—things that *could* be true, but of which he had no proof.

They were just no closer to figuring out who was behind these murders and sabotages, let alone if mermaids were responsible. So he entered the tavern with a preoccupied mind and a heavy heart. He stood inside the doorway for a moment, letting his eyes adjust. Even at this time of day, with the morning sun blazing outside, the tavern's common room was dim. Private dining rooms occupied the tavern's eastern wall, so the windows there were closed off, shutting out most of the sunlight.

Once his eyes had adjusted, he spotted Perpetua sitting by herself at a small table. His spirits lifted a little. He placed a quick order for breakfast, then went to join her. She was eating toast and sipping a cup of hot chocolate (a more popular choice than tea here in the Mariner Kingdom, Demetri had noticed). Her dark eyes were as faraway as his own thoughts had been.

"Morning," he greeted her, sinking into the seat opposite her.

Perpetua's gaze swept over him critically. "You look…"

"Tired?" He sagged back in his chair. "Hot? Hungry?"

"Tired seems about right." She sipped at her chocolate. "Kinsley said there was another body found this morning. What did it look like?"

Demetri was rather taken aback by her conversational tone. As though they were discussing the possibility of rain later, not corpses. "You really want to know?"

Perpetua nodded, lifting her toast to her lips.

Demetri hesitated. "Ah...while you're eating?"

"What does that have to do with anything?"

"Well." Some people had more of a stomach for this sort of thing than he did, he supposed. Actually, going by the others he'd encountered—Sabine, Captain Gage, Briar, Garrett—almost everyone had more of a stomach for it. "It wasn't actually a body. It was a severed arm."

"Severed," Perpetua repeated. Demetri watched her for some sign of revulsion or fear, but all she did was furrow her brow. As though she was befuddled by this. "Like, with a blade?"

"No, I wouldn't say so. More...ripped off."

"I see."

"Also, the arm was covered in scales."

"*Scales?* It had scales?"

"Mm-hmm." Demetri turned aside to accept a cup of tea from the auto-waiter. It scurried back to the bar, weaving through the tables. "So everyone thinks it's the arm of a mermaid. I'm not even convinced those scales are real. But we'll know more once the body has been examined by the coroner."

"A mermaid." Perpetua leaned back, looking troubled. "A mermaid's severed arm."

"So that was my morning." He affected a flippant tone. "What plans do you have for today?"

Perpetua shook herself and straightened. "Briar wants to go to the beach later. When she's done working on her submarine."

Demetri took a long sip of his tea, inhaling the lemony scent. There was nothing so calming as a nice cup of tea. He eyed Perpetua over the rim of his cup, noting her unenthusiastic expression. "But you don't want to?"

"I'm a little sick of the beach," she admitted. "Of the ocean. I feel like I practically used to live there. Before."

"Well, then let's do something else."

"Me and you?"

"Sure." Demetri froze with his cup halfway to his lips. Was this a bad idea? He wasn't sure, exactly, where he and Perpetua stood these days. He had been rather open about courting her before, what with the kissing and taking her to the ball. But he'd meant what he'd said that night—it wasn't fair of him to court her while he struggled with feelings for Briar.

But did that mean he couldn't be friends with her? He didn't even know if Perpetua was interested in more than that. Given everything that had gone on with her family, she probably hadn't given *him* much thought.

"Hmm," Perpetua said, drawing him out of his thoughts. "All right."

Well, he supposed that settled that. For today, at least. "What do you want to do?"

Perpetua seemed to consider this very seriously. "What *is* there to do?"

"Around here? Oh, many things, I'm sure."

"I want..." Perpetua traced a finger over the dark tabletop, following its serpentine lines. "I want to do something I've never done before."

"Like what?"

Perpetua lifted her gaze, and he couldn't tell if the look on her face was amused or rueful. Perhaps both. "The things I have not done would probably amaze you."

"All right," Demetri said with a small laugh. "Well. Let's see." He clasped his hands together, trying to think of something—something fun and easy, something available, but perhaps not something a local Moselle girl might have done before.

Then it came to him. Leaning forward, he asked, "Have you ever been horseback riding?"

One of the perks—the only real perk, so far as Demetri was concerned—of playing the "prince" for the Mariner counts was he had access to anything at Mariner Castle. He could do without most of it—he had become accustomed to life without the finer things. But he no longer owned his own horse; the one Garrett gave him had run off during a storm. He had been looking at buying one not long ago, but then he'd moved to Moselle for the summer and found he had no need of one.

But he missed riding. It was something he had enjoyed since he was a small boy. So this was not the first time he had made use of the Mariner Castle's stables, though it was the first time he'd brought someone with him.

"I've seen people riding horses," Perpetua said as they emerged out into the riding enclosure. Demetri usually rode around the castle's extensive grounds, but since Perpetua had never ridden before, they would stay within the enclosure. "Capital guard and such. But it still seems like madness to me."

Demetri glanced at her. "Are you sure you want to try?"

"Yes." Perpetua's tone was almost defiant.

"It really isn't difficult," Demetri assured her. "The horse does most of the work."

It was not so hot here on this high, grassy hill. The enclosure was ringed in by thick woodland, cultivated for the castle grounds. A mixture of dark, shady cedar trees and soaring poplars surrounded them, providing protection from the midday sun. A blustery breeze wound through the trees, rippling over the pale-green grass.

When the stable workers brought out their horses—the same dappled gray Demetri had ridden before, and a red dun mare—Perpetua eyed them with a curious glint in her eye. Still, she was plainly unsettled. "What if it—the horse," she said, stumbling over her words, "can tell that I'm..."

When she didn't finish her sentence, Demetri turned to face her, placing his hands on her shoulders.

"Horses don't care what you are," he told her firmly. "They don't even care if you're afraid, contrary to popular opinion. They only care that you're honest with them."

"Honest?" Perpetua echoed, her brow wrinkling.

"Mm." Demetri stepped back, crossing to his dappled gray. He ran a slow hand over the horse's neck, the gray's coat smooth and soft beneath his palm. The horse tilted his head towards him. "When I was eight," he said, "I fell from my horse while riding." He'd been thrown, actually, but he didn't want to alarm Perpetua. "After that, I was afraid to ride again. My cousin Kol—" A small lump grew in Demetri's throat, as it always did when he thought of his long-dead family "—kept telling me I had to stop being afraid if I wanted to ride again, because horses can sense fear."

"Can they?" Perpetua asked, her eyes wide.

"I suppose they can. But that doesn't matter." Demetri threaded his fingers through the horse's silvery mane. "I couldn't just stop being afraid. But I did want to ride again. So when I finally worked up enough courage to try, I just had an honest conversation with my horse. I let her know I was afraid, that it wasn't personal, and that I just needed a little help from her."

"And that worked?"

"It did." Demetri gave the gray one last pat. "So there's nothing to worry about. Because your horse will understand, so long as you don't try to hide from it."

Perpetua nodded, and just like that, the troubled look in her eyes vanished. As though she had willed her worries away with hardly any effort at all.

Demetri and one of the stable workers helped her mount the mare. The stable hands claimed the mare had a mild temperament, but even so, she stamped nervously when Perpetua came near. But as Demetri turned to mount his own horse, he could hear Perpetua whispering to the mare beneath her breath, and by the time he was in his saddle, both she and her mount seemed calmer.

They walked the horses for a bit, Demetri demonstrating how to direct the horse and answering her questions, most of which had to do with him and his own riding experiences. The afternoon turned balmy as the sun moved across the sky and the wind rustled the leaves on the trees.

"How do you make the horse run?" Perpetua asked suddenly, after they had completed a walk around the enclosure.

"Well, horses don't run, exactly. They gallop."

"How do you make it do that?"

"You sort of lean forward," Demetri said, demonstrating this, "and then you give it a bit of a kick and—"

"Like this?" Perpetua adjusted her foot to do just that.

And then, before he could stop her, she was galloping.

Demetri gaped after her. The whip-like shock that surged through him eased a bit when she did not immediately fall off, though he did kick his own horse into a gallop after her. She had enough of a head start that by the time she reached the opposite end of the enclosure, he was still a ways behind. But when she wheeled the horse around, he realized she was laughing—a wild, free, pealing laugh that she couldn't seem to control.

Demetri slowed his horse to a walk, his racing pulse slowing. "You," he said, and he couldn't contain the grin spreading across his face, "are totally mad."

"Mad?" Her horse stood still as she waited for him to reach her. With some effort, it seemed, she got her laughter under control. "What makes you say that?" Her eyes glittered with mirth.

"You could have fallen off that horse."

"But I didn't. And what is the point of riding a horse if you can't run?"

"Gallop," Demetri corrected. "Want to race to the other end?"

They did race, and Perpetua won, and not because Demetri let her. Though he was a bit distracted, watching tendrils of her warm-brown hair trail her in the wind, admiring the graceful arc of her neck, and catching snatches of her exhilarated laughter.

"I changed my mind," he told her as they slowed their horses. "You're not mad. You're fearless."

"Oh, I don't know." Perpetua lifted one shoulder in a shrug, but there was something plaintive about the gesture. "There are a lot of things I'm afraid of."

Demetri shook his hair back from his face. "Like what?"

Perpetua didn't answer at first, and Demetri felt stupid for asking such a personal question. It was just that it had always been easy to talk to Perpetua about anything. There was something so *open* about her, so genuine and uninhibited.

So fearless.

"I'm afraid," she said slowly, as though just working this out for herself, "of not—living."

"Of dying?"

"No. Not exactly." Her eyes fixed on a spot between them, on a single blade of grass, perhaps. "I mean, of not...feeling, not experiencing...everything. Everything there is."

Sometime later, as twilight encroached upon the castle, staining the sky a rosy hue and dampening the humidity, the two of them sat out on the bluff behind the castle, watching the hazy light on the horizon fade as the sun sank below the sea. Demetri was exhausted again, but in the most perfect way, and he tipped his head back with a long sigh.

"It's weird, seeing the sea like this." Perpetua's voice was a gentle hum, mirroring the distant rumble of the waves far below. "So far away, but still beautiful."

Demetri murmured in agreement, though he'd closed his eyes.

"Where did you live before?" Perpetua asked suddenly.

"Before I came to Moselle, you mean?"

"I mean, before. Because you're a prince. Did you live in a castle like this one?"

"Well, I—wait." Demetri's eyes flew open. "How did you know—"

"—that you're a prince?" Perpetua turned a wry gaze on him. "Doesn't everyone?"

He supposed, by now, everyone did. It was no wonder Perpetua had heard it from someone. He ran a hand down the side of his face. "And here I thought I was so stealthy."

"Why did you want to hide it?"

Demetri let his hand fall. "Oh, I don't know. It wasn't that I *didn't* want you to know, it's just—I'm really not—" He bit the inside of his cheek. "I'm not really a prince. Not anymore."

And he told her then. Everything. All of it. Everything that had happened to him. Briar's curse, and the djinn that took him captive. He did not dwell on what that had been like for him, but he didn't hide the trauma it had bred in him either. And he told her what had happened once he was freed—meeting Garrett, waking Briar, the corpse monsters, realizing he had to leave his old life behind and find a new one. By the time he finished, the setting sun had vanished below the horizon, leaving only an imprint of crimson light awash over the bay.

When he was done, Perpetua said, "That's what you meant. When you said you lost everything."

"Yes."

She pulled her knees up to her chest and rested her cheek against them. Her eyes crinkled in distress, and it was a minute before he realized the distress was for him. "So this other prince...Garrett...I don't understand. You said he's your friend."

"One of the best."

"But he has everything *you* had. Your kingdom, your home—your—well—"

"Briar?" Demetri felt a smile tugging at his lips. That he could manage that while thinking about Briar felt good. "Well, for one thing. She was never *mine* to give or for anyone to take." He shook his head. "I know it sounds weird, but Garrett wasn't responsible for anything that happened to me. And he did everything he could to help me." He paused. "I'm sorry, by the way."

"About what?"

"That I...never mentioned that Briar and I had been involved. Romantically, I mean."

Perpetua was quiet for a moment. Then she said, "I already knew."

"What?"

"Briar told me."

Demetri chanced a glance at her. But she didn't seem upset. Her eyes were soft as she said, "It doesn't matter. We're friends, aren't we?"

"Yes. Demetri's voice was rough. It was a relief to hear her say this, to know she didn't expect anything from him. But there was something troubling about it too, and he couldn't work out why.

"So you don't mind then," Perpetua pressed, "about Briar and Prince Garrett?"

"No," he answered honestly. He had never had to pretend about that, never.

"But how?"

That answer was easy too. "I love them both." He lay back, pillowing his head against the fine, downy grass. "And when you love someone, you only want for them—whatever will make them happy. No matter the cost to yourself." He closed his eyes again. "And Briar and Garrett make each other happy."

Perpetua was quiet for so long, she might have disappeared. Demetri had no way of knowing with his eyes closed, the breeze whispering over his face and the grass tickling his ears.

Then she said, her melodious voice very close, "I hope someday I know what it's like. To love like that."

Demetri turned his head. Perpetua lay beside him, inches away, staring up at the sky. He thought of her family, and what wretched people they must be, that she didn't already know a love like that. The thought burned.

He shifted his hand around until it bumped into hers. And he didn't take it, but just let it rest there, his fingers touching hers. "I hope you do too."

17

MONSTROUS

"**P**ERPETUA!" BRIAR CALLED. "COME on! It's just down here!"

Perpetua licked her lips as she eyed the shoreline. She knew she was being paranoid—it was the middle of the day, so they were not likely to run into any naiads out here—but for some reason, she could not shake the edginess that had come over her as she'd followed Briar down the rocky hillside.

Briar had taken the day off from her work and insisted Perpetua accompany her to the beach for the afternoon. Not the main beach, where most of the humans liked to go—Briar said it was becoming too crowded. Instead, she'd chosen a more private spot she'd discovered when she'd first arrived in Moselle. It was quite close to the tavern, a little ways north from the main beach.

Perpetua clambered the rest of the way down the hillside until she came out onto a narrow strip of sandy beach, sequestered between the rocky crag on their right, and a murky stretch of marshland on their left.

"Here we are!" Briar beamed at Perpetua. "What do you think? Nice and quiet, yes?"

"Yes." Placing her hands on her hips, Perpetua eyed the spot. "But isn't this where you found those—er—remains?"

"Why, yes." Gallia, one of Briar's guards, turned a flat look on her princess. "Yes, it is."

Briar waved a dismissive hand. "Oh, that was further down that way." She pointed vaguely southward. "It's fine. Anyway, Gallia, weren't you the one who didn't like all those men gawking at you on the beach last week? Well, there's no men to gawk here, are there?"

"Except that one." Perpetua pointed at another of Briar's guard, the only male to accompany them. He stood up the hillside, fully dressed, at a vantage point where he could see their surroundings.

"Yes, except Aden, but he doesn't gawk," Briar assured her. "At anyone, apparently."

"He certainly shouldn't be gawking at *us*," said Sabine, another guard. "He's on duty. Too bad for him. Me, I'm not wasting another second standing around. I'm getting in the water."

They had to change first. Perpetua still could not believe the lengths to which humans would go to for *propriety's* sake. She had been dumbfounded to learn humans went swimming in *clothing*—it seemed so much more convenient to just strip. Then again, from what she had seen, most humans didn't actually swim. They just waded into the shallows and splashed around. What was more, they couldn't change into their "bathing costumes" (as Briar called them) back at the tavern, because they couldn't walk the streets in them. The main beach had changing stalls, but here, in this isolated spot, they took turns changing in the seclusion of the trees at the end of the narrow beach.

"But if it's just us," Perpetua asked, as she and Sabine waited for Briar and Gallia to change, "why can't we just change out here? What does it matter?"

Sabine frowned. "Well—I mean—*Aden* can still see us here."

"But Briar said he doesn't gawk."

"But...he's still a *boy*."

Perpetua just stared at her. Sabine stared back, apparently having no further explanation to give. Perpetua sighed inwardly and turned away. *Humans.*

Once Briar and Gallia emerged from the trees in their strange bathing costumes—a sort of one-piece suit made up of short trousers (Briar called them *bloomers*) and a long-sleeved top—Perpetua and Sabine ventured into the swampy woodland to do the same.

It was quite dark in this cove. The trees surrounding them were massive, the biggest Perpetua had ever seen. Their trunks were like the legs of a great beast, knobby and entrenched in the shallows, growing right out of the water. Overhead, their broad canopies blocked out the sky, their branches hung with knotted strands of moss.

There wasn't any dry ground, but there was an old dock, rickety but safe enough to stand on. Perpetua and Sabine changed quickly. Sabine seemed eager to get out in the water, but Perpetua's haste was spurred by something else. That edge she couldn't seem to shake. A tension that had settled right betwixt her shoulder blades. As she shimmied out of her dress, the tension grew, a horrible knot forming at the base of her neck. It was like—it felt like—

Like someone was watching her.

Perpetua froze with one leg in mid-air, preparing to step into her bathing costume. She tossed a glance over her shoulder at Sabine, but the soldier seemed oblivious, still changing at the end of the rickety old dock.

Slowly lowering her leg, Perpetua swept a long, searching glance over her surroundings. Her gaze traveled over the gargantuan tree trunks, spotted with pale lichen, over the dark, cloudy water, reflecting the murky outlines of the branches overhead. The water was still here in this cove, almost eerily so. Still and rank.

Except for a rippling back in the trees, near the opposite end of the dock.

Perpetua watched the water ripple outwards from a swathe of shadows. It could have been caused by anything, she supposed. A turtle slipping off the shore into the shallows, or a fish cresting the surface. She stared hard into the trees there, into the shadows, looking for any sign of movement. Any slight shift in the darkness...

She crept down the length of the dock, around a bend concealed by the massive trees. It could just be an animal or the sun moving through the canopy, shifting the shadows...

"Perpetua?" Sabine called, her voice distant and uncertain. "Where are you?"

Perpetua glanced back. She couldn't see Sabine anymore, though she knew the soldier wasn't far. Just around that bend in the dock. She opened her mouth to call back—

—just as an arm wrapped around her middle, a hand closing over her mouth.

A *scaled* arm. A *clawed* hand.

"Don't make a sound," a voice hissed in her ear, "or I will kill her."

The gasp building in Perpetua's chest froze, stuck just south of her throat. She couldn't breathe, and not because of the hand over her mouth. Because of the fear inside her, making her pulse skitter. Filling her lungs, pushing out all the air.

She recognized that voice. She would recognize all three of them, she thought, for the rest of her life.

Meliora. One of the Ternion.

"I mean it." Meliora's voice was a whispered snarl. "I will kill them all. Your friend there. The boy guarding the hillside. And the two pale ones on the beach. I will kill them all if you don't do exactly as I say."

The two pale ones. Gallia, she meant—and Briar.

A strange thing happened then. The fear that had Perpetua quivering like a clump of fronds vanished a little. Just a little, making room for something else. Another feeling surging inside her. Making her feel strong, like steel.

Anger.

Because Meliora was threatening *Briar.* And Perpetua did not like that at all.

"Perpetua?" Sabine called again. Her voice sounded closer this time, though she was still out of sight.

"Tonight," Meliora growled in her ear. "You will meet me. In your cave. Tonight at dusk. Do you understand?"

Still roiling between fear and steely anger, Perpetua jerked her head in assent.

"You had better," Meliora whispered. "Or I will come back and kill them all. Don't think I will not, *naiad.*"

And then she was gone. The heavy weight across Perpetua's middle, the damp palm over her mouth. Gone. Gulping in an unsteady breath, Perpetua whipped around.

There was no sign of Meliora. She had vanished.

"Perpetua! There you are!"

Perpetua turned back as Sabine appeared around the bend. The soldier looked half-relieved, half-exasperated. "Didn't you hear me calling you? Where did you go? You're not dressed yet? I—" Sabine broke off, tilting her head. "Are you all right? You look..."

Perpetua could only imagine how she looked, standing there in her undergarments, clutching her bathing costume in one hand. She could imagine the wild look on her face, an outward depiction of the turmoil inside her.

Because Meliora wanted to meet her. Tonight. At her cave. And Perpetua had no idea why.

Nadalia had not said a word about Meliora when they'd met at Castel's house. Neither had Sohalia said anything when she'd demanded her favor of Perpetua.

Perpetua didn't know where Meliora's loyalties lay. With Nadalia. Or Sohalia.

⸺◇⸺

The sun had sunk so far below the horizon, only a rim of sunlight remained, casting a pearly sheen over the sea. It was quite beautiful, Perpetua noticed, but standing here, in the lagoon she had once called home, she was in no mind to admire beauty. Fear had carved a hollow space into her middle, leaving her faintly queasy. She remembered the threats Meliora had made on Briar's life and tried to recall the steeliness that had awoken inside her. The *strength* she'd felt.

But that strength was nowhere to be found. Perpetua removed her short boots and stockings before venturing over the slimy black rock outside her cave. Her skirt trailed in the frothy water. She ducked into the cave, leaving the balmy breeze for muggy, dank darkness.

Inside the cave, a naiad waited for her.

Meliora.

"You came," Meliora said. In the greenish light of the algae on the walls, her white skin was paler than ever. It was a stark contrast to her long dark hair and her scales, a black as true as night. Unlike her Ternion counterparts, she was petite, but no less intimidating. "I half-suspected you wouldn't."

Perpetua's hands curled into fists. "Did I have a choice?" she asked, surprising herself with her own daring. Perhaps there was some steel in her after all.

"You had plenty of choice." Meliora's voice was not like Nadalia's—toneless and smooth—but like gritty sand rubbing over skin. She seemed perpetually angry, her dark eyes flashing with every word. "You can't care all that much for those humans you're living with. Their deaths would have been merely an inconvenience, surely?"

Perpetua bit her tongue. Better, perhaps, not to let on how she felt about those humans. "A big inconvenience. I need those humans to survive in their world."

Meliora gave an annoyed flick of her fingers. "And so here you are. Let's not waste any more time. It's been nearly a fortnight since we first contacted you. Have you learned anything?"

Perpetua didn't have to feign the confusion that must have shown on her face. Since *we* first contacted you? "Learned anything about what?"

"About Sohalia, of course!" Meliora snapped. "And what she's up to! You said she intended to collect a favor from you. Has she?"

A fortnight ago. Of course. It had been about two weeks since she'd left Castel's house—since Nadalia had told her what, *who*, Castel really was.

Perpetua let out a breath through her teeth. When Meliora had said "we," she hadn't been sure if she'd meant her and Nadalia—or her and Sohalia. "You're working with Nadalia."

"Of course I am! Nadalia is my—" Meliora broke off, scowling. "Yes. So? Has Sohalia made contact?"

Perpetua didn't answer right away, trying to think. Her insides were still a mess of fear, standing here before one of the Ternion, being threatened again. And yet, there *was* something else too. She was tired of being threatened, she was *tired* of being stuck in the middle of whatever games the Ternion were playing with each other. After all, how could she know for sure who Meliora was working with? She might be allied with Sohalia, trying to see if Perpetua would betray the sea witch, or maybe she was working her own angle and just wanted to know what Nadalia was up to, or maybe—

Perpetua grimaced. The possibilities were endless, and they made her head hurt. "How do I know you're working with Nadalia? Why isn't she here?"

"She's busy," Meliora growled. But the look that passed through her eyes was different this time. Dark and troubled.

Suddenly, Perpetua recalled the discovery Demetri had made over a week ago. The remains that had been discovered down the beach. Not human remains, but something else. An arm.

A *scaled* arm.

Perpetua hesitated. "Busy, or—or missing?"

Meliora snapped her head around. "What are you talking about?"

Perpetua shriveled beneath Meliora's glare, but she tightened her fists and stood her ground. "The humans found...an arm. A severed arm. But with claws and scales. *Green* scales."

For a moment, it was as though Meliora had forgotten how to speak. Then she said in a hushed voice, "A naiad?"

"I don't know. I didn't see it myself, but..." She'd heard from Sabine that the coroner had ruled out a hoax. "The humans think so. They said the scales were real."

Meliora's white face went even paler in the sickly light. Lowering her head, she whispered, "*Nadalia.*"

Perpetua stared. Just a few weeks ago, she might not have recognized the throbbing twang coloring Meliora's voice, but she knew it for what it was now—sadness. Real sadness. Grief, even.

"She's been missing almost since she went to speak with you." Meliora's voice bore an edge.

Perpetua's heart tripped over itself. "I—I didn't—"

"I know you didn't." The glare Meliora shot her was half-hearted, weighted with loss. "This was *Sohalia*. She must have found out—and this was her retribution. Against Nadalia. Against *me*." Perpetua watched as Meliora sank onto a rock, dropping her face into her hand. "She was my daughter. My *last* daughter."

Perpetua felt glazed, her own shock like a fog separating her from the naiad before her. She still couldn't quite believe it—a *naiad*, breaking down like this. One of the Ternion, the most feared creatures Perpetua knew. And she called Nadalia her *daughter*. That was a human word, a human concept. Naiads did not have family any more than they had friends.

When Meliora lifted her head, her eyes were as hard as jet. "Sohalia will do the same to you, you know. Now that you've left her pet witch. So if you know anything—"

Perpetua took a step towards Meliora, shivering in the damp. "She wanted me to keep an eye on Princess Briar. Briar's working on a submarine—that's a kind of ship that goes under the water. Sohalia wanted me to keep her updated on it. She wanted to know if the princess was looking for some kind of mineral."

She said all this very quickly, in one breath. But it was not the threat of Sohalia that made her say it. It was something else. Perpetua couldn't quite explain it, but something about the pain in Meliora's voice when she spoke of Nadalia—it made something *twist* inside Perpetua. She thought of Briar and Demetri, and she thought about something bad happening to them. She thought about Sohalia hurting them.

The thought made Perpetua sick.

"This mineral," Meliora said. "What was it?"

"She didn't say. She just wanted to know if Briar was looking for it." Perpetua cast her mind back, trying to remember. "She said something like, that if Briar *wasn't* looking for it, she would have to 'come up with something else.'"

"Why would she be interested in some mineral? Or a submarine?" Meliora murmured. "What else did she say?"

"Nothing. And I haven't seen her since she first talked to me. That was over a month ago."

"And *is* the princess looking for this mineral?"

"Yes." Perpetua only knew that because it was the reason Briar had extended her stay in the Mariner Kingdom. She didn't know if the princess had found anything.

"Hmm. Well." Meliora flexed her fingers. "If Sohalia hasn't come after you, perhaps she's decided she doesn't need you. In which case, you're no use to me either."

Perpetua shifted, puddled water lapping over her bare feet. But Meliora didn't seem to be threatening her. If anything, her words sounded like a dismissal. Which was a relief, really...except...

Reaching for that steel again, Perpetua asked, "Why do you think Sohalia is interested in Briar?"

"I've no idea." Meliora sounded distracted. "That's what I'm trying to figure out. At any rate, it's not your concern. Unless Sohalia asks something else of you, in which case—"

"I think it is my concern. I'm risking my life by telling you this, and Princess Briar is my friend."

"Your friend," Meliora scoffed. "As though you were truly human. As though you *cared* about her."

"Maybe I do."

Meliora looked at her. Slowly, the scorn faded from her eyes and was replaced by a strange, curious light. She stepped towards Perpetua, closing in on her. Perpetua's pulse picked up, thrumming inside her, but she stood still as Meliora encircled her.

"I know Sohalia returned your claws and fangs," she said, inspecting Perpetua from head to toe. She stopped and peered into Perpetua's face. "When did you last feed?"

"I..." It had been weeks. She hadn't fed once since she'd left Castel's house. "About—three weeks ago. I think."

"You don't remember?"

"I—"

"Because you're looking rather *peaked*." Meliora's tone was almost suspicious. "Why haven't you fed again?"

Perpetua closed her eyes. She knew she would need to feed on another human, and soon. Oddly enough, she found the hunger easier to suppress these days, but that did not mean her body didn't need the sustenance. If she didn't feed soon, she would die.

So why hadn't she?

When Meliora spoke next, her voice was oddly soft. "You don't want to."

Perpetua's stomach gave another funny twist. "No. I mean, yes—I will—it's just..." She sagged a little. "It's weird now. Now that I live with them. That's all."

Meliora was still staring at her, but the hard lines on her face eased out. "We weren't always like this, you know."

"What do you mean?"

Meliora stepped back. "We naiads. You know, many years ago, we lived in the sea? In fin-form?"

Perpetua nodded warily. Truthfully, she'd always thought those stories little more than rumor, but if Meliora, one of the Ternion, said it was true, then she supposed it must be. It was a strange thought, naiads living under the sea.

"We didn't have another form. Well, we could take human-form, but it was even more limited than what we have now. Human-form was only for mating, so we could take it once a year within a certain window. We couldn't assume it whenever we wanted. And we certainly didn't have *this* form." She gestured at her scaled body, her webbed feet and hands. "We didn't have claws or fangs. We didn't feed on humans, you see."

Perpetua felt gutted, like a fish on a hook. She'd heard the stories about naiads living in the sea, but she'd *never* heard of naiads who didn't feed on humans. "Then what happened? How did we become like this?"

"No one knows for sure." Meliora retreated from Perpetua, deeper into the cave, the murk swallowing her petite form. "There was a story I used to hear. When I was younger. Of an ancient temple belonging to our gods, the sea gods. The legend said if a naiad sought out this temple, she could ask a boon of the gods. And that boon would be granted, so long as the naiad offered—in exchange—a single drop of blood into the sacred pool at the temple. Of course, as these legends go, no one could ever find the temple."

Meliora's voice floated out of the shadows as she continued. "Naiads used to say the reason we changed is because some foolish young naiad found the temple. And the boon she asked for was that all naiads be granted a human form—a *real* human form, one we could take whenever we wanted. And the sea gods agreed. But when it came time to repay the boon, the naiad refused."

"She wouldn't give a single drop of blood?" That was nonsense, Perpetua thought. How many times had she bled a little, accidentally scraping against a coral reef or a jagged rock? It was nothing. Had this naiad been afraid to bleed? Or just stupidly proud, stupidly selfish?

But Meliora said, "It's just a story. Probably not true." She turned towards Perpetua, her face lit by the algae's ghoulish light. "Just an old legend used to explain what happened to us. Anyway, as the story goes, when the naiad refused to give her blood, the boon she'd asked for went wrong. Our new "human" forms became twisted. We could walk on land, but we craved the sea. We became monstrous, a thing to be feared. We became killers." Meliora's voice dropped low. "*Hunters.* Forced to feed on humans. As though to ensure we could never be accepted among them.

"We used to live far from here, did you know that? Much further south along the coast. But we've had to migrate over the years. After a while, the humans start to notice how many of their kind are missing or being killed."

"That's why you made the Ternion dictate. The recent one. About taking food off the docks."

"Yes. We will likely have to migrate again soon."

Perpetua touched a hand to the rock beside her, grounding herself in its damp cold. She felt tiny, trying to connect herself to these naiads of the past, who lived so far away and never fed on humans. She couldn't quite accept it. "You said this was just a story. How do you know the whole thing isn't a story? That naiads were ever any different than we are now, that we never fed on humans—"

"I know it," Meliora said coldly, "because I lived it."

Perpetua clamped her mouth shut.

"I was just a child when the change took us." Meliora's hard voice turned brittle. "The memory is distant, but I *do* remember. I remember my life before. Living deep in the sea. I remember my mother's face, and the things she used to say to me. She spoke of caring for me, she spoke of things like...love..." Meliora paused. "And I remember the change. It was *painful*. Pain like I had never known and have never known since. And once we changed, it all began to fade. My memories. Things that had once mattered. Those things my mother said to me. Even my mother herself. We grew distant. I began to care for myself."

Perpetua understood. That was the way of a naiad. Mothers did not care for their offspring. A naiad survived on her own, or she didn't. Perpetua couldn't remember the naiad who had birthed her; she wasn't sure she had ever known her. What Meliora was speaking of—that sounded more the way humans did things.

"It was all so long ago." Meliora's voice drifted, as though drifting back through the years. "Decades past. Maybe a century. I've lost count of the years. But I am one of the few still alive who remembers. Who lived through the change."

Perpetua felt numb. She felt *unstable*, the threads of her reality coming apart. "That's why you called Nadalia your daughter. Because you remember how we used to be."

"Yes." Meliora drew her lips to a thin line. "I've birthed many daughters over the years. And for a long time, I tried to raise them like I was raised. I tried to care for them." She shivered, her eyes as dark as the depths of the cave. "You see, I changed like the others, but...there was always that part of me that remembered. And when I remembered, I *wanted* to care again. I wanted to feel that way again, to feel..." She trailed off, then added, "I never seemed to relish the killing like the others did. I have to feed on humans, of course, but I've always hated it. I tried to find the worst ones. Murderers and criminals."

A small shock ran through Perpetua. *Never seemed to relish the killing*. These words resonated with Perpetua, striking something deep. She had always thought she was the only one, the only strange one. The only one who tried to resist giving into the bloodlust, who hated the way it took her over. She hated it even more since becoming human.

Meliora suddenly looked weary. "But it's hard. It's gotten harder over the years. I call Nadalia my last daughter, but I think I have others. I just stopped caring for them. It's become so hard to remember—why it matters, why it *should* matter—"

"Why?" Perpetua whispered. "Why were you different?" *Why am I different?*

"I don't know. But I wasn't the only one. There were some few of us who were different, a few others who lived through the change. Including Sohalia."

"*Sohalia?* But she doesn't seem...um...like you. That is, she seems—"

"Twisted?" Meliora cut in. "Mad? Self-serving?"

"Well. Yes."

"She's always been self-serving." Meliora snorted. "But I remember her as a young naiad, before the change. She wasn't so bad. She was very clever and very curious. She wanted to know how things worked, she wanted to explore the vast reaches of the ocean. A bit naïve, perhaps, but..."

"So what happened? If she was like you, if she didn't like to kill—"

"Yes, she resisted the bloodlust. But the years have been even harder on her. Thanks to her *magic.*" Meliora's voice warped around the word "magic," as though it was something particularly distasteful, like rotted carrion. Nadalia had spoken of magic the same way.

"Nadalia said Sohalia gained her magic the same way all human witches do," Perpetua recalled. "And that it twisted her. Made her insane."

"Yes," Meliora said grimly. "Witches, you see, gain their powers by making a deal with dark forces. Sohalia made her deal...oh, I don't remember when. Sometime after our first move. I told her it was a bad idea, but, as I said, she had always been curious. Always eager to dabble in otherworldly affairs."

"She became a witch just because she was curious about it?"

"Oh, no." Meliora shook her head. "No, she became a witch because she thought she could help us. She thought if she became a witch, then she could find a way to save all of us. To change us back into what we once were. Living in fin-form, beneath the sea."

"She thought she could change us *back?*" Somehow, of everything Meliora had told her, this was the most unbelievable. Because— "But you said she's self-serving."

"She is," Meliora muttered. "Oh, she claimed she just wanted to help, but I think she fancied herself a savior. The savior of the naiads. I think she wants the credit. That's always been her way. Thinks very highly of herself. I think that's why she thought she could do it. Become a witch, and still retain that part of herself that was good. But something in the magic twisted her. I don't think naiad blood and human magic were meant to mix."

"Yes..." Perpetua recalled how strange Sohalia had seemed to her. As though she was not quite right. Nadalia had said something similar. "So that's why you want to know what she's up to? You don't think she wants to save the naiads anymore?"

"Even if she does, I'm worried how far she might go," Meliora said. "For some time now, I've suspected she's up to something very bad indeed. Something dark. And she won't tell me what it is. She used to confide in me, but she's become so *secretive*—and if she's really killed Nadalia—" Meliora choked on her daughter's name. "Then she really has gone too far. She's crossed a line, and I fear how many more she is willing to cross. In pursuit of what*ever* she's after. I fear whatever it is could be dangerous for us all...naiad and human alike."

18

PREDATOR

PERPETUA LAY AWAKE FOR most of the night, staring into the darkness, haunted by the rumble of the ocean through the open window. The little sleep she managed was tattered, interrupted by evil dreams of vicious sea gods and orphaned naiads and witches working dark magic.

When she finally dragged herself from bed sometime close to noon, she found herself alone. Briar had already gone for the day to work on her submarine. Perpetua had gone with her once or twice—not that she was much help—but she found herself wishing she'd gotten up earlier so she could have gone with her today.

Because the last thing she wanted was to be alone. Alone with her thoughts.

She ran a hand through her bedraggled hair, then rubbed at her tired eyes. Last night, in the cave with Meliora, she'd gotten so caught up in the naiad's tale. She'd felt so *connected* to it. But now, in the morning's stark light, she wished Meliora hadn't told her any of it.

After all, what was she supposed to do about it? She couldn't stop Sohalia, whatever she was up to. Meliora had told her to report anything else the sea witch asked of her, but Perpetua didn't think Sohalia would approach her after all this time. She hadn't bothered to seek Perpetua out, either to punish her or extract more favors from her. And Perpetua wasn't about to go looking for the sea witch. Not if Sohalia had decided to leave her be.

And anyway, Perpetua thought, splashing cold water onto her face, maybe Meliora was wrong. She only *suspected* Sohalia was after something dangerous. She didn't actually know. Either way, it seemed best to leave all that to Meliora. She was a Ternion naiad; if anyone could handle the sea witch, she could. What could she, Perpetua, be expected to do?

It had nothing to do with her, she told herself firmly. Besides, she had other, better things to think about.

Like Demetri.

A hazy image of Demetri's face formed in her mind, and all thoughts of Meliora and her tragic tale fled. Over the past couple of weeks, Demetri had found few new leads in his investigation, so he'd had a lot of time to spend with Perpetua. They'd done all sorts of things—horseback riding and shopping and hiking and playing cards. They'd visited a pub or two, and watched fireworks on the beach, and eaten ice cream in the town square. Demetri had even taught her the basics of fighting with a sword.

The only problem was, Perpetua was fairly certain she had lied to Demetri when she'd told him they were just friends. Or rather, when she'd implied she *could* just be friends with him. Because the more time they spent together, the more she felt she wanted to be much more to him.

She was going out with him again tomorrow. And that was all she wanted to think about right now. Not Meliora and her gloom-and-doom fears.

❖

The next day, late in the afternoon, Perpetua stood before the long mirror in her room at LeBeau's. She didn't know where Demetri was taking her this evening—he'd said it was a "surprise"—so she was unsure what to wear. She'd chosen a dress of mint-green satin with capped sleeves, neither too fancy nor too simple. She gathered her long hair up in one precarious hand and snatched a few pins off the armoire. Then she paused, staring at her reflection.

Meliora had been right when she'd said Perpetua looked peaked. Her cheeks had a hollow, sunken-in look, and the cast of her skin had gone sallow around her eyes. She felt well enough, but she knew how quickly that could change. She would have to hunt soon—she would have to feed on another human. The thought made her stomach twist.

The door to the room swung open, and Briar trudged in. It was late in the afternoon, and Perpetua supposed she had finished her work for the day. The princess looked exhausted, but when she heard Perpetua was going out with Demetri, she immediately came to help pin her hair.

"There," Briar said when she was done. Perpetua's hair was now gathered in a tight bunch of curls at the nape of her neck.

"Perfect." She set to work on Perpetua's skirt next, draping it over the bustle and pinning it back.

A sudden tide of feeling swept over Perpetua, dizzying in its intensity. When Briar finished with her skirt, she turned to face the princess. "Thank you," she said, trying to inject her gratitude into her voice.

Briar waved a nonchalant hand. "It's nothing."

"No, I mean—thank you." Perpetua struggled to put these feelings—feelings she didn't quite understand—into words. "Not just for—but for everything. For letting me stay with you and being my friend and...just everything."

Briar seemed pleased. "Well. You're welcome. But you don't have to thank me for being your friend. I could thank you for that as well."

"I don't really...have many friends."

Briar shrugged. "I didn't always either. Not for a long time."

The princess disappeared into the washroom to clean up, and Perpetua departed, distracted and troubled. That was something else that had changed in the last couple of weeks. She had really, truly found a friend in Briar. And she appreciated that.

She had thought Castel was her friend. He wasn't, of course—he'd only been spying on her for Sohalia. But the difference went beyond that. Castel had seemed to like having her around. He'd been generous about giving or buying Perpetua things. But he had never concerned himself with how Perpetua was doing, how she felt. He hadn't, she realized, really *cared* about her. Not like Briar and Demetri did.

Demetri met her downstairs in the common room. He was not dressed too formally, in a blue waistcoat and a dark necktie, so Perpetua supposed her own dress was appropriate.

"Ready to go?" Demetri asked.

"I think so," Perpetua said, "though it's difficult to know without knowing where we're going."

Demetri laughed. "That would spoil the surprise."

They had a bit of a walk through town, heading inland. Further inland than Perpetua had ever been. They walked until the town began to thin out, the buildings growing further apart, the hum and bustle of the docks and town center fading into the distance. They walked until they came upon a vast, green square, the ground covered in lush grass. In the distance, children ran and played, and other people lay out on blankets, sunbathing.

But on the closer side of the green, a long, wooden platform stood, and before it rows of wooden benches. There were chairs on the platform as well, and many people—some of them sitting, others milling around. The people were all dressed in black and white, and they carried different objects in their hands—instruments, she realized, recognizing some of them from the ball at the castle.

"It's the Mariner Symphony," Demetri explained. "They put on free performances once a month."

Perpetua ran over these words in her head as she stared at the platform. *Symphony. Performances.* "It's music," she deduced, a delighted smile spreading across her face.

"Come on." Demetri took her by the hand. "Let's find a place to sit."

They found two empty spots on a bench three rows from the front. Demetri talked a little about musical performances he'd been to before, and Perpetua listened eagerly, picking up new words—*symphony, musicians, stage, violin, conductor.* Then the crowd grew quiet, and Demetri sat back, and then—

Then the musicians began to play.

It was quiet at first. Hushed. Barely there, like the soft, distant roar of the ocean. Then one of the musicians—one of the violins—began to play its own tune over the gentle roar. Its song was like birdsong—not the screeching of a gull, but a sweet, lilting melody, like the birds Perpetua heard in the early morning hours when she couldn't sleep. It trilled, the song sweeping through high pitches, growing in speed, growing in intensity.

And then, with a great rush, the rest of the instruments joined the birdsong, and then it wasn't just birdsong, but something earthshaking, something vital, something massive beyond Perpetua's understanding. And whatever it was rushed *into* Perpetua, sweeping her breath away. The music swelled, growing too big, and Perpetua felt fragile, like cracked glass that might shatter at a single touch. But she couldn't break away from the rapture of the music, and she didn't want to. Not ever.

When the first piece was over—when the music went silent, and the void began to fill with the sound of people clapping—Demetri leaned over and whispered, "Are you all right?"

Perpetua tore her gaze from the stage and looked at him. It was only then that she realized her eyes were brimming with tears, her hands bunched tightly in her lap. But she was smiling too, and she couldn't stop. The dichotomy was thrilling and bewildering, and Perpetua, who had no words, only nodded to reassure him.

The music continued, the symphony playing three pieces in all. When it was over—when it was all, tragically, over—Perpetua stood and clapped with everyone else, and then she and Demetri left the stage behind, taking a wide path that meandered through the edge of the park, beneath a range of leafy green trees. The sun had disappeared far to the west, beyond the trees and the town, but the vast light it cast lingered around them. Perpetua was surprised it was still so early; if she'd had to guess, she'd have thought they'd been listening to the music all night. She had been so completely entranced by it.

They stopped to sit on a mossy stone bench beside a small pond, because it was quiet and still there, and because Perpetua felt dizzy and bursting, still exhilarated.

"What did you think?" Demetri asked, once they were comfortably seated on the secluded bench.

Perpetua drew in a deep breath, dispersing some of the restless tension within her. "It was..." She racked her muddled brain for some adequate description, some word that could encompass everything she had felt.

"Amazing?" Demetri suggested. "Beautiful? Breathtaking? Am I on the right track?" His smile faltered. "It wasn't ghastly, was it?"

Perpetua let out a punchy giggle. "No. Not ghastly. It was all of that. All those things you said. But also...more." She shook her head. "I don't know the words to describe it. I think maybe there *aren't* words."

"Yes," Demetri murmured. "I don't think there are."

Perpetua let out another breath, gazing up at the treetops. Their drooping branches swayed in the gusting breeze. She felt lighter than she had in days. Though the music had long stopped, it hadn't faded from Perpetua's mind, from her heart. It played on inside her, crooning, her own personal serenade.

And Demetri. Demetri sat so close beside her, she could feel the warmth of him bleeding into her. She looked at him. He gazed out at the little pond, his demeanor as relaxed as hers, his eyes as bright. He gazed at the pond, and she gazed at him, and that crooning inside her deepened, the song playing on.

Oh, sea gods. She did not want to be friends. She wanted more. She had never *stopped* wanting more. That feeling that had made her spare his life, that inexplicable connection, drawing her to him again and again—it was still there. It still pulled at her, hooking her like a fish and reeling her in. Reeling her into him.

He turned to look at her, and suddenly they were *so* close. Elbows knocking into each other. The light in Demetri's gaze didn't fade, but he looked uncertain now, his eyes crinkling. But he didn't draw away, and—slowly, hesitantly—his hand shifted on the bench, brushing against hers.

Perpetua turned, facing him more fully. Demetri hooked two fingers over her hand. They gazed into each other's eyes a moment longer, the both of them leaning in. And then a little more. And then...

He kissed her.

Or maybe she kissed him. She wasn't sure where it started, but her eyes fell shut and their lips met and it was better, even better than she remembered. A little thrill arced through her body, setting off fireworks inside her, suffusing her with heat. She placed a hand flat against his chest as her lips parted beneath his, and she could feel the thrumming of his heart beneath her palm, beating as intensely as her own—

And then he pulled away.

Perpetua caught her breath on a gasp. He didn't just pull away. He *yanked* back from her with his whole body, retreating into the corner of the bench. She was so startled, she had to reach out a hand to steady herself.

"I—I'm sorry." Demetri's face was washed of color. "I can't."

Perpetua stared at him dumbly. The fireworks inside her fizzled and died, turning to ash. It took a long time for his words to sink in. When they finally did, the understanding was swift and brutal.

"Because of Briar?" she asked.

Demetri looked stricken. "I..."

"What if I don't care?" Perpetua challenged him. *Demetri, he said it was a mistake, inviting you to to the ball*, Briar had said. *Not because he doesn't like you. Because he didn't want to hurt you.* If he couldn't kiss Perpetua because he didn't want to hurt her, shouldn't she get some say in that?

"Don't care?" There was a bitterness in Demetri's eyes. "You mean you wouldn't care if I was kissing you and thinking of her?"

Well, when he put it that way, it sounded indefensible. Perpetua ran her hands over her hair, her fingers knotting in the curls behind her neck. "What, then, Demetri? You go on loving her, and she goes on loving someone else, and you never...never—" She broke off, hearing the cruelty in her words. "I'm sorry. I didn't mean..."

"I just—" Demetri fumbled. "I just need time."

"But don't you..." Perpetua's voice became small and tenuous. "Don't you feel...anything...for me?"

She hardly dared look at him. When she finally managed it, she found him as evasive as she was, his eyes darting around, looking everywhere *but* her. "I do—I mean—we're friends. Aren't we? Isn't that what you said?"

Perpetua's heart plummeted like a stone. "Friends." That horrid word again. And yes, she had said that, she *had*, but— "Then why do all this?" She threw an arm out to indicate all of it—their secluded spot here, the symphony in the park. Everything they'd done, all the time they'd spent together.

"I—well." Demetri looked at her, and she hated the lost expression on his face. She *resented* it, because how dare he be so lost and confused, when to her, it was so very *clear*. "You said you wanted to do things you'd never done before. That you wanted to experience everything…"

So that's all this was, then. That was all *she* was. A project. Something for him to work on, just like the murders he was investigating. "Right," she said softly. "And now I've experienced *this* too."

"Perpetua—"

Perpetua jumped to her feet. She didn't want to hear anything else. He'd said it all, really. All that needed to be said. She left him behind, walking as fast as her human legs would carry her, and then, once she was sure he couldn't see her anymore, she began to run back into town.

It grew dark, twilight falling around her. The glow of the streetlamps punctuated the black night. Perpetua ran until she didn't know where she was, and then she stopped, her legs quivering.

Her chin quivered too. Perpetua realized she was crying again. She couldn't stop the tears—big, fat tears, falling rapidly from her eyes. She tried to breathe, tried to blink them back, but still they kept coming.

It was all too much. The feelings inside her were too big, too *many*, swinging so suddenly from one to the next. The elation that had rushed through her as she'd sat in the park, listening to the music, making her lightheaded. The warmth and intimacy burning in the pit of her stomach as she'd kissed Demetri. And now *this*—the pain clawing at her, trying to cleave her in two. She hated it, she hated it all, she hated Demetri and she *hated* crying over him, *again*, and she hated being human, she hated *every part of it*—

Fighting for breath, she staggered away, retreating into a narrow alley between two houses, leaving the light. Then she summoned her claws. That crimson haze fell over her eyes, tinging the brick wall before her red. Her jaw unhinged, making room for her sharpened teeth. And finally, *finally*, the tears stopped, drying up at once.

Perpetua breathed in deep. She placed a hand against the wall and leaned into it, though she felt much better now, much steadier. More like herself.

"Miss? Are you all right, miss?"

Perpetua whipped around before she could think.

There, at the mouth of the alley, stood a small boy. A child, hardly old enough to be out on his own. His dusty blond hair glimmered in the flickering light of the streetlamp behind him. And though Perpetua stood deep within the alley, ensconced in shadow, it was clear by his pale face that he could see her clearly—the girl with blood-red eyes and teeth like a shark.

He didn't run. He didn't scream. He just stood there, rooted to the spot. And as Perpetua stared at him, she realized how very *hungry* she was. Her body was weak with the need for human sustenance. The hunger bored through her, making a hollow chasm of her insides. Her claws twitched, desperate to tear into flesh. It was *agony.*

And the boy just stood there.

For a moment—how long, she didn't know—Perpetua imagined what it would be like to rip out his little throat and feast on him. And though her mouth watered at the thought, something else rose within her, at odds with her hunger. Something heavy and cloying, climbing up her throat.

We became monstrous, a thing to be feared.

Killers. Hunters.

Perpetua sucked in a tenuous breath as Meliora's words rang in her head. She was going to be sick, she thought, she felt like she was going to be sick. And then she remembered something else Meliora had said—

I never seemed to relish the killing like the others. I wanted to care.

Taking in another shallow breath, Perpetua forced her fangs away. Her jaw snapped back into place. And she stared at the little human before her. He hadn't moved, she realized, because he was frightened. He was frightened of her, and rightly so, because she was salivating at the thought of *eating* him. A *child*.

He was just a child.

Perpetua swallowed, fighting the urge to vomit. "G—*go*," she croaked. "Go now. Run."

The boy managed a shaky step back, his terrified gaze fixed on her face.

"Go!" she repeated. "*Run!*"

This time he heeded her, as though she'd compelled him with the Voice she no longer had. He fled into the main street. But Perpetua just stood there, unmoving, long after his flapping footsteps faded. She stood there and breathed, and breathed, and breathed. She breathed until the agonizing hunger inside her dulled to a mere ache, held at bay by the horror of what she'd almost just done.

19

DOOMED

PERPETUA DIDN'T EMERGE FROM that alley until a long time later. How long, she wasn't sure. But by the time she stumbled back onto the main street—a human girl again—she had realized there were two things she needed to do.

Neither of these things particularly appealed to her. But she was beginning to understand that sometimes, people had to do things they didn't want to.

So as the moon glinted overhead, peeking through wispy clouds, she made her way to the finer end of Moselle. To a part of town she hadn't been to in weeks.

To Castel's huge, gleaming white townhouse.

She couldn't bring herself to knock on the front door. She didn't know what she would do, standing there, waiting for him to answer. So instead, she watched from a block away, crouched behind an iron bench and a large wastebin. The stink of the bin's contents was not pleasant, but oddly, it eased Perpetua, helping to keep the hunger at bay.

When she finally spotted Castel exiting through the front door, she waited another five minutes. Then she scurried across the street to the house.

She still had a key. And he had not changed the locks.

Inside, the house was dark. She stood in the entrance hall until she could make out the the great, winding staircase. She took the stairs two at a time, practically hauling herself up by the varnished balustrade. Then, at the top of the stairs, she entered Castel's room.

Unlike last time, she didn't root through his things or make a mess. She just stepped back into a corner, not quite hidden behind the emerald-green curtains, and there, she waited.

Hours passed. Perpetua knew she could very well wait all night. But she was in luck. She didn't hear the door when it opened downstairs, but she heard his heavy footfalls, and as those footfalls grew louder, Perpetua grew her claws and fangs.

The door drifted open, and Castel stepped into his bedroom.

For a moment, Perpetua took in the sight of him, and it was a strange sight, so unlike the man she remembered. His shoulders were slumped, his head bent. It was such a weary, troubled pose that Perpetua almost wondered if it was really him.

She only wondered for a moment. Then his head snapped up, and though he couldn't have seen her in the dark, his gaze zeroed in on her. "Have you come to kill me?" he asked, his tone as careless as ever.

Perpetua stepped forward. Castel reached over to wind up the bulb latched onto the wall by the door, twisting it a couple of times. A scant glow washed over the room. Only then—once she was sure he had seen her, red-eyed and clawed and fanged—only then did she allow her fangs to shrink back. "No," she said.

"Hmm." Castel's gaze flicked over her, and if there was any doubt that he had known what she was, that doubt was gone. He was utterly unsurprised to see her like this. "Because last time you were here, you left my room quite a mess."

Perpetua retracted her claws, her vision returning to normal. "Sorry about that."

Castel's head jerked. "*Are* you?"

Perpetua reflected on this. "No. I'm not."

Castel nodded, as though this was exactly what he had expected. He stepped further into the room, shrugging out of his coat and draping it over his cast-iron bed.

Perpetua cut right to the chase. There was no point drawing this out. "I need your help."

"That's rich."

"Is it?" Perpetua asked sharply. "After what you did to me, is it really?"

"What I did to you." Castel looked disparaging. "You mean, taking you in, buying you clothes, providing shelter and food and money—"

"I *mean*, concealing what you are from me."

Castel reached up to loosen his tie. "I could say the same about you, darling."

"Except you always knew what I was. Because you work for Sohalia." Perpetua was annoyed that this still stung—this betrayal, this rejection. "That's the only reason you approached me at the ball, isn't it? That's why you took me in—to keep an eye on me. To spy for her."

"Oh, Perpetua, that wasn't all." Castel turned wide, innocent eyes on her. "I *was* looking for someone to party with that night. And as it happens, I did enjoy your company. Quite a lot."

"That doesn't make you my friend."

"No," Castel said coldly, "it doesn't. But that's nothing personal, love. I don't have any friends. I can't afford them."

Perpetua crossed her arms over her chest, leaning her hip into his cherrywood bureau. "And what about Kinsley?"

Castel froze in the act of removing his tie. It was only for half a second, but Perpetua saw it. When he spoke, his voice was stiff. "What about Kinsley?"

"Well, I assume if you can't have friends," Perpetua said, watching him closely, "you can't have lovers either."

Castel laughed brazenly. "I've had plenty of lovers, my dear."

"One you actually *care* about, I mean."

"I don't care about Kinsley." If Castel was lying, he did a good job of it, but that didn't mean anything. Perpetua already knew he was a good liar. He met her gaze, dispassionate and detached, before stepping past her to perch on the foot of the bed.

"So you're just spying on him, then. Like you spied on me. Or rather, *using* him to spy on Princess Briar."

"Sohalia is rather interested in her, I'll give you that."

"Why?" Perpetua asked.

"I've no idea."

"And if you did, you wouldn't tell me, would you?"

"No. I wouldn't. I like my life, thank you very much. Rather, I like being alive. I'm in for quite a nasty, eternal existence after I die, you see. That's what comes of being a witch." Castel leaned over, bending to undo the buttons on his shoes. "But I'd guess that when you said you wanted my help, you weren't looking for information on Sohalia. I'm going to guess this is about you and your...well-being." He straightened, his eyes traveling over her.

"Only, you don't look so good, Perpetua dear. You're looking a little *underfed.*"

"What do you know about it?"

"Really, nothing. It is truly a guess. I've never seen what happens to a naiad who doesn't feed on humans."

"But you know what Sohalia did to me. You know she made me human. But I still have to feed."

"Yes," Castel said. "So what's the problem? Are you looking for a provider? You want me to procure warm, living bodies for you, the kind that won't be missed? I suppose it's more difficult now you're living among humans. More difficult to be unobtrusive about it, I mean."

"That is not the problem," Perpetua snapped. "As though you don't *know.*"

Castel tilted his head up at her. "I think you're overestimating the depth of my knowledge when it comes to you naiads. Or maybe overestimating how much Sohalia trusts me."

Perpetua closed her eyes. "When she made me human, she made me...*human.*"

"Still not following."

"I don't *want* to feed on anyone!" Perpetua burst out. "Don't you get it? It took a while, and I still don't—I don't know exactly what's happened to me or why. I don't know if this was part of her spell, or if it's just—if this is just—" She pressed her lips together. She didn't want to say too much—she didn't want to expose any weakness. And it wasn't like Castel cared. But for the first time in weeks, here, in Castel, was someone she could talk to about this. A *human* she could talk to. No matter how bad a human.

"I care, Castel," she said in a low voice. "I didn't used to. Killing humans, feeding on them—it was easy. I never gave it a second thought. It's not that I knew I was doing something bad and did it anyway. I didn't think of it as bad. It was just survival. Humans were prey, nothing more. But now..." Perpetua shook her head, her wavy tresses sweeping over her shoulders. "I can't do it. I almost killed a *child* today, a child whose only crime was stopping to ask if I was all right. And I felt—I felt—" She gulped back more words, fearing she'd said too much.

Castel stared at her. There was a peculiar look in his eyes, very different from anything she'd seen there before. It was not indifference, not insolence or cheek. It was something much more serious than that. "You've developed a conscience."

"What's that?"

"I'll give you a clue—I buried mine a long time ago." He flashed a bleak smile and leaned forward, his hands on his knees. "But your body still craves human sustenance? You still *need* to feed on humans. Is that why you look so ill?"

"Yes."

Castel went silent for a moment. He gazed out the long, paned window across his room, out at the starry night sky and the winding rows of townhouses beneath it. Then he said, "I don't know what you think I can do about it."

"Do some spell or something. Something so I don't have to feed on humans."

Castel looked skeptical. "That would mean making you fully human."

"Can't you?"

"I doubt it. That goes beyond the physical, you see, and messing about with souls and spirits will take far more skill than I have. At the very least, it would take some time to figure out. Probably more time than you have. But—" Castel rose to his feet and crossed the room to his wardrobe—the one where Perpetua had discovered all his witchy things. He popped open the hidden drawer and rummaged through it before pulling out a long, thin vial of clear liquid and a small packet of violet petals.

"I can give you something that will take away the craving." Castel stood with his back to her as he began mixing things together, so she couldn't see what he was doing. "Your body will continue to weaken. You'll still die if you don't feed. But take this for now, and maybe I can find a more permanent solution in the meantime."

Perpetua watched him, staring intently at the spot between his shoulder blades. A dark suspicion stole over her, one she couldn't ignore. Even though she had come here for his help—even though she had preyed on the hope that she wasn't wrong about his feelings for Kinsley. "Why? Why do you even care, Castel? Is this about Kinsley?"

Castel let out an aggravated growl. "No, it is not about Kinsley. Shut up about Kinsley, all right? I don't *care* about Kinsley. I don't."

He was a little too adamant, Perpetua thought, for someone who didn't care.

"I don't even care about you," he said, turning to face her. He held the thin vial between his fingertips and swirled it around. "But she didn't give you a choice, love." Castel's mouth formed a hard line. "And I don't like that. I may be a killer—all witches are—but I got into it with my eyes wide open. I am what I am, and I made that choice a long time ago." His eyes grew distant, and in their depths, Perpetua felt like she could see his years. "I damned my own soul. And I take issue when others don't get the same choice."

He held out the vial to her. "So. Here you go. Shake it up well before you take it. It should last a week or two. Come see me if you need more. But I fear, darling, you may be dead by then."

The second thing Perpetua needed to do was seek out Meliora.

She remembered Nadalia's instructions about how to summon her. She assumed the same would work for Meliora. So now, in the early hours of the morning, she waded into a shallow, secluded inlet just out of town. There, she submerged herself in the water and called for Meliora.

She dreaded facing Meliora even more than she'd dreaded asking Castel for help. Because a part of her—a not-so-small part of her—still wanted to run from all of this. A part of her still wanted to pretend she'd never learned the things Meliora had shared with her, about the naiads of old, about how they'd been different once. It was...painful...to think about. And she still didn't know what she could do to help stop Sohalia. But. She should at least offer, she thought. Offer to help Meliora with whatever she could.

Of course, she was not so selfless as all that. *Still a monster,* she thought wryly. Meliora wasn't a witch like Sohalia, but she was a member of the Ternion. An old, powerful naiad. If anyone could help Perpetua—if anyone could teach her *not* to be a monster—it was her.

So after calling for Meliora, she made her way home on foot. Not back to the tavern—back to her cave, the home she'd left behind. By the time she reached it, the sun was peeking over a pale pink horizon, casting shimmering rays over the sea. And when she climbed down into the cave, leaving behind the burgeoning daylight, she half-expected to find Meliora waiting for her there, just as she had the last time she'd come here.

But she wasn't there. No one was. The cave was empty.

Perpetua let out a little sigh. She hoped she wouldn't have to wait long. This cave had been her home once, but now—as she ventured warily into its damp, gloomy reaches—she found it cold and uninviting. And rather creepy.

She perched on the least-wet boulder she could find and waited, arms folded across her chest. As the minutes passed by, the light outside the cave growing stronger and brighter, Perpetua found her chin drooping onto her chest, sleep tugging at her eyelids...

A scuffing sound at the cave entrance broke through her drowsiness, and Perpetua bolted awake. She leapt to her feet as a long, lean shadow cast itself over the pitted cave wall, the shadow of a figure with two legs, two arms, and long, dark hair...

Perpetua's breath stuck in her throat. Had she been foolish to come here? After all, Meliora wasn't the only one who knew this cave had been her home. Sohalia knew too—

The figure casting the shadow stepped into sight, pale daylight framing a hazy outline around them. And though the shadow had been large, the figure itself wasn't. It was a petite woman. A woman with ivory skin.

Perpetua sagged in relief. "Meliora. For a minute, I thought you were—"

She broke off as Meliora took an unsteady step into the cave. And as the daylight receded from the cave entrance, shaded over with passing clouds, Perpetua saw Meliora's face was terribly gray. One tremulous hand clutched at her middle where...

Where her scales had been slashed and torn, deep rents exposing glistening blood.

Meliora managed one more staggering step. Then she collapsed, her scaled legs giving out beneath her.

"No!" Perpetua darted forward. Not soon enough to catch the wounded naiad, who sprawled on the ground, her body spasming. As Perpetua reached her, dropping to her knees, Meliora gasped, a spittle of blood leaking from her lips.

"No, *no*," Perpetua moaned. Hope scrabbled inside her, desperate to find purchase, but as Perpetua peeled Meliora's hand back from her bleeding torso—as she took in the cracked scales and deep gouges—she knew at once that Meliora had been damaged beyond repair. Perpetua had dealt such damage with her own claws. She knew what a killing blow looked like.

Given the amount of blood staining Meliora's black scales, running all the way down her legs, it was a miracle she wasn't dead yet.

"H-had to—get here." Meliora's voice cracked like a thin shell, her words barely intelligible. "H-had to—"

"It's all right." Perpetua sat back on her heels, lifting Meliora into her lap. She didn't know if she was trying to comfort Meliora or herself as she said, "It's fine. I can go get help, I can—" She looked around wildly.

A grating sound left Meliora's lips. It was a moment before Perpetua recognized it as a laugh. "Help? From...who?" She coughed, more blood wetting her lips. "Y-your—human—friends?"

"Maybe," Perpetua whispered. "They could help. They *would*."

"No time." Meliora's words grew more broken. "No time f-for...that."

Perpetua felt like she was sinking, a stone cast into the ocean. Sinking straight down into the seabed. *I need you. I need you to help me!* "Please," Perpetua begged, "you can't die." Without thinking, she snatched up Meliora's hand. It was horribly cold.

"Listen. Sohalia—" Meliora slurred the sea witch's name. "She wants to *k-kill*...no...to trade...the princess."

Perpetua's chest grew tight. Kill Briar. *Trade* Briar? For what?

"She will...do it—on—" Meliora's eyes fluttered. "The. Sol-stice."

"The summer solstice?" The summer solstice was days away. "But what is she trying to do?"

"She needs—the p-power from...the solstice. To open—she n-needs..." But whatever she meant to say next was smothered in a wrenching cough. It ripped through Meliora. Perpetua clutched the naiad's hand more tightly than ever. Panic swam inside her, and she had to do something, *anything*, to stave this off, to *save her*, but there was nothing...

There was nothing she could do.

The realization struck Perpetua so hard, she went numb. Inside and out.

Meliora's eyes fluttered again. Perpetua stared down at her. She wanted to say something comforting, but she didn't know how. She tried to think of what Demetri would say, or Briar; she tried to remember all the kind words they had given her. But they felt so far away. So far away from this cold, remote cave.

And Perpetua was a stone, stuck fast in the seabed, sand and silt billowing over her. Burying her hard and fast.

But as Meliora's eyes began to glaze over, she tried to lift her arm, spasming as she reached for Perpetua. "Are you—crying—for m-me...naiad?"

Perpetua blinked. She *was* crying. Tears spilled down her cheeks like a drumming rain. A sob built in her chest, the terrible pressure pushing at her lungs. But Meliora was wrong; it wasn't for *her* that Perpetua was crying. It was for herself, for her pitiful, stupid self, because she *needed* Meliora, the solstice was only three days away and now she would be all alone, she couldn't stop Sohalia by herself, and even if she did, she was still *dying*, and there was nothing she could do about it—

But Meliora's fading voice was filled with amazement. "Sh-she...finally...d-did it."

Perpetua leaned in close. "What?"

"So—halia. She finally—" Meliora swallowed, the movement slow and painful. "Or m-maybe...it was never hers—to give. Maybe...it was...yours...to..."

Her words were cut off by another blood-soaked cough. This one went on for quite a bit longer than the last, and Perpetua bent her head over the naiad, rocking back and forth, squeezing her hand, as though if she held on tightly enough, she could keep Meliora from slipping away.

When the coughing ended and the shuddering stilled—when Meliora looked up at her—her face changed. "Nadalia," she whispered.

Perpetua could not stem the tide of her tears. She didn't know if Meliora thought *she* was Nadalia, or if she was just thinking of her. Thinking of her dead daughter, in these last moments.

"I—w-wish—you…" Meliora's words trailed off, growing weak. "Wish *I* could re-member…how it feels…to…lo-v…"

Her voice died as her head lolled to the side. And her hand grew limp in Perpetua's, going slack.

"*No*," Perpetua wailed. The sob in her chest finally broke free. She gathered the tiny naiad in her arms, hugging her to her chest. "No, *no*—I *need* you, I need your help—I *can't do this*—"

Her sobs echoed through the cave like the cries of some dreadful creature. She cried for herself, and yes, she cried for Meliora. Meliora, who had survived so much, withstood the monster within for so long, only to die in this wretched cave. And she cried for them all, for all the broken naiads, who didn't even know they were broken, who had no idea of the darkness that awaited them all.

20

UNVEILED

"D EMETRI! WHAT ARE YOU doing here?"

Demetri blinked as he stepped out of the castle and into the sunlight glaring across the outer stone bridge. A white carriage stood before him, and climbing out of it was Briar. She was accompanied by Tory and Kinsley, but they hung back to speak to the carriage driver.

"Briar." Demetri shook himself. He'd been caught up in his own thoughts, thoughts muddled by lack of sleep. Last night, after his...evening out...he'd gone straight home and retired to bed early, to no avail. He'd lain awake for hours, unable to sleep.

His mind full of Perpetua. And the disaster he had made of things with her last night.

"Erm." Demetri rubbed a hand over his face. "I had a meeting with the counts this morning. They wanted a report on my investigation. Not that I had much to say," he added sourly. "In fact, I had nothing to say."

"Well." Briar stepped forward, shaking a few strands of hair from her face. She was dressed sharply in snug trousers, a frilly white blouse, and a tweed corset. "That's good, isn't it? I mean, there haven't been any more attacks or deaths, so far as you know."

"Yes, and with no leads on the person—or creature—behind the first ones." Demetri gestured at her. "What are you doing here?"

Briar gave a dramatic sigh. The sunlight glimmered over her white-blonde head, giving it a lustrous sheen. "Alas, I am also here to meet with the counts. About extending my work on the submarine again. I'm cleared for another week, but I'm hoping to get more time. Well. I telegraphed King Victor, and he said I should ask them first. If they say no..."

"He'll force the issue?"

"More or less." Briar smiled, but it faded quickly as she ran a critical eye over him. "Are you all right, Demetri?"

"Hmm? Oh, yes. Fine."

"How was your evening with Perpetua?"

Demetri felt his stomach drop. Perpetua. He merely had to blink his eyes shut and he saw her face, so beautiful and so wretchedly sad. *Don't you feel anything for me?*

"Demetri?"

"Fine," he repeated. "It was fine."

"Are you sure?"

"Of course I'm sure."

"Oh, all right, then." Briar placed a hand on her hip. "I suppose that's why you came home so early last night, *alone*. And why Perpetua didn't come home at all."

"She didn't come home?" Demetri fretted. "Are you sure?"

"Yes, I'm sure. We share a room, don't we? Don't worry," she added. "It's not the first time she's stayed out. Her family may be a horrid bunch, but she has lived here in Moselle a lot longer than us. I won't worry unless she doesn't turn up later today. Anyway, so? What happened?"

What happened? Demetri wiped a hand over his mouth. That was the problem—he wasn't sure he knew. Or rather, he wasn't sure he understood. He'd spent his whole walk home from the park thinking about his conversation with Perpetua, going over it in his head. "Do you remember," he said, "at the ball, when I told you I shouldn't have brought Perpetua? Because it wasn't fair to her?"

"Yes."

Demetri exhaled. "What if I'm just making excuses?"

"What do you mean?"

He'd done it before. He'd done it with Briar when he'd ended their relationship last year. At the time, he'd told himself it was because he was causing her memory lapses, that he was making things worse for her. But the truth was, he'd needed to end things for *himself.* He just hadn't realized it at the time.

He was beginning to wonder if he wasn't doing the same thing again. "I keep thinking I can't be with Perpetua because I'm not ready to move on," he said.

"From me, you mean?" Briar asked cautiously.

"I don't think it's about you, Briar. Not really." Demetri looked her in the eye and found it was not difficult to do so. "I think it's more that I'm just—that it's me, that I'm too—too messed up for another relationship. And I'm worried all I'll do is bring my mess into her life. I don't want that. She has enough problems of her own—"

"Yes," Briar cut in. "She does. And being friends with us—spending time with *you*—has helped her deal with those problems."

"Did she tell you that?"

"Not in so many words." Briar squinted up at the sky as a mass of clouds shifted over the sun, dimming its light. "But I can tell. Look. Just consider a few things, all right? First of all, I don't think you're as messed up as you think you are. Secondly, Perpetua knows about all that, doesn't she? I mean, you told her about your past, and she knows about us—and has she ever expressed she has a problem with that?"

"No." In fact, she had indicated just the opposite. *"What if I don't care?"* she'd asked.

"Then, thirdly, I suggest to you," Briar said, her voice oddly gentle, "that maybe a new relationship is what you *need*, Demetri. Maybe being with Perpetua could help you like it's helped her. I've seen the way you are with her, Demetri. When you're with her, you seem...happier. Certainly happier than you've been on your own."

Demetri nodded slowly.

"Just think about it." Briar peered up at the castle behind him. "Well. I'd best not put this off any longer." She turned to wave her guards forward. "You can take my carriage back to Moselle, if you like. I have a feeling I'm going to be here a while."

They parted ways, Briar flanked by her guards as she trudged into the castle, Demetri climbing into her carriage. It was a castle carriage, manned by a driver who nodded cheerily when Demetri instructed him to take him into Moselle.

The morning was warm and muggy, so Demetri leaned his head out the window as the carriage trundled down the paved path. He breathed in the salty ocean air, occasionally catching a glimpse of the sea through the cedar trees dotting the low cliff-side. The sky was still cloudy, and beneath the muted sunlight, the ocean was a grave blue.

Halfway to town, Demetri's eyes caught on a tiny speck in the distance, moving through the patchy grass off the side of the road. As they came closer, Demetri realized the speck was a person, and once they were closer still, he recognized the person.

It was Perpetua.

Demetri frowned. She was garbed in the same dress she'd worn to the park yesterday, and though his nerves fluttered seeing her, they were dampened by his concern. He couldn't help but wonder where she was coming from.

"Perpetua!" Demetri called, tapping a hand outside the carriage to ask the driver to halt. As the carriage slowed, Perpetua looked over her shoulder at him. Her expression—a little empty, a little distracted—did not change as her gaze fell on him, but she did wait while he climbed out of the carriage and jogged over to her.

"What are you doing out here?" he asked, a little out of breath.

"Walking," she answered tersely.

Right. Of course. "Are you going back to town? You can ride with me."

Perpetua's gaze traveled from him to the carriage, then back to him. "No. I want to walk."

"Oh." Demetri shoved his hands into his pockets, trying to hide his awkwardness. Perpetua did not seem particularly upset by his presence, but neither did she seem welcoming. It was like she barely realized he was there. "Well. Do you mind if I walk with you?"

Perpetua shrugged again. Demetri trotted back to let the driver know he could return to the castle. By the time he turned around, Perpetua was walking again, but slowly enough for him to catch up.

"So," Demetri said, "where are you coming from?"

Perpetua glanced at him. She was silent for so long that Demetri began to think she wasn't going to answer. Then she said, "Home."

"Home. You mean, your family's home?"

"Yes."

"Oh." No wonder she looked so troubled. No, not troubled, he thought, peering at her unobtrusively. She looked *worn*. "Erm. Do you want to talk about it?"

"Not really."

"Right."

They both fell silent. Demetri couldn't think what else to say, and he found his thoughts drifting back to his conversation with Briar. *Maybe being with her could help you like it's helped her. When you're with her, you seem happier.*

He had thrown his heart and soul into his relationship with Briar. He did not know how to do it any other way. But so many things had gone wrong, and now—was it possible he could have something new, something better, with Perpetua?

He looked sidelong at her. He took in her long, dark hair, streaming down her back, and the curve of her mouth, somehow sad and faraway. She was something special, he realized. She was kind and funny and genuine. And she had courage, he thought, like no one else he had ever known. Oh, he knew people who were brave. Garrett was brave; he would take on a troll twice his size, any day. Briar was brave; she had risked everything to take down the dark fairy, a creature stronger and more ancient than any other.

But Perpetua had *courage*. The courage to try new things. The courage to speak the truth, even when that truth might hurt her. When he'd first met her, he'd viewed her as a sort of counterpart to Briar; an easier alternative. But she was more than that, she *deserved* more than that. Why was he only just now seeing that?

And he decided, right then and there, that he had to at least *try* to have something with her. Whether he was ready or not.

"Perpetua..." he started.

"Hmm?"

Demetri dithered, looking aside. Their path had begun to wind closer to the cliffside, which had sloped down so steeply, it could hardly be called a cliff anymore. The rocky beach was only a short drop below. They were so close to the sea, Demetri could hear the waves rustling over the shore.

"I wanted to talk to you," he said, his voice horribly stilted, "about—something."

He hadn't realized he'd stopped moving until Perpetua stopped too, turning to face him. She coiled her hair with one hand, pulling it over her shoulder, and as she looked at him, her gaze sharpened. As though she had only just realized he was there. "I—" She sucked in one of her angular cheeks, her eyes complicated. "I need to talk to you too. I need to tell you something. I'm just...not sure how to say it."

"Whatever it is, you can tell me."

"I'm afraid you'll be angry."

"Me?" Demetri almost laughed out loud. "Angry with you? Perpetua, after last night, *you're* the one who should be angry."

"This isn't about that. I mean, this is completely—" Perpetua jerked, her eyes fixing on something behind Demetri. Then she lurched towards him. "Demetri—no!"

Demetri didn't even have time to be confused, much less turn around. Something knife-sharp raked across the back of his neck, and then he was knocked aside with a bruising hit that sent him sprawling. He landed flat on his back, stunned with pain, gasping for air. And as he lay there amidst the grass, a dark-haired head came into view, leaning over him.

It was not Perpetua.

"Don't move," the owner of this head said.

Demetri stared into the face looming over him. It was a girl, a girl with sleek black hair and narrow eyes. Narrow *red* eyes—red from eyelid to eyelid. There was something weird about this, something that tugged at Demetri's brain, but it didn't seem very important. The important thing was this girl's voice—how beautiful it was, like the sweetest melody he'd ever heard.

"Get away from him!" another voice rasped. This voice was not so beautiful—familiar, but nowhere near as compelling as the red-eyed girl's voice. "What do you think you're doing?"

"What does it look like?" The red-eyed, black-haired girl grasped Demetri by the shoulder, hauling him to his knees. He caught his breath as a burning pain erupted from the back of his neck, at odds with the hazy bliss stealing over him. "I'm hunting, Perpetua. I'm *feeding*. That's what we do."

"Not on this human."

Demetri breathed past the pain, the scene before him coming into focus. *Perpetua.* Of course Perpetua was there; how could he have forgotten?

"What's so special about this one human?" This came from the red-eyed girl, only her voice didn't sound so lovely anymore. She stood beside Demetri, holding him upright in an ironlike grip. Out of the corner of his eye, Demetri saw that the hand wrapped around his arm had long, sharp claws—claws that dug into his skin. His sleeve felt hot and wet, beginning to soak through with blood. *His* blood.

"Perpetua." Demetri struggled to think. A word ghosted across his brain, a familiar word. *Mermaid*. "What is going—"

The red-eyed girl bent to look him in the eye. "Don't talk."

Demetri clamped his mouth shut, another tendril of blissful fog creeping over him, putting his brain to sleep.

"Leave him alone, Tatiana," Perpetua snapped. "You can't have him."

"And how do you propose to stop me?"

"I—" Perpetua began, but then she whirled around. Demetri followed her with his eyes and watched as a second girl emerged from below the cliffside, crawling over the edge like a spider. She had tangled golden hair and red eyes to match the other girl, and—Demetri realized, as he slowly regained some coherent thought—scales. Crimson scales covered her legs and torso, leaving only one arm bare.

Mermaid, he thought again.

"Hello, Perpetua." The golden-haired, red-scaled mermaid stalked forward like a lion in the grass. She circled Perpetua. "Tatiana told me you'd become a real human, but I didn't believe her. Even after you *shot* me on that boat—"

"I'm not a human," Perpetua growled. "Tatiana doesn't know what she's talking about."

"Really?" The golden-haired mermaid stopped to face Perpetua. "Because she's been following you all over town when she can. Watching you. And she says you spend quite a bit of time as a human these days. More time than is possible."

"*All* of your time," the other girl—*mermaid*—spat.

"That's not true," Perpetua said stubbornly. "Go away, Candelaria. Leave us be."

"Us?" The golden-haired mermaid let out a peal of chilling laughter. "*Us? You* and the human?"

"I mean it."

"I'll tell you what, Perpetua," the mermaid said. Perpetua had called her "Candelaria." "Prove Tatiana wrong. Prove to me you're still a naiad, and I'll leave you alone."

Perpetua went very still. Demetri's eyes flicked back and forth between her and the mermaid Candelaria. His thoughts were spinning in jumbled circles, still foggy. None of this made sense. Why did Perpetua know these mermaids? Had she just said she wasn't human? And what was that word...*naiad*...what did that mean?

He settled his desperate gaze on Perpetua. Her eyes found his. He didn't like the fear he saw there. The kind of fear that meant something terrible was about to happen.

"Demetri," Perpetua whispered. "I'm sorry."

Then she began to change.

The fingers on her hands elongated, her nails sharpening into points. There was a horrible *cracking* sound, and her jaw changed shape, growing longer to make room for two rows of shark-like teeth. And her eyes—*her eyes.*

Her dark, hooded eyes turned scarlet from rim to rim, as though they had filled with blood.

Demetri still couldn't speak. He couldn't move. But neither of those restrictions tamped down the horror rising in his throat. He felt boneless, *senseless*, trying to convince himself what he was seeing wasn't real.

Perpetua was a mermaid.

Perpetua was a *mermaid.*

No. She couldn't be. Demetri felt like he was floating, straight up out of his fogged-up brain. Because this was madness, this couldn't be happening, his eyes were wrong, because what he was seeing, what he was *seeing* just. Didn't. Make. Sense.

Blam. Blam. Blam.

Shots rang out, cracking through the air. The mermaid beside him let out a screech so tearing and high-pitched, it stung his ears. Her grip went slack, claws ripping free of him as she spasmed and slumped to the ground. At once, the last of the haze clouding Demetri's brain vanished, and he fell forward onto hands and knees, pain flaring down his shoulder and across his back.

Somewhere nearby, men were shouting. Demetri thought he heard his name. He caught his breath and glanced aside, staring at the fallen mermaid beside him. He saw now that she had scales too, brown scales, but more importantly, he saw she was dead. Someone had shot her, twice in the back and once through the throat.

An animal-like snarl tore his attention from the dead mermaid. He jerked his head up as Perpetua flung herself at Candelaria, who was trying to flee. The two of them tumbled until Perpetua pinned the mermaid beneath her, slamming her into the ground. "Where do you think you're going?" Perpetua hissed, her words horribly distorted by the fangs in her mouth.

Another shot *cracked* the air, and the bullet snagged the ground, inches from Perpetua and the other mermaid. Perpetua jerked her head up as Demetri lurched to his feet, whirling around.

"Stop!" he yelled, holding up his arms. There were men coming towards them, men on horseback in green uniforms, all armed with pistols. "Don't shoot!"

The herd of soldiers was still a ways off, but they were closing in quickly. Demetri spun around. Perpetua was on her feet, tugging Candelaria up with her. They both froze when they saw Demetri, and Candelaria opened her mouth to speak.

Demetri spoke first. "Go, you have to go." The words tripped from his mouth. "Quickly. Before they get here."

Perpetua met his gaze. As he watched, her fingers shrunk, claws vanishing, and the red faded from her eyes.

Too late, Demetri thought dazedly. It was all much too late.

"You're letting us go?" Candelaria snapped. Her voice was harsh and grating, with none of the melodious compulsion the other had used. "*Both* of us?"

Demetri tore his gaze from Perpetua long enough to look at her. "Look, I've heard what those soldiers mean to do to you all if they catch you. They want to cut your tongues out, and that's just to start." He threw a glance over his shoulder. "You can try to kill me again sometime, and I'll try to kill you right back. But I draw the line at maiming and torture."

"She won't try to kill you again." Perpetua flashed a glare at Candelaria. "You can be sure of that."

"Good. Now *go*."

Candelaria turned to flee, but Perpetua didn't move. Her eyes—her beautiful brown eyes, the eyes Demetri knew so well—fixed on him. "What about you? They'll see that you let us go—"

"I'll tell them you mind-controlled me!" Demetri waved a frantic hand. The earth trembled as the horses galloped towards them, their hooves like thunder as they drew close. But he wasn't only worried about Perpetua getting caught. He was just desperate for her to be *gone*, because seeing her there—looking so *normal* again, looking just like any other girl—

It was too painful. He couldn't stand it.

"Just go." His voice turned to stone. "Before I change my mind."

Perpetua's jaw tightened. She cast him one more look, and then she turned and ran after Candelaria. The two sprinted through the cedar trees, straight for the cliffside. And as the capital guard reached him, flinging themselves from their saddles to seize him by the arms, they raised their pistols, firing into the line of trees.

Too late, Demetri thought again. For the mermaids were already gone, leaping off the low cliff into the water below.

21
CONTRITION

BRIAR HAD NOT MENTIONED her unsettling conversation with Castel to Kinsley. She wasn't really sure what to say. It was only one conversation, after all. Kinsley obviously knew the man better than she did. And she couldn't say exactly what about Castel had thrown her off—it was just a feeling, and if she couldn't articulate that feeling, she wasn't sure she could trust it.

She had let Perpetua know she'd run into him, and that he'd asked about her. Perpetua had looked at her rather blankly when she'd mentioned her brother, until Briar clarified by naming him, "Castel."

"Oh," Perpetua had said. "Him."

"How many brothers do you have?"

Perpetua had only waved a vague hand, indicating, Briar supposed, quite a few.

But she had decided not to mention anything of Castel to Kinsley. And she supposed she never would have, except—while waiting for a carriage in the courtyard of Mariner Castle, after her meeting with the counts—Kinsley said, "All right. What's wrong with you, Your Highness?"

"What?" Briar looked blankly at him. She stood on the bottom step at the back of the courtyard, the towering front doors tightly shut behind them. "What are you talking about?"

Kinsley stood beside her, hands clasped behind his back. He cast a sidelong glance at her. "We've not spoken much lately."

"Yes, well, whose fault is that," Briar said tartly. Considering he spent all his free time *out* nowadays. With a certain someone. "You've not been around much."

"Well, when I've been around," Kinsley said, unperturbed by her tone, "you're always sneaking me weird looks."

"I am not."

"You are too."

"I am no—" Briar broke off before they descended into a childish argument. She glowered at Kinsley, who merely returned a neutral gaze, waiting her out. Briar sighed. "I ran into Castel. A couple of weeks ago. Near the submarine."

Kinsley blinked, as though whatever he had expected her to say, it was not this. Evidently, Castel had not mentioned their little meeting. "And?"

Briar shrugged.

Kinsley looked amused. "You didn't like him."

Briar pulled a face. "That seems a strong way of putting it. It was only a short conversation, and—did you know Perpetua is his sister?"

Kinsley surprised her with a nod. "Not at first. It wasn't until our third outing that he told me. I gather Perpetua had mentioned you, and he made the connection."

"Hmm." Briar shifted her weight, crossing her arms over her chest. The sun had climbed high enough that it shone over the courtyard's high walls, its heat beating down upon them. Where *was* Tory with that carriage?

"What did he say to you?" Kinsley asked calmly.

"Nothing, really, it was just..." Briar hesitated. "He seemed a bit—well—" She cast him a furtive glance.

Kinsley arched an eyebrow, infuriatingly patient.

"—dodgy," Briar finished.

Kinsley laughed. That surprised her even more; rarely did she hear Kinsley laugh like that—so openly, so uninhibited. It transformed his face completely. "Your Highness, there's no 'seems' about it. Castel is definitely a bit dodgy. More than a bit."

"And you're all right with that?" Briar narrowed her eyes. "You *like* that? Is that your type? Dodgy men?"

"Hardly."

"So...?"

Kinsley rolled his shoulder back, looking pensive. After a moment, he admitted, "I grant you this courtship with Castel has been...rather more wild than usual for me. But it's nothing I can't handle, Briar, and nothing I've felt uncomfortable with."

"And he's worth it?" Briar pressed.

Kinsley didn't answer right away. He gazed up at the blindingly sunny sky, squinting. It was with an air of quiet self-consciousness that he said, "I believe so. It's hard to explain, but...he sees me. Somehow. Even after knowing me for only a few weeks. He really sees me."

"I see you," Briar grumbled.

Kinsley looked amused again. "Are you jealous, Your Highness?"

"Don't be stupid."

"I can love you and other people, Princess."

"Shut up, Kinsley."

Kinsley laughed again, though it was a quieter laugh this time. But Briar, feeling uneasy, couldn't help but notice Kinsley's use of the word "love." Perhaps it had only been meant in jest, but somehow, Briar thought not. It was clear that—no matter how short a time they'd known each other—Kinsley's feelings for Castel were already quite serious. And she worried about that. She worried for Kinsley.

She never wanted to see him get hurt.

"Your Highness!"

Briar turned, spotting Tory as she sprinted across the courtyard, her ruddy cheeks redder than ever. As she stumbled to a halt in front of them, Briar peered out through the arched entry, eyeing the bridge outside and the road beyond it. She didn't see a carriage.

"What's wrong, Tory?" Briar asked. "Where's—"

"Your Highness—it's Prince Demetri." Tory heaved a breath.

"Demetri? He's gone back into town."

"No. He's here. They've brought him back here. And he needs your help."

<hr>

It was dusk by the time Briar returned to LeBeau's. A full day, spent at the castle. A full ten hours.

And in that ten hours, everything had changed.

Beneath the dim glow of the gear-bulb fixture, Briar watched Demetri head into his room, head bowed. She'd offered to stay up with him, grab a drink down in the common room, but he'd said he was exhausted and wanted to get some sleep. She was sure he *was* exhausted. Exhausted and troubled. And how could he not be, after everything he'd been through today, after everything—

Everything he'd discovered.

Not thinking about that, Briar told herself sternly, heading down the corridor for her own room.

The Mariner counts had held Demetri at the castle for hours. Despite his claims that the mermaids—or whatever they called themselves—had mind-controlled him, they'd arrested him and threatened to lock him up. It had taken considerable persuasion and negotiation from Briar to get them to release him. In the end, it was really the threat of retaliation from King Victor that had done it.

Briar slumped as she reached the door to her room and dug her key out of her pocket. A full day, lost. A full day's work on the submarine lost. But then, she reminded herself, that didn't matter anymore. The counts had grudgingly agreed to release Demetri, but they'd revoked his authority to investigate the mermaids, and then, they'd revoked Briar's permission to work on the submarine. Even threats of King Victor hadn't persuaded them on that point. They'd insisted it was a matter of security, and stiffly maintained they wouldn't change their minds until this "mermaid business" was wrapped up.

"Or until Victor convinces them otherwise," Briar muttered, stepping into her room. She let out a long sigh as she eased the door shut. Her sitting room was cloaked in shadow; night had fallen. A soft breeze whistled through the window, fluttering the lacy curtains. Briar set her key on a small table—

Then she froze. Cocking her head, she frowned at the open window.

She hadn't left it open.

Her senses sharpened, tension seizing every muscle in her body. Slowly, she scanned the room, her eyes lingering on every shape in the darkness, every shifting shadow—

But it wasn't movement that alerted her to the intruder. It was a pair of blood-red eyes, beaming in the darkness.

Briar managed to stifle a swift stab of fear, seeing eyes like that, eyes like *them*, here in her dark room. Though her heart gave an erratic skitter, Briar remained outwardly calm as she zeroed in on the person sitting on Perpetua's bed in the corner.

On *Perpetua*, sitting on her bed in the corner.

Briar cleared her throat and took another step into the room. "I didn't expect you to come back here."

"I'm not staying." As Perpetua's voice floated out of the darkness, her red eyes vanished. Briar could just make her out as she leaned over to wind up the lamp on her bedside table. It dimmed on, the white glow bright but small. Perpetua sat cross-legged on the bed, wearing the same mint-green dress she'd left in yesterday, the same dress Briar had helped her with.

Stones, was that just yesterday? It felt like a lifetime ago. She imagined Perpetua felt the same. Given the state of her dress—the hem muddy and water-stained, the satin ripped and wrinkled—the last twenty-four hours had been no picnic for her either.

But then, how could she have any idea what Perpetua felt? She didn't know if mermaids felt anything. The thought was another *stab*, one that made her go cold inside. "So why are you here?"

"I was worried about Demetri," Perpetua said.

"That's rich."

"Is he all right?"

All right. Now Briar went hot, anger flashing through her like a bolt of lightning. "The counts have released him, if that's what you mean." Briar yanked open a drawer on the end table beside her, checking the loaded pistol she'd left inside was still there. She didn't really think she'd need it, but then, how could she be sure? How could she be sure of anything, so far as Perpetua was concerned?

She slammed the drawer shut. "He's here. Safe in his room. But, no, Perpetua. I really wouldn't say he's *all right.*"

Briar looked up. Perpetua met her gaze. Briar couldn't read a damn thing on her face, and for some reason, that made her even angrier.

"You're upset," said Perpetua. As though just now deducing this.

Briar didn't answer. She simply turned away as she shrugged out of her short coat. Then she started yanking the pins out of her hair, one at a time. Stones, but they were tucked in tight. She could feel a headache forming at the crown of her head, throbbing dully.

"You're upset with me," Perpetua said.

"What makes you say that?" Briar yanked out another pin.

Perpetua was quiet for a moment. Then she said, "I thought we were friends."

"*Friends?*" Briar spun around. "I thought that too, Perpetua. But do mermaids even have friends? Do you even know what that means?"

Perpetua looked at her, her face solemn. "Naiads."

"What?"

"We're called naiads," Perpetua explained. "Not mermaids."

Briar stared at her for a moment. Then—forgetting her hair, leaving half of it pinned back and half of it tumbling over her shoulder—she sank down onto an upholstered ottoman, dropping her head into one hand. "Right. Naiads."

"And you're right," Perpetua said softly. "Naiads don't have friends. They wouldn't even understand what the word means."

Briar lifted her head. "They? Not 'we?'"

Perpetua regarded her with an odd expression. A little wary. A little resigned. And just as exhausted as Briar was. Maybe even more so. The exhaustion in Perpetua's eyes seemed to extend deep inside her.

"I'm not really one of them," the mermaid—naiad—said. "Not exactly. Not anymore."

"Then what are you?" Briar demanded. "No, I have better question. *Why*, Perpetua? Why do all this?"

"All this?"

"Why pretend to be human?" Briar waved a slightly hysterical arm, trying to encompass it all—the time they had spent together, the friendship they'd built, or rather, that Briar *thought* they'd built. Every conversation they'd had, sharing a room here. Stones, Perpetua had saved her life from those—from those other— "Why pretend to be our friend, why live here with me—why any of it?"

"I wasn't pretending to be your friend." Perpetua's voice held a note of pain. As though *she* was the one who was hurt. As though she had any right to feel hurt. "I am your friend. And I thought you were mine."

"I thought I was too!" Briar surged to her feet, driven by a new spark of exasperation. "But now—I don't understand any of this, Perpetua. Seriously, please, explain it to me, because I don't understand! What *are* you, and why—"

"I was a naiad," Perpetua interrupted her. "I was just like the others. But then the sea witch cursed me, and I became...this." She gestured at herself. "Sort of human. Sort of not. But mostly human, I think."

The words washed over Briar, endless thoughts and feelings tumbling through her. When she finally opened her mouth to respond, she wasn't sure what was going to come out.

"What, by the Gift, is a sea witch?" she asked.

"She's a naiad. Who is also a witch."

"Like a *witch*? An evil witch, casting spells and hexes and such?" Briar rubbed a hand over her eyes. "Huh. All right. And she hexed you...why? For a lark?" Briar knew well enough there were witches—and other creatures—happy to go around cursing people on a lark.

But Perpetua shook her head. "It was a punishment."

"For what?"

"For Demetri. For saving Demetri. For saving a human."

Briar stared at her again. Her thoughts were ordering themselves now, pushing past the hurt and anger and fatigue to make sense of things. And now, a last, vital piece of the puzzle fell into place. "The shipwreck. You saved Demetri from the shipwreck, didn't you? You brought him back to shore."

Perpetua nodded wearily. "Yes. And ever since then, my life has been turned upside down."

"Do you regret it? Saving him?"

Perpetua twisted her lips. "No. I can't regret it. Not when—" Her voice grew a little hoarse. "Not when I think about him. I can't regret it."

She looked up at Briar. The glare of the lamp beside her was reflected in her eyes, giving them an eerie, haunted look. "I tried not to lie to you. To all of you. I *tried* not to. What I said about my family casting me out, having nowhere to go—that was true, in a way." She clenched her fingers into the sheets beneath her. "But I *couldn't* tell you the whole truth. Not with Demetri hunting naiads, not after—with everything I've done, every person I've—" She broke off.

But Briar knew what she'd been about to say. "Every person you've killed." The dread that rose within her was a quiet, insidious thing. "Which is...how many, exactly?"

Perpetua only gave her a wry look.

"Right." Briar lowered herself back down onto the ottoman.

"It's just what they do." Perpetua pulled her knees up to her chest, wrapping her arms around herself. "What *we* do. We're hunters. Predators. We *have* to feed on humans to survive. Otherwise..." She trailed off. "There's no malice in it. It's just about survival. Naiads don't *care* about humans. Any more than you care about anything you eat."

"Then why did you save Demetri?" Briar asked intently. "I mean, I assume you were there to hunt. But you spared his life. More than that, *you saved him*. Why?"

Perpetua managed a tiny, tired smile. "I still don't know. There was just something about him. And then he spoke to me, and—I don't know. I couldn't kill him." She clenched her lips tight. "I won't do it anymore. I *don't* do it anymore. Killing humans. Even if—I won't."

"Why?"

"I can't." A weird look flashed over Perpetua's face. "That night on the boat. At the party. When they attacked you. The other naiads."

Briar felt cold fingers slide into her chest and curl around her heart. At the thought of those red eyes. At the memory of what had happened that night. "Yes? What about it?"

"You could have killed Candelaria—the naiad. From what I saw, you could have killed her. But you didn't."

Briar leaned back, curling one leg towards her. Yes, she had spent a lot of time thinking about that attack. A lot of time wondering why she hadn't killed that creature. She hadn't *decided* not to. She'd just...frozen. Working out the why, though, had taken a bit longer.

"I killed someone. Once." Briar's breath felt uncertain in her chest. "I say someone, but she wasn't really a person. She was a monster. And I *had* to kill her. She would have killed me, and a lot of other people. She wanted to kill everyone." Briar pursed her lips. "For a long time, I told myself I didn't really kill her. That I had just made it possible for her to die. But that's just semantics, really. I did kill her."

For a moment, there was only the sound of the wind and the ocean, furling in through the window. Then Perpetua said, "And it bothers you. That you killed her." She looked a part of the night, sitting there on her bed. Her dark hair framing her face, her brown eyes fathomless. "Even though she was a monster. Even though she would have killed others, killed you."

"Well. Yes." Briar looked at her frankly. "Would it bother you?"

Perpetua inhaled a shaky breath. "If you had asked me that a few weeks ago, I would have said no. But now..."

"What's changed?"

"You," Perpetua whispered, "and Demetri. Before I met you two, I didn't care about anyone. And no one cared about me."

Briar's tired, fragile heart gave a lurch. Because she knew that feeling. Until she'd met Demetri, eighty-two years ago, she'd been the same way. She'd lived in her castle, surrounded by people, but with no one who cared about her. And no one for her to care about.

It was a horrible, lonely way to live.

"I was kind of empty inside," Perpetua said. "Or like I was a shadow, and not a person. That's what it is, to be a naiad. To be a monster." She tossed her hair back from her face. "And I think part of me knew I was missing something, but I didn't know what. Until I met you two." Her voice turned rough. "So you see, I wasn't pretending to be your friend. I didn't know what it *meant* to be a friend when I first met you. But you taught me. And I still want to be your friend. If I can be."

Briar looked at her. Perpetua's dark eyes shimmered in the lamplight; they were filled with tears. Briar didn't cry, but she *felt* it, on the inside. Her chest was in shambles.

"So," she managed to say, "tell me about this sea witch, then."

Perpetua let out a breath. A single tear spilled down her cheek, but she dashed it away. "Yes. I should. Because apparently, she's after you."

"What? Me? Why?"

And Perpetua told her. She laid everything out, relating a tale of sea creatures who lived deep in the ocean until they became monsters. A tale of a naiad who became a witch so she could save her people. A witch who now meant to trade Briar for something.

"This sea witch," Briar said, once Perpetua had told her everything. She was on her feet again, pacing back and forth in the dark room. "What did you say her name was?"

"Sohalia."

Sohalia. Briar thought of the woman she'd met that first day out on the beach. The one who'd called herself *Sohi.* "Yes. I think I met her. She's the one who got me looking for elarium in the first place. But what does she want with it?"

Perpetua shook her head. "I don't know. Meliora didn't say anything about it before she died. All she said was Sohalia wants *you.* That she wants to trade you. On the summer solstice."

Briar chewed her lip. "So we need to find out exactly what she wants."

"I think I might know someone who can tell us." Perpetua hesitated. "Only, you're not going to like it. Rather, you're not going to like how he knows."

"All right." Briar tried not to shiver with the foreboding that trickled through her. "Who are we talking about?"

22
GATEWAY

BRIAR GLANCED DOWN THE long, cobbled street, eyeing the row of massive townhouses. They loomed like watchful beasts in the darkness, the windows built into their faces like a great many eyes staring down at them. Briar was all too aware of the number of *people* who could be staring down at them through those windows. "Hurry up, will you," she muttered.

"It's—not—working," Perpetua huffed. "The key doesn't work!"

"Looks like he changed the locks on you."

"I was just here last night. Or. The night before last, I suppose." Perpetua turned to face Briar, blowing a stray lock of hair from her face.

"And apparently, he spent the day changing the locks." Briar peered around the side of the house. "Don't worry. Just follow me."

"What are you going to do?"

Briar edged around the house, venturing down a narrow alley. Most of the fine houses on this street butted right up against each other, but Castel's gleaming white house sat at the mouth of a town square where several broad avenues converged. Briar continued down the alley, around the house, until she'd gone as far back as she could go. There was a broad window back here.

Briar removed her coat and wrapped it around her hand.

Then she punched straight through the paned glass, smashing the window.

From behind her, Perpetua said, "I thought you might pick the lock or something."

"Oh." Briar motioned for Perpetua to step through the jagged opening in the window. "I could have done that, I suppose." *But smashing through this prick's window felt really good*, she thought.

Castel deserved a lot more for deceiving Kinsley. A *lot* more.

Briar climbed in after Perpetua and found herself in a small, dark room. Her eyes adjusted quickly as Perpetua marched to the door. "Come on. Castel's room is upstairs."

Briar followed her down a winding corridor and up an elaborate staircase. They'd rung the doorbell before Perpetua tried her key, and there had been no answer, so they were fairly certain the witch wasn't home. Still, Briar tensed as Perpetua pushed open the door to Castel's bedroom. The room was awash in darkness, but Perpetua stepped inside and leaned over to wind up a lamp. The dim glow emitted through the emerald shade showed an empty bedroom. Castel wasn't there.

Briar let out a long breath. "So I guess we wait."

Perpetua drifted across the room and pushed aside the dark curtains there, peering through a large window. The glass was black and opaque in the night, only vague shapes and outlines visible outside.

"Briar?" Perpetua said.

"Hmm?"

"How was Demetri? Really? I mean—I know he's not all right, but..."

Briar sighed. "Well, when we got back to LeBeau's, he was mostly just exhausted. But I'm sure he feels the same way I did."

"He let us go," Perpetua said softly. "Me *and* Candelaria. I knew he would get in trouble for it. *He* had to know. But he still let us go."

"Yes, well, that's Demetri for you. Always trying to sacrifice himself."

"What do you mean?"

"That's just what he's like." Briar shrugged. "He'll do anything for the people he cares about."

Briar's gaze snagged on a tall, black bookshelf in the corner of the room. Crossing over to it, she scanned the spines, then began pulling books out one by one, flipping through them. She popped one open and her eyes bulged. She snapped the book shut, thankful her rotting condition made it impossible for her to blush. "That is *not* a spell book."

"No, it's not, princess. It's far more entertaining."

Briar whirled around.

Castel stood in the doorway.

"Though I'm not sure why you're looking for such a thing here." Castel stepped into the room. "Or why you're—" He broke off as his eyes fell on Perpetua, standing in the corner. His expression barely changed, save for a tightening around his eyes.

"Perpetua." His voice was low and dangerous. "I have to say, I didn't expect to see you back here so soon."

"Or at all," Perpetua shot back. Briar felt strangely proud of her for standing up to Castel. "Since you changed the locks. I guess you didn't mean it when you said you'd keep helping me? When you told me to come back in a few weeks?"

"Actually, I did," Castel said tersely. "Believe it or not, changing the locks had nothing to do with you, Perpetua dear. You see, I thought I could trust you."

"*You're* one to talk about trust." Briar stalked forward, facing Castel head-on. "After all the lies you've told. And not just to me."

A flinch spasmed through Castel. It was so small and so subtle, Briar might have imagined it. "So I assume you've told Kinsley everything you know about me?"

"No, I haven't." She watched Castel closely for another reaction—another flinch, a change in his expression—but his gaze was unruffled. Hardening her voice, she added, "But I will. Unless you want to tell him yourself."

Castel snorted. "Why would I do that?"

"I don't know. Maybe because it's the kind of thing that *should* come from you? Given how much he cares about you and all?"

"Does he?" Castel asked idly. "Care about me?"

Briar dug her fingernails into her palms. "You tell me."

Castel's expression still didn't change, but there was something about him—an edge in his eyes, a tension in his body. As though he were a puppet whose strings had been pulled taut. But then he shrugged. "You can tell him whatever you like, princess. I don't need him anymore." An aggrieved look flickered over his face. "Not that I got anything useful from him. He's very loyal to you."

White hot anger lanced through Briar. "I could kill you."

"I very much doubt that." He looked past her, his gaze fixing on Perpetua. "Anyway, I'm hardly the only one who has lied. Or has dear Perpetua told you what *she* really is?"

"She's a naiad. And you're a witch. Minion to the same witch-naiad that turned Perpetua into a human."

Castel rolled his eyes. "I'm no one's *minion*." He stepped further into the room, flicking on a second light. His bright crimson coat and matching tie seemed at odds with the room's dark furnishings. He moved right past Briar, towards his bed, and for a moment, Briar thought he was going to lie down on it. But instead he bent, rooting out something from beneath his mattress. He straightened, holding the object out to Briar.

It was a book. A very old, very tattered little book. His spell book, she presumed.

"I believe you were looking for this," he said, "though I don't know what good it will do you."

"None at all, I'm sure," Briar replied, matching his tone. "Actually, we were hoping you could do the spell work. Or give us some information. About what Sohalia is up to. And how to stop her."

Castel looked amused. He glanced between her and Perpetua, as though waiting for one of them to say, "Only joking!" When neither of them did, he tossed the little spell book onto his bed. "And why, by the Gift, would I do that?"

"You said you'd help me." Perpetua stepped out of the shadow of the curtains, her hands curled into fists.

Castel was unmoved. "Yes, I did. But not by betraying Sohalia." He sat back on his bed, stretching his legs out and crossing them at the ankle. "I'll admit, I don't care for her that much. Not anymore. I think she's quite mad. But she is very powerful. More powerful than me. And if I betray her outright—say, by giving you all information on her—she *will* kill me." He lifted a hand to inspect his nails. "Besides, I don't know what she's up to. So far as I know, she has always had one goal."

"Which is?"

Castel said, "When I first met Sohalia—a long, *long* time ago—she was obsessed with finding a way to save you naiads. She's changed a lot since then, but I've never heard her talk about anything else."

Briar narrowed her eyes. "Not even me? Or didn't you just admit you were using Kinsley to get information about me?"

"Did I?"

"You did," Perpetua pressed. "*And* you said you didn't need him anymore."

"Suggesting Sohalia's already got whatever information she needs," Briar said flatly. "So what was it? Something about the elarium? We found a deposit, but I don't see how she could know that. Unless Kinsley told you something."

"I already told you," Castel said, "I didn't get anything from Kinsley. And I don't know anything about any elarium. The only thing she wanted me to do was monitor how long you were staying here this summer. In fact, my little flirtation with Kinsley was less about getting information and more about *influencing*."

"Influencing Kinsley? To do what?"

"To stay here. Rather, to make *you* stay here."

"But stay here for what?" Briar burst out. When Castel simply turned an impassive look her way—either unwilling to share more or as clueless as he claimed—she spun away, pacing back and forth. "All right. Well. The summer solstice. We know she has plans to do something then, right?" She glanced at Perpetua. "What else did your friend say?"

"She said Sohalia needs the power from the solstice," Perpetua said. "She said Sohalia plans to *trade* you on the solstice. And something about opening something?'

Castel's careless gaze sharpened.

"What?" Briar glowered at the witch. "Does that mean something to you?"

Castel stared at her for a long moment, his expression still unchanging. He was very good at that, Briar thought. Keeping everything off his face. Only this time, there *was* something, deep in his eyes. Something haunted.

"She wouldn't," he said at once.

"Wouldn't what?" Briar demanded. "What do you know?"

Castel looked between her and Perpetua. Then he stood abruptly, so abruptly that Briar took an involuntary step back.

"Even she wouldn't be that mad." Castel's tone was abstracted, as though he was speaking to himself. He ran a hand through his hair until it was quite disheveled. "What am I saying. Of course she is. I've been afraid of her doing something like this for a while now."

"Are you going to explain anytime soon?" Briar asked, exasperated.

"Look." Castel ran both of his hands over his face. "When I say Sohalia has gone mad, I mean that quite literally."

"The Ternion thought so too," Perpetua cut in. "Meliora and Nadalia. They seemed to think naiads were never meant to become witches. Meliora said naiad blood and witch magic shouldn't mix."

"I think it's a little more complicated than that," Castel's eyes narrowed pensively. "You naiads live with a certain bloodlust. A thirst for killing. Sohalia used to be quite good at fighting that bloodlust, but it was a constant struggle for her. Then she became a witch, and you see, we witches *also* live with a darkness inside us. Not quite the same as what the naiads experience, but...." He tapped a finger against his chin. "When Sohalia became a witch, she suddenly had *two* demons inside her, figuratively speaking. Two little devils sitting on her shoulder, whispering in her ear. Begging her to kill, to give into the darkness. I think that's enough to drive anyone insane."

"Right." Briar had no trouble believing that. "So what is it you think she's doing, then?"

Castel let out a long sigh. "For all I knew, there were plenty of reasons Sohalia might want you here, princess. But if you're talking about her opening something on the solstice, trading you..." He looked right at Briar. "Kinsley really was loathe to talk about you. He would never divulge any secrets. But he mentioned something in passing once—something about a creature he came across. A djinn?"

Briar froze, a chill whispering at the back of her neck.

"I see you *do* know what I'm talking about," Castel said grimly. "Kinsley didn't go into details—when I say he mentioned it in passing, I mean that—but given what I know of djinn, *and* of your story, I can guess the rest. A djinn fed off you, I presume, while you were asleep for a century? Dragged you down into its little hellscape, its *shadow world*, and fed off your life force?"

"It wasn't a century," Briar said tightly. She wasn't sure why, but Castel confronting her with this truth was deeply unsettling. "And I don't remember it. But that's what happened. Or so I'm told."

"So you can see why the whole lot of them would love to get their hands on you? For all eternity?"

Briar frowned. "The lot of who?" When Castel only held her gaze, his eyes bleak, she said, "The *djinn*? But they're all confined to that shadow world. I thought they could only get to me in my sleep—unless you're saying Sohalia plans to put me under another enchantment—" The chill tickling the nape of Briar's neck solidified, closing around her throat. That's what had happened to Princess Snow. Her evil witch of a stepmother had put a sleeping hex on her.

But Castel said, "I doubt it. A witch's hex isn't strong enough to hold out against a djinn's magic."

"Meaning what?"

"Meaning, if Sohalia put a sleeping hex on you and the djinn proceeded to feed off you, you wouldn't last long. You'd die and be of no use to the djinn at all. But if Sohalia opened a gateway into their world—say, with the power of a solstice behind her—she could hand you over to them. Forever."

"And she can do that?"

"*Can* she? With the power of the solstice, yes, I would think so. *Should* she? That is a different question entirely." Castel shook his head. "Opening a gateway would be incredibly dangerous. Opening a gateway would give the djinn a chance to escape."

Briar swallowed. "And why do you care about that?"

Castel smiled thinly. "What makes you think I do?"

"Call it a hunch." Briar didn't like relying on *hunches* and "gut feelings," but then, this particular hunch was built on what she could see right before her. Castel was clearly disturbed by the idea of Sohalia opening this gateway. What she didn't know was why. "See, I would think a witch, of all people, wouldn't care one whit about djinn and what they do."

Castel let out a huff. "Look, there are plenty of witches out there—like Sohalia—who don't mind trading favors with djinn. But that's because they're idiots. That's because they don't know what I know. They don't know…"

Briar eyed him. "They don't know…?"

"How dangerous djinn are." Castel never broke eye contact with Briar, but she had the distinct impression that he'd meant to say something else. "They don't understand that allowing the djinn to roam free would upset the magical balance this world teeters so precariously on. But I know better. Unfortunately," he grumbled.

"Unfortunately?"

"What can I say, princess?" Castel sank back onto his bed, looking weary. "Knowledge is a curse."

Perpetua stepped forward. She'd gone quiet, listening to Briar and Castel's exchange. Now she turned her gaze on Castel. "And what exactly does Sohalia want?"

"I believe we just established that."

"We established she wants to *trade* Briar to these djinn," Perpetua clarified. "A trade means she will get something in return. What is she getting?"

"I've no idea." Castel dropped his face into his hand. "For all I know, she's getting a way to save you naiads. I told you, she's always been obsessed with the idea. It happens, sometimes, with mad people. They fixate. She probably doesn't really *care* about saving you all, but she can't let it go. It's the only thing she's lived for all these years."

Briar said, "Well, it doesn't really matter, does it? Whatever her ultimate goal, we need to find a way to stop her."

Castel looked up. "You want to stop her, princess? Leave. Go back to the Glen Kingdom. Better yet, go home to the *Mountain* Kingdom. Where you'll be hundreds of miles out of Sohalia's reach, surrounded by an army of corpses to put between you and her. If she can't trade you, then she's got no reason to open any gateway."

"We don't know that for sure." Briar chewed her lip. "She could have contingencies. And even if she doesn't, she's not going to give up, is she? She'll keep trying to get...whatever it is she's after, whether I'm here or not. We need more information, and we need to stop her. So." She placed her hands on her hips. "Are you going to help us, Castel?"

Castel met her gaze, unabashed. "There's still the little matter of her killing me if I betray her."

"I would think that's worth the risk, given how concerned you seem about these djinn escaping."

Castel folded his arms across his chest. "Look, I'm not even sure what I could do. I don't know what she's planning. She won't tell me just because I ask. As I mentioned, she's a bit more powerful than me."

Briar gritted her teeth. She jerked her chin at Castel's spell book. "Does she have one of those? And might it conceal notes or clues to what she's planning, or how to stop it?"

"Ye-es. Possibly." Castel's tone made it clear just how tenuous he thought that 'possibly' was.

"Well, it's a start. Where would she keep it?"

Castel looked from her to Perpetua. "She *will* kill me if she finds out I told you anything."

"Yes, yes." Briar waved a negligent hand. "Honestly, I don't really care what happens to you, Castel. In fact, *I* would very much like to kill you for deceiving Kinsley. You do know he's probably the most decent person in the entire world?"

"Yes." Castel smiled, and it was an oddly genuine smile. "I know."

"But," she went on, "for Kinsley's sake—for the sake of *his* feelings—if it ever comes up, I won't tell the sea witch you helped us."

"Doesn't mean she won't find out."

"Well, that's the best I can do. Now. Are you going to help us or not?"

Castel let out a long sigh. "She has a yacht. Docked just outside town. It's a private marina, but there's no security. That's where she keeps everything she uses for spell work, including all her books." He leaned back on his hands. "It also happens that I am meeting her this afternoon. Here. Which means she definitely *won't* be on the yacht."

23

INCENDIARY

B RIAR CROUCHED BENEATH THE rocky formation lining
the strip of beach where Sohalia's yacht was docked. Beside
her was Demetri, perched with his arms slung over his shoulders.
He looked nervous, shooting frequent glances around them,
even though they were well hidden within this stony trench.

"You didn't have to come, you know," Briar told him. "In fact,
you don't have to be part of this at all. My guard and I can handle
it—"

"No, no." Demetri waved a hand. "Evil witch, looking to open
a dangerous portal. I'm here to help. As usual."

When Briar had returned to LeBeau's that morning, she'd
wasted no time filling Demetri in on everything she'd learned.
And Demetri, of course, had not hesitated to offer his help.

Of course, it helped that Perpetua wasn't here, Briar thought.
Castel had cautioned against Perpetua accompanying them to
the yacht. Sohalia, he claimed, was not happy that Perpetua had
turned out so poor a spy. He didn't think the sea witch was angry

enough to go looking for Perpetua, but if she were to turn up in her domain...well, the sea witch would kill her in a heartbeat, he'd said.

"I can't help you," he'd told Perpetua, "if you die first."

It wasn't until later—after they'd left Castel's house, after they'd parted ways—that Briar had thought to wonder what it was Castel was helping Perpetua with.

Demetri peered around, his expression edgy. "I just think maybe we should have brought more than two guards."

"This is a reconnaissance mission, Demetri," Briar pointed out. "Or maybe it's theft. I don't know. Either way, stealth is required. And typically, the more people you have, the harder stealth is. Trust me, two guards is sufficient."

"That's what Garrett said when we took six men into your castle to rescue you. And look how that turned out."

Briar couldn't help but smile. "I was just thinking about that. Not when you two first came to the castle, but later. When the two of us waited to get back in through the sewage tunnel. Doesn't this remind you of that?"

"I suppose so," Demetri said heavily. "Hopefully this turns out better than that did."

"What are you talking about? I defeated the dark fairy! I broke the curse! Saved my kingdom!"

"I got stabbed."

"Oh. I forgot about that."

"*And* ended up with a broken hand."

"Well, that was on you," Briar said primly. "If you'd stayed out of it like you were supposed to...but *no.* You had to go and try to be the hero."

A smile tugged at Demetri's lips. "I didn't want to be a hero. I just didn't want you to sacrifice yourself. I thought it had better be me instead." His smile vanished. "Sometimes I still think that would have been for the best."

"Oh, Demetri." Briar cast her eyes heavenward. "You don't have to be so maudlin, you know. I mean, why would you even say something like that? As it turned out, *no one* had to sacrifice themselves, did they? I found a loophole."

"I know." Demetri let out a long exhale. "It's just...what have I done since? All these months gone, and I've still no idea what I'm doing with my life. So far, being a mermaid hunter has turned out as spectacularly awful as every other thing I've tried. For the Gift's sake, the girl I was beginning to love turned out to *be* a mermaid."

Briar blinked at him. "Were you? Beginning to love Perpetua, I mean?"

"I don't know." Demetri ran a hand over his face. "That's just it, Briar. How can I know? How can I know how much of what I felt for her is real? I don't even know when Perpetua became human, when she lost her ability to control people. So she very well may not have been human when I..."

*When he...*what? Briar wondered. But he didn't extrapolate, and she didn't ask. "Look," she said, considering her words carefully. She knew he was angry with Perpetua. Hurt and angry. Of course he was. But. "Perpetua was a monster, Demetri. All the naiads are. But they didn't choose it. They were made to be that way. Sound familiar?"

Demetri met her gaze. "You aren't a monster, Briar."

"And neither is Perpetua. Not anymore." Briar slouched, stretching her legs out. "She may have lied to us, Demetri, but it wasn't *all* a lie. I believe that. You just have to decide if you believe that too."

Before Demetri could reply, a shadow fell across them, and they both jumped, looking up. But it was only Kinsley, his rifle slung over his shoulder. Before Kinsley had become Briar's bodyguard, he had served under Garrett as his primary sharpshooter.

"Tory says the boat's clear," he told them. "Do you still want me up on the navigation deck?"

Briar rose from her hiding spot. "Yes. Just in case."

"All right." Kinsley lowered his rifle, hefting it in both hands. "You know, you still haven't explained exactly what we're doing here, Your Highness. Or how you found out about this yacht."

Briar hesitated, throwing a glance at Demetri. Demetri sent her a blank look. She hadn't told *him* how she'd found out about the yacht either, though she was fairly certain he'd inferred Perpetua had told her about it. There hadn't really been time to get into the details, and besides...

She dreaded telling Kinsley the truth. About Castel.

"It's kind of a long story." She turned back to Kinsley. "I'll fill you in on everything once we get back to LeBeau's."

"Fair enough. Give me about ten minutes to get set up, and then you two can follow. Tory will be waiting on the main deck."

He set off across the narrow beach. Briar watched him go, checking her timepiece to measure out ten minutes. It was a long, tense ten minutes, and neither she nor Demetri spoke as they waited. *It's fine*, Briar told herself, *everything is fine*, and it was. Sohalia was not here; there was *no one* here, no one in sight. Tory had already cleared the yacht, and Kinsley would be place if, by some mad chance, something went wrong.

Yet Briar could not shake the nagging feeling crawling up her back.

Once their ten minutes was up, she and Demetri hurried across the beach and down the long stone pier. The yacht's main deck was not tall, but just tall enough that they had to use the netted rigging hanging down the side of the boat to climb into it. Briar made it first, leaping onto the deck. She cast a quick glance around, then turned to help Demetri up. He had a more difficult time than Briar, half-falling onto the deck.

"All right." Demetri heaved a breath as he straightened. His eyes swept across the deck. "Empty. Good."

"Yes..." Briar glanced up at the navigation deck, but she couldn't see Kinsley from here—which was the point, of course. He was meant to be hidden. And the rest of the deck *was* empty, so why did she still feel uneasy?

Then she realized.

"Wait a minute," she said, "where's Tory? Kinsley said she'd wait for us here."

"She is, princess. She's waiting right here with me."

Briar felt as though someone had reached inside her and grabbed her by the windpipe. She spun around.

The deck was not empty. There, standing on the top stair leading out from the cabin, was *her*.

Sohi. The woman from Briar's worksite. Tall and lithe, lustrous black hair framing her long face. Just as Briar remembered her. But instead of the gauzy white dress she'd worn that day, she stood before Briar clothed only in scales. Glittering blue-black scales that covered most of her body. And the dark eyes Briar recalled were red from lid to lid.

Not a woman at all. Not *Sohi*.

Sohalia. The sea witch.

Beside her, Demetri reached for his pistol. But Briar did not reach for hers. Because the sea witch was not alone.

Tory stood before her. Sohalia held her by the shoulders, razor-sharp claws dangerously close to the soldier's throat.

"Put your guns on the deck and kick them towards me," Sohalia commanded. "And get down on your knees and stay there."

Her voice was not the lyrical, lulling tone the other naiad had used on Briar. If anything, the sea witch's Voice was harsh and grating, like metal scraping against metal. The sound of that voice clanged in Briar's mind, making her head instantly ache. Stones, she felt as though her ears were bleeding, and yet, even so—she could not resist the compulsion in that voice. Just like before, at the steamboat party.

She and Demetri immediately obeyed, dropping their guns and kicking them away. Then they knelt. Briar's mind was not so foggy as it had been the last time this had happened to her, but it *was* hard to think, that screeching voice ringing in her ears. She winced, tilting her head as though she could shake the compulsion free. As if she could just get that ringing to *stop*, and then she could fight it.

If Sohalia noticed her internal struggle, she wasn't concerned by it. "Now, then." The sea witch smiled at Briar. "Princess. So good of you to deliver yourself here. I had planned to abduct you the night before the solstice, but now that won't be necessary. I can hold you for a few days, I'm sure. Especially now you're not working on that submarine. There won't be anyone to miss you."

Her guards would miss her, Briar thought, the ones that weren't here. Aden and Alec, Gallia and Sabine. But she wasn't going to tell the sea witch that. Instead, she settled for her most lethal glare.

"Ah," Sohalia said, taking in her expression. "Yes. I imagine you're wondering how I knew you would be here."

"I don't have to wonder." Briar spoke through gritted teeth. "*Castel.*"

"Unfortunately, no. That little traitor didn't tell me anything. He will have to be dealt with. No..." Sohalia ran one long, pointed claw down Tory's arm, casually slicing through her navy blue coat. "It was Tory here who told me your plans."

"What?" Briar's heart stuttered in her chest. "That can't..." She trailed off, focusing on Tory's face for the first time. The soldier's eyes were glassy and unseeing, untroubled by what was happening here. Of course, the sea witch would have compelled her not to fight, just like she had done to Briar and Demetri. But somehow the vacant look in Tory's eyes went even deeper. As though Tory herself wasn't in there anymore.

Icy tendrils slithered around Briar's heart. Tory was *completely* under Sohalia's control.

"She first came to my attention when I caught her following Perpetua." Sohalia ran her claw down Tory's arm again, this time drawing a long, thin line of blood that glistened through the tear in her coat. "Tory was much cleverer than the lot of you. She suspected Perpetua. She could tell there wasn't something quite *right* about her. I compelled Tory to keep her suspicions to herself.

"Then when Perpetua proved a most terrible spy, I made Tory my spy instead. She was the one who told me of all your plans. That you had decided to prolong your stay to search for elarium, as I suggested. That you found a deposit nearby. And after you told her about your plans this morning over breakfast, she came straight to me and told me everything. She's been quite useful." The sea witch gave a long, bored sigh. "But now that you know, she's no use to me anymore."

With a swipe of her arm, Sohalia dug her claws into Tory's middle and tore through her, rupturing flesh and sinew. Tory didn't even scream as she collapsed to the floor, blood pooling across the wooden decking.

Demetri cried out, but Briar's scream stuck in her throat. She stared at Tory, slumped on her side. The glassy look had left her eyes. Though she still didn't move or make a sound, Tory's gaze was pained and frightened. Tory had served in Garrett's company before joining Briar's guard; she had been one of the few soldiers to survive the foray into Briar's corpse-ridden kingdom. She had always been there, ever since Briar escaped her cursed castle. And now she lay here, bleeding to death, and Briar couldn't do a thing to help her. She couldn't fight. Couldn't *move*.

"Shame," Sohalia said indifferently. "But I hate to let a good meal go to waste." She stretched her lips in a grisly approximation of a smile. Her jaw *cracked* as it snapped out of place, her teeth growing into hideous fangs. She lunged for Tory—

Then a shot blasted out, exploding through the air. Sohalia stumbled, the bullet taking her in the back. As she staggered around, another shot rang out, the bullet burying itself in her shoulder.

Kinsley, Briar thought, desperate with hope. She still couldn't see him, hidden up on the navigation deck, but if anyone could take Sohalia out from that vantage point, he could...

But before a third shot could come, Sohalia—doubled over, but still on her feet—shot an arm out, splaying her fingers wide. A rifle flew from the navigation deck, sailing clear over the yacht's railing and splashing into the water below.

No, Briar thought frantically, *Kinsley*—

Sohalia curled her arm in towards herself. Briar's hopes turned to ash as Kinsley appeared from over the railing of the navigation deck, dangling in the air, the toes of his boots scraping the floor. He didn't fly as swift as the rifle had but instead drifted forward with inexorable slowness. The furious grimace on his face made it clear he was fighting the sea witch with everything he had, but she was too powerful, even with two bullets in her.

"*So.*" Blood bubbled over Sohalia's lips as she spoke. Her jaw had snapped back into place, her fangs retracted. As Kinsley reached her, floating down from the navigation deck, she snapped her hand down by her side, as though bringing a dog to heel. Kinsley fell to his knees.

"You're Castel's little pet, aren't you?" Sohalia breathed. "Perfect. I can use you to teach him a lesson."

Fear surged through Briar with blinding clarity. Crisp, bright, and sharp. "No. *Don't!*"

Sohalia trembled from head to toe, but she kept her footing as she grasped Kinsley, taking his black-haired head between her hands. She bent close, her face inches from his, and began to whisper so quietly, so unintelligibly, that Briar couldn't hear what she was saying. It could have been a spell, a command, anything—

Then Kinsley began to scream.

It was a terrible sound, starting deep in his chest and ripping through him. As though Sohalia had reached down his throat and pried it from him with her clawed hands. The anguish in that scream was beyond pain, beyond terror. It was madness itself given voice. Kinsley writhed in her grip, clutching at her wrists, his feet scrabbling uselessly against the deck—

"Stop, stop!" Briar cried. She struggled, delving deep into the corners of her mind, searching for a way out of this mental prison, but it was no use. She could not get up. She couldn't retrieve her pistol, she couldn't fight, she *couldn't get to Kinsley*. She struggled and struggled, and after what seemed an eternity listening to Kinsley's wretched screams, all she managed to do was fall forward onto her hands.

Sohalia had ordered her to kneel and stay there. She couldn't disobey.

Then she felt a hand on her wrist. Briar tore her gaze from Kinsley long enough to look down.

It was Tory. She had dragged herself across the deck, leaving a long, crimson streak in her wake. Her breaths were short and ragged, her shredded coat soaked with blood. Painstakingly, she pointed at Briar's waist.

Briar looked down. There was a little pouch tied to her waist, a little pouch Briar had grabbed at the last minute before setting out from the tavern. *Just in case*, she'd thought. *Just in case.*

The little pouch contained a single grenade.

"She didn't tell you—not to use it." Tory's voice was a broken whisper. "She—didn't say—not to kill her."

Briar stared at Tory. Comprehension rushed through her like a tidal wave. She fumbled for the pouch, loosening the drawstring to pull the grenade out. Trying to be careful, trying to push her frantic fears aside—trying to ignore Kinsley's screams—she set the grenade down by her knee and dug a box of matches out of her coat pocket. Fumbling, she pulled a match from the box and struggled to light it.

Across the deck, Sohalia finally released Kinsley, flinging her arms wide. Kinsley slid back across the deck as though she'd physically pushed him, boneless, tumbling down the stairs into the cabin below. He had finally stopped screaming.

Briar's match flared alight. Head pounding, heart quivering, she picked up the grenade and lit the fuse.

"Hey." She straightened up on her knees. "Sea witch."

Sohalia turned.

Briar drew her arm back and hurled the grenade at Sohalia.

Sohalia—reacting instinctively, as Briar had hoped—lurched and caught the grenade. Barely. Cradling it in the crook of her arms, she frowned at it.

Her eyes widened. She dropped the grenade and turned to run, but there was no time.

The grenade exploded, blasting through the air with a deafening roar that whistled through Briar, shutting out the screeching ring of Sohalia's compulsion. Heat arced outwards, engulfing Briar in a cloud of black smoke. Briar choked, a metallic tang coating the back of her tongue, but as a wave of splintered boards and debris swept towards her, she found she could finally move. Grasping Demetri by the sleeve, she dove backwards, ducking down to shelter against the onslaught.

24

WILLING

PERPETUA TUGGED A HAND through her windswept hair as she left the hospital, stepping beneath the awning stretching over the front steps. She hadn't been allowed in yesterday, but Briar had told her she should come back today.

To visit Kinsley.

Really, she had gone to visit Briar. She didn't see much point visiting Kinsley. He had no physical injuries—he had survived the explosion more unscathed than anyone; being down in the cabin had protected him. But his mind was broken. Beyond repair. The doctors said they had no way of healing him; they didn't even know what was wrong with him.

Perpetua knew. Once Briar had described what Sohalia had done, she understood. The sea witch hadn't used magic to break Kinsley; she'd merely used her Voice. She had delved into his mind and tangled it in a morass of compulsion. Perpetua couldn't imagine how to begin to undo the damage.

Perpetua had apologized to Briar more than once for bringing this to them, for putting them in such danger. But Briar, with a hollow voice and weary eyes, persisted it was not her fault. Perpetua hoped Briar knew it was not *her* fault either. The princess refused to leave Kinsley's side, even though he simply lay in his bed, awake and silent, staring sightlessly at the wall.

At least he was alive. Unlike Tory, who—by the time they'd all emerged from the wreckage of the yacht—had bled to death from the wounds Sohalia had inflicted. As for Sohalia herself, Briar was certain she had been killed in the explosion. Although they had searched for her body and found nothing, she had been too close to the blast, Briar said, to survive.

"Perpetua."

Perpetua glanced up, startled. She still stood outside the hospital, and there, climbing up the steps before her, was—

Demetri.

Perpetua felt her throat grow tight. She hadn't seen Demetri since—well, since Tatiana and Candelaria had attacked him. When she'd been forced to show him what she was.

"What, uh…" Demetri mounted the top step, and Perpetua shuffled back to give him some room. "What are you doing here? I mean…" He rubbed a hand over his chin.

"Just visiting Kinsley," she said stiffly. "And Briar."

"Right. Of course." He stuffed his hands into his pockets. "How is Kinsley?"

"The same."

"Right." Though he'd seemed distracted when he'd asked the question, his reaction was anything but. Perpetua saw the way his face fell.

Perpetua cleared her throat. "I've been back to Castel's house. I was hoping he could...but he wasn't there. Some of his things have been cleared out too. I think he's gone."

"Gone for good?" Demetri pursed his lips. "Well. He was supposed to meet Sohalia that afternoon, wasn't he? And she didn't seem surprised to learn he'd betrayed her. Maybe she...I mean, before she ambushed us on the yacht, maybe she..."

He didn't have to say it. Perpetua had considered the same possibility. Perhaps Sohalia had killed Castel before she'd gone to deal with Briar and her people. Then again, she considered it just as likely that Castel had run off in the wake of the disaster at the yacht. What did he care, Perpetua thought bitterly, if that left Kinsley without anyone who could help him?

"Well." Demetri sighed. "He may not have been able to do anything for Kinsley anyway."

"Yes."

The two of them stood in silence for a moment. Eyes evading, feet shuffling, hands fidgeting. Finally, Perpetua said, "You should go in. Briar said visiting hours end soon." She started down the steps, ducking her head. "Goodbye, Demetri."

She half-hoped he would call after her. But he didn't.

It was just as well. Being around Demetri was too difficult. Because despite everything that had happened, a tiny, traitorous part of her still yearned for him. For that old easiness between them. But, she reminded herself, deflating, even if they could get that back, there was no point. Even with Sohalia dead—perhaps *especially* with Sohalia dead—there was no point.

Sohalia and Castel had been her last hope of finding a way to live as a human, to live without taking another life. Or to be turned back into a naiad, though she wasn't sure she wanted that. She didn't know *what* she wanted, what she might have chosen. Perpetua was honest enough with herself to admit—somewhat shamefully—that her decision to die rather than feed was harder to face now she had little else to worry about. She had considered doing like Meliora had, feeding only on despicable humans, the worst criminals. But she wasn't sure if she could manage that, and she didn't know what kind of life it would be.

She wasn't sure it was a life she wanted.

Perpetua trudged down the street, turning southeast. It was misting lightly, rain so scarce it was more like humidity ghosting down from the clouds. Perpetua's loosely-belted dress grew damp, and by the time she reached her destination—that huge, pristine townhouse in the upper side of town—she was shivering.

Perpetua couldn't stay at LeBeau's any longer, not with the capital guard looking for her. But Castel was gone, so Perpetua had spent the last couple of nights here in his big house. Now, as she stepped inside, she shut the door and leaned back, squeezing her eyes shut. Then she straightened, pushing herself away from the door. Around her, the cavernous vestibule was awash in shadow, vast and empty. The marble colonnades stretched up towards the high ceiling. With sadness weighing her down—or maybe that was just exhaustion—she took a step up the winding staircase, leaning heavily into the balustrade.

Out of the corner of her eye, the shadows shifted.

Perpetua froze. Gripping the railing, she turned.

A figure emerged from the darkness, limping out of the curving corridor to the right. A tall, willowy figure—though hunched over—moving slowly with one hand pressed against the wall. Blood dripped from the figure with every lurching step, red droplets glistening over the tiled floor.

"Hello, Perpetua," Sohalia said. "Fancy meeting you here."

Quiet horror crawled up Perpetua's throat. She had known, some part of her had *known* the sea witch couldn't be killed that easily. Even still, she clutched at the balustrade, her knuckles pale and tense. It was debilitating to realize that, in spite of all the ways she had changed, in spite of everything she had been through, Perpetua's fear of Sohalia was as strong as ever. As strong as it had been the last time she'd faced her, that night on the stone pier, all those weeks ago.

"No," Perpetua whispered. "But you're—"

"Dead?" Sohalia let out a raspy laugh. "I came very close, Perpetua, but as you can see..." She gestured weakly.

Yes, Perpetua could see. The left side of Sohalia's face was scalded, the skin red and blistering. A bald patch marred her head where a clump of hair had burned away. Her left arm was burnt too, the scales charred and black. The blood that dripped onto the floor seeped from a glistering wound on her right side.

It was not so bad as the wound she had dealt Meliora, Perpetua thought with a shudder. Not so bad as the wound that had *killed* Meliora. Clenching her lips together, Perpetua asked, "And now you've come to kill me?"

Sohalia let out another terrible laugh. "Kill you? Perpetua, I had no idea you were here. I merely stopped by to pick up some supplies. Mine were all destroyed in the explosion."

Supplies. Supplies for witches, Perpetua supposed. "All his things are gone."

"Not quite." Sohalia leaned heavily into the wall. "He has more hidden in the kitchen. But if you don't mind, I think I will just...rest here a moment."

Perpetua looked at her, some of her fear leaking away. Some. She watched as Sohalia turned to face the wall, breathing shallowly.

"Where is Castel?" Perpetua asked. "Did you kill him?"

"Do you really care?" Sohalia's smile was more like a grimace. When Perpetua didn't answer, she said, "He's been dealt with."

Perpetua's stomach clenched. What did that mean? Was it still possible he could help her? Or had Sohalia really killed him?

"As for you..." Heaving in a rattling breath, Sohalia straightened, turning to face Perpetua. "I *was* very disappointed in you, Perpetua. Only days after I asked you to keep an eye on the princess, you left her company."

"I went back," Perpetua said shakily.

"Yes, I know. But by then, I had a much easier source of information."

Tory, Perpetua thought. Sohalia had used a level of compulsion on Tory that Perpetua could not imagine. Like what she'd done to Kinsley.

Sohalia was so powerful. How could any of them ever stop her?

"The truth is—" With a wince, Sohalia pushed herself off the wall. Perpetua watched with bated breath as the sea witch managed a step on her own. Then another. And another, coming closer to the staircase. Closer to Perpetua. "I don't want to kill you, Perpetua. You may look like a human, but at heart, you are still a naiad. And the last thing I want is to kill a fellow naiad."

Perpetua choked at that. "You killed Nadalia. And Meliora."

"Meliora…" Sohalia staggered, grasping at the balustrade. Perpetua clenched her teeth against a whimper, climbing further up the staircase. "Meliora…and Nadalia…wanted to stop me."

"Yes, they wanted to stop you." Perpetua tried for a defiant tone, but her voice sounded small in her ears. "From opening a door into this shadow world, from making a deal with those dangerous creatures—"

"From *saving* us all." Sohalia's knees buckled as she reached the stairwell, and she sank onto the first step. "I can still do it. And they wanted to get in the way of that."

Perpetua realized her jaw was hanging open and shut it quickly, her teeth clacking together. "That's why you're doing this? You're still trying to save the naiads?" She hadn't really believed that either. Even though Castel had thought so, it had been easier to believe Sohalia's goal was more nefarious.

But Sohalia peered up at her and said, "Of course. Saving our people, putting us right—that is all I have ever wanted. If I give the djinn what they want, they will help me. Help me change us back into what we once were."

Perpetua's mouth went dry. Sohalia couldn't see it. Even if her intentions were noble, she was still risking too much. Because what the djinn wanted was Briar. "There has to be another way. Another way to save us. One that doesn't involve these djinn and their shadow world—"

Sohalia said, "Oh, there is."

What? Perpetua was sure she must have heard wrong. "What are you talking about?"

"There is another way." Sohalia's voice was old, so old and tired. "The only problem is, it's impossible."

"What way?"

"The same way that got us into this mess. Bargaining with the gods."

Perpetua looked down at the sea witch, sitting about six stairs below her. "You don't mean that old story Meliora told me? About the naiad who found the ancient temple and asked for a boon? But that's just a legend..."

She trailed off, taking in Sohalia's face. The ironic little twist to her lips. The resentful look in her dark eyes.

"It's just a legend?" Perpetua whispered. "Isn't it? The sea gods, the temple—"

Sohalia made a quiet sound in the back of her throat. "That's what everyone always said. But, oh, if you knew me, Perpetua. When I was young. I told you, didn't I? That you remind me of myself. I was as foolish as you are. I was *idealistic*. I had such dreams. I believed."

And suddenly, Perpetua understood. The words were out of her mouth before she could consider how ridiculous they were, how impossible. "You were the young naiad. The one who found the temple and asked the sea gods to give us human-form."

Silence met this pronouncement. Perpetua waited for Sohalia to deny it. To laugh and tell Perpetua how silly she was. But the sea witch said nothing.

She didn't deny the tale.

"You..." Something surged inside Perpetua, a hot, blazing emotion. "You were the naiad who wouldn't give a drop of blood to appease the gods!"

"Oh, *really*," Sohalia snarled. "There are no gods, Perpetua. And it wasn't a drop of blood that was required of me. It was *lifeblood*. For my boon to be granted, I had to die."

Perpetua leaned back, feeling dizzy. "You had to *die?* But you didn't...and that's why the boon went wrong? But wait, if there are no gods, then how—"

"There are no gods," Sohalia repeated. "I believed there were. Just like I believed the pool and the ruins I found were the remains of some sacred temple. Well, perhaps they were. But they carried no power of their own. Rather, the power was all around me, leeched into the ground, the rock."

Perpetua listened to all of this and understood none of it. "You're not making sense."

Sohalia sighed. "I was foolish, Perpetua. I really was quite like you. We naiads lived in the sea, in fin-form, and we were happy, I suppose. But I wanted more. Not just for myself, but for all naiads. The sea was ours, but I thought—with a new form, a 'human-form'—we could walk the land too. Explore new territory. And I wanted that for us. I wanted to give that gift to my people."

Perpetua remembered, then, what Meliora had said about Sohalia. *I think she fancied herself a savior.* And Perpetua could see that. Sohalia wanted to give her people a "gift," but what she really wanted, Perpetua thought, was to be known as the one who'd given them that gift.

"Most of the other naiads thought it was silly, of course," Sohalia went on. "And when I decided to seek out the temple from the legend, no one took it seriously. After all, everyone knew that temple wasn't real, and even if it was, no one had ever found it. No one believed in me except for one naiad. My best friend, Damonica. When I set out to search for the temple, she came with me. And we found it. Together."

"And you made your boon? You asked for all naiads to be given human-form?"

"First, I bled." Sohalia tilted her head back to look at her. "I gave a drop of my blood into the pool. Yes, I did that much, Perpetua. And when I did, I was *transported*. Somewhere else. Everything went white, and I heard them. I heard *it*."

"Heard what? The sea gods?"

"That's what I thought at the time. Since I've become a witch, I know better. There are no sea gods, Perpetua. There is only nature. The primal forces that hold this land together. Something greater and more terrible than you can possibly imagine." A shudder ran through Sohalia, and when she spoke again, the faraway tone in her voice shifted, turning hard. "Whatever it was, that power—it said it would grant my boon. But I had to offer something in return. Lifeblood. It required a sacrifice. A soul."

A soul. Perpetua shivered. Castel had spoken of souls, but Perpetua didn't really understand what the word meant.

"Of course, I didn't want to die," Sohalia said frankly. "I wanted to enjoy our new form with the rest of the naiads. But that was all right, I thought. After all, I hadn't come to the temple alone. There was someone else who could die for my boon."

"Your friend. Damonica? She offered to be the sacrifice?"

"She didn't offer." A frown touched Sohalia's face. "I didn't bother to ask. Sometimes I wonder if I had—would that have made a difference? Would that have made it all right? Or did it have to be *me*, no matter what?"

Perpetua gazed down at her, puzzled. "You didn't ask? You mean..." Comprehension dawned slowly. It crept up her throat like a black mold, horrifying, suffocating, expanding. "You *killed* her? You didn't ask, didn't explain—you just took her life? Your best *friend?*"

"You sound so shocked. As though you wouldn't do the same. Are you thinking of your precious human boy, perhaps? Dear Demetri? You wouldn't sacrifice him for something you wanted so dearly?"

No. Of course she wouldn't. Perpetua felt sick at the thought. Sohalia should know better, she thought furiously. She, Perpetua, had already made that choice. The night of the shipwreck. And it had cost her everything. But—just like she'd told Briar—she didn't regret it. If she could go back and change it, she never would. She would *never* kill Demetri.

Meliora had been right about the sea witch. *She has always been self-serving.* It was clear that even before the change, Sohalia had never cared about anyone but herself. She'd wanted to give the gift of human-form to her people because she'd wanted the praise, the *gratitude*. And if she wanted to save the naiads now, it was for the same reason. Or because—as Castel had claimed—she was obsessed, insane. Unable to see her way through anything else.

Perpetua let out a long exhale. Slowly—still poised to run upstairs, if need be—she sank down onto her step. "So your boon went wrong because you sacrificed someone else? That's why we became monsters?"

"What I did wasn't a true sacrifice," Sohalia murmured. "I know that now. That's why I wonder, if I had just asked her, and she had been willing—perhaps that would have been enough."

"I don't understand."

"Of course you don't. And therein lies the root of the problem. That's why another boon cannot work." Sohalia smiled at her. "It took me a long time to figure it out. I told you before, when I became a witch, I learned things. Like what kind of forces govern this world. And the subtle intricacies that guard the laws of sacrifice."

She leaned back, her head lolling against the railing. "Asking for a boon to be granted requires a sacrifice. And the very nature of sacrifice requires a *willing soul*. It requires a comprehension of...of feeling, of love. Of the value of a stupid, single life. Do you imagine you comprehend all that, Perpetua? You don't. When I made you human, I didn't make you *human*. I told you that before. Perhaps you've felt new feelings these past few weeks. Perhaps you even care for that human boy. But love, Perpetua? Do you think you know what it is to love?"

Perpetua's chest felt tight again. No, she didn't imagine she understood love. Not for a second. She remembered asking Briar, so many weeks ago, how she knew she loved her prince, Garrett. And she remembered her frustration at Briar's answer: *I just do.*

She didn't understand any better now than she had then. Sohalia was right. It was beyond her comprehension.

"I didn't understand it myself," Sohalia said softly. "Because I was young and foolish. And now—thanks to my boon, thanks to what we've become—there is not a naiad alive who can understand it. Because we have no souls."

"I don't know." Perpetua's voice twisted with rancor. "You seem to understand it rather well."

"Well enough to explain it, perhaps. But that's not the kind of understanding I mean. I'm not talking about something you understand here." Sohalia tapped her scalded head with one, long finger. "I almost remember it. Feeling that way. I was young, but

I caught glimpses of that understanding. But now it is beyond me. Beyond all of us."

Perpetua cocked her head. "But it's not beyond the humans. Does it have to be a naiad who makes the boon? Couldn't a human do it for us, and then—"

Sohalia cut her off with a cruel laugh. "A human? Oh, Perpetua. You really don't understand, do you? The sacrifice must be made *willingly*. And what human would do that? What human would give their life for us?"

Demetri would, Perpetua thought. *Briar would*. Of course, she didn't want them to. She could never ask them to do that. The thought of either of them dying made her chest hurt.

"You really do remind me of myself," Sohalia mused. "I used to admire the humans, Perpetua. That's why I wanted human-form. I thought we could walk among them. Befriend them. But that's another thing I've learned. Humans are not worth befriending. They are faithless, contemptible, helpless creatures. Not one would give their life to help us."

She was wrong. So very wrong. But, Perpetua thought, with a sinking feeling, it didn't matter. She could never ask Briar or Demetri to sacrifice themselves. She leaned her forehead against the banister, the varnished wood cool against her skin.

It really was hopeless. For all the naiads. For herself. A chill, cold and dark, trickled down Perpetua, hardening around her heart. For the first time, she really felt it. Making it all real.

There was no hope for her. Either she would have to live like a murderer, feeding on humans. Or she would have to die. There was no other way.

No other way...except Sohalia's way. And that was no way at all. Was it?

"Why Briar?" Perpetua asked, so quietly, she wasn't sure Sohalia would hear her. She breathed the words into the banister. "Why does it have to be her? Why did those djinn ask for her?"

"Well, they didn't." When Perpetua snapped her head up, Sohalia clarified, "Not specifically. They want royal blood—blood from the original five royal families. So far as I know, Princess Briar is the only one alive who fits that requirement. The Glen line is a new line. The other lines have all died out or vanished. I think Briar has a cousin up in the Mountain Kingdom, but there's no time to get to her now." Groaning, Sohalia stood. "I chose Princess Briar because she was convenient."

Perpetua eyed the sea witch cannily. Sohalia leaned so heavily into the railing, it rattled beneath her weight. "And how do you plan to get Briar? Can you even take human-form right now?" Usually, such terrible damage as Sohalia had suffered would prevent such a thing.

"No, I cannot." One of Sohalia's grotesque smiles stretched across her face. "That's why *you're* going to bring her to me, Perpetua."

Perpetua felt as though her stomach had dropped out beneath her. "What? No, I won't—I would never—"

"Why not?" Sohalia looked madder than ever, a sinister glint in her dark blue eyes. "I've been thinking about it as we've been sitting here, chatting. *You* can bring her to me."

"She's my friend."

Sohalia laughed. "Oh, Perpetua. Is that what you think? You forget, I had that human soldier under my control. And she told me *everything*. Including why you ran off with Castel. Your human boy, he loves Briar, doesn't he? And so long as she's alive, he can never love you. Don't you see, if we hand her over to the djinn, that will solve all your problems. If the djinn can help me restore the naiads, then I'm sure they can make you human—*really* human. That's what they do; they grant wishes. And with Princess Briar gone, you can be with your human boy. With Demetri."

Perpetua stared down at her. She felt dizzy. The stairs seemed to sway. This was madness. Sohalia was mad, just like everyone said. And yet...the way she laid everything out, the way she explained it all...

It didn't sound so mad.

Except if Perpetua went along with her, she would have to betray Briar. Something she could never do. Could she?

"It's your only choice, Perpetua." The look in Sohalia's eye turned knowing. "You know it is. Bring Princess Briar to me, tomorrow, an hour before sundown. You can bring her to your old cave—that's close enough."

"Close enough to what?"

"The spot where Princess Briar found her elarium deposit." Sohalia's smile widened. "You didn't think I asked her to search for elarium for no reason, did you? The elarium will provide a good focal point for my spell. A spot rife with magic."

Perpetua shook her head. She didn't understand any of that. But she didn't need to. She wasn't going to bring Briar to Sohalia. Sohalia could wait for her out there. Sundown would come and go, and nothing would happen. The sea witch wouldn't be able to complete her spell.

That's all there was to it, Perpetua thought, but she trembled. She *wouldn't* betray Briar. Not even to save her own life.

She wouldn't.

She wouldn't.

25

SOLACE

DEMETRI TRAIPSED UP THE stairs in LeBeau's, longing and dreading to reach his room. Longing, because he was exhausted, and the thought of collapsing onto his bed sounded wonderful. Dreading, because he doubted he would be able to sleep no matter how tired he was. Just like last night, and the night before that, and the night before that. He would lie awake for hours. Alone with his thoughts.

He trumped up the last few steps and down the dim corridor. When he reached the door to his room, he stopped, fumbling for his key in his pocket, glancing aside—

He frowned. There was a figure at the end of the corridor. Someone sitting against the door to Briar's room. One of her guards? But Briar was still at the hospital; when he'd left earlier today, she'd said she would stay the night there. Demetri had assumed her guards would too. So who—

The figure shifted, turning their head into the light of the shaded gear-bulb fixture beside the door. And—to Demetri's amazement—he saw it was Perpetua.

Perpetua. Demetri stood frozen, fingers clutched around his key. The key to his room. But he didn't move, didn't turn to open his door. He just stared at Perpetua.

She hadn't seen him. She sat there, arms wrapped around her knees, hunching in on herself. She looked about as miserable as he felt. After he'd discovered she was a mermaid—no, a naiad—he hadn't seen her for days. He'd kind of thought he might never see her again. And now, here he was. Running into her twice in one day.

Before he could stop himself, he said, "Perpetua?"

Perpetua whipped her head up. "Demetri." She scrambled to her feet. "I didn't—I was looking for Briar. I know I shouldn't be here, but. I need to talk to her. I wanted to talk to her."

Her words washed over Demetri. She wore the same dress she'd been in earlier, a simple seaside dress of white muslin. It was free of lace or ruffles; there was only a pale rose ribbon, wrapped around her waist.

He was still so at odds with himself when it came to Perpetua. After having some time to think, he'd realized it wasn't so much *what* she was or what she'd done. Briar was right—it seemed the naiads did not have much choice over what they did. Having been through something similar with Briar and her people, he understood that. No, what really cut him was the lie. It hurt, feeling like he did not know her, thinking she had not trusted him enough to tell the truth. Of course, he had been hunting naiads most of the time he'd known her. Except for that first time he'd met her on the docks—

That first time they'd kissed.

A lump formed in Demetri's throat. Thinking of that hurt the most.

He realized he was still staring. "Erm. Briar. Right. Well, she's still at the hospital. When I left, she wasn't planning to come back tonight. Sabine said they would try to convince her to come get some rest, but. She didn't sound hopeful."

Perpetua nodded. Her face was drawn and ashen. Or perhaps that was just the dim lighting. And she was shaking, he realized. She stood with her arms folded tightly over her chest. Cold? he wondered, but that didn't make sense. It wasn't the least bit cold in the tavern; if anything, the narrow, airless corridor was too warm.

"Well." She evaded his gaze. "I'll just wait for her, then. I'll—I'll wait in the back stairwell. No one will see me there." She turned to go.

"Perpetua," he called. "Wait."

Perpetua halted, tensing. Without turning to look at him, she said, "Yes?"

Demetri hesitated. Some part of him wondered why he was doing this, why he didn't just let her go. That would be easier, surely. "Are you all right? You look..."

Now she turned, a strange expression on her face. "I'm fine."

"Right. Good." Demetri tapped his fingers against his chin. "It's just..."

"Yes?"

"There's, uh—there's something I wanted to ask you." And here it was. The question he'd been so afraid to ask. The answer he desperately needed.

Perpetua faced him head-on, still hugging herself. She looked eaten up by the shadows, standing just out of the light. "What is it?"

Demetri took a deep breath. "It's about the night we met. That night on the docks. I was wondering..." His voice wilted. "Were you still—I mean, had the sea witch cursed you yet?"

"No. I was still a naiad."

"So, you still had your—" He gestured towards his own throat.

"My Voice? Yes."

"And did you use it on me?"

Perpetua didn't answer right away. She stood there, silent and still. Then she took a slow step towards him, and another. As she passed into the light, Demetri saw the gray color in her cheeks had deepened into a dark flush.

"Ye-es," she confessed. "I made you answer my questions truthfully. About who you were. Looking back, I should have just *asked* you, but. I didn't know any other way then." Shaking her head even more frantically, she added, "I mean, that's no excuse, I didn't mean to—"

"What about when you told me to kiss you?" Demetri cut in.

Perpetua blinked. For a minute, the question hung between them. Demetri's heart quivered like a fish on a hook, waiting to discover its fate.

Then Perpetua said, "Oh. *No.* Demetri, no. I swear it. I didn't compel you to kiss me. I just asked."

Rather than relaxing, Demetri's chest tightened. "Why?"

"I'm not sure. I wanted to see if you would do it. On your own. I wanted..." Her eyes darted around him.

But as Demetri looked at her, his own uncertainty began to dissipate. Like a black cloud that had been hanging over him, drifting away. The quivering inside him was still there, but it felt different now. "I've been wondering. I was so afraid...but it was just me. I wanted to kiss you."

Perpetua jerked her head, looking startled by his reaction. For a long moment, they stood there, Perpetua unsure and expectant, Demetri mulling over everything she'd said, mulling over his own feelings.

Then he said, "You shouldn't wait in the stairwell. For Briar, I mean. I know it's not used much, but someone might see you. And with the capital guard still looking for you—"

"Oh. Right." Perpetua looked down at her feet. "Of course. I'll go, then."

"No," Demetri blurted out, and Perpetua looked startled again. "That is, what I meant was, you shouldn't wait out in the open." He rubbed a hand behind his neck. "None of Briar's guard are here either, but. You can wait in my room. If you like. That is, to see if she comes back tonight."

Perpetua looked like she needed a moment to process all this. Demetri didn't blame her; he was babbling like a fool. Weakly, he gestured towards his door. "So would you like to? Wait in my room?"

Perpetua didn't answer right away. Her expression was un-readable. Then—after a long moment—she nodded.

Expelling a silent breath, Demetri turned and unlocked his door.

As soon as the door shut behind them, Demetri began to regret asking her in. Not because he begrudged it of her—it really would be absurd for her to sit in the stairwell all night—but because it suddenly occurred to him that they would be in here, the two of them, *alone.*

And he had no idea what to say to her.

So he offered her a glass of wine, and when she accepted, he gratefully busied himself, setting his sack coat aside and pouring a cup for each of them. Perpetua sat in the wooden chair beside the table as she sipped her wine, while Demetri leaned against the weathered wardrobe and took a gulp of his, eying her over the rim of his cup. They were quiet for several minutes, and then Perpetua said,

"Are you sure it's all right? Me being here?" Her voice was soft and rough at the same time, her words tip-toeing over broken glass.

"It's fine." When Perpetua turned a skeptical eye on him, Demetri added, "Really. It's been quiet here. Briar and the guards have been at the hospital round the clock, and I've been, well..." He shrugged. "I haven't been sleeping much. I haven't had anything to do." He dared a glance at her. "There's been no one to talk to."

"And you hate that," she murmured into her cup. The words were said absently, yet for some reason, they sent a rush of warmth into Demetri. That she knew him so well. That here was someone who knew him so well.

"Yes," he said. It seemed such an inadequate response.

They sat in silence for a moment. Then, without looking at him, Perpetua said, "That wasn't the first time we met, you know."

"Er—what?"

"That night on the docks. When I kissed you." Her face was oddly guarded. "I thought Briar would have told you. That was the second time we met. The first time was the night of the shipwreck." She hesitated. "I saved you. I brought you back to shore."

Demetri stared at her. *The night of the shipwreck...*

Of course. It finally made sense. How he'd survived, how he'd ended up at that pier. He should have realized before now, he should have thought to ask—as much as he had gone over everything in his head, these past few days...

"To be perfectly honest, I was there to feed." The words tumbled from her. "I can't pretend I set out to save you, or anyone. But when I saw you, I couldn't do it. I couldn't kill you. I don't know why. There was just something about you. It was the weirdest feeling. I looked at you, and it was like—like I knew you already. Like we'd met before, or—" She shook her head. "I still don't understand it. But I saved you. I swam that little boat back to shore, and...well, you know the rest."

There was just something about you. Like I knew you already. Demetri felt his throat grow tight. Hadn't he always felt that way about Perpetua? How easily he had connected with her—how she had just seemed to fit, like she was meant to be there. Meant to be in his life.

He watched her now, taking in the tentative way she sipped at her wine. The way she balled her hand in her lap, the way her large dark eyes wandered around the room. And Demetri realized—with another quiver in his chest—that she was still the same person he had always known.

Briar was right. It hadn't all been a lie.

She was same girl he'd kissed on the docks. The same girl he'd sat beside in the carriage on the way to the ball. The same girl he'd taken in when she had nowhere to go. The same girl who'd galloped fearlessly the first day she rode a horse. The same girl who had cried when she'd heard the music at the symphony.

The same girl who had saved his life before she'd even known his name.

He hadn't realized, until now, that he'd felt like he lost her. But now he had her back.

Or maybe she had never gone anywhere to begin with.

"Well," he said. "Thank you."

She made a rueful sound. "You don't have to thank me. Not after everything—"

"But I want to. So. Thank you."

Perpetua gave an awkward nod.

Demetri took another long drink from his wine. "So what did you want to talk to Briar about?"

"Oh." Perpetua shot him a glance beneath her lashes. It was an oddly fragile glance. "It was nothing, really."

"Just wanted to check on her?"

"Yes," Perpetua said, but when she raised her cup to her lips, Demetri noticed she was shaking again. So much that she had to grip the cup with both hands to keep her wine from sloshing over.

"Are you sure you're all right?" Demetri set his cup aside and crossed the room to her. "You don't look well. I mean—you look tired."

The timorous look on her face made his heart twist. "You're the one who hasn't been sleeping. Didn't you say that?"

"Yes, well..." Demetri rubbed a hand over his forehead. "I'm not really an example to live by. Where have you been staying? Somewhere with a proper bed, I hope." *Somewhere with a proper roof,* he thought uneasily. Stones, he hoped she hadn't been sleeping outside somewhere.

"What does it matter?"

"Well, perhaps you need a good night's rest and—"

"No," she interrupted. "I mean, why do you care?"

Demetri paused. The question was more than fair. And she hadn't said it with any hostility or bitterness. She just looked at him with such *openness.* With such a real desire to understand him.

Demetri swallowed. It was such a characteristic look from her. A look he had come to know well.

"I care," he said raggedly," because I care."

Perpetua frowned.

"About you, I mean," he clarified.

The open look on Perpetua's face shifted, darkening. Turning to doubt.

"Perpetua." Demetri crouched before her, taking her hands in his. From this angle, the muted light of the gear-bulb lamp cast its glow over her face, bathing her in its warmth. "I'm sorry."

"You haven't done anything to be sorry for." Perpetua tugged at her hands in his, but halfheartedly.

"I'm sorry I didn't tell you before now," he said, "but it doesn't matter to me, Perpetua. It's taken me some time to work it out. But now that you're here, it feels so obvious. It doesn't matter what you are, mermaid or naiad or whatever. It doesn't matter what your life was before."

Perpetua's eyes glimmered. "Even if I was a monster?"

Demetri shrugged. "Briar was a monster too. Perhaps I have a thing for monsters." When Perpetua didn't smile, he added, "Perpetua. You *aren't* a monster. Not in the way you mean."

Perpetua took in a shaky breath. Demetri realized her eyes glimmered because they were filled with tears.

"I've spent a lot of time with you this summer," he told her, "and one thing I know for sure is this: You live better, care better—*love* better—than any human I've ever known."

"No, I don't." Perpetua's words were tenuous with tears. "I don't even know what love is."

Demetri let out a low laugh. "No one does. That's why it's so tortuous." He squeezed her hands. "I know this, Perpetua. Monster or not, you are worthy of being loved. And I think one day...when I'm a little more whole—" His voice knotted in his throat. "I think I could love you. And if that's not enough, I understand, Perpetua. But I don't want to lose you. No matter what."

Perpetua gently tugged one of her hands from his, but she didn't pull away. She simply rested her palm against the curve of his chin. Demetri leaned into her touch.

"It is enough." A tear spilled down her cheeks. "And I don't want to lose you either. No matter what."

"All right." Demetri rubbed his thumb over the damp track on her jaw. "Why are you crying?"

"I can't help it." Perpetua sounded so genuinely frustrated. "It keeps happening. You humans cry over everything."

"I suppose we do," Demetri murmured. Then he leaned in and kissed her.

When he'd kissed her before, he'd been hesitant. Some part of him beating a warning in his head, fearing her, fearing what she could mean to him. But this time, he didn't hesitate. He kissed her deeply, as though he could fall right into her.

And Perpetua did not retreat. She kissed him just as searingly, her body arcing into him. Wrapping his arms around her, Demetri stood, pulling her flush against him. He kissed her until he felt dizzy, until his breath faltered in his chest, until he staggered. Kissing her was more intoxicating than any wine. Then he realized he actually *was* staggering, stumbling back until his legs hit the bed.

Perpetua clutched at him as he fell back, pulling her down onto the bed. One of her hands raked through his hair, her fingers sweeping along the nape of his neck, and he shivered. They curled around each other, and as Demetri trailed his lips along Perpetua's jaw, a puff of air escaped her, the breath ghosting over his neck.

It wasn't until Demetri had his hand inside the collar of her dress, caressing her bare shoulder—it wasn't until Perpetua had all the buttons of his waistcoat undone—that he came to his senses. "Erm." He gently untangled himself from her, falling back on the bed. "We should probably stop. Not because I *want* to stop, it's just—"

Perpetua rolled onto her side to look at him, pillowing her head against her arm. Her eyes were huge and beautiful and darker than ever, gleaming like stars in a black night sky. She didn't look hurt by his words. A little crease formed between her eyes, and she said, "Because it's not proper?"

"Well." Demetri gave a self-conscious cough, then reached out to smooth Perpetua's hair back from her face. "I mean, I know I said that was all a load of hogwash, but—"

"No." Perpetua sighed regretfully and sat up, kneeling before him. "You're right." A frown tugged at her lips. "But I don't want to leave."

"You don't have to." Demetri pushed himself upright, running his hands over his tousled hair. "We can still talk. And you haven't finished your wine—although maybe that's not the best—"

"Is that a violin?" Perpetua pointed into the corner.

"Oh. Yes." Demetri turned to look. The violin case was a dark burgundy, and at the sight of it, his chest gave a complicated tug. Longing knotted with hesitation. Pleasure bleeding into grief. "My friend Emile recently inherited it from his uncle. But he doesn't play, and he knew I did, so he was kind enough to give it to me."

"You play?" Perpetua asked, a breathless catch in her voice.

"Well. Yes. Though it's been a while." *Eighty-two years.*

Perpetua's gaze latched onto him. Weirdly, Demetri saw his own mess of emotions reflected in her eyes.

"Could you play for me?" she asked.

In that moment, Demetri could not have said no to her for all the world.

So he played. And at first, his fingers felt stiff, and the bow seemed to scratch against the strings, but he played and played, and soon his fingers loosened up, and the bow remembered its way. And Perpetua listened, and they drank their wine, and they kissed again, and Demetri played some more. And then—when it grew very late, or perhaps very early—Perpetua curled up on his bed and closed her eyes, and Demetri sat beside her, propped against the headboard, and he played into the night, the violin's song weaving a thread between them, with one end corded around his heart, and the other around hers.

26

INDEBTED

PERPETUA WOKE SLOWLY. LASSITUDE dragged at her eyelids, urging her back to sleep. To sink into lovely dreams of pale-green grass, a gentle breeze soughing through her hair, warm hands on her skin and soft lips pressing kisses into her neck—

Dreams of Demetri.

Perpetua opened her eyes. She found her face half-buried in a lumpy pillow, facing a wall of wooden slats. She was in Demetri's room. She had fallen asleep to the lulling sound of his violin. Rolling onto her back, she glanced aside, expecting to find him asleep next to her, or perhaps on the floor like the last time she'd stayed here.

Instead, he was nowhere. Demetri was gone.

Perpetua bolted upright, but almost as quickly, she relaxed. She didn't know how long she'd been asleep, but it felt like hours. If it was morning, perhaps Demetri had gone down to the common room for breakfast.

Morning. The morning of the solstice.

A sick feeling fluttered in Perpetua's chest before she could remember why. Then she did remember, and the panic intensified, twisting her stomach in knots.

Sohalia. Sohalia was still alive.

And she wanted Perpetua to bring Briar to her. To trade her to the djinn.

Perpetua knocked her head back into the metal bedframe, sagging. She reached for those pleasant feelings she'd woken with but couldn't find them. They were just dreams now, fading away. Last night, with Demetri—that may as well have been a dream too.

She had lost any hope that Demetri would forgive her, that he could look past what she was. So to see him again—for him to invite her to stay, to kneel before her and tell her that one day, he could love her—to kiss her again—

Yes, it had felt like a dream. A dream that was too good to be true. Because she had known, even then, that no good could come of renewing their friendship. Even if that was all it was.

She had no future.

Perpetua let out a long sigh, hugging her arms across herself. After she'd left Sohalia last night, when she'd come here to LeBeau's...sea gods, what had she been thinking? She didn't know, she didn't *know* what she'd been thinking, and that was terrifying. She'd come to see Briar, but she truly didn't know, even now, if she'd come to tell the princess that Sohalia was still alive, or—

Or if she'd come to do as Sohalia had asked. Lure Briar away from the tavern. Bring her to Sohalia.

It was madness. She could see that now. It was a good thing, really, that she'd run into Demetri. She didn't know if it was being with him or just getting a good night's sleep, but either way, she could see it now. Had she *really* been considering going through with Sohalia's plan? Yes. Yes, she had.

Shame burned through her. Sitting there with Sohalia, in the darkness of Castel's house, she had allowed fear to take hold of her. Fear of the sea witch, fear of the fate that awaited her. She had allowed herself to get swept up in Sohalia's insanity.

But now, in the light of the new day, she could see that that's what it was: insanity.

There was no way she could help Sohalia.

There was no way she could risk so much by helping her trade with these djinn.

There was no way she could betray a friend. And Briar was her friend.

She wondered if Briar had ever returned from the hospital last night. Stiffly, Perpetua climbed out of bed. Leaving her shoes behind—sprawled at the foot of the bed, where she'd kicked them off—she left the room.

She padded down the corridor, barefoot and silent. When she reached Briar's room, she raised a hand to knock but paused. She didn't want to wake Briar if she was sleeping. So she turned her head aside, straining to hear anything in the room. Any voices, any movement.

She heard nothing.

But she *saw* something. Movement at the end of the corridor. At the top of the back stairs.

A flash of color. A flash of *red.*

Instinct made Perpetua go stock-still, breath freezing in her chest. She stood like that for a moment, then wheeled around silently. Holding her breath, she crept down the corridor, her steps so sinuous and slow, the wooden floor didn't emit a single *creak*.

She stopped just short of the stairs. Long enough for a crimson haze to fall over her vision. Long enough for her fingers to elongate into claws.

Then she spun, whipping an arm out and wrapping her fingers around the neck of the naiad hiding in the staircase. She hauled the naiad out, pinning her against the wall.

"Candelaria," Perpetua said evenly. "What are you doing here?"

Candelaria bared her shark-like teeth.

Perpetua tightened her grip. "Well?"

But Candelaria surprised her. She snapped her leg up and delivered a solid kick to Perpetua's middle, sending her reeling. Perpetua choked on a gasp and stumbled, barely catching herself before she could tumble down the stairs. She blinked rapidly, clearing out the spots encroaching on her vision, and as she caught her breath, she growled, preparing to lunge at Candelaria.

But Candelaria held her hands up, fingers splayed, poised halfway between a fighting stance and a pose of surrender. "Don't make me kill you," the naiad hissed. Her golden hair straggled around her face. "I could do it easily. Looking the way you do."

"The way I do?" Perpetua said evenly. "And how is that?"

Candelaria jerked her chin. "Like a shriveled shrimp. Like you haven't fed all summer."

Perpetua clenched her hands into fists. Well. That was true enough. *Could* Candelaria take her down so easily? Probably. Perpetua was starting to feel the hunger now. In waves of weakness that came out of nowhere, making her dizzy and tired. In sudden pangs that stabbed and lingered, gnawing on her insides.

Still. She wasn't going to let her guard down. "Tell me what you're doing here."

"Why should I tell you anything?"

"Maybe because you're alive because of me," Perpetua snapped. "You could be dead right now, like Tatiana. With a bullet in your chest."

Candelaria let out a trill of laughter. She relaxed, dropping her hands and straightening out of her predatory crouch. "Because of *you?* I'm alive because of your pet human. He's the one who let me go."

"I'm surprised to hear you admit that."

"It's the truth. Unfortunately."

"Unfortunately?"

Candelaria bared her teeth again, and Perpetua tensed. But the golden-haired naiad snarled, "I will *not* live in the debt of a human, Perpetua. That is beneath me. I—" She grimaced. "I have been staying close to him. Watching him. Waiting to see if I can repay him somehow."

"*Repay him?*"

"Save his life, perhaps." Candelaria waved a hand. "Anything. Just so I do not have to go around with this debt hanging over my head. A debt to a *human.*"

Perpetua goggled. She shouldn't be so surprised, she supposed. Gratitude was foreign to a naiad, but a debt wasn't. That was a matter of pride, not gratitude. Still, she didn't think most naiads would extend the concept to a human. Then again, most naiads weren't as prideful as Candelaria.

"Well." Perpetua rubbed a hand over one eye. "Go downstairs, then. You can watch him eat breakfast. Maybe he'll choke on a piece of melon and you can save him."

Candelaria cocked her head. "He's not downstairs. He left…oh, just a little while ago."

"What? To go where?" Perpetua tried to keep the alarmed note out of her voice.

"How should I know where he went? He's *your* pet human." Candelaria ran her fingers over a strand of her hair, the gesture sulky.

"His name is Demetri. And I thought you were staying close to him!"

"Yes, well, as much as I want to repay my debt, I'm not going to risk my *life* for him. And he left with that man, that witch. The one you were living with. And by the look of it, he didn't want to go anywhere with him, so. Intervening would have meant pitting myself against a witch. I'm not an idiot."

Perpetua struggled to parse all this out. "He left with the man I was living with?" That could only mean— "*Castel?* Demetri left with Castel?" She thought Castel was dead. Sohalia said he'd been dealt with. "Wait. And you're saying Demetri didn't *want* to leave with Castel? Then why would he?"

Candelaria gave her an impatient look. "I don't think he had much choice. The witch had a tight hold on him, marching him down these steps and out onto the street. No doubt he was using some kind of magic. *I* don't know. I don't understand much about human interactions, Perpetua, but I know predator and prey when I see them. The witch was the predator. Your human toy was the prey. That much was clear." She waved another hand. "Oh, and he—the witch—said something like, 'I don't want to have to come back here and hurt Perpetua, but I will.' Some kind of threat like that."

Perpetua felt like there were spiders crawling up her spine. "But why?" she asked, dismayed. Speaking more to herself than to Candelaria. "I thought Castel was *dead*. Why would he come here, why would he take Demetri..."

"He said he was under orders," Candelaria said idly. "The witch? The one you call Castel. He said he had no choice but to her follow 'her' orders."

Her orders.

Sohalia. Of course.

Perpetua reached out, taking Candelaria's arm in a bruising grip. The naiad winced and protested, but Perpetua ignored her, shaking Candelaria until she looked her in the eye. "Candelaria. Tell me everything you saw. Everything you heard."

"I already have."

"Are you sure?"

Candelaria rolled her eyes heavenward. "The witch said something else about you. Something like...that the sea witch knew you would never go through with it, and 'any royal blood will do.'"

Perpetua caught her breath. *Any royal blood will do.* "No." When Sohalia had mentioned the royal bloodlines yesterday, she hadn't mentioned Demetri. Perpetua had assumed Sohalia didn't know he was a prince, or that he wasn't an option. She didn't really know what was meant by "original royal family." But if Demetri belonged to one of those families, if he had the kind of blood these djinn wanted...

And Sohalia had known Perpetua wasn't going to bring Briar. Perhaps she had realized that after Perpetua left. Or perhaps she had only ever suggested it to throw Perpetua off. There was no telling.

Perpetua bit her tongue, trying to shove down the panic rising inside her. But it filled her lungs, pushing out all the air until she felt like she couldn't breathe.

Demetri. She had to get him back. She had to save him.

There was only one thing she could do, only one thing she could think of.

She needed Briar.

27

ALLIED

"**B**RIAR. BRIAR, WAKE UP."

Briar couldn't suppress a moan as she came awake. It felt like she'd only put her head down a few minutes ago. She'd stayed at the hospital until midnight. That was when Sabine and Gallia had dragged her out, assuring her Kinsley would be fine with Aden and Alec for the rest of the night.

If Briar was honest with herself, she'd been too tired to argue. So she'd allowed her two guards to lead her back to the tavern and up to her room, where she'd fallen face-first onto her bed and gone straight to sleep.

A few minutes ago. Surely it had only been a few minutes ago. "What?" she grumbled, spitting hair from her mouth and rolling onto her back. She blinked groggily at the two, hazy figures leaning over her, expecting Sabine and Gallia.

The figures came into focus. And they were not Sabine and Gallia.

They were Perpetua. And a naiad.

One of the naiads who had tried to kill her.

Briar shot up straight. Too quickly. Her head banged into one of the metal bars on her headboard, and she sucked in a breath, wincing. "What, by the Gift—" Touching her head gingerly, she scooted back, looking from the golden-haired naiad to Perpetua. "Perpetua? What is going on? What is *she* doing here? And how did you even get in here?"

"I broke down the door," the golden-haired naiad said.

"Sorry," Perpetua added. "Not just for the door, but for waking you like this. Candelaria—" She glared at the naiad beside her "—isn't going to hurt you. I promise. But there's a lot to explain, and not a lot of time to do it, so...I'm sorry. All right?"

Briar scrubbed her hands over her eyes, then tugged a hand through her mussed hair. "Uh. All right. I suppose." She blinked at the golden-haired naiad, who wasn't wearing her scrappy little dress this time. No, she stood here—in Briar's bedroom—decked out in full *naiad*, blood-red scales covering her body, all the way up her torso and creeping over one shoulder and arm.

"Briar, listen," Perpetua said. "Demetri is in danger. I think Sohalia has him."

That caught Briar's attention. Shock zapped through her like a bolt of lightning, burning away the last of the sleep tugging at her. She focused on Perpetua. "What are you talking about? Sohalia is *dead*, the explosion—"

"—burned her badly, but she's still alive," Perpetua cut in. "I saw her, Briar. Yesterday. I *spoke* to her. She's weak and injured, but very much alive. Last night," she barreled on, forestalling Briar as she opened her mouth to interrupt, "I was here with Demetri. But when I woke up, he was gone. Candelaria here—"

She looked at the red-scaled naiad "—has been stalking Demetri for reasons too bizarre to explain right now. But she saw him leave." She jerked her head at Candelaria. "Tell her what you told me."

As the naiad repeated everything she'd seen and heard, Briar listened, trying to remain calm. So far, her confusion was outweighing her fear for Demetri, but she could feel that too. Lurking beneath the surface. Perpetua was not so calm, tugging anxiously at her hair while Candelaria spoke. When the naiad got to the part about *why* she took Demetri—instead of Briar—Briar went cold inside. *Any royal blood will do.*

"No," she breathed. "That's not—but of course. *Why* didn't I think of that?" Wasn't that what Dev, the djinn who'd used her, told her all those months ago? It was fairies who had sealed the djinn away, confining them to their shadow world. The fairies had used their own blood to do it, and so fairy blood was the key to freeing the djinn. The original five royal families had been gifted fairy blood, and they carried it in their bloodlines to this day.

If Sohalia needed someone descended from an original royal line to trade to the djinn, she had precious few options. Briar was one of those few.

And so was Demetri.

Heart thudding in her chest, Briar looked up at Perpetua. Judging by the devastation on Perpetua's face, she knew exactly what Briar was thinking.

"She told me yesterday," Perpetua whispered. "When I saw her. But I never thought—she said you were the only one. I didn't realize *he* was. Otherwise I would have warned him." Perpetua's voice turned shakier with every word; Briar could tell she was on the verge of tears. "But I didn't, I didn't even tell him Sohalia was alive. I didn't think it mattered. I didn't know she had Castel to help her."

"All right." Waving an impatient hand at Candelaria—who still loomed at her bedside—Briar swung her legs over her bed, standing. "Perpetua, listen. It's not your fault. We're going to get him back."

"Look at you." Candelaria eyed Perpetua in disgust. "Blubbering like a human. It's pathetic."

"If you don't shut up, I'm going to make *you* blubber," Briar snapped. "Now just—"

The door to her bedroom opened wide, banging off the wall. Briar jumped, spinning around, but it was only Sabine, Gallia, and Alec, bursting into the room with pistols raised. They didn't drop them, and it was a second before Briar realized it was because Candelaria was there.

"It's all right," she told them. "She's not going to hurt anyone. You can put your guns down."

Sabine eyed the naiad. "She might have made you say that."

"Well...she didn't," Briar said lamely.

"She might have made you say that too."

Candelaria snarled. "I can stand here in silence for the next several minutes and prove I haven't used my Voice. But in the meantime, the he-witch is getting further away with *Demetri*, and since we only have until noon to retrieve him, I would think you would not want to waste time."

"*Who* has Demetri?" Sabine asked, but Briar turned to Perpetua.

"We have until noon?" she asked. Trying to hold her fear at bay.

Perpetua nodded miserably. "She told me sundown. But that must have been a lie. Candelaria heard Castel say the spell would take place at noon." She pinched at her eyes with her thumb and forefinger. "I know where they're going though. I guess it could have been another lie, but—I don't know where else she might be."

"Then that's where we'll go." Briar turned back to her guards, frowning. "Alec, what are you doing here? I thought you were at the hospital with Kinsley."

Alec had lowered his pistol, but he licked his lips, still eyeing Candelaria. "Aden's there. But that man from the capital guard turned up—Captain Gage. He said something terrible is going down at the submarine site. That's why I came to get you. But..."

Briar felt a sinking in her stomach. "What are you talking about?"

"Apparently, some of the counts went down there early this morning to make an inspection. Looking to see what would need to be dismantled, now you're not working there anymore. But Captain Gage said something attacked them. Something *not human*. He didn't seem to know how to describe it. He said it moved fast, and the people it attacked..." Alec looked a little green. "He said it was bad. Very bad."

Briar swore. She began to pull on her boots and harness vest. Once she was done, she left the room, heading down the back stairwell. Everyone followed in her wake, silent. She trotted down the stairs, taking them two at a time, and by the time she emerged at the bottom, stepping outside into the morning sunlight, she realized what she would have to do.

And she hated it.

She turned to face the five people behind her.

"If there are people being attacked at the submarine," Briar said heavily, "then I can't just leave them to die. We have to stop these not-human attackers, whatever they are. Some of us, anyway."

She met Perpetua's gaze, afraid of what she might see there. But there was no recrimination in Perpetua's eyes. Only a stubborn look. "I'm going after Demetri."

"Of course." There was no question of that. "Sabine, I want you to go with her. And Candelaria—"

"I don't take orders from you," Candelaria snarled, "and I am *not* going anywhere near the sea witch. Unlike Perpetua, I don't have a death wish."

Briar bit back an impatient snarl of her own. "You don't even know what kind of monsters we'll be dealing with at the submarine."

Candelaria shivered. "Anything is better than the sea witch."

"Fine. You come to the submarine. Gallia, you'll go with Sabine and Perpetua." Briar took in a deep breath.

"You're not coming with me, are you?" Perpetua asked.

"I can't." Much as she wanted to. It would be so easy. Briar didn't know who was at the submarine site, she didn't care about anyone there. Not personally. Not like she cared about Demetri. But— "No one knows the submarine like I do. If those monsters get into the vessel, I have the best chance of tracking them down and stopping them. We don't know what they are, but..." She shrugged. "Hopefully, I'll be a match for them."

"It's all right. I understand." Perpetua looked at Briar a moment longer, then took her hand and squeezed it. "Just be careful. Do what you have to."

Gratefully, Briar squeezed her hand back. "You too. On both counts."

⎯⎯◆⎯⎯

When they reached the submarine site, they found the remnants of a massacre. Even from outside the barbed wire enclosure, Briar could see something was very wrong. The beach was silent and still, but not empty. The large pavilion in the center had collapsed, and other were strewn all over the place. And not only supplies. Briar spotted dark lumps spotting the sandy ground.

Once inside the enclosure, the picture got worse. Blood spattered the sand like some bizarre art display. The dark lumps Briar had glimpsed were bodies. All still. All dead. And not just dead, but...

Briar peered at one of the bodies. Judging by what was left of the sage-green uniform, it was a capital guardsmen. His chest was caved open, as though some savage autopsy had been performed on him. The other corpses were gruesomely identical, bodies split apart, spines torn asunder through their ribcages.

"What did it?" Alec had a pistol drawn as he turned left and right. "And where is it now?"

"In there." Candelaria pointed a webbed finger.

Briar and Alec turned to look. She was pointing at the submarine, docked in the bay. From here, Briar could see the submarine's tower, the long, cylindrical entrance down into the vessel. Its round door stood open, and the steel rim was stained with blood.

"Good guess," Briar muttered. "Come on."

They moved down the length of the wobbling gangplank, then clambered over the topside of the submarine. Briar took the lead, climbing up the rungs in the tower. At the top, she paused, staring down into the submarine. Darkness stared back at her, a silent abyss.

She glanced over her shoulder at Alec and Candelaria. Then she jumped, straight down the tower, into the submarine.

Her boots hit the floor with a ringing *thud*. Briar stilled, listening, but she heard nothing. As Alec descended the tower more slowly, using the ladder built into the interior, Briar turned in a circle, her gaze sweeping the shadows. The submarine should have been lit by gear bulbs strapped to the walls, but they were all out. The only light was the cloudy daylight beaming down through the open tower.

Alec reached the bottom, joining her. He fiddled with a small, handheld lantern, an invention he and Briar had devised together. As he wound it up, Candelaria leapt down just as Briar had. She hit the floor more quietly than Briar, her webbed feet making no noise as she landed in a crouch. When she straightened, raising her head, Briar saw her eyes had gone scarlet.

Briar clenched her hands into fists. It was hard not to flash back to the night of the boat party, when this very creature had attacked her. She found herself waiting with bated breath, watching the naiad. Waiting for her to attack.

But she didn't. Candelaria only bared her teeth and snapped, "What?"

"Nothing," Briar said quickly. She cast around for something to fill the awkward moment. "Er—are there no male naiads? I haven't seen any."

"No," Candelaria scoffed. "No males."

Briar frowned. "But then, how do you—I mean..." She trailed off, waiting for the naiad to infer her meaning. When Candelaria only stared at her, she added, "...procreate?"

Candelaria gave a haughty toss of her head. "We mate with human males. Then we eat them."

"Oh." Briar coughed in an attempt to hide her urge to gag. "That's very...efficient."

If Briar was not mistaken, Candelaria actually looked pleased by this assessment. But when the naiad stepped past her, Briar exchanged a look of panicked horror with Alec.

"Something smells strange in here." Candelaria lifted her head. Her features, already distorted by the fangs protruding from her mouth, wrinkled further.

"Strange how?" Briar supposed quite a few things in a submarine might smell strange to a naiad.

Candelaria met Briar's gaze. "Like death."

"Right." Briar turned to Alec, but he was still fiddling with the lantern, looking frustrated. It was only a prototype and still a bit faulty. The light it emitted was bright white like any gear bulb, but its glow was narrow and limited, barely encompassing the three of them.

"It'll have to do." Alec flipped the light between Briar and Candelaria. "So? Any idea which way to go?"

Before they could answer, a loud *clanking* sound echoed down the corridor stretching before them. This was followed by a long, thin scream that ended abruptly, leaving them in ominous silence.

"Well," Briar said, "I'm guessing we should follow the screams."

They started down the corridor with Candelaria in the lead. They heard no more screams, but when they reached a fork at the end of the first corridor, Candelaria lifted her head and closed her eyes, scenting the air. Then she nodded, turning right.

Briar glanced at Alec. He crept beside her with his pistol raised, held steady with both hands. Briar had taken the small lantern so he could do so, even though he needed the light more than she did. He caught her glance and offered a tight smile. "Aden will be disappointed he missed this."

Briar smiled back. She very much doubted that. Alec was probably glad his brother was safe back at the hospital. For her part, Briar was trying very hard to focus on the task at hand, but her mind kept wandering to the others. She hated that she couldn't go to save Demetri. "I hope Perpetua is all right. I hope she can manage with Sabine and Gallia."

Up ahead, Candelaria made a disparaging sound. "What does it matter?"

"Excuse me?"

"Ah, I suppose you are concerned for your *friend*. Demetri." Candelaria shook her head. "I always forget how importantly you humans regard each other."

"Yes, we're weird like that," Briar said dryly. "Anyway, it's not just Demetri I'm worried about. I'm worried about Perpetua too." *And Sabine. And Gallia.*

Now Candelaria let out a derisive laugh. "Why?"

"Because she's my friend," Briar snapped. "I don't want anything to happen to her."

Candelaria flicked a glance over her shoulder. They were nearing another fork in their path, and there, the gear bulbs lining the corridor were still on, though very dim. As though they were burning out. But the low lighting helped illuminate Candelaria's scornful expression as she said, "I repeat, what does it matter? She will be dead soon anyway."

These words hit Briar like a punch in the throat. "What? What are you talking about?"

"It's easy to see." Candelaria's tone was dismissive. "She is starving. Wasting away. Her human body must be killing her."

It had been a long week. Most of which Briar had spent cooped up in a tiny hospital room, sitting at Kinsley's bedside, feeling helpless. And now she was here, in her submarine, creeping in the darkness, primed for an attack from some unknown entity. Perhaps that was why, as Candelaria casually spoke of Perpetua dying, Briar lost her temper. Before she knew what she was doing, she grabbed Candelaria by the arm and wrenched her around, so hard she could have dislocated the naiad's shoulder.

Candelaria hissed in pain, but Briar didn't care. She shoved Candelaria up against the wall and glared, heedless of the naiad's shark-like teeth, inches from her face.

"Explain," Briar growled. "What do you *mean*, Perpetua is starving?"

Candelaria bared her teeth, stretching her jaw wide. "Naiads must feed on humans. To go without a human meal will eventually mean a slow, painful death. Perpetua may walk around like a human now, but I know what a starving naiad looks like. If she doesn't feed soon, it will get bad for her. Very quickly."

Briar processed these words rapidly. As though her brain was working on automatic gears, she flashed back to something Perpetua had said.

I don't do it anymore. Killing humans. Even if—I won't.

Even if. *Even if.* Briar stared at Candelaria without really seeing her. She had thought Perpetua was going to say, *even if I become a naiad again.* But that wasn't it at all. The sea witch stuck Perpetua in human-form, but she must have left her with a need for human sustenance. Perpetua still needed to feed on humans to survive.

But she wasn't. She wasn't going to.

Even if it killed her.

"No," Briar muttered. "She can't—that can't—"

Candelaria gave her a shove. Briar, startled, lost her grip and stumbled back. The naiad snarled, threatening, but Briar faced her down. "I can break both your arms this time, if you like."

"Sorry to interrupt." Alec's voice was small and timid, very unlike him. "But I think there's something down there."

Briar turned, then followed his line of sight. He was staring down another narrow corridor, branching off to the left.

Briar knew the submarine well; even in the dark, she could place their whereabouts. That narrow corridor was a maintenance shaft; it ended abruptly about twenty paces down. With the gear bulbs out, the shaft was pitch-black, the darkness so absolute, even Briar's keen eyes couldn't pierce it. Though the submarine was not submerged, there were no windows here, nothing to let in a little light.

"Something moved." Alec's voice was hushed. "Like a shadow."

Briar still clutched the lantern. She raised her arm, extending the light towards the dark corridor. The tiny white glare didn't illuminate much. Briar swept her arm left to right, but the light was just too small to show anything more than a few feet down the corridor.

Warily, Briar inched forward. One step. Then another. She continued to sweep the light from side to side, looking for any hint of movement—

The light caught on a flash of white in the darkness. Not a bright white, like the glow of the lantern. A dull, discolored white—like the white of a bone.

Then the light went out.

"*Stones.*" Briar gave the lantern a little shake, then turned it around to inspect the gears on the bottom.

"Briar," Alec said in a warning tone.

"Hang on." Quickly, she wound the lantern up. The wind-up knob was so small that it was hard to grasp; that was something they would need to consider for future models. After a few turns, the light flickered on again, but it was unsteady, a pulsating glow, dimming on and off.

"Briar—" There was an edge of fear in Alec's voice now.

Frustrated, Briar raised the lantern again, pointing it down the dark shaft.

She caught another bone-white flash. Closer this time.

The light flickered off. Briar gave it a shake.

The light flickered on.

This time, she spotted the vague outline of *something* down the corridor, about eight paces away. A white figure, solid but not quite right, the joints of its limbs oddly formed, its torso twisted and gaunt—

The light went out again.

"Damn it!" Briar slapped a hand against the lantern.

"Briar!" Alec cried.

The light flickered on again. Briar lifted it—

And something ran past her, knocking her off her feet.

28

SUBSTITUTE

DEMETRI STRUGGLED AGAINST HIS bindings, but it was no use. The scratchy rope tied around his wrists was thick and secured with a dozen different seamen's knots. There was no way he could ever get it undone, not without help.

And he had no help. The black, rocky bluff Castel had rowed him out to was deserted, a raised ridgeline protruding into the ocean. A very small patch of sand at the base of the promontory was the only thing resembling a beach, the only spot to moor a vessel. The shoreline ended abruptly in a line of shallow caves extending along the cliffs. According to Castel, these were the caves where Briar's team had discovered elarium.

But no one from her team was here now. There was no reason they should be, with the submarine project shut down. And it was hardly a place anyone would come for fishing or leisure. It was isolated, far from Moselle or the castle. Far from everywhere.

Sohalia stood on the edge of the bluff at the farthest point reaching out over the sea. It was not a terribly high cliff, and the sound of the waves breaking against the rock was thunderous, making it difficult for Demetri to hear the sea witch's chanting as she prepared her spell.

When they had first arrived, Castel dragging Demetri by his bound arms, Sohalia had only said, "So good of you to join us, *Prince* Demetri. Do you know, I had no idea the boy Perpetua saved was a prince? Much less one descended from an original royal line. It wasn't until I was chatting with Count Reynard a few days ago—*suggesting* he take a large party to inspect the submarine site today—that I discovered it. And a lucky thing, too. I understand the fairy blood runs stronger in females, but the djinn will be satisfied with you. I think they're getting desperate. They know they have few options left."

Now, as Sohalia used a sharp stone to scratch a symbol into the rock around her, Castel hauled Demetri back to the opposite end of the promontory, sitting him down firmly. "You sit *here*," he told Demetri. "Right here."

"You don't have to do this, Castel," Demetri said through gritted teeth. He squeezed his hands together, straining against the bindings. It might be no use, but he had to try *something*.

"Yes, so you've told me. About ten times already." Castel rolled his eyes as he knelt to bind Demetri's ankles. Demetri tried to kick him, but the witch gave a flick of his fingers and a sharp little jolt *zapped* through Demetri's limbs. It was a small pain, there and gone, but it was enough to jam his muscles, temporarily paralyzing him. "Say it again, and I'll gag you."

"You're the one who told Briar how dangerous this was," Demetri argued. "You said the djinn couldn't be allowed a chance to escape."

Something flashed through Castel's eyes, but he didn't pause as he knotted up the rope around Demetri's ankles. "And I stand by what I said. But in case you haven't noticed, I don't have much choice." He looked up, meeting Demetri's gaze. "She's more powerful than I am. And witches can't just do whatever we please, believe it or not. The forces we serve don't like it when we go around helping the needy."

"Is that why you didn't stick around to help Kinsley?" Demetri demanded.

Castel didn't answer that. He merely finished tying off Demetri's bindings. Then he said, "Now. You sit *right here*. Understand?" His gaze darted past Demetri, over his shoulder. There was something...emphatic...in his gaze. "Right here. *Exactly* right here."

Demetri scowled. Where else was he supposed to go? Even if he could get to his feet, he could hardly hop very far with his ankles bound.

"Castel!" Now Sohalia's voice carried over the crash of the sea. "Once you've secured him, go below and make sure no one disturbs me."

Castel patted the bindings around Demetri's wrists, as though checking they were secure. When he spoke next, his voice was so low, Demetri almost didn't hear him. "Once she starts the spell, she won't be able to break from it. Understand? She won't be able to divert her magic anywhere else."

Then—clapping a hand on Demetri's shoulder—he stood and backed away, vanishing down the winding path to the beach below.

Demetri stared after him. Had he just said...? Had Castel just given him a warning? *She won't be able to divert her magic any-*

where else. Meaning, she wouldn't be able to attack him with magic. She would be vulnerable.

And what was all that about sitting *right here?* There was nowhere to go, with Sohalia ahead of him, Castel down below, and behind him—

Demetri twisted to look. Behind him. Where Castel had been looking a moment ago.

Behind him was a mass of junk. A damp, tattered net clung to the uneven edges of the crag, and tangled up in it were clumps of seaweed and varied debris, bits of wood and empty bottles and scraps of cloth. It was not a tall cliff and, Demetri realized, when the tide was high—especially if the water was rough or choppy—the waves must reach all the way up the crag here. Carrying all this debris from the ocean, litter and wreckage from ships lost at sea. Demetri scanned the netting for anything he could use to cut his ropes, anything he could use as a weapon—

And then he spotted it. Not just something he could *use* as a weapon. But an *actual weapon.* A long, thin blade. Glinting beneath the shards of sunlight peeking through the clouds.

It was a rapier.

It was *his rapier.* The one he'd lost in the shipwreck.

Demetri gaped, his jaw hanging open. *What are the odds...?*

He cast a glance at the sea witch, chanting at the end of the bluff. Her back turned towards him. Distracted by her preparations. Castel had gone, climbing down to the beach to stand guard.

Demetri cast one last glance at Sohalia. Then he started scooting, shoving himself backwards, heaving with all the strength in his body to get to that blade.

<h1 style="text-align:center">29</h1>

<h1 style="text-align:center">DEMONIC</h1>

BRIAR LANDED *HARD*, FACE-FIRST, her head cracking against the metal floor. She lay there, chest aching, face throbbing, trying to process what had happened. But she was so stunned, it felt like she'd vacated her body. Had someone—*something*—just run into her? And then she remembered the twisted figure she'd glimpsed down the dark maintenance shaft...

She groaned, stirring on the floor, trying to get a hold of herself. She heard voices nearby, Alec crying out and Candelaria snarling. But Briar couldn't speak; all the air in her lungs had rushed out of her. She gasped for breath.

Then something gripped her by the shoulder. Cold, slender fingers. Wrenching her around, rolling her onto her back. Briar blinked, her vision coming into focus.

The face that loomed before her was unlike any Briar had ever seen. She had stared into the ghastly, rotting face of her own cousin, she had stared into the pitiless black eyes of the dark fairy.

She had gazed upon the terrifying faces of the naiads, seen their blood-red eyes and gaping jaws filled with serrated teeth.

But *this* face...this face...

This face was more terrifying than all of them. Because it *wasn't* a face. It was like a mask. Bone-white, features crude and distorted, as though it were a sculpture half-formed. A nub of a nose, protruding from the center of its face. Eyeless sockets set over hollow cheekbones. And a mouth that did not open, lips melded together.

For a moment, Briar lay there, transfixed by the dreadful sight. Horror had her by the throat, pinning her down. And then, just as she realized she needed to fight back, to shove the creature away—

It was gone.

Briar lay still a second longer, staring up at the metal piping in the ceiling. She could feel her pulse racing in her neck, she could hear her blood pumping in her ears. Her body, preparing for a fight. Unwilling to believe she was safe.

Then another face loomed over her, this one much more welcome.

It was Alec.

"You all right?" he asked.

Briar ran her tongue over her teeth, coming back to herself. Her breath came in shallow bursts, her forehead smarting and her chest heaving, but she seemed all right. A little bruised. Gulping, she took the hand Alec proffered her and climbed to her feet.

"What *was* that?" she demanded. "And where did it go?"

"It ran off." Alec looked around, his face nervous. "I'm not sure where—"

"It was a demon." Candelaria's voice was a low growl. "A demon from the underworld."

Briar and Alec turned to stare at her.

"That's a *thing?*" Briar demanded. "A demon? Seriously?"

Candelaria lifted her hands. "I've never seen one. But I've heard stories. Stories about the sea witch summoning dark creatures to do her bidding."

"Well, that's just perfect," Briar grumbled.

"You think Sohalia summoned this thing and sent it here?" Alec shook his head. "But why?"

"Probably to keep us distracted. So we couldn't come after her. Unfortunately, it's worked." Briar's voice turned sour. "We can't let that thing loose. We have to stop it before it kills anyone else."

"But which way did it go?" Alec picked up the lantern, which Briar had dropped. It was back on, the light bright and steady. That figured.

Another scream echoed down the corridor, distant but clear. Full of terror.

Candelaria raised an eyebrow at Briar. "Let me guess. Follow the screams?"

"You're catching on."

They set out again, moving more quickly. Once most of the adrenaline had seeped out of Briar's body—*most* of it—her scattered brain calmed, and her thoughts returned to Perpetua. She fretted even more about the naiad's safety now that she knew Perpetua was dying. *Why* hadn't she said anything? Briar hoped Perpetua wasn't going to do anything reckless.

But she couldn't help Perpetua now. She could only hope that Gallia and Sabine would watch out for her. All Briar could do was focus on the here and now. Fortunately, that was not difficult to do. Every now and then, another scream punctuated the eerie silence as they crept down the corridors, each one louder and closer, echoing off the metal walls. Briar became more and more certain of where they were headed. As they came upon another fork in their path and swung left, she saw she was right. Just down this corridor was—

"The control room," Briar whispered.

A dim emergency light blinked overhead, illuminating the metal door to the control room. It stood open, a long streak of bright red blood smeared down its center. Just outside it lay a grisly corpse, one of the crewman, judging by what was left of his uniform. The body was identical to those they had seen outside, cleaved down the middle with its ribcage cracked open, divested of its insides. The crewman's eyes bulged, staring sightlessly at the ceiling.

Briar shuddered, but there was no time to dwell on the corpse. Frantic screams and panicked shouts came from inside the control room. Moving swiftly but silently, Briar approached the door and peeked around it, glimpsing the interior by the low glow of the gear bulbs inside.

The room was in chaos. It was a small, semi-circular room, lined with metal panels and mechanical control boards. A handful of seats were arrayed along these controls, but no one sat in them now—even though the room was filled with people. It looked like they had all come here to hide, albeit unsuccessfully. Either they had not gotten the door secured in time, or the demon had managed to get through it.

Briar counted fourteen people in all, four of whom were already dead. One corpse was strewn across the control board on the right, while the others lay spread-eagled on the floor, their middles split open, their faces fixed in frozen screams. Those still alive included three nobleman, identifiable by their fine frock coats, two guardsmen, and a handful of servants and engineers.

And the demon.

Most of the people cowered where they could, hiding beneath the piloting gear and control panels, though there wasn't much room to do so. As Briar watched, the misshapen demon grasped a guardsman by the ankle, yanking him out into the open. The guardsman flailed and screamed as the creature descended upon him.

"At least it is only one." Briar glanced around and saw Candelaria and Alec had come up behind her. Candelaria's eyes had gone red again. "Best to let it keep attacking the humans. That will keep it distracted."

"We're not doing that." Briar watched as the demon set its sight on a new victim at the back of the room—Count Reynard. "I'm going to distract it. Alec, get as many people out of here as you can. Candelaria, once the demon's attention is on me, see if you can attack it from behind."

"It is fast." Candelaria sounded dubious.

"So am I," Briar said grimly.

She crept into the control room. She moved a good ways from the door—she didn't want to block the exit for Alec and the others—then hurled her tiny lantern at the demon, adding a touch of supernatural strength into the throw. The lantern streaked across the room like a bullet, hitting the demon squarely in the back.

The demon turned. Its eyeless gaze seemed to zero in on Briar, its ill-formed features tightening in a grimace.

"Demon!" she called. "Try your luck against another monster, why don't you?" She moved slowly, inching to the left. Circling.

The demon followed, tracking her movements.

Then it ran at her.

It *was* fast. It could have bowled her over in a second, but when it moved, Briar did too. Summoning a burst of speed, she zipped to the left, out of its reach. She couldn't sustain that speed over long distances, only in short bursts. But that was all she needed.

Now on the opposite site of the room, Briar faced the demon. It stood in the spot where she had just been. If it was frustrated or baffled, Briar couldn't tell; that mask-like face betrayed nothing. It simply fixed its eyeless gaze on her, then dashed at her again.

Briar summoned another burst of speed, flitting away. She ran this way and that, racing from one spot to another. The problem was, she didn't have a lot of room to maneuver, and fatigue snuck up on her quickly. She began to lose sight of where she was running, growing dizzy, her vision swimming before her. As she summoned another burst of speed, sprinting to the far end of the room, she *crashed* into the pilot's console and stumbled back, nearly losing her footing. Dazed, she staggered around, coming face to face with a gibbering Count Reynard.

Then the demon slammed into her from behind.

Briar toppled over, choking on her own breath. Her chin banged against a large screw in the metal floor, and it sliced through her skin. A ringing pain shot up her jaw. Gasping, shuddering, she tried to get an arm under her. She managed to roll onto her back—just as the demon lunged for her, pinning her to the floor.

Briar tried to kick at the demon, but that was difficult. Her legs felt like jelly, drained of all energy; her muscles had seized up tight. One of her arms was constrained by the demon's leg as it straddled her. Briar reached up with her free arm, but before she could get a hold of the bone-white creature, it leaned over her, pressing its long, bony fingers into her middle.

Then it began to *dig*, its fingers burrowing straight through her flesh.

An unbidden scream rose in Briar's throat, ripping free of her. The pain was like a thousand fiery blades, worse than any pain she had ever experienced. Her legs kicked now, flailing of their own accord as she writhed beneath the demon, desperate to get it off her, to kill it, to *make it stop*.

And then it did stop. The demon reared back, and the pain in Briar's middle dulled to an intense throbbing as its fingers pulled free of her. Over the demon's shoulder, Briar glimpsed Candelaria. The garnet-scaled naiad held the demon fast in her clawed hands, and as Briar watched, she sank her shark-like teeth into the creature's neck.

Now it was the demon who writhed. No scream issued forth from its welded lips, but it twisted this way and that, struggling to break free of Candelaria. Briar reached up, leaning forward to get a hold of the demon's head. Its white flesh was icy cold and strangely hard, as though it really was made of bone.

Summoning the last of her strength, Briar snapped the creature's neck so violently, its faceless head spun all the way around.

The demon went limp. Candelaria leapt back, shaking her head furiously. The demon corpse collapsed atop Briar.

"Disgusting," Candelaria spat. Black blood stained her mouth and teeth, dripping down her chin.

Briar grunted, trying to push the corpse off of her, but she felt too tired to move. She craned her neck to look at Candelaria. "You took your time."

The look Candelaria gave her was full of disdain. "You said to wait until you had the demon's full attention. I judged that to be when you were screaming on the floor."

Briar rolled her eyes. "Get this thing off me, will you?"

Candelaria bent and grasped the corpse by its bony shoulders, heaving it off Briar and tossing it away. She paid no heed where she threw the creature, and it nearly hit Count Reynard, who still cowered nearby. He lurched aside to avoid the corpse, skittering away.

"Thank you," Briar said to Candelaria. She sat up slowly, wincing, putting a ginger hand to her middle. Her fingers came away red with blood, but the wounds didn't seem too deep. "All right there, Count Reynard?" she asked.

The count whimpered in response.

"Right." Briar winced again as she rolled forward, climbing to her knees. "Listen. I don't suppose this might be a good time to discuss reinstating my privileges to work on this submarine?"

30

BLOODED

PERPETUA BREATHED IN DEEPLY as they neared the black, sea-spattered promontory jutting out into the sea. She tasted salt on the air, and something sharp and *charged*. There was a storm nearby, she thought, though she couldn't hear any thunder. But dark clouds gathered overhead, encroaching on the cliff face, restless and jagged. The shrouded sun shifted beneath them, uncertain through the haze.

It was a troubled, bated morning. And soon it would be over.

It was nearly noon.

The bow of their dinghy *thudded* against the shoreline as they came aground beside another, slightly smaller rowboat. Sabine leapt out of the prow, splashing through the shallows, and began tugging the boat the rest of the way in, lodging it in the sludgy sand. "All right," she said, "Briar said this line of caves was full of elarium; they found traces of it all over the rock here. So we just have to figure out exactly where the sea witch is doing her spell and—"

She broke off as the beach gave a shudder, trembling around them. Then a beacon of blinding, blazing white light burst into the air, stretching up from the tip of the promontory. Perpetua peered up, shielding her eyes, but she couldn't see Demetri or Sohalia. Only that vortex of light, spinning all the way up into the low-hanging clouds.

"I think we found her," Gallia drawled.

"Yes," Perpetua whispered.

"Well, come on, then." Gallia leapt out of the boat as well. "Let's get this—"

But whatever she meant to say was cut off. Something *hit* her—an invisible force, jolting through her body. Gallia stiffened, going rigid like a board. Then she collapsed to the beach, falling face-first into the sand. Sabine whipped around, reaching for a pistol, but she, too, dropped like a sack of stones, sprawling across the ground.

Perpetua's cry of alarm died in her throat as a figure emerged from one of the caves across the small beach. A figure she recognized.

It was Castel.

Perpetua snatched up her pistol from the bottom of the boat, but by the time she straightened and aimed, cocking it back, Castel faced her dead-on, his arm stretched towards her. "Don't," he warned.

Perpetua kept her pistol trained on him. "What did you do to them?"

"They'll be fine." Gone was Castel's breezy demeanor, his careless tone. Now he was all business, unflinching, his eyes hard. "Might have a pair of raging headaches when they wake up, but they will wake. In an hour or so."

Perpetua clenched her jaw. Without dropping her gaze, she stepped out of the dinghy. She had never gone back for her shoes before they'd left, and the sifting sand beneath the shallows tickled through her toes. The hem of her white dress trailed in the foamy water.

"Where is Demetri?" Perpetua flicked her gaze up at the promontory, only for a second. "Up there?"

"Turn around, Perpetua," Castel said evenly. He, too, had not dropped his arm. "Get back in your boat. Take the guards with you. And leave."

"No."

"Don't make me stop you."

"Would you?" Perpetua challenged him. "Would you stop me?"

In answer, Castel gave a sharp twist of his wrist. Before Perpetua knew what was happening, her pistol jerked from her hand and flew, spinning through the air to splash into the sea, far from the shore. Perpetua swore, following the flight of the gun before whirling back to face Castel.

"I can stop you without hurting you," he said. "I can knock you out, same as your friends there. But I'd rather not do that. There'd be no one to row you away from here, and I really think that's best. Just in case this all goes sideways, and Sohalia actually opens her gateway."

"You think she won't?" Perpetua demanded. "I don't see you doing anything to stop her."

"No, but your little friend Demetri might, if he's clever enough."

"So let me go help him!" Perpetua took another step out of the water, then froze when Castel clenched his hand into a fist.

"Castel. *Please*. I know you don't want this. Just let me pass, let me go up there, Sohalia will never know—"

"Why? *Why* do you care so much?" Castel let out a hoarse laugh. "I sold my soul, but you don't even have one. Not according to her." He jerked his head up at the cliffside, at the blazing bolt of light shooting into the clouds. "So why does it matter so much to you, Perpetua? Demetri, the princess, this *world*—why do you care?"

"I just do," she said, and the words echoed strangely through her, thrumming a familiar tune. "Please, Castel. I can't leave Demetri up there alone, facing this alone. I *have* to help him." She narrowed her eyes. "Maybe you're the one who should row away from here. Back to the mainland. Go to the hospital. See if you can do something to help Kinsley. To *save* Kinsley."

Castel blew out a breath. "You don't understand. None of you do. It's not that simple. There are consequences, all right? Consequences to my using magic to save people. Putting that little potion together for you was one thing, but healing someone—there are consequences."

"And Kinsley's not worth it?"

Castel didn't answer. A muscle worked in his jaw. Then—with a long, regretful sigh—he dropped his arm. "Just go before I change my mind. But don't expect any help from me."

Perpetua didn't hesitate. Pulling Sabine's pistol from the fallen soldier's holster, she ran across the beach, tearing past Castel. "Don't worry," she muttered as she passed him. "I won't."

The winding path up the cliff was hardly a path at all. Perpetua scrabbled up it, fingers and toes curling around the grooves in the rockface, hauling herself up as quickly as she could. By the time she reached the top—panting, sweating, hair slick and plastered to her face—her hands were scraped raw. Blood seeped from a cut in the sole of her foot. As she straightened and limped across the top of the crag, she left a trail of bloody footprints behind her, staining the rock red.

She looked around for Demetri, but he was nowhere to be seen. Shielding her eyes against the blinding white light, Perpetua limped forward, peering down the bluff.

Sohalia stood at the edge of the promontory, at the furthest point. The white light arcing up into the sky came from some kind of symbol she had etched into the floor of the rockface. The sea witch stood before the light, arms raised to the sky. She faced the sea, her back to Perpetua.

Her back to Demetri.

Demetri. Who sprinted down the length of the bluff, slipping and sliding over the wet rockface, a long, thin sword clutched in his hand. He ran at Sohalia, raising his blade. He had nearly reached her—he was steps away—

Then Sohalia turned. She caught Demetri by the scruff of his neck, wrapping one hand around his throat.

"*No*," Perpetua cried. As Sohalia caught Demetri's wrist in her other hand, forcing his blade away, Perpetua began to run too. Her bare feet didn't slide over the rock as much as Demetri's boots had, but with every slapping step, pain cut through her, slicing her skin open anew.

She didn't care. She ignored the pain, her gaze fixed on the fight ahead. Demetri and Sohalia struggled hand-to-hand, gripping each other, shoving, fighting for Demetri's sword. Behind them, the blazing white light stretched into the sky, molten sparks rushing from the symbol etched into the rock. As Perpetua closed in on the edge of the promontory, she skidded to a halt, raising her pistol to take aim.

She couldn't get a clear shot. She was so close, it should have been impossible to miss. But Demetri and the sea witch were so close together, entangled as they fought, pushing each other this way and that. Frustrated, Perpetua tossed the pistol aside. Summoning her claws, she ran at the sea witch's unprotected back. But she hadn't taken two steps before Sohalia gave Demetri a savage shove, sending him sprawling. His sword clattered to the ground as his head *slammed* into the sharp black rock.

Letting out a cry of rage, Perpetua launched herself at Sohalia, wrapping one arm around her neck and stabbing her claws into her side—the side that was already wounded.

Sohalia gasped, her body spasming, back arching in pain.

Perpetua yanked her claws free, preparing to sink them in again. But Sohalia—with another violent spasm—shook Perpetua free of her.

Perpetua fell back. She managed to keep her footing, landing in half a crouch, claws dripping garnet blood.

And Sohalia whipped around and raked her claws down Perpetua, slicing through her from neck to hip. Her claws dug deep, shredding through Perpetua's flesh, mangling her insides. And when she ripped her hand free, staggering back, blood spurted from Perpetua like spilled wine, drenching her dress.

Time seemed to slow.

For a second—a long, drawn-out, eternal second—Perpetua stood, wavering, her legs growing weak. The pain was a distant thing. Or maybe it was so close, she couldn't pick it apart from everything else. The damp of the ocean, spattering her. A rush of cold, enclosing her heart in ice. Wind flinging her hair around, tickling her face.

Perpetua stood there. For one, long second.

Then she fell, boneless, crashing into the rocky ground.

A dull roar filled her ears. She wasn't sure if it was the ocean or the wind or more shouting. Perhaps all three. She lay on her side, one arm pinned by her body, soaking in the pool of blood gathering beneath her. The scarlet film blanketing her vision had gone, but everything was still blurry, as though she was looking through a bowl of water.

She saw a disoriented Demetri snatch up his blade and teeter to his feet. She saw Sohalia spin to face him, lurching. She saw Demetri plunge his sword into Sohalia, piercing her chest, the tip of the thin blade peeking through the other side of her. She saw him pull his sword free, and she saw Sohalia fall.

And the sea witch lay dead before her, dark eyes wide and unseeing as she stared at the sky.

The rock rumbled around Perpetua. She blinked slowly—and it was hard, very hard, to get her eyes open again—and saw the column of blazing light falter, sparks sputtering out. Then the light vanished, collapsing in on itself, and it was gone.

Perpetua saw all of this. And all the while, her blood pooled beneath her, running along the fissures in the rock, crimson tendrils creeping further and further away from her.

Her vision grew hazier. She could barely see Demetri as he fell to his knees, arms stretched towards her. But before he could reach her, he, too, collapsed onto his side, his eyes fluttering shut. She could barely see a second figure—Castel—running towards them. He was calling to her, shouting, but his words were muffled, distorted, impossible to make out. She thought she heard her name—*Perpetua, Perpetua*—but that was it.

And then a strange thing happened.

Perpetua's blood left her body, sluicing down the cliffside like a cleansing rain. But something else was rushing *into* her. Something in the rock, something she was suddenly aware of. It was warm and bright, like veins of molten gold buried deep inside the cliff. She felt it through the layers of stone beneath her; it burned so hot, how could she *not* feel it? How had she not felt it before?

And then—from somewhere deep inside the rock—it spoke. A rumbling, resonant voice, echoing around her.

Blood has been offered.

Blood has been accepted.

A request may be heard.

And then, the world went white.

31

REPARATIONS

PERPETUA FLOATED. BODILESS. PAINLESS. Formless. She just...existed. Somehow.

The space she existed in was all white. Or, no, not white. It was a pale, shimmering gray. The gray shifted around her like wispy clouds drifting through the sky. But not quite like that. The gray *undulated*, as though there were figures inside it, moving, pulsating.

Existing.

"What's going on?" Perpetua asked. Well. She didn't really *ask*. She couldn't speak. She didn't have a mouth. Or ears, or any kind of body, or...anything. Yet despite her lack of mouth, someone—some*thing*—must have heard her. Because a voice answered.

You have offered blood. You may make a request.

The voice was vast, coming from everywhere, and at the same time, coming from nowhere. It echoed *through* Perpetua, through her formless self. It was terrifying in its intensity, in its enormity. Yet there was something comforting about it. The way it thundered through her was almost calming.

Perpetua was so caught up in the *feel* of the voice that it took her a moment to process its words. "A request?" she repeated. "What kind of request?" And what did it mean about blood? She had offered blood?

Then she remembered.

The bluff. Sohalia's spell. Sohalia's *claws*. Shearing through her. Stealing her life.

And her own blood, gushing over the cliff...

The memory shook her, though it was hard to feel the full extent of fear, here in this soft, gray space. Perpetua set the feeling aside, still puzzled. Her blood spreading over the rockface—and now this voice, this *thing*, said she had offered blood...

Why did this sound so familiar?

You may ask a boon, the voice told her. *Whatever you desire. You may ask.*

A boon...

And Perpetua remembered. Sohalia's story. How she had sought out the old temple from legend. How she had offered a drop of blood and been granted a boon. But only in exchange for a sacrifice. For her own life.

She had offered a drop of blood, but what else had she said? Something about how the power wasn't really in the temple, but in the ground. In the rock. And she'd offered her drop of blood and been transported...someplace else...

Comprehension blazed through Perpetua, but only for a second. She still didn't understand. There had been something special about the place Sohalia had traveled to, even if it wasn't the temple itself. There had to be. People went around bleeding on rocky surfaces all the time, and they weren't offered boons. "Why?" Perpetua asked. "Why me?"

The voice rumbled around her. *You have offered blood.*

"Yes, but how did you...receive it?" she asked. "How did I reach you? Who *are* you?"

The voice rumbled again, but there were no words Perpetua could understand.

There must have been something special about the place where I fell too, Perpetua thought. There was no other explanation. Maybe all the magic Sohalia had been doing—hadn't she said something about it being a good spot for her spell, for some reason...? Perpetua couldn't remember.

Well. She supposed that didn't matter. In fact, none of it mattered. "And in return?" Perpetua asked. "If I make a request. What do I have to give in return?"

Lifeblood. The answer shivered through Perpetua. *A sacrifice.*

Perpetua felt as heavy as a stone. "I have to die."

Yes.

"But I can't," Perpetua said, frustrated. Really, if this voice—entity—was as powerful as it seemed—as Sohalia had described—shouldn't it know this? "I don't have a soul. I can't be a sacrifice."

Another rumble. If Perpetua wasn't mistaken, she thought she sensed confusion in that sound. In the feel of it. *What is a soul?*

"You know," Perpetua huffed. "A soul. The thing that makes you—able to understand. To understand sacrifice, and feelings, and—" She tried to remember what else Sohalia had said "—the value of a stupid life. And love." She suddenly felt small, so small. "A soul is what makes you able to love."

The voice spoke again. *You love.*

"What?"

You feel. You love.

"No, I—" Perpetua started, but then she fell silent. The wispy gray around her began to shift more intently, as though something large was moving through it, making it billow and whorl. Flashes of light appeared in the gray, short, quick bursts.

And then images formed before her. Images of herself. Images from her life.

Memories.

Briar, standing in a dark room. The room they shared at the inn. Her pale face shone in the darkness, her gray eyes filled with pain. Because Perpetua had lied to her. In that moment, Perpetua had hurt too. Knowing she'd hurt Briar. *I still want to be your friend*, the Perpetua in the memory said. *If I can be.*

The image blurred and faded, and another one took shape. Demetri, sitting beside her in the gray-green grass. The two of them overlooking the sea at dusk, watching the sun sink below a smudgy horizon. He told her about his past, about the sleeping curse and the imprisonment he'd endured and everything he'd lost. And the Perpetua in the memory ached for him, knowing what terrible things he'd been through. *That's what you meant*, she said to him, *when you said you lost everything.*

The image faded again. This time, the one that replaced it was of Meliora. Meliora as she bled to death in Perpetua's cave, as she shuddered and coughed in Perpetua's arms. *Are you crying for me, naiad?* she asked in her weak, broken voice.

Perpetua clenched tight, watching Meliora die again. Watching all these memories. She'd thought there was no pain in this gray place, but she was wrong. She had no body to feel physical pain, but there were other kinds. "So love is pain?" Perpetua felt cold and empty. "Is that what you're saying?"

Sometimes, the voice answered. *Not always.*

More images appeared, more quickly this time, forming, blurring, and fading in rapid succession. Briar smiling in the mirror as she helped Perpetua dress. Demetri laughing and brushing his arm against hers as they sat on the edge of the pier. Briar squeezing her hand as they parted ways this morning. Demetri kneeling before her, telling her she was worthy of being loved.

You live better, care better—love better—than any human I've known.

"But he was wrong," Perpetua said. "I don't even understand it. I don't know what it *means...*"

No one does, Demetri's answer echoed back at her.

Why do you care so much? Castel had asked. *I sold my soul, but you don't even have one. So why?*

I just do, she'd answered. *I just do.*

When you love someone like that, Demetri had said, speaking of Briar and Garrett, *you only want for them...whatever will make them happy.*

"No," Perpetua whispered. But something else quivered through her. Not the voice, not the power of this place. Her own comprehension. Her own understanding. "It's not possible..."

But hadn't she said she could never ask Briar or Demetri to sacrifice themselves? Hadn't she decided she couldn't betray Briar, even if it meant she, Perpetua, could finally have what she wanted? Because she cared about Briar. She cared about Demetri.

She loved them.

And now Meliora's voice echoed through her. Her last words, as she lay dying in that cave. *Are you crying for me, naiad?*

And she had, Perpetua realized. She had cried for herself, yes, but she'd also cried for Meliora. And she'd cried for the naiads, all of them doomed by Sohalia. Forced into this monstrous life. Never even knowing what they suffered, what they were missing.

She finally did it. Or maybe it was never hers to give. Maybe it was yours to take.

"I can do it?" Perpetua asked, hardly daring to believe it. Her formless existence here felt fragile and unsteady, as though she would come apart and drift away into the wispy gray. "I can save the naiads? They can be what we once were? No killing, no feeding on humans, just ...living in fin-form, living in the sea? Like we used to?"

The voice rumbled in answer. *If that is your wish.*

"And in return..."

Lifeblood is required, the voice flooded through her. *A sacrifice must be made.*

"Is it really a sacrifice though?" Perpetua asked softly. "I'm already dying. I don't have a choice."

But the voice thundered in disagreement. *There is always a choice.*

She supposed that was true. After all, she held a lot of power here. She could ask that she be healed, her life restored. She could ask someone else to make the sacrifice for her. Demetri would do it.

But she had already decided. She didn't want that for him. And more importantly—she didn't want that for the naiads. She wanted *them* healed. She wanted them whole. She wanted to save them.

Her brethren. Her sisters.

"All right," she said. "That's my boon. Save the naiads. Undo Sohalia's mistake. Make them what they once were." She paused. "And one more thing..."

The voice listened to her request. Then it rumbled its assent.

And the gray around her receded, dissolving into a burst of light.

Perpetua blinked her eyes open. The light that met her was not as bright as the burst she'd just experienced, but it was harsher. Blistering. Real.

She was back.

She expected pain, but there was no pain. Just a deep cold seeping through her, making her numb. Making it hard to move. Hard to breathe. That blistering light was too bright to make anything out. Everything blurred together. She felt dampness on her cheeks, sea spray misting over her. She tasted it on her lips, briny and gritty. She heard the tumbling, booming crash of the ocean.

She tried to speak and choked. Her throat felt full. Only a soft, mewling noise escaped her, little more than a breath.

"Shh, love," a voice murmured nearby. Very near. "Don't move. I've got you."

Perpetua blinked her eyes, and the blurry lines before her coalesced into a figure she knew. A dark head, blocking out some of the light.

"Ca—" She drew in a gurgling breath. "Cas...tel."

"Right in one, darling."

"Thought you—weren't—gonna h-help."

A hand squeezed her arm. Castel's hand. "Strictly speaking, I didn't help. I waited until the sea witch was dead, stabbed by your dear prince here."

"De-metri." Perpetua tried to lift her head, but she couldn't manage it. "Where—"

"He's right here. He'll be all right, love. Just knocked his head too hard when he fell." Castel lifted her gently, pillowing her head in his lap. From this angle, propped up, Perpetua could see Demetri. He lay right beside them, eyes shut, a bit of blood wetting his hair.

"Help h-him." Perpetua tried to reach for him, but her arm merely flopped, boneless. "Please—"

"He's all right. He's breathing, I checked." Castel smoothed a hand over her hair. "I'm going to help you first."

"Help...me?"

"Yes." Castel's voice turned scratchy. "I know I said I couldn't. That there would be consequences. But I don't care, Perpetua. I can help you. I can heal you."

"N-*no*," Perpetua croaked. She tried to lift her arm again and kept trying until she caught a fistful of Castel's sleeve. "Don't. Don't—heal me. I can—save them. All. The naiads. I can...d-do what she did. Sohalia. I can...fix it."

"What are you saying?"

"Have to—sacr-ifice." The words were getting harder to get out. A spasm racked Perpetua's chest, and it was a moment before she could draw another gurgling breath. When she spoke, it was not seawater she tasted on her lips, but the metallic tang of blood. "Life...blood. And my...boon...will be granted." She tried to focus on Castel's face. "You know. Don't...you?"

"Perpetua." Castel laid his hand over hers. "I don't know. I mean, what you're saying—I've heard stories, but I don't know—"

"I c-can do it." Perpetua drew another rattling breath. "Just have—to let me...go."

Castel interlaced his fingers through hers. "And what if I don't know want to?" he asked, his voice cracking. "I can do it, Perpetua. I can save you. Damn the consequences. Just let me heal you."

Perpetua tried to squeeze his hand, but she didn't think she managed it. She felt untethered. As though her body was dissolving around her. As though she was drifting away. But Castel must have felt something because he leaned in close to catch her reply.

"Save it for Kinsley," she whispered. "All right?"

"Oh, Perpetua."

"P-promise. Me."

"I promise." Castel shuddered around her. "I promise."

The blistering light was fading now. She couldn't see Castel anymore, not even a vague outline of his dark head. But she could still feel the pulse of his chest as he breathed, in and out, in and out.

"Cas...tel."

"Yes, love?"

"C-can you..." She fought for a breath, fought for this one last thing "...sing?"

Castel laughed a pitiful, broken laugh. "I'm a terrible singer, darling. Completely tone-deaf."

But if there was one last thing Perpetua wanted to hear in this world, it was music. "Please…"

"Oh, all right," he said, his voice tight with tears. And he began to sing. She couldn't make out the words, but the song flowed through her, pulling her under into a blissful, quiet dark.

The last thing she heard, though, wasn't Castel's song. It was his weeping.

She forgave him for that.

32

HEALED

B RIAR WINCED AS SHE stood up, a throbbing *pang* hitting her ribcage. Where that demon had dug its fingers into her. She was fairly certain that, had she been a normal human—that is, were it not for the supernatural side effects of the rotting curse—she would be much more severely injured. As it was, she was only mildly discomforted. Her face actually hurt a lot more.

It had taken some time, but they—she, Alec, and a grumbling Candelaria—had finally gotten all the survivors out of the submarine and safely up the beach. Candelaria had not wanted to help, and it was only after she (grudgingly) mentioned her debt to Demetri that Briar managed to convince her, assuring her that helping them would appease that debt. More or less.

The only problem was, now that everyone was safe from the demon, free of the submarine, and sitting out beneath the open sky, many of them—especially the remaining noblemen—eyed Candelaria with mingled trepidation and suspicion.

"They are all *staring* at me," Candelaria said.

"Well." Briar coughed, turning to face Candelaria. "None of them have seen a naiad before." *Let alone been saved by one.*

"They will try to capture me. Kill me." Candelaria bared her teeth. "I should kill them first."

"We just saved them."

"So?"

"Look." Briar placed a hand on Candelaria's scaled shoulder. The naiad whipped her head around, growling, and Briar quickly dropped the hand. "You have an opportunity here. *You helped save them.* Maybe this is a chance to show them naiads aren't all bad. Maybe this is a chance to convince them to stop hunting you."

"*We* hunt *them.*" Candelaria looked nonplussed. "Why should they stop hunting us in return?"

Briar had to admit she didn't have an answer for that. "Look, I'm just saying—"

But she was interrupted as Candelaria let out a long, choking gasp. The naiad doubled over, clutching her middle as though she'd been shot. For a moment, Briar had the wild thought that she *had* been shot, that one of the people on the beach was trying to kill her, just like she'd said. But then she realized she hadn't heard gunfire, she hadn't heard *anything* except for that strangled sound Candelaria was making.

"What's wrong?" Briar half-reached for the naiad, then thought better of it. "Candelaria. What's going on?"

"Briar?" Alec, who had been walking among the survivors, checking on each of them, hurried forward. "What's happening? Is she hurt?"

"I don't know." Briar watched, baffled and helpless, as Candelaria slumped to her knees. Her golden hair had fallen forward around her face, but then the naiad snapped her head up. Her eyes were wide, bulging from their sockets.

"Help—me—" she gasped.

"I don't know what's wrong. Are you hurt?"

Alec shifted uneasily, glancing from the naiad to the people behind them. Briar could hear them muttering, the low hum of their voices anxious and disturbed. But Briar couldn't worry about them right now.

"Help—" Candelaria flung an arm up, grasping Briar by the wrist. Briar took in a sharp breath as the naiad's claws pierced her skin, drawing blood. When Candelaria managed to lift her head again, her eyes had gone red from brim to brim. "*Help me—*"

The anxious murmurs behind her turned to cries of alarm. Without really meaning to, Briar clutched at the webbed hand Candelaria had wrapped around her, wincing. She'd only thought to try and loosen her grip, but—almost as soon as Briar touched her—the naiad's hand began to *change*.

The claws vanished, shrinking back into her fingers. Briar had seen that before, but this time, the change didn't stop there. The webbing between the naiad's fingers shrank too, melting into nothing. Then her *scales* began to fall off, sloughing right off her skin. Briar dropped Candelaria's hand in a flash, expecting to see the naiad's skin turn raw and red, like the skin beneath a scab. But it didn't. The scales fell away from her body—crumbling to dust as they hit the ground, bleeding into the sand—and revealed smooth, beige skin, the same color as her one bare arm.

"What the—" Briar stumbled back a step. "What is *happening—*"

As the last of the scales fell away from Candelaria, Briar looked her full in the face. As she watched, the red slowly bled from the naiad's eyes. With a final shudder, Candelaria blinked hard, bowed her head—and then slumped forward, barely catching herself with her hands.

When she looked up again, her eyes were just blue. A deep, glittering blue, like the sea.

"What—" Candelaria gasped. "What—*how*—I—"

"You're—" Briar looked her over from head to toe. "You look *human*. Really, actually—you look—"

"Really naked," Alec said.

"Alec!" Briar whirled on him. "Yes! She is! So—!"

Blushing, Alec spun to face the other direction. Briar rushed towards Candelaria and knelt before her. The naiad—if that's what she was anymore?—wore a look of complete shock. As Briar reached her, Candelaria began to tremble. She pressed a shaking hand to her chest.

"What's wrong?" Tentatively, Briar placed a steadying hand on Candelaria's shoulder. She waited for another growl from the naiad, but there was none. Instead, Candelaria gulped in a breath. "Are you hurt?"

"I'm—" Candelaria croaked. "I—" She looked up, and Briar was startled to see her eyes glisten.

Then she burst into tears. Great sobs racked through her, and she fell into Briar. Even more startled, Briar wrapped an arm around Candelaria's shaking shoulders.

"All right," she said, twisting around awkwardly as she held the weeping naiad. "What the hell is going on?"

⫷◆⫸

It was nearly two hours later before Briar discovered what was going on. What had *happened*. And once she did—once she finished listening to the tale from a red-eyed Demetri—she wanted to cry too.

But she didn't. She never did.

"She sacrificed herself," Demetri said shakily. They sat in Briar's room at LeBeau's, Briar on her bed, Demetri in a chair across from her. He wore a bandage around his head, expertly wrapped by Sabine. He'd refused to go to the hospital. "I didn't really—Castel explained it—he said it was old magic, very old—"

Briar stirred at that, lifting her head from her knee. "Where is Castel? He wasn't with you."

But Demetri only shook his head. "I don't know. He disappeared when we docked back here. I didn't even notice..."

Briar curled her fingers into her palms, clenching them tight. The mention of Castel brought Kinsley to the forefront of her mind, and a new wave of grief washed over her. Kinsley, Perpetua. Tory.

Sohalia had been stopped. She was dead.

But the cost had been so high.

The next morning, Briar found herself at the hospital again. She'd finally convinced Demetri to get checked out, only by reminding him that Kinsley was still at the hospital, and he could stop by to visit once he'd been seen to. So he'd been led off to an exam room, and Briar found her way to Kinsley's room, taking her usual seat at his bedside.

She sat in silence for a long while. A shaft of sunlight pierced the dull, gray hospital room, shining through a small window. It was the first sunlight she'd seen in days, but Briar barely noticed.

Leaning forward, she pressed her forehead into Kinsley's shoulder.

"I wish you would get better," she whispered. She was fully aware of her use of the word 'wish' and didn't regret it. If her djinn was anywhere around right now, she would gladly spend the third wish she swore she'd never use. "I wish you would get better so I could talk to you. So much has happened..." She trailed off. If Kinsley recovered, she would have to tell him that Tory was dead. That Perpetua was dead. That Castel had lied to him and used him.

She didn't care. She would gladly have all those painful conversations. If only he would come back to her.

But Kinsley did not stir. He did not look at her or give a reply. He only stared blankly ahead. His room here in the hospital was a private one, though it was a small, joyless room. She supposed all hospital rooms were joyless. She should bring him some flowers, she thought. Something to brighten it up.

The door creaked open. Briar lifted her head as Aden walked in. The dark circles beneath his eyes were nearly as prominent as Briar's. "Gallia is going to run out for a late lunch, Your Highness." His soft voice was like a balm, so different from his boisterous twin brother. "Do you want anything?"

"I'm all right." Briar rubbed a hand at her temple. "But you should wait and ask Demetri."

"I'll tell Gallia." Aden looked at Kinsley. "There's been no change?"

"No." Briar pushed her hair back from her face. "Garrett and his father are coming here in a few days. To re-negotiate with the counts about the submarine." Her heart lifted at the thought of seeing Garrett, but a dark shadow shot it down. "He doesn't know about Kinsley yet. Garrett." Her voice cracked. Garrett had lost soldiers before, but Kinsley had been in his service longer than most. "I don't know what I'm supposed to tell him."

"That's easy, Your Highness," Aden said steadily.

Briar looked at him in surprise.

"You tell him Kinsley did his job," said Aden. "He protected you, and he followed your orders. That's all."

"Yes," Briar said bitterly. "He followed my orders. And now…"

"Prince Garrett will understand, Your Highness." Aden clasped his hands behind his back. "Soldiers have died and been injured following his orders too. I guarantee you none of us have ever resented him for it, because none of those casualties came needlessly. They always came fighting for what was right. And what we did here was right."

Briar set her hands on her knees. "Thank you, Aden."

"Not at all, Your Highness."

Suddenly, there was a shout from out in the corridor, followed by the shuffle of hurried footsteps, a dull *thud*, and a cry of pain. Aden whipped around as a voice sounded out from outside—Gallia's voice. "What are you doing here? You can't go in th—*oof*."

Then Castel rounded the doorway and stepped into the room.

Briar leapt to her feet. "What are you doing here? What did you do to my guards?"

Castel didn't answer. He didn't look as though he'd even heard her. There was something strange about him, something *charged*. As though a current of energy ran through him. As though, if Briar reached out and touched him, the very air around him would shock her. His dark eyes blazed with that crackling energy, his gaze bent on Kinsley.

Aden reached for the pistol at his waist, but without even looking at him, Castel gave a dismissive flick of his wrist. Aden shot across the room and slammed into the wall, crumpling in the corner.

"Hey!" Briar whirled on Castel. "What do you think you're doing? You can't just—"

Castel flicked his hand again. This time, Briar was the one who slid across the room, though she managed to remain upright, the soles of her boots squeaking over the tiled floor. She skidded back until she *thudded* into the wall, hard enough that her breath reverberated in her chest.

Castel stepped right up beside Kinsley. Briar tried to push herself away from the wall and found that she couldn't, pinned by an invisible force. As though a great, monstrous hand pushed against her chest, holding her in place. "Hey! Get away from him!"

Castel ignored her. As Briar watched, struggling and helpless, Castel took Kinsley's head in his hands. He began to mutter beneath his breath, the words too soft for Briar to make out. There was something oddly lyrical to his words, his voice swaying like the boughs of a tree in a gentle wind. Briar found herself hypnotized by the sound until something pierced through it, something sharp and frightening.

The way Castel stood there, holding Kinsley's head, murmuring—it was so like what Sohalia had done. When she had destroyed Kinsley's mind.

"Stop," Briar whispered, unable to pitch her voice louder. "Please, stop."

But Castel did not stop. Still mumbling, he leaned forward and touched his forehead to Kinsley's. It was only for a few seconds, but in that moment, something... *something*... seemed to pass between them. A sliver of a shadow. A ghostly fragment.

Then Briar blinked and the shadow was gone.

Castel let go of Kinsley, stumbling back from the bed. Briar glimpsed his face and saw it had gone gray and chalky. His eyes were bloodshot, as though *he* was the one who hadn't slept in three days, and his whole body stooped forward, his knees buckling.

And then Kinsley emitted a deep, gravelly gasp.

Briar's eyes widened. She suddenly realized she could move again, and she lunged forward as Kinsley arched in his bed, his entire body spasming.

"Kinsley!" Briar reached for him but froze as he arched a second time, and then a third. Terrified, uncertain, Briar grasped his arm. Another spasm rocked through him, and then he shuddered, falling limply against his pillows, one arm dangling off the side of his bed.

"Kinsley? *Kinsley!*" Briar had never felt so helpless in her life. Her eyes roved over Kinsley, looking for some sign of life.

Then she whirled on Castel.

"What did you do to him?" She was on Castel in a flash, snatching him up by the scruff of his neck, her fingers wrapping around his throat. She lifted the witch easily, slamming him into the wall and pinning him there, just as he had done to her with his magic. "What the hell did you *do to him?*"

Castel didn't answer. He couldn't. For as soon as Briar pinned him to the wall, Castel began to *flicker.* A bright, white light surged through him, over and over again, bolts of lightning arcing through him. Briar stared, aghast. With each burst of light, Castel flashed back and forth between the Castel she knew—the living, breathing Castel—and some kind of *wraith*. The wraith-like Castel was skeletal, shriveled, cheeks sunken in, eye sockets empty, limbs wasted away and hands curled into twisted clumps.

"What the hell—" Briar choked.

The blinding light flashed one last time—then flickered out. Briar released Castel as though he'd burned her, though in truth, she hadn't felt anything as she'd held him there. Castel fell like a stone, sagging to the floor, his chest heaving.

"What the hell," Briar repeated, numb.

"What—the hell—is right," Castel croaked. He sucked in another breath and it juddered through him like a wheel spinning off its axle. He lifted his head.

A shock of hair at his temple had turned white. Pure white.

"What just happened?" Briar demanded. "What did you *do?* What happened to you?"

Castel shoved trembling hands through his hair. After another deep breath, he staggered to his feet, one hand laid across his ribcage and the other grasping at the wall. "The forces I do business with," he said weakly, "don't like me to use magic for good."

"For good," Briar repeated. "But. What *happened* to you?"

Castel flashed a look at her. It was something like his usual blasé smile, but there was a darkness in it. A haunted look. "I just lost a fifth of my life."

Briar gaped at him.

Castel turned to go, still pressing one hand to the wall. When he reached the doorway, he looked over his shoulder at Briar. "Tell him goodbye for me, will you?"

Then he was gone.

Aden groaned as he climbed to his feet. "Are you all right, Your Highness?"

"Fine," Briar said faintly. "I—that was—"

"Princess?"

Something swooped through Briar. A ghost, cutting through her and stealing her breath. She clutched at her middle.

Then she whirled around.

Kinsley sat upright in bed, staring at her—not with the glazed, vacant look he'd had since Sohalia's attack, but really *staring* at her, his eyes focused and puzzled. "What's going on?" he asked. "Where am I? Is this—what happened?"

Briar's hand flew to her mouth. "By the Gift." She caved in on herself, her shoulders slumping forward. For a moment, she really thought her legs were going to give out beneath her. Disbelief and exhaustion and relief crashed into her with equal force. "Kinsley. *Kinsley*. Are you—stones—you're all right? You know who I am?"

"Princess Briar." Kinsley's brow furrowed. "Of course. Is this a hospital? How..." He rubbed a hand over his cheek. "The yacht. We were on Sohalia's yacht—but what happened?" He blinked at Briar. "Why are you looking at me like that? Your Highness, are you all right?"

Tears pricked at Briar's eyes. "Yes, I'm all right," she said. "I'm more all right than I've been in days."

33
SOULFUL

DEMETRI WAS TUGGING ON his boots when the knock on his door came. He knew who it was, though he'd been hoping to leave before she got here. Not because he didn't want to see her, but because he didn't want to answer any questions.

He didn't want to answer any questions about where he was going.

Still—though he briefly entertained the idea of pretending he was not there—he crossed the room and opened the door.

"Oh." This was Briar's greeting. She looked surprised, as though she had expected someone else to answer the door to his room at LeBeau's. "You're—are you going out?"

Demetri tried to look nonchalant. "I'm just getting dressed. It *is* ten in the morning."

"I know, but—Sabine told me—" Briar broke off, casting her eyes down.

Demetri stepped back and gestured for her to come in. Sabine told her what? That he hadn't left his room in days? Except for the two times Sabine had dragged him downstairs for a meal.

"Well." Briar stepped inside, looking around the small, dim room tentatively. She wore a dress for once, a kind of naval seaside dress in dark-blue linen with large bronze buttons down the front and a ruffled white underskirt. "Kinsley is out of the hospital. He was stuck there longer than he should have been. I think the doctors were rather confused about his recovery, but I didn't know how to explain that a witch healed him."

"So he really is recovered?" Demetri asked. "Completely?" This, at least, was good news, though it was difficult for even that to pierce the dark cloud that had descended over him. He felt a bit selfish about that—that he couldn't even be happy for Kinsley, for Briar.

"He's the same old Kinsley," Briar confirmed. "He doesn't remember anything. He says one minute, we were on the yacht, fighting Sohalia, and the next—he woke up in the hospital."

Demetri nodded. He stood facing Briar, trying to hide his impatience.

"Anyway," Briar said, "my guard and I are going up to Mariner Castle. Garrett and his father arrive today. Sabine told you they were coming?"

"Yes." That was the reason for the dress, then.

"Did—" Briar cleared her throat. "I thought you might want to come with us. To see them. They're staying at the castle since they've come to make nice with the counts, well, and I doubt King Victor would stay here, but—"

"It's all right. You can go without me."

Briar wrung her fingers together. "Are you sure? I know Garrett would like to see you."

"Perhaps I'll come on later," Demetri said vaguely. "I've got something to do first."

Briar nodded, though she still looked uncertain. "Well. I don't know about you, but I'll probably be in Moselle for a while longer. Assuming the negotiations between the counts and King Victor work out. I'll probably be here the rest of the summer. Besides, I told Candelaria I would do what I could to help her and the naiads. They want to stay around here, I think, but it will take some time to convince everyone they're no longer a threat."

Candelaria. The name cut through Demetri. Not because of Candelaria herself, but because of the reminder her name brought. The reminder of Perpetua and what she had done. Castel had explained it to him that day, as they'd rowed away from that terrible bluff, back to Moselle. He had explained what little he knew. He'd told Demetri a story, an old legend about blood offerings and ancient powers and boons and sacrifices. He'd told Demetri what Perpetua had said. That she believed she could save the naiads. Undo the damage that had been done.

Demetri had not believed it until he saw Candelaria in the common room at LeBeau's, in human-form, a *real* human form. Not the kind of glamour she had assumed before. And when she'd returned to the sea later that day, her legs had melded into fins, and she'd disappeared into the ocean's depths. But not before Demetri spoke to her. Not before he heard the choked tears in her voice as she tried to process every emotion she was feeling for the first time.

And Demetri had known then. It was all true.

Perpetua had saved the naiads.

"I talked to her last night." Briar looked a bit awkward, twisting to one side, her eyes hovering near Demetri without really looking at him. "Candelaria. She said you talked to her too. Just yesterday."

Demetri stiffened. He turned aside, fiddling with the loose handle on his cabinet. "Yes. I did."

"She wouldn't tell me what you talked about."

Well. Demetri *had* asked the naiad to keep their conversation private. "It wasn't anything, really. I just asked her a bit about...Perpetua."

That much was true.

"Oh. Well." Briar lifted her gaze to his face. "Are you all right, Demetri?"

"Sure," Demetri said, his voice hollow. "I'm fine."

"I mean, I know you're not."

"Why did you ask, then?"

"I just meant..." Briar looked at him with such open consternation. "Will you be all right?"

Demetri looked at her. There was no polite way to express his incredulity at this question, no way to say what a stupid question it was. He was not all right. He knew that much. He had no idea if he would be. Perhaps he would be. Perhaps tomorrow. Or five days from now. Or a month from now, or a year from now. Or maybe never.

All he knew was, right now, it felt like never.

"I'll be fine," he told Briar. "I just need to get going."

"Oh. Me too, I suppose." Briar smoothed a hand over her knot of hair. "I'll see you later then. Maybe tomorrow."

"Right."

Briar left. Demetri waited ten minutes, just to be sure he wouldn't run into her out in the corridor or downstairs, and then he left too. He left his room, left the tavern, and left Moselle.

He walked south down the coast. It was quite a trek, over rocky shores that could not properly be called a beach. He walked through scrubby grass and wooded marshland, his path curving along the bay. He walked, following the directions Candelaria had given him. He walked until he found it.

The cave where Perpetua had lived. The lagoon she had called home.

The cave was a bit difficult to get into, almost entirely surrounded by water. Demetri scrabbled over slick black rock, a narrow bar jutting out of the salty shallows, though he slipped near the end and found his leg submerged up to his calf. Then he ducked into the cave.

Inside, it was dim and damp. Demetri knew he had the right place because of all the little added touches in the cave, evidence that a naiad-human hybrid had lived there. A bowl carved out of stone. A bed of moss. A pair of boots. A pair of boots, which Demetri found hilarious. Since Perpetua had so rarely worn shoes.

But that was all. All that was left of her.

The day was sunny outside, treacherously sunny, but little of the warmth reached inside the cave. Only a mugginess in the air, and even that was disturbed now and then by a cool breeze rippling over the puddled water, flaring through the fuzzy algae carpeting the walls.

It was cold and dank and dark, and Demetri found that both comforting and distressing. Comforting, because it felt so much like he did on the inside. Distressing, because a part of him wanted to stop feeling that way, though he didn't know how.

With a sob trapped in his chest, Demetri slipped down onto his knees. The cave floor was hard and unforgiving, slicing through him.

He had come here because he wanted to be with Perpetua. He had come here because he thought, maybe, he might feel her here, in this place where she had lived all alone. But there was nothing but emptiness here, an emptiness that Demetri thought she must have felt day in and day out when she was a naiad. Before she learned how to feel.

Maybe that meant he could stop feeling here. Maybe, if he stayed long enough, he would.

He sat there, in the damp cold. The day passed by outside, the shadows on the wall shifting as the sun moved through the sky. The occasional breeze turned into blustery gusts of wind as the tide rushed in, close enough that Demetri could hear it hurtling over the rocks outside.

The sky darkened through the cave opening, the algae on the walls pulsing with an eerie light. Dusk fell over the cave, shutting out the last of the sun. Demetri was so, so tired; it seemed ages since he'd last slept properly. The last time had been with Perpetua the night before the solstice, the night he'd played his violin for her.

He was so tired. He lay back on the floor, the rock wet beneath him, seeping through his clothes. He didn't know how long he lay there in the dark, exposed to the worst elements of the cave. The cold leeched into him, settling into his bones. His body vibrated with a shaking he could not stop. A blissful numbness came over him, his thoughts turning hazy. He closed his eyes and waited for the numbness to take over completely, to take his heart and soul so he wouldn't feel anymore.

But it wasn't working. He couldn't quite remember why he felt so terrible, so heavy and empty all at once. He didn't know where it came from, this pit opening inside him, a blackness he couldn't escape.

Perpetua.

Perpetua. Why did she have to leave him? Why hadn't she waited for him, why hadn't she saved herself? He would've saved the naiads for her, he would have sacrificed himself. That would have been better. It seemed such a terrible waste, that Perpetua was gone—wonderful, bright, fearless Perpetua, who still had so much to live through, so much she hadn't experienced.

But Demetri should have died a long time ago. He was a relic of a time long past, an imprint of a life long gone. In all the months that he'd been free in this new world, he'd never quite figured out how to live again.

"Demetri."

And now, as though it couldn't be any worse, he was hearing her voice in his head.

"Demetri. You have to get up."

Get up? He didn't even remember lying down. He didn't know where he was. Down at the bottom of some deep abyss, that was where.

"You have to get up, Demetri. You're going to freeze to death."

There was a pitiful, pained, whimpering noise. It was a moment before Demetri realized it had come from him.

"Demetri. Get up. Get up now. Get up get up get up get up—"

"Stop," Demetri moaned. He opened his eyes.

A white shadow leaned over him.

"Stars and—" Before he knew what he was doing, Demetri shot straight up. Feeling rushed back into his body, none of it good. A deep ache in his back and shoulders, an icy chill shuddering through him from head to toe. His fingers were so numb they stung, and his head throbbed.

But he hardly noticed any of it. All he noticed was the white wisp of a figure floating in the air before him like some kind of ghost. It had to be a ghost because it wore a face that looked vaguely like Perpetua.

"Perpetua?" Demetri whispered. His throat was so dry, the name barely made it past his lips.

The wispy figure regarded him. It was not formed like a human, not really. For one thing, it was quite small. Smaller than a human, smaller than a fairy. And the white, shimmering strands emanating from the figure made its body fluid, changing, though he glimpsed an arm here, a torso there, as though the figure was trying to remember what a human looked like.

But it did have a face. And though it was hard to tell—because of how blindingly white it was—the face looked like Perpetua's. It had her angular chin, her high cheekbones, her hooded eyes.

"I'm not Perpetua," the figure said.

Demetri's heart felt like it had shattered into a million pieces. Again.

"But there is a part of me that was her," it continued. "That part of me has her memories, her feelings. I know who you are, Demetri."

"But..." Demetri croaked. "You're not Perpetua."

"Not precisely."

"What—what *are* you?" Demetri rubbed the heel of his palm over his eye. Perhaps he was hallucinating. Perhaps he was still lying on the floor of the cave, slowly freezing to death, having a full-on hallucination.

"I'm not entirely sure. A remnant, I think. Something left of the sacrifice Perpetua made." A somewhat familiar, playful smile flickered over the figure's face. Perpetua's face. "Maybe I'm a *ghost*," it said, adopting an eerie tone.

"That's not funny."

"No. I suppose not." The smile vanished. "Demetri, you can't stay in this cave. You'll die if you stay here."

"I'm not sure I care."

"Yes, you do. And so does Perpetua."

"You're not her," Demetri retorted. "You just said you weren't. I don't know *what* you are—a byproduct of my dying mind, probably—but you aren't her. You don't know what she wants."

"What I just said," the figure replied primly, "is that a part of her is me. I *do* know what she wants, and what she wants is for you to not die, Demetri. You're supposed to live."

"But I would have died instead," Demetri protested. "I could have been her sacrifice. Why did she get to decide?"

The figure regarded him gravely. "Because they were *hers*. The naiads. She knew you would have died in her place if she'd asked. But the naiads—their pain, their suffering, their *wound*—belonged to her. They were hers to save, and she wanted to do it. Don't try to take that away from her." The figure drifted closer, peering at him. "Does that help?"

Demetri shrugged, feeling dazed. *Don't try to take that away from her.* Oddly enough, it did help. He felt...lighter. Just a little. As though a single stone had been lifted from the pile of wreckage burying him. And he felt a little chastised, for taking the sacrifice Perpetua had made and wallowing in it. Taking on guilt that wasn't his to bear.

"Anyway," the figure said, "I don't think you understood my full meaning."

"About what?"

"You're supposed to *live.*" The figure's tone was reprimanding. "Not just be alive. But *live.* Don't you remember what you told Perpetua the night before the solstice? You said she lived better than any human you've known. That's what you're supposed to do, Demetri. Live like Perpetua would. Do everything you can. Not just what you think you should do, not just what you think is required of you. But everything. Everything there is."

"That seemed a lot easier when she was still living too."

The figure considered this. "Well, I'm here. I don't think I'm going anywhere. I can stay with you, if you want. "

"Is that a good idea?"

"I don't know. I don't think there's ever been anyone like me before. I suppose I can do what I want."

"But I mean—what will other people think when they see you?"

"You can only see me right now because I'm allowing you to," the figure told him. "No one else has to see me. If you don't want them to."

Demetri scrubbed his hand through his hair, ruffling it. A part of him still wasn't sure if this was real, or if he was dreaming, or if maybe he was already dead. "You say a part of you was Perpetua."

"Yes."

"If I tell you that I love her..." Demetri squeezed his fingers together. "Will she hear that?"

"Do you? Love her?"

Demetri stared at the figure. She held his gaze until Demetri couldn't hold hers anymore. With a groan, he dropped his head. "I don't know," he confessed. "I don't know how I feel about anything anymore. Perpetua, Briar—"

"It doesn't matter, anyway," the figure cut in. "That's not what mattered to her in the end. What mattered is she learned how to love. She learned the kind of love you already have, Demetri. In your friends, in Briar and Garrett. She learned to love you like that, and she loved Briar like that. She only wanted you both to be happy." The figure cocked her head. The gesture was so hauntingly familiar, so like Perpetua, that Demetri felt gutted. "You did that for her, Demetri. You could still do it for others. Are you really going to give that up? Here, in this cave?"

Demetri clamped his lips together. He was quiet for a long, long moment.

Then he said, "No."

"Good. You have to get up then."

You have to get up. Demetri swallowed. "You said you could stay with me."

"Yes."

"What am I supposed to call you? If you're not Perpetua."

"I'm not her." A hand formed from the figure's wispy strands, and she ran a finger over her lips, looking pensive. "But a part of me is. So perhaps you could just call me Perpetua."

Demetri let out a slow, tremulous breath. "All right."

"All right." Perpetua fixed him with an expectant look. "Well?"

"Well, what?"

"I told you, Demetri." Her face softened. "You have to get up."

Demetri clasped his shaking hands together. He knew he had to. And it should have been easy. All he had to do was stand. He had done it millions of times before.

Swimming across the ocean seemed easier right now.

"Here." Perpetua stretched two misty tendrils towards him, and the tendrils became arms. Hands. "I'll help you."

Demetri only looked at her.

"She's not here anymore, you know." The ghostly figure's gaze swept over the cave. "No part of her is. It's just a cave."

"I know," he whispered.

"So just get up, then." She waved her misty little hands.

Demetri took a breath. Then he reached out. He expected his hands to pass right through Perpetua's wispy ones, but they didn't. Her hands closed around his, and they were not warm, or cold, or anything, really. But they were solid.

She tugged at him. And in one, fluid movement, Demetri rose to his feet.

The moment he did, Perpetua was gone.

⫷◆⫸

It was nearly midnight by the time Demetri arrived at LeBeau's, shivering and sore. The walk back had been miserable, and not only because he felt like he was leaving Perpetua behind. Not only because he was alone. He did not want to be alone right now. He knew that decisively. Over the past several days, he had wrestled with the simultaneous desires for company and solitude, but now, he knew he didn't want to be alone.

It was almost midnight, though. Demetri didn't know if Briar and her guard had returned from the castle or if they'd stayed for the night, but even if they were here, he couldn't wake them now. Though Briar might still be awake...

But when he trudged into the tavern's common room, he spotted a familiar face in the back corner. Surprised, he weaved through the empty chairs and tables until he reached Sabine.

"What are you doing here?" he asked. "No, what are you doing up?"

Sabine lifted a steaming cup of tea at him in greeting. "I'm always up this late. Not an early riser by nature."

"So you all came back? From the castle, I mean?"

"No. Just me." Sabine looked him over bluntly. "You look terrible."

"I feel terrible." Demetri pulled out a chair and slumped into it. "Never spend the night in a cave. It's a bad idea."

"Doesn't sound like something I'd try, but thanks for the advice."

"Wait, did you say you came back here alone?" Demetri signaled the auto-waiter for a cup of tea, then turned back to Sabine. "Why?"

"Actually." Sabine set her cup down and looked at him carefully. "Princess Briar and Prince Garrett sent me. To you."

"I don't understand."

Sabine reached into the pocket of her unbuttoned coat and pulled out a sealed roll of paper. "This is from Prince Garrett." She handed the paper to Demetri, who took it, mystified. "You can read it later. The gist of it is, Prince Garrett would like to hire you—sort of. Or contract you on from time to time. As a kind of outside consultant."

Demetri stared at her. "Huh?"

"Well, you have garnered a bit of a reputation as a monster-hunter."

"A failed one, maybe." Demetri took his cup as the auto-waiter rolled up. "I was meant to be hunting naiads, and the whole time I was courting one and didn't know it." A pinprick of pain poked him in the chest, but he did his best to ignore it.

"Well, you can't be successful all the time. Anyway, should you accept the prince's offer, I'm meant to stay on with you—as your guard, friend, business partner. Whatever works for you."

Demetri eyed her over the rim of his cup. "They've sent you to babysit me, haven't they?"

The look Sabine gave him was disdainful. "I'm not babysitting anybody. Look, I don't even know you that well, and I can see you're miserable on your own. And you *are* qualified to hunt down the weird and supernatural, which, as I told you, appeals to me. So?" She lifted an eyebrow. "How about it?"

Demetri mulled it over. "If I say yes. Do we have to start now? Go over to the castle, I suppose—"

"It's an open offer. Prince Garrett made that very clear. If you want to think it over and talk to him later, that's fine." She sipped at her tea. "I can stay with you. If you don't mind."

Demetri set his cup down. He stretched in his chair, twisting to one side, then the other. As he did, his eyes roamed over the common room, taking in all the empty chairs, the quiet, the stillness.

Then he saw it. A flash of white out of the corner of his eye, near the bar. Slowly, he turned to look.

She was there. That wispy white figure. Perpetua. Floating behind the bar, drifting in circles. She caught his eye and smiled.

"Demetri?"

Demetri turned back to Sabine. "I would like to think it over. Garrett's offer, I mean." He didn't really want to see them right now, Garrett or Briar. They would only mother him, or tip-toe around him. Sabine, though—well, it was like she said. She was no babysitter.

"You know," he said, "from what I recall, the Glen Kingdom used to boast an excellent symphony. Back in my day."

"They still do, from what I've heard. I've never been myself."

"I think I'd like to go. This weekend, maybe."

"Well. There's a train leaving for the Glen Kingdom tomorrow morning."

"Good." Demetri leaned back in his chair. "And perhaps by next week, Garrett will be back home too."

"Perhaps so."

They sat there a while longer, finishing their tea, chatting about nothing in particular. When they were finished, they stood and left the table, heading upstairs to their respective rooms to pack. And behind them, flitting through the air, was a misty wisp of a figure. A remnant. A ghost.

A soul.

READ ON FOR AN EXCLUSIVE BONUS CHAPTER

While Perpetua is at Castel's house, discovering exactly what he is, Castel takes Kinsley out to an underground club. But the crowd is a little too dangerous, even for Castel...

Haunted

CASTEL PUT ON HIS most devilish smile. "Tell me what you're thinking."

Kinsley studied their surroundings. His eyes swept over the flickering bulbs on the wall, the peeling black paint covering the long bar, and the smudgy glasses in the hands of the pub's patrons. All three of them. The place was quite empty, as it almost always was.

"Not really your sort of place, is it," Kinsley noted. His face was wonderfully blank, his gaze giving nothing away. Kinsley wasn't an evasive person, Castel thought. Just very discreet. And very polite.

Two traits that made him very intriguing.

Castel beckoned to Kinsley as he crossed to the back of the pub—a very short distance to cross, as the pub was smaller than most of the rooms in Castel's house. "First of all, every place is my sort. And secondly—this little hole-in-the-wall isn't our final destination."

He led Kinsley through a swinging door at the back of the pub, then down a short flight of steps. There were more doors at the bottom. One led to the pub's storeroom. The other was a squat, nondescript door that most people would have overlooked.

Castel rapped on this door five times. Three measured knocks, followed by two staccato taps.

A voice called through the door, "Password?"

"I don't really think that's necessary." Castel's reply was airy but pitched loudly enough to be heard through the door.

There was a pause. Then a little slot near the top of the door slid open. A pair of dark eyes peered out, landed on Castel, and widened. The slot slammed shut.

"Well," said Kinsley, "this is all very mysterious."

Castel glanced at him, and they shared an ironic smile. It had only been a little over a week since the two of them had met at one of Darcy's infamous boat parties. A meeting that Castel considered an unqualified success. Not only had he stolen a kiss from Kinsley that night, but he'd also secured a promise for a night out with him. Since then, they'd been out a couple of times, frequenting various parties and upscale bars. They'd even had a very civilized dinner at Castel's favorite, most expensive restaurant.

But tonight, Castel wanted something a little more illicit. A little more *underground*. And he had business to conduct. So he could kill two birds with one stone.

About thirty seconds later, the slot on the door shot open again. This time, a pair of jade-green eyes peered out. Then the door opened wide, revealing a woman on the other side. "Well, *well*," she said. She was very short, with a head of very red hair, and garbed in a corseted blouse that was *very* tight. "Look what the cat dragged in. Is that really you, Castel?"

"It's me." Castel put on another smile, but this one was a bit different than the one he'd showed Kinsley. This smile had a hint of malice in it. "It's been a while, Scarlett."

If Scarlett perceived the threat in his smile, she didn't let on. She lounged against the doorframe, looking unconcerned. There was nothing to say her own smile wasn't genuine. Except for a coldness in her eyes—but that was just Scarlett. "Well, whose fault is that? I haven't seen you at my club in some time."

Castel injected a little more danger into his smile. Showing his teeth. "Your club has been rather hard to find, darling. Almost as though you didn't *want* me turning up."

"Oh, please." Scarlett rolled her eyes. "It's true I've been forced to go more underground than usual. But to assume that's about *you*, Castel, is—well, rather like you, I suppose. Always the narcissist." Scarlett finally turned to Kinsley, and the coldness in her eyes vanished. Kinsley, Castel had noticed, had that effect on people. "And who is this handsome fella?"

Kinsley's smile was completely genuine. No coldness. No hidden threat. "I'm Kinsley."

"What you are—" Scarlett took Kinsley by the arm, ushering him inside "—is much too good for this scoundrel." She jerked her head at Castel. "That, I can already tell."

Kinsley sent Castel a mirthful look over his shoulder. "Oh, I'm fully aware."

That surprised a laugh out of Castel—a laugh so real, he startled himself. A laugh that came from deep down inside of him. His heart gave a peculiar little shiver, drawing out a feeling he hadn't felt in a long time.

A feeling he couldn't afford to feel.

Scarlett led them down a short corridor that opened into a vast, opulent room. Much more opulent than one would expect, considering it was essentially a basement. Gear-bulbs shaded in garnet and gold cast a low light over the space. Round tables covered in rich cloths filled the room, set before a small stage where a brass band played sensual music. A long bar lined one entire wall, and the glasses being served there were not smudged, but sparkling crystal.

Kinsley shot Castel another look, though Scarlett still had him by the arm. "Like I said," he murmured, and Castel acquiesced with a nod and a smirk. Perhaps he *did* have a certain sort of place.

Scarlett gave Kinsley's arm a noticeable squeeze. "So, what's your story, then?"

"Kinsley is a guardsman," Castel told her. "Serving a most important royal person."

He was pleased to see the slight widening of Scarlett's green eyes—just the smallest hint of alarm. But she played it off with a laugh and turned back to Kinsley. "Oh, dear. I do hope you're not here to take down my illustrious little place of business."

"Hardly," Kinsley said dryly. "The royal I serve wouldn't concern herself over a place like this. In fact, she'd probably be delighted to frequent it."

Scarlett let out a whoop of laughter. "You must be talking about that Princess Briar, aren't you? The one working on that submarine? I heard she was at one of Darcy's parties last week. Made quite an impression on a lot of people, from what I heard."

"Oh, dear," Kinsley muttered.

"Well, much as I'd love to spend the whole night with you two gentlemen, I've plenty other patrons I need to see to." Scarlett finally relinquished Kinsley, stepping back. "Enjoy yourselves, and Kinsley, mind yourself with this one." She dipped her head at Castel. "He's all charming smiles, until it's too late." She flashed her own smile as she departed—one that made Castel think she hadn't missed his own threats before.

Kinsley arched an eyebrow at Castel. "Old friend of yours?"

"Friend," Castel said breezily. "Business acquaintance. Nemesis. What's the difference, really?" He cast one last look after Scarlett, watching the woman sashay across the room and disappear behind the bar. "One thing's for sure. She runs the best underground club in the kingdom." Castel turned back to Kinsley. "And fortunately, I managed to get tonight's location. So." He swept his arm out. "I propose a few shots first, and then—"

"Actually," Kinsley interrupted, "I'll take the lead tonight."

Castel blinked. That was the second time he'd been surprised. That was not a sensation he was used to. "Is that so?" A slow smile spread over Castel's face. "And what exactly did you have in mind?"

"You'll see," said Kinsley, and Castel tried not to notice the decidedly knowing glint in the soldier's eyes. He tried not to notice the way it made his stomach flip.

So he followed Kinsley's lead. It was a most unusual experience, Castel thought, letting someone else be in control. He could not remember a time when he was not constantly planning, always five steps ahead of everyone around him. That was not to say that he was never spontaneous, that he never lost himself to a little partying and drinking. But he was never as careless as he seemed. He couldn't afford to be.

But for tonight, he followed Kinsley. He followed him right into a high-stakes card game taking place in the back corner of the club, far from the music and quite private. Castel opted not to play, sitting back and watching Kinsley instead. He was surprised yet again to find Kinsley in his element, and judging by the reactions of the other players, he was not the only one.

As Kinsley shuffled the cards for a third round, Castel leaned in close to him, resting his elbow over the lacquered table. "And how did you ever get so good at cards?"

"That's what I'd like to know," grumbled the man on Kinsley's other side. He was an older gentleman, and a noble, if Castel was not mistaken, though he'd taken care to dress informally. Castel had been raised among nobility; he knew an aristocrat when he saw one, no matter what he wore.

Kinsley's reply was smooth, the little smile on his lips unaffected. "I'm a guard. And what do guards do all day?"

The nobleman eyed him. "Guard people, I presume?"

"Yes. But guarding people involves a lot more sitting around than most people realize." Kinsley dealt out the cards around the table, five to each player. "So we guard. And we play a lot of cards." He leaned back in his seat, eyes narrowing as he studied his new hand. "Of course, we typically play for much different stakes."

"Like what?" asked the nobleman.

"Like privy-cleaning duty."

Another laugh escaped Castel, and yet another when he saw the look on the nobleman's face. Kinsley's gaze left his cards long enough to sneak a glance Castel's way, one that Castel caught. Castel didn't move from his position—leaning forward on the table, his arm so close to Kinsley's, he could feel the warmth of him through the fabric of his shirt. Without taking his eyes off

Kinsley, Castel brushed his knuckles along the back of Kinsley's hand. The barest touch. Just a whisper.

He was rewarded when Kinsley sucked in a breath, low in his throat. Castel held in a smile and leaned back in his seat. He didn't want to distract Kinsley *too* much. Not while he was besting everyone in this card game.

The truth was, Kinsley was a constant surprise, and that was what Castel liked so much about him. Being surprised. Watching him surprise others. On the face of it, Kinsley—unfailingly polite and dedicated—seemed like the perfect conquest for Castel. One might be forgiven for thinking Kinsley naïve, uneducated in the ways of the world. Especially the darker, more wicked ways. But Castel had quickly learned Kinsley was far from that. He was somehow both worldly *and* decent, perhaps the most decent man Castel had ever met.

That was a rare combination. One Castel was sure he might never see again, even if he lived a thousand years.

Which he very well might.

Castel's smile slowly slipped off his face. The fact was, Kinsley *wasn't* just another conquest. Not even close.

He was a job. And Castel couldn't forget that.

Sohalia certainly wouldn't.

Castel rubbed his thumb over the ring on his forefinger. His gaze was still fixed on the card game, but he was distracted, quickly losing track of each player and their moves, of the low conversation between Kinsley and the others. Sohalia worried him. Rather, her recent behavior worried him. She'd always been a little unhinged, but then, Castel didn't know a witch that wasn't. In one way or another. He probably was himself. He was just better at hiding it than most.

He was young for a witch. *Give it time*, he thought.

Still, the way Sohalia had been acting lately—she was beyond desperate to achieve her aims. And working against some kind of deadline, though she wouldn't tell Castel what it was. The summer solstice, perhaps? There were all kinds of terrible spells she could pull off with the power of the solstice. But what was she after?

He wasn't sure he wanted to know. And it wasn't his business to know.

He had other business to be about.

Leaning in close to Kinsley again, he excused himself, murmuring something about fetching another drink. Kinsley nodded without sparing him a glance, his gaze fixed on his hand of cards, an adorable little crease marring his forehead. Castel sauntered off, making for the long bar.

He spent a few minutes chatting up the bartender, his outward demeanor relaxed, his tone a little flirtatious. Playing just a little tipsy. Inwardly, he kept a sharp eye out for a familiar flash of red hair. When he finally zeroed in on his target, he slid off his seat and made his way around the bar, slipping into a small back room. It was a storeroom, lit by a single gear bulb swinging from the ceiling, and filled with stacks of crates and shelves lined with liquor. Castel didn't bother to quiet his footsteps and Scarlett—bending over something in the corner—turned around when he entered the room.

"Castel." The smallest hitch of her eyebrow betrayed her surprise. And the smallest fluttering of her fingers betrayed her nerves. "Lost your handsome soldier already, have you?"

Castel's smile was humorless. "Hardly. He can take care of himself for a few minutes."

"You're out of your depth with that one, you know."

Castel's heart missed a beat. "What do you mean?" he asked, then cursed himself for letting the words escape him.

"Nothing." Scarlett's smile was catlike. "Only, he's not your usual type, is he?"

Dropping all pretense, Castel said in a hard voice, "What makes you think you know anything about my type?"

Scarlett let out a laugh. She turned to face him with a glass in one hand and a bottle of liquor in the other. Castel recognized the label on the bottle. It seemed she'd been helping herself to the expensive stuff.

"Oh, Castel." Scarlett fluttered her eyelashes at him in an exaggerated fashion. "I know because I've been trying to seduce you for years. But I'm just not *innocent* enough for you, am I?"

"More like you're not man enough," Castel drawled. "Literally."

Scarlett lifted her glass to her lips, inhaling the scent of its contents. "All I'm saying is, that young man out there is not so gullible as your usual conquests. And I think you know it."

Castel didn't like how closely her words echoed his own thoughts. Eager to move on from this conversation, he said bluntly, "You've been avoiding me, Scarlett."

"I've done nothing of the sort."

"You've been moving your little establishment here more often than usual. Twice in the last month, I thought I'd tracked you down, only to find you'd just gone. So what's going on? And don't give me that piffle about it not being about me."

"It's *not* about you." Scarlett's voice didn't waver, but neither did she meet his gaze. "Look, the whole town is on edge. All these murders and disappearances—all this talk of *mermaids*—"

Now she cut a glance in his direction. "And while most people seem willing to attribute everything to them—rightfully so, I'm thinking—the capital guard are on alert. Looking for any other illicit doings." She shrugged. "I'm not taking any chances."

Castel crossed his arms over his chest, pinning her with a shrewd look.

But Scarlett was unimpressed. "Look, you're here now, aren't you? Relax, Castel. I'm not dodging you *or* your mistress. Come on, sit." She took her own advice, perching upon a crate. "Have a drink with me." She proffered her bottle of liquor, the greenish liquid sloshing inside.

"I'll pass."

"So mistrustful."

Maybe he was, but he had good reason to be. Especially around someone like Scarlett. Scarlett was a viper. A necessary evil. Castel had known her for a long time, and though they always played at friendliness, they were both very aware that was all it was. A play. They did their little dance, putting on false smiles until one or the other had what they wanted. Sometimes, they both got what they wanted.

Castel had a feeling this was not going to be one of those times.

"So you have what I need, then?" he asked. "More to the point, you have what *Sohalia* needs?"

Scarlett didn't answer right away. She swirled her glass round and round, gazing into it. Then she downed the contents in one go. "Times are hard right now, Castel. Not just for me. For any witch." She poured herself another glass. "Truth is, nothing's really been the same since Delphine got herself locked up. Until her antics with the king, most people had all but decided witches didn't exist anymore. Then she had to go and make herself queen, and of course, it all blew up in her face."

Castel made no comment. She wasn't wrong about any of that—Delphine certainly had done a lot of damage, but that was nothing new. Delphine had been doing damage for centuries. Scarlett was trying to change the subject. Or make excuses. Either way, he wasn't going to be led by her.

"And now there's this new witch hunter running around." Scarlett's eyes had gone a bit unfocused, her cheeks flushed. "Have you heard about him? They say he killed some witch down south when he was just a boy. Now he's got Adela on the run, chasing her around half the country."

Castel scoffed. "Adela has never been very powerful."

"But she does know how to stay alive." Scarlett tossed back her second glass. She wiped her mouth with the back of her hand. "She's a good sight older than you or me. Older than Delphine, even. It would be a fine thing if some *child* took her out."

She stood then, setting her glass and bottle aside. Swaying slightly.

"This is all fascinating," Castel said, "but it doesn't answer my question. Have you got what we need or not?"

Scarlett stepped towards him, a little unsteady on her feet. "My answer," she said as she neared him, "is *this*."

Too late, Castel noticed the look in her eyes. They weren't unfocused at all, but hard as emeralds. Before he could think to defend himself, she snatched up his hands in hers, gave them a tight squeeze, and hissed a sharp word.

Invoking a hex.

Castel gasped. Heat suffused his body from the inside out, as though the blood in his veins had begun to boil. The sensation

was so overwhelming, so all-consuming, that he didn't even notice as Scarlett dropped his hands and backed away. He staggered,
and when the arm he flung out failed to catch on anything, he
toppled into a stack of crates and crumpled to the floor.

The sudden heat began to subside at once, its potency fading,
but it did not leave him entirely. He lay slumped against the
fallen crates, sweating profusely, flushed and feverish. His body
felt wrung out, as though that torrent of heat had sucked all the
life out of him. He didn't think he could move.

Scarlett's smug face came into focus, looming over him. "Poison. And not just any poison, my dear. A very special one of
my own making. It was dormant in your bloodstream until I
activated it just now." She glanced aside, and Castel followed her
gaze to the bottle of liquor she'd been drinking. "Oh, I knew
you'd never accept a drink from me. But, chummy though you
may be with my bartenders, they are *mine*. They work for me.
And they'll serve you whatever I tell them to."

Castel tried to speak. He wet his lips, but before he could get
any words out, something flashed through his mind, blinding in
its intensity.

An image. Hazy, indistinct. Colors blending together. A face,
Castel thought, but he couldn't quite make it out. And yet,
something inside him responded to the blurry image, some deep,
subconscious part of him. Emotion surged through him, unwelcome, unbridled emotion. It made him want to weep.

"You're in for quite a trip." Scarlett's voice came from somewhere above him, but he couldn't seem to find her face again. His
surroundings blurred, tilting dangerously. "One you probably
won't survive. I would tell you to let that sea witch hag of yours
know I won't be running errands for her anymore, but, well..."

She trailed off. A moment later, Castel heard the squeal and *thud* of a door swinging shut, and then the light went out, leaving him in darkness.

Need to get up, he told himself, *need to get out of here—*

It was a laughably useless thought. He couldn't even feel his legs. He wasn't sure which way was the floor and which way the ceiling. As another hazy image flashed through his mind, a strange feeling rose inside him, bubbling up his throat. A second later, he heard weak, wheezy laughter coming from somewhere.

Then he realized it was coming from him.

Another image flashed. This one was easier to make out. A pair of boys, running through a wood filled with soft, dewy daylight. One of the boys had dark hair and an impish smile. *Me*, he thought, *that's me*, and then he knew who the other boy was, even though he'd forgotten his face decades ago—

Another swell of emotion filled his chest. Pushing out all the air, leaving him choking. Choking on a sob.

The images kept coming, faster and faster. Not just images. Memories. And with each one came a fresh surge of *feeling*, his emotions swinging from elation and joy to despair and fear. Too fast to process, too fast to manage. But he felt it *all*. Castel had spent most of his life learning how to ignore his emotions; he was a master at compartmentalizing every aspect of his life. But Scarlett's poison seemed to have stolen that ability, and now it all washed through him, every suppressed emotion, every painful memory—

It was going to kill him. That seemed strangely fitting.

Castel did not know how long he lay there, succumbing to Scarlett's poison. It felt like forever. But then the light overhead flickered on, blindingly bright.

A voice said, "Castel? Are you in here?"

Kinsley.

The name broke through all the bright, hazy images, even though—for just a moment—Castel couldn't remember who Kinsley was.

Then a face appeared in his line of sight, leaning over him. A pale face set beneath a head of black hair. And he remembered. *Oh. Right. Kinsley.*

Kinsley cursed softly, putting a hand on his shoulder. "What happened to you?"

Castel tried to answer, but when he opened his mouth, all that came out was a raspy giggle.

"All right." Kinsley leaned in towards him, ducking to get an arm around his shoulders. "Come on. Stones, you're burning up. Come on, up you get—"

A gasp escaped Castel's lips as Kinsley hauled him to his feet. Another gush of heat rushed through him, as though the movement had exacerbated the poison in his bloodstream, sending it racing through his veins. He gasped again and managed his first word since Scarlett had taken him by the hands. "Can't—"

"Yes, you can. I've got you. Come on, there's a back door nearby—it's not far—"

Castel didn't know how they made it. He still couldn't feel his legs, yet somehow, he stumbled alongside Kinsley, his feet dragging over the floor. Images continued to flash through his mind. He could barely see the way ahead as they wound through a narrow corridor. When they reached the back door, Castel heard a burst of music from the club's main room, but then Kinsley kicked the door open, practically dumping Castel onto the stoop outside.

"By the Gift," Kinsley muttered as the door swung closed behind him, shutting out the sound of raucous music. The street outside was dark and quiet. A breeze whistled past them, but Castel barely felt it. It was like a single drop of water in a desert. The heat inside him was too strong, pumping through him, burning him alive.

"Hang on," Kinsley told him. "I'm going to see if I can find us a carriage. I'll be right back."

Castel wanted to tell him not to leave him, but by the time he remembered how to speak, Kinsley was already gone, vanishing up a small flight of steps and down the street. Castel sat slumped at the base of the steps, leaning against the pub's exterior wall, barely upright.

Get a hold of yourself, he thought. *You can fight this. Burn it out. Think, damn it!*

Focus, he had to focus. If Scarlett had just hexed him, he'd likely be doomed. But she hadn't. She'd poisoned him. He could fight that. He could burn it out, he just had to focus long enough to gather a little strength—

The swift patter of footsteps announced Kinsley's return. "I found a carriage, it's coming round." He knelt before Castel, his face swimming into view. His blue eyes were tight with concern. "Castel?" He touched gentle fingers to Castel's face. Rubbed his thumb down his jaw. Because he was crying, Castel realized. The inane giggling had given way to a tide of tears, streaming down his face.

Focus, he reminded himself. *Focus.*

And suddenly, he could. Kinsley's touch grounded him long enough to push away the next image in his head. He reached up and grasped Kinsley by the wrist, holding on for dear life.

He plunged into the well of magic inside him. Plumbed its depths, his reach like the roots of a tree delving deep into the land. He gathered as much power as he could, and then—

He flooded his own body with it. Let it fill him. The magic raced through his veins, a wildfire far more intense than Scarlett's poison. It raged through him, burning every drop of that poison to a blackened crisp. Until it was gone, purged from his body. Leaving him alive—and exhausted.

"Castel? *Say* something, damn it."

Castel gulped in a ragged breath. The images were gone, the swell of feeling gone. He felt strangely empty in the wake of it all. And so, *so* tired. His body began to topple to the side. Kinsley reached out and steadied him.

"I—didn't—" Castel mumbled. On the street above them, a carriage trundled into view, slowing to a halt at the curb. It was an old-fashioned carriage, with a driver and two horses.

"Didn't what?"

"Didn't—take anything." It was still hard to speak. Castel's tongue felt too thick for his mouth.

"I know."

"Scarlett drugged—what?" Castel blinked, forcing his eyes to focus on Kinsley. "You know?"

"Believe it or not, it was rather obvious that woman had it in for you, Castel," Kinsley said dryly. "From the moment we walked in. So I kept an eye on her. When you followed her behind the bar, and then she came out and you didn't, I figured I'd better go look for you. That's why I took us out the back door. Thought it best we avoid her."

Castel mulled all of this over as Kinsley—with the help of the driver—lifted him to his feet, hauled him up the stairs, and got him into the carriage. Though he still felt out of it, his thoughts a jumble, he had enough presence of mind to marvel at Kinsley's skills of observation. Not to mention his discretion. Then again, he was a bodyguard.

The carriage started up, the horses' hooves *clop-clopping* over cobbled stone. Castel swallowed and tried to ignore the swaying movement as they jostled down the street. He felt queasy. The poison was gone from his body, but, as Scarlett had been sure to tell him, it hadn't been just any old poison. It was a hex in liquid form, and its effects lingered in his body, in his mind.

Those memories lingered in his mind. Haunting him.

He was crying again, he realized. His body felt so completely beyond his control. It was terrifying, not to mention humiliating. If there was one thing Castel hated it, it was losing control. But if Kinsley noticed his silent tears, he didn't say anything. He simply sat beside him, one arm looped through Castel's. Castel closed his eyes and sagged into Kinsley.

He didn't know how long they rode in the carriage. Castel thought he must have dozed off because suddenly, the carriage was drawing to a halt and Kinsley was climbing out.

"Where are we?" Castel mumbled as Kinsley heaved him out of the carriage.

"LeBeau's." Kinsley nodded to the driver, then helped Castel down a dark alley. "Don't worry, there's a back staircase. And luckily for you, being head bodyguard grants me the privilege of a private room."

It took some time for Castel to process all of that. LeBeau's. The tavern Kinsley was staying at. The tavern Princess *Briar* was staying at. Castel certainly did not want to meet her in this state.

For a lot of reasons. "I should go home," he said, but by this time, they were inside, halfway up a flight of wooden stairs.

"Well, we're already here." Kinsley grunted, towing Castel by his arms as they lurched up the last few steps. "And I don't think I should leave you alone tonight. Come on, my room's just here." He led Castel to a door only a few paces down from the staircase. Kinsley leaned Castel up against the wall, and he managed to stay upright long enough for Kinsley to unlock the door and grab hold of him again.

They tottered inside. The room was dark. Kinsley lowered Castel onto a bed, gently laying his head against a pillow. Castel sank into the mattress and found he could move enough to lift his legs onto the bed by himself.

"I'll be right back," he heard Kinsley say. "I'm going to get some clean water. And maybe some tea." He was gone before Castel could form a reply, the door latching shut behind him.

Castel released a long, heavy sigh. The bed he lay on was narrow and lumpy, but in that moment, it felt like heaven. He rolled onto his side, pressing his sticky face into the pillow. He didn't think he had any more tears in him, and if he did, they were going to stay where they were.

Well, for a third rendezvous, this wasn't terrible, he thought. Now that the worst effects of the poison were wearing off and fatigue sinking in, he was beginning to feel a bit punchy. *I let a woman drug me and started crying. Very attractive.* He'd had worse outings. With worse men.

He felt a twinge in his chest. Far, far worse men. Compared to Kinsley, everyone was worse. He really shouldn't stay here, he thought, under the same roof as the princess Sohalia was after, and in such a state, but there was no way he could get out of this bed on his own. Much less make it down the stairs. Burning out Scarlett's poison had taken every drop of magic he had in him. He had no strength left.

And though it was stupid—so, so stupid, so *weak*—he wanted nothing more than to lie here and let Kinsley take care of him.

Kinsley returned after a few minutes, bearing a tray with a clean cloth, a jug of water, and a steaming pot of what smelled like ginger tea. "Still awake?" Kinsley spoke in a low voice, easing the door shut.

"This," Castel said, his voice muffled by the pillow, "is the smallest bed I've ever slept in."

Kinsley let out a snort of laughter. He turned to place the tray on a round table, then wound up a small lamp in the corner. It flickered on, the light thankfully dim. "It's about ten times better than my bed back home in the barracks."

"That is appalling. I feel terrible for you."

"Yes, well, what can I say. I don't love everything about my job."

Castel shifted his head, watching Kinsley as he busied himself pouring a cup of tea. "Me too."

Kinsley glanced over his shoulder, then turned to bring him the tea. He set it on the small bedside table. "'Me too?' Meaning, you also don't love everything about my job? Or yours?"

"Both, I suppose." Castel eyed the cup of tea, barely lifting his head. "I don't think I can drink that."

"Well, it's there if you want it." Kinsley retreated, sinking into the chair at the table. He rubbed his hands over his face, showing just how tired *he* was. "I didn't think you had a job. Besides partying professionally."

Castel closed his eyes. "We all answer to someone, Kinsley."

Silence fell over them. Castel lay with his eyes shut, carefully inhaling the spicy scent of the tea. It didn't make his stomach turn. Perhaps he should try to drink it. The problem was, the thought of propping himself up enough to do so—without spilling it all over him—sounded far too difficult.

He wished for sleep, but despite his exhaustion, it felt just out of reach. The events of the night lay heavily on him, pulling his thoughts in a million different directions. He still hadn't regained full control of his emotions. He should never have been so stupid to let Scarlett fool him, pretending to be drunk, getting him to let his guard down. He would have to decide if it was worth it to let Sohalia deal with her or not. But that was a decision for tomorrow. He couldn't think it through right now. Not with this fatigue burying him, not with Kinsley sitting there, not with...

Not with those memories haunting him.

Castel inhaled a silent breath. The benefit of living so long meant one eventually forgot all the painful moments. All the lost loved ones. All the shameful mistakes. But Scarlett's poison had brought them all back, and they weren't so easy to banish now.

He opened his eyes and found Kinsley watching him. Keeping vigil. Probably worried he would choke on his own vomit or something. The churning in Castel's gut intensified, making him feel sicker than ever. Kinsley shouldn't be worried about him at all. He wouldn't be, if he knew what Castel really was. If he knew that their meeting at the boat party had been no accident.

Castel swallowed, his mouth feeling dry. "Aren't you going to ask?"

Kinsley, leaning back with his hands clasped behind his head, said, "Ask what?"

"Why Scarlett…drugged me." He nearly slipped and said *poisoned*. That would invite some unwanted questions.

Kinsley looked amused at this. *Amused*. "I gather you two had some kind of dealings that went south."

Well. He was not wrong. "You don't want to know the specifics?"

"I don't need to."

For some reason, this answer made Castel feel even worse. "Why not?"

"What?"

"Why not?" Castel felt warm again, uncomfortably so. Fever flushing through him. Remnants of Scarlett's poison, not quite done with him. "Maybe she was right to drug me. Maybe I wronged her."

"I somehow doubt that."

"*Why?*" Castel pressed. "You don't know me, Kinsley. Not really." They'd met little more than a week ago. As though that was enough time to get to know someone, *really* get to know them. Enough time to judge a person's true character.

Enough time to fall for them.

But Kinsley leaned forward in his chair. His blue eyes ensnared Castel. "Believe it or not, I'm a fairly good judge of character, Castel. I have to be. It's part of my job. That's how I knew Scarlett was up to no good." A faint smile touched his lips. "And that's how I know—while you were *also* up to no good—you didn't mean her harm like she meant for you."

Castel stared at him. Then he let out a hoarse laugh. "You think I'm harmless."

"Well, I didn't say that."

"Good, because I'm not." Castel closed his eyes again. He couldn't bear to keep looking at Kinsley. *I'm a good judge of character.* The words stabbed at Castel like a knife. *Oh, but you're not. Not as good as you think.* Another wave of emotion rocked him, but this one wasn't brought on by the lingering poison. This feeling was familiar to Castel because he lived with it constantly. He managed to keep it at bay most of the time, but it was always there, hovering just out of sight.

Hatred. Hatred for himself.

Castel clenched a hand into his pillow, then rolled onto his back. "I'm not harmless, Kinsley." His voice was like splintered glass, unrecognizable to himself. "I've done plenty of harm. More than most people."

Kinsley's answer was unbearably kind. "I'm sure that's not true."

"I killed someone."

Silence met these words. Castel stared up at the ceiling, unwilling to look at Kinsley. His eyes stung. He cursed silently, realizing it was more tears prickling at his eyes. Threatening to escape. He blinked hard, smothering them before they could.

Then Kinsley let out a breath. "Who?"

Castel answered in that strange, broken voice. "The first boy I loved."

"What happened?"

"What does it matter? I said I killed him, didn't I?"

"You killed him?" Kinsley repeated. His tone was infernally knowing, infernally patient. "Or you feel responsible for his death?"

Same difference, Castel thought. Killed him, got him killed. The result was the same. He rolled onto his other side, facing the wall. Turning his back on Kinsley. As though he could escape the impossible understanding in Kinsley's voice. The *sympathy*. Stars and stones, anything but sympathy. It was far too close to pity. And he didn't deserve either.

But Kinsley wouldn't let him escape. Too late, Castel glimpsed a shadow moving on the wall, cast by the scant light of the lamp. Kinsley's shadow. Hovering over him. He felt the mattress give as Kinsley perched behind him, his knee settling against Castel's back. When he spoke, his voice was so close. "I find it hard to believe that you would simply murder someone you loved."

Castel said, "I may as well have."

"That's not the same thing."

A tremor shook through Castel. He wanted to push back, to insist Kinsley was wrong. Wrong about him, wrong about his past. But he was so tired, a new wave of exhaustion sweeping over him. Then Kinsley laid a hand over his arm, squeezing his shoulder, and the touch was too tempting to fight. Too comforting to resist.

So when Kinsley leaned back against the headboard and pulled Castel towards him, Castel didn't protest. He shifted around, curling into Kinsley, nestling his head in the crook of the guard's neck. Kinsley wrapped an arm around him. Warm, protective. Consoling. And as Castel's eyes fell shut, sleep finally dragging him under, his last thought was that he had been wrong about two things.

The bed wasn't so small after all.

And a week was more than enough time to fall in love with someone.

Don't Miss the Next Book in the Series!

When all the evil witches from the fairy tales decide to work together, the hunter Ansel and daredevil Prince Garrett take them on, battling hexes, faceless demons, and a particularly tenacious black cat...

AVAILABLE NOW

In this Rapunzel-inspired novella, Demetri and Sabine get more than they bargained for when they investigate a ghost story in a dark forest. Sign up for the author's newsletter and download your copy of *Don't Go Into the Woods* for FREE!

WWW.ELIZABETHKKING.COM

Scan the QR code below to sign up now!

THE FIVE KINGDOMS

The Mountain Kingdom

Princess Briar's home kingdom. Currently ruled by Briar's cousin.

The Glen Kingdom

Originally ruled by Demetri's family, the Georgas, until their fall. Currently ruled by King Victor and his son, Prince Garrett.

The Mariner Kingdom

Princess Snow's home kingdom. Last ruled by her father, King Laurent, until their deaths. Currently ruled by a council of lords.

The Forest Kingdom

A fallen kingdom. The last king vacated the throne 150 years ago.

The Desert Kingdom

Located far to the south. Little is known about this kingdom.

MAGICAL ELEMENTS

Fairies

These woodland creatures can be identified by their green skin, petite statures, black eyes, and enormous wings. They mostly live in the north. Though at peace with humans, they retain the ability to curse them. They are forbidden to kill humans, and humans cannot kill fairies without dire consequences.

Djinn

Mortal enemies of the fairies, the djinn have all been confined to a shadow world. Theirs is the ability to grant wishes. They can gain strength and even freedom from their confinement by feeding off the life force of those descended from the original royal families. They can be identified by the blue markings on their faces; however, they have the ability to shapeshift into other forms.

Witches

Witches are not natural to this world. They can only access magic through fairies, usually by spilling (and even consuming) fairy blood. Witches also must make a deal with unknown dark forces to access magic. This deal grants them long life, but guarantees an eternity of torment once they die.

Naiads

Also known as mermaids, the naiads once lived deep in the sea. Now they dwell in caves and lagoons along the coast. They are solitary creatures, and must hunt and eat humans to survive. They have multiple forms, but their natural form is marked by red eyes, scaled bodies, enormous teeth, and claws.

The Gift

This term commonly refers to the pact that ended the ancient war between fairies and humans. Specifically, the Gift was a gift of fairy blood, bestowed upon the five original royal families. The descendants of these families carry fairy blood in their veins.

Elarium

A mineral unique to the Five Kingdoms, which is capable of powering various devices, including bulbs, mechanical devices, vehicle engines, and more.

Acknowledgements

Writing a book often seems like a solitary endeavor. And while many hours are spent sitting alone at my desk, there are so many other people who play a crucial part in the process.

First and foremost, I have to thank my beta readers: Rachel, Sarah, and Emilie. Your comments, feedback, and advice have been essential in shaping this story. After spending hours working alone on a book, there is always a moment of doubt in which I think—is this all just trash? Will I have to scrap the whole thing? But the thoughtful criticism and praise you all provide reassures me every time. Thank you.

To the team at Miblart, including Tania and my brilliant cover artist—you all constantly amaze me with your dedication, patience, and understanding. As someone who knows a little bit about graphic design but is far from an expert, I know I can be an exacting client! But you all display such kindness and hard work, always going the extra mile. Thank you so much.

To Saumya Singh, who created the beautiful map in this book—thank you so much for bringing the Five Kingdoms to life with your gorgeous artwork.

To my parents, who truly are my biggest supporters—this book, like all my stories, would not exist without you. Thank you especially for listening to my editing woes, stepping in when I needed help, and encouraging me to never give up on my writing dreams. And to all the family members who have given me so much love and guidance, who have bought, read, and spread the word about my books—thank you so much. I am so blessed to have such an awesome family.

Finally, to all the librarians, booksellers, and readers—none of this would be possible without you. All your support and love for my books helps more than you know. I appreciate so much the thoughtful reviews you leave, the orders you place, the posts you share on social media, the people you tell, and the kind words you send. And even if all you do is read—that alone means so much. That means *everything*. A story cannot truly live until it is read. Thank you all for giving my stories life.

ABOUT THE AUTHOR

ELIZABETH K. KING is a fantasy and horror writer. Over the years, she has nurtured her love of monsters through TV shows like *Buffy the Vampire Slayer, Supernatural,* and *Grimm.* She spends her time writing in her gothic study and roaming the Shire (her backyard) with her cocker spaniel, Blue. She lives in Houston, Texas.

You can find Elizabeth online at www.elizabethkking.com, on Instagram @elizabeth_k_king, and on her Facebook page, Elizabeth K. King, Author.